continued . . .

"A fun twist on typical witchy mysteries . . . with a delightful cast of characters." —The Mystery Reader

"Four magic wands for *A Witch Before Dying*—get your copy today!" —MyShelf.com

It Takes a Witch

"Blending magic, romance, and mystery, this is a charming story."
  —*New York Times* bestselling author Denise Swanson

"Magic and murder . . . what could be better? It's exactly the book you've been wishing for!"
  —Casey Daniels, author of *Supernatural Born Killers*

"Blake successfully blends crime, magic, romance, and self-discovery in her lively debut. . . . Fans of paranormal cozies will look forward to the sequel."
  —*Publishers Weekly*

The Goodbye Witch

A WISHCRAFT MYSTERY

HEATHER BLAKE

AN OBSIDIAN MYSTERY

OBSIDIAN
Published by the Penguin Group
Penguin Group (USA) LLC, 375 Hudson Street,
New York, New York 10014

USA | Canada | UK | Ireland | Australia | New Zealand | India | South Africa | China
penguin.com
A Penguin Random House Company

First published by Obsidian, an imprint of New American Library,
a division of Penguin Group (USA) LLC

First Printing, May 2014

ISBN 978-0-451-46587-0

Printed in the United States of America
10 9 8 7 6 5 4 3 2 1

Chapter One

"Do you think I can get away with murder?"

The back door slammed, punctuating the startling question as Starla Sullivan rushed into the kitchen of As You Wish, my aunt Ve's personal concierge business that doubled as our home. Or, more appropriately, the old Victorian housed a business.

Sudsy bubbles slid down my fingers as I set down the pot I'd been washing. Early-afternoon light streamed through the window over the sink as I dried my hands with a dish towel, turned off my iPod (silencing Eliza Doolittle singing about all kinds of loverly things), and studied Starla more carefully. Normally I'd laugh off such a question. Murder? Impossible. She was the most even-keeled, joy-filled witch I knew. But panic clouded her usually sparkling blue eyes, and a touch of fear slid down my spine.

"Maybe," I said honestly. Since moving to the Enchanted Village last June, I'd learned a thing or two about homicides as I'd helped solve several local cases. There were ways to get away with murder if you planned carefully enough. I'd picked up a few tips and tricks to evade the police—but couldn't imagine ever implementing the knowledge. I wasn't usually the murderous type, either, unless my family and friends were threatened. Then, look out. The mama bear in me wouldn't back down.

As I watched Starla pace nervously, I had the uneasy feeling this was one of those times. "Why? Who do we need to kill?"

Holding on to a thread of hope that she was simply venting and hadn't really turned homicidal, I'd purposefully kept my voice unnaturally light. My dog, Missy, formally known as Miss Demeanor, looked up from her bed near the mudroom door, and cocked her head as though understanding the seriousness of this conversation.

"*We*, Darcy?" Tears brimmed on the corners of Starla's light lashes.

"Obviously I'm not letting you do it alone. If you deem that someone needs to go, then I trust your instincts. *Patooey.* I spit on that person, and that's saying something, because you know I hate spitting."

A mourning dove cooed from the windowsill as sunbeams fell across Starla's face, making her look more angelic than usual, despite her sudden affinity for murder. A quivering smile spread across her face and lit her from the inside out. Then a passing cloud blocked the sun, her smile faltered, the tears fell, and she suddenly threw herself into my arms and started sobbing.

A lump lodged squarely in my throat as I held her tightly like I used to do with my younger sister Harper. Because I was the only mother figure she had ever known— our mom died the day she was born—Harper had always turned to me for affection. But at twenty-three and fiercely independent, she rarely needed my soothing anymore.

I held on to Starla tightly. As I consoled, I noticed her skin felt chilled, probably a result of the icy air outside. January in the Enchanted Village, a themed neighborhood of Salem, Massachusetts, was about as cold as I'd ever experienced. The village had already received more than a foot of snow this month alone, and it was only two weeks into the New Year.

"Oh Starla, what's wrong?" I whispered, rubbing her back as she trembled beneath my hand. "Did Vince do something?"

Vincent Paxton was Starla's boyfriend, and someone I didn't quite trust. Not yet. Maybe not ever. He was a Seeker, a mortal who longed to become a Crafter, like Starla and me. I was a Wishcrafter, a witch who could grant wishes, and she was a Cross-Crafter, a hybrid witch. She was part Wishcrafter (her predominate Craft) and part Bakecrafter (she had zero skills in the kitchen), the opposite of her twin brother, Evan, who owned the only bakery in the village.

There were many things I didn't like about Vince, including his past history as a murder suspect with questionable morals, and only a few things I did. One was how much he obviously cared about Starla. But if he'd hurt her . . .

"It's not Vince." Sniffling, she backed away from me. As fast as she could wipe them away, more tears filled her blue eyes.

"Then what?" I asked, an ache growing in my stomach.

Right now I wished with all my heart that I could take away the obvious pain she was in. But one of the frustrating rules of being a Wishcrafter was that I couldn't grant my own wishes.

Her voice cracked as she said, "He's back."

"Who's back?" I suddenly wished my aunt Ve was around in case Starla needed additional moral support. Plus, I had no doubt she'd help us hide a body if need be. But she was out of town for the day on an As You Wish assignment.

Starla began pacing again, her boots hitting the wood floor with the force of her anxiety. With each pivot, her blond ponytail swung out behind her, slashing the air. "Kyle. Kyle's back."

I knew of only one Kyle in her life, and simply hearing the name come from her lips was enough to make my blood run cold. "Your ex-husband Kyle?" I said in a hushed breath. "Are you sure?"

"I'm fairly sure. I was wrapping up my afternoon rounds on the village green when I saw him near the ice skating oval. One minute I'm snapping shots of a toddler wobbling on the ice, and the next my cozy happy world fell apart."

In addition to being a part-time photographer for the town newspaper, *Toil and Trouble*, Starla owned Hocus-Pocus Photography and was often out and about in the square, snapping pictures of tourists—mementos the visitors could purchase on their way out of the village.

"Could it have been someone who looks like him?" I speculated. "Maybe his twin brother?"

Kyle and Liam Chadwick were fraternal twins, but looked very similar. Kyle's whole family (his mom, his dad, and his two brothers) still lived in the village—they owned Wickedly Creative, an art studio just beyond the square. It was excruciatingly awkward when Starla bumped into one of them.

"No, it wasn't Liam. It was Kyle. I'd know him anywhere. Fortunately, I had the sense to take pictures of him just to be sure—and to show the police. He's back."

"Let me see the pictures." I'd seen Kyle Chadwick's face often enough on the wanted poster in the village police station to know what he looked like.

Her hand fluttered to her chest, where her camera usually hung. But it wasn't there.

"My camera!" she cried. "I was so freaked out at seeing him that my legs went weak. I had to sit down for a second, and I must have left it on a bench near the skating rink. I have to go back and get it."

"Let me call Harper. She can get there faster than you." That, and I was starting to realize I needed reinforcements. If it was Kyle she had seen . . . this was big news. Big dangerous news. "Hold on a sec."

Tears spilled down Starla's face as she nodded. I quickly ducked into the As You Wish office, closed the door a bit, and dialed my sister at her bookshop, which was just across the street from the ice rink.

"Spellbound, this is Harper."

"It's me," I whispered into the phone.

"What's wrong, Darcy?"

She knew me too well, picking up on my anxiety from only two little words. "It's Starla. She left her camera on a bench near the ice skating rink. Can you go get it?"

"Why'd she leave it? What's going on?"

There was no point in trying to be deceptive with Harper. She would get the information out of me eventually. "She accidentally left it there when she saw Kyle Chadwick."

There was a beat of silence before she said, "Kyle Chadwick, her lousy stinking rotten jerk face of an ex?"

The description fit. "Yes. Well, she thinks it's him." I explained the situation.

"For the love," Harper muttered. "Did she call the police?"

"I don't know." The office was its normal mess—a source of contention between Aunt Ve and me. Today the clutter only added to my stress level. I pulled my long ponytail forward over my shoulder and fussed with the dark strands of my hair.

"If she hasn't she should."

Harper was right. The sooner the police were involved with this, the better. "Can you get the camera? It'll be nice to have confirmation that Kyle is in the village when the police get here."

"I'm on it." She hung up.

Setting the phone into its dock, I let out a long sigh. Chill bumps covered my skin, and my hands shook as I walked back into the kitchen.

Starla had quit pacing and now sat on a kitchen stool with my aunt's gray-and-white Himalayan, Tilda, curled in her lap. Tilda seemed to have a sixth sense for when people were upset. Despite her persnickety disposition, she almost always set aside her normal crankiness to offer comfort to people in need. This time was no different.

I often wondered if Tilda was a familiar—a Crafter who took on the form of an animal after death—but if she were one she wasn't letting on. Other familiars I knew, like my mouse friend, Pepe, and the scarlet macaw that lived next door, Archie, had no trouble speaking to me. If Tilda was a familiar, she was giving me the silent treatment.

Pulling up the stool next to Starla, I said, "Did you call the police?"

She buried her face in Tilda's fur. "I didn't. I snapped the pictures of him, and then kind of froze. I started shaking. I don't remember much after that—only running here." Tears swam in her eyes. "Maybe it wasn't him. Maybe I'm making a fuss out of nothing. Maybe my mind is playing tricks on me. It is almost the anniversary of when he was arrested, and it's been on my mind."

Maybe. But I'd like to be sure—for her sake.

It didn't escape my notice, either, that she referred to the upcoming anniversary as when he was *arrested.* But in a few days it will have been two years since Kyle Chadwick had attempted to strangle her.

My hands curled into fists as I said, "We should call Nick."

Nick Sawyer wasn't only the village's police chief. He was also . . . mine. We'd been dating since summertime. We'd had our ups and downs, but right now we were in a good place.

"Only Nick for now, okay?" she said, putting her hand on my arm. "I don't want . . ."

I reached out and held her hand. "What?"

"It's just that when Kyle was arrested . . . there was so much scrutiny."

"That makes sense. He was charged with a horrible crime."

"Not only scrutiny of him, Darcy. Of me. People didn't want to believe what happened. . . . They accused me of lying. I don't want to go through that again. At least not until I'm sure that the man at the rink was really him. The pictures will prove it."

"I'll call Nick's cell phone, not the police station," I said, conceding to her wishes.

"Okay."

I dialed, but Nick didn't answer. I left a message for

him to come over as soon as he could, that it was important.

"I can't stop shaking," Starla said, absently watching her hand tremble.

I couldn't blame her. It had to have been such a shock to see her ex-husband. A man she once loved with all her heart.

A man who'd tried to kill her.

Tilda's purrs filled the air as Starla asked, "Why would he come back?"

"I don't know." According to Aunt Ve, one of the best gossipers in the whole village, Kyle had escaped jail and disappeared right after being charged with Starla's attempted murder. No one had seen hide nor hair of him in two years. He was still a fugitive.

I'd lived in the village for less than a year, so I had never met the man, but I hated him with every drop of blood in my body, as did everyone who loved Starla. Why would he risk surfacing in a place that knew him so well? It didn't make sense. I hoped with all my heart that she'd been mistaken. That he wasn't here in the village. But I doubted she would have had such a visceral reaction if she hadn't been certain.

The back door swung open, and Harper hurried inside, a fancy camera in hand and her cheeks bright red. Whether the color came from the freezing temperatures or from her agitation I wasn't sure. She tugged a stocking cap off her head, leaving her pixie-cut light brown hair sticking up in static-filled tufts.

Setting the camera on the counter, she went over and hugged Starla, who might be my best friend but had quickly become like family to all of us. She was practically another sister to Harper, another niece to Aunt Ve.

Missy came off her bed and barked. She probably felt the tension in the air and didn't like it much. I scooped her up and held her close. Her heart beat furiously against my hand.

Harper and I hadn't known a thing about Kyle Chadwick until a month ago when Starla opened up to us, telling us her fateful story of love gone wrong. According to Ve, Starla didn't talk much about her tumultuous marriage at all, telling people only that she was divorced and that it most certainly hadn't been amicable.

That had been an understatement of a lifetime.

It was a miracle she was sitting here.

There was a tap at the back door, and Nick stuck his head inside. "Darcy? You called?"

Missy squirmed, and I set her down. She bounded over to the door as I waved him inside. He bent down to rub Missy's ears before coming into the kitchen.

All it took was one look at our faces before his dark eyes shifted from curious to on-the-job. "What's going on?"

Standing close to him, I felt the warmth of his body heat and moved a little closer. I cared for him more than I ever dared admit. I was working up my nerve to confess those three little words, even within the silence of my own head. It had been a long time since I'd said them to a man—my ex-husband had been the last, and we'd been divorced for years now. But even as lousy a husband as Troy had been, he had been a saint compared to Kyle Chadwick.

Starla related what she'd seen on the village green and fresh tears filled her eyes. "Except for being a lot thinner, he was exactly the same as he was two years ago. The same haircut—long and shaggy—and the same square face, the same piercing blue eyes. I always thought that if he came back he'd wear a disguise. Change his hair color, grow a beard. But no. He was just . . . him. And he was watching me."

I shivered.

Harper shuddered.

Nick dragged a hand through his dark hair. He knew the history of Kyle Chadwick, the village's most notorious fugitive. "Starla, are you sure it was him?"

"The longer I sit here, the more I doubt myself. But I took pictures. They'll prove it one way or another." She pushed the camera toward him. "You know what he looks like, right? From his mug shot and the wanted posters?"

Fortunately, Kyle was not a Wishcrafter—or else his photos would be nothing but bright starbursts. He was a Manicrafter, a witch with magical hands. And he was most likely a sociopath.

"I'd know his face anywhere." Nick drew in a deep breath as he reached for the camera and flicked the power switch. He hit the button to review the photos and clicked and clicked and finally looked up at Starla.

"What?" she asked, lifting off the stool at his strange expression. "It's him. Isn't it him? I know it's him."

"How many pictures did you take this afternoon?" he asked.

"Of just Kyle or of everyone?"

"Everyone."

"Hundreds. I was wrapping up my afternoon rounds when I saw him."

Nick's brown eyes were flat and unreadable as he turned the camera around. "Then it looks as though someone might have tampered with your camera."

"What do you mean?" She grabbed for the Nikon and let out a little cry.

I leaned over her shoulder as she continued to click a button, despite the message on the review screen.

Folder Contains No Images

There was no photo of Kyle.

There were no photos at all.

They'd all been deleted.

Chapter Two

None of us knew what to say as a stunned Starla stared at the camera. Finally she broke the thick silence. "I don't know what happened to the pictures."

"Could you have accidentally deleted them?" Nick asked. "Sounds like you were in a bit of shock."

Her shoulders hunched in a shrug. "Maybe."

Maybe, maybe, maybe.

I was beginning to hate that word.

Harper's small fist banged the countertop. "No, that's not what happened. For the love. It's obvious he erased them. He saw that you left your camera behind and took the opportunity to wipe the camera's memory clean. I'll go ask around the rink, see if anyone saw something."

"No," Nick said in a determined tone. "I'll go. This is police business. If Kyle Chadwick is back in town, then the *police* will look into it. He's a fugitive, a dangerous one at that."

Nick and I had gone through a rough patch around Halloween after Glinda Hansel, a village police officer, had complained that I was too involved with an ongoing murder case and that Nick had violated regulations by sharing information with me. She had not so subtly threatened his job if he kept it up.

The shake-up had created a wedge between Nick and me. He'd become overly sensitive about keeping me out of police business, and I'd become resentful that I had to share everything I learned about the case with him but he couldn't tell me a thing.

I'd been relieved when that case had ended (thanks mostly to my sleuthing), and we'd been able to put it behind us and move on.

Until now, apparently.

Harper's big elfish eyes narrowed—she hated to be challenged—but then her gaze flicked to me. I silently begged her to let it go.

"Fine," she said. "You look into it."

"Thank you," I mouthed to her.

"Listen," Nick said, his gaze sweeping over all of us. "I know this situation is upsetting, but until we know anything for certain, let's not get ahead of ourselves. I'll let patrol know to keep an eye out for Kyle Chadwick, that there's been a possible sighting in the village. I'm going to make a call." He spun and went out the back door.

A gust of icy wind swept inside and swirled around my feet as I watched him go. Starla didn't stop him, so I figured she'd come to terms with taking her plight public.

I hated what I saw in her eyes. The angst. The despair.

"I don't want to go through this again," she whispered.

Putting Missy on the floor, I wrapped my arms around Starla from behind, resting my jaw on the top of her head. "We're not going to let anything happen to you. As soon as Ve gets home, I'll talk to her about casting one of her famous protection spells, too."

Sometimes being a witch came in handy.

"Thanks," she murmured. Tilda let out a *reow* as Starla scooped her up and passed her off to me. "I think I'm going to head home and rest for a while."

Tilda squirmed in my arms, and then leapt out of them and raced up the back staircase. I didn't take her abandonment personally. Though we'd had a rough start, we got along fairly well now as long as I remembered that Tilda was boss. "You can stay here, Starla." I didn't like the idea of her being alone right now.

The zipper on her coat stuck and she gave it a good yank, drawing the metal tab up to her chin. "That's all right," she said. "I just want to be home."

"Will Evan be there? Or is he still at the bakery?" Harper asked.

The siblings shared a brownstone together, along with Starla's tiny dog, Twink, who, though adorable, couldn't protect her from a gnat, never mind a deranged ex.

"He's out delivering a cake," she said.

I doubted Evan even knew what was going on since Starla had run straight here after seeing Kyle. But if he wasn't around . . . "I can call Vince." I was proud of myself for making that offer without a hint of animosity in my voice.

With fists balled at her side, twin red spots bloomed on her cheeks. The angst had shifted out of her eyes, replaced now with a simmering fury that made her blue irises appear purple. "I'll be fine."

I had the feeling she was talking more to herself than us.

Her knuckles had turned white from clenching her fists so hard. "I refuse to let him do this to me again. I will not be a victim."

"Damn right," Harper said in solidarity. "Thatta girl!"

Resolutely, Starla nodded, picked up her camera, and turned toward the back door. She took a few calming breaths, inhaling softly and barely exhaling. "I can do this."

"Of course you can," I said, wishing she'd just stay.

"Okay, I'm going." She took two steps forward, then stopped. Another step, then stopped. "Really, I am."

When Nick opened the back door, Starla took the opportunity to rush out, flying past him as fast as her booted feet could carry her. He pressed himself against the door to avoid a collision.

"I'll follow her," Harper said, giving my arm a quick squeeze, before she, too, blew past Nick.

Missy bolted out the door, too, and I hollered, "Make sure the gate's closed!" That little dog was sneaky as could be and had run off more times than I could count. She never failed to return home, however, so I wasn't *too* worried.

Nick closed the door and said, "Did I miss something?"

"A demonstration of courage at its finest," I said.

"Starla's a tough cookie."

I didn't agree. If Starla was a cookie, she was a Mallomar. Tough on the outside, yes, but one crack revealed a marshmallow middle. Right now she was putting on a courageous act.

But I was a big believer in the "fake it till you make it" philosophy she was using. If she could make it through this test of her fortitude, she could make it through anything.

Nick said, "The village force is on high alert, and I sent Glinda over to interview Kyle's family. She's a friend of theirs, so hopefully they'll open up to her."

Glinda. Great.

"Is there anything magical I need to know about this case?" he asked.

Nick had grown up mortal but had been tuned into the witchy world around him, thanks to his deceased ex-wife Melina. She'd been a Wishcrafter who gave up her Craft to let him in on her secret world once they were married, making him a Wishcrafter-by-marriage (known as a Halfcrafter in our circle). He had no powers but he was privy to the magical world in which he lived and was able to help raise his twelve-year-old daughter Mimi as a Crafter. She had inherited her mother's Wishcrafting abilities and was slowly learning the ins and outs of the Craft.

Mimi and I had a lot in common.

My father had also been mortal, and my mother had also lost her Wishcrafting abilities when she told him of the magic she possessed. Unlike Nick, my father wasn't supportive of the witch world and insisted his children be raised as mortals. I liked to think that my mother would have eventually changed his mind, but she never had the chance. There had been a car accident when she was pregnant with Harper—my mother had died. Harper was born prematurely.

My father never told us of our heritage, and it wasn't until after his death that we learned of our abilities from Aunt Ve. It didn't take long after that for Harper and me (and Missy) to pack up our lives in Ohio and move here to the Enchanted Village.

"Kyle Chadwick is a Manicrafter, so this definitely is not a mortal case." I was still a little shaky as I walked back to the sink and picked up the pot I'd abandoned when Starla had come in. "But I don't think his Craft has anything to do with him being a sociopath."

"What kind of abilities do Manicrafters have?"

Drawing my hands out of the soapy water, I wiggled my fingers at him. "Manis have magical hands. They are exceptional with tactile adeptness. They're great with delicate work, small objects, and arts and crafts. As you probably know, Kyle's mom, dad, and brothers are all artisans and own Wickedly Creative."

"Mimi loves that place."

"She does?" How didn't I know that?

"Glinda teaches basket weaving there, and has taken Mimi there a few times to paint ceramics and take some classes. They did a glassblowing class last weekend. Mimi couldn't stop talking about it."

Glinda again. She was a Broomcrafter, so basket weaving was right in her wheelhouse. She was extremely adept at woodworking as well. I sponged down the inside of the pot and rinsed it clean. I couldn't help but feel an ache bloom in my chest. Mimi hadn't said a word about the outing to me, and I'd seen her every afternoon this week. Four days and not a word about glassblowing with Glinda.

Letting out a sigh, I supposed I couldn't blame Mimi for keeping mum. She was a smart girl and sensed the tension when Glinda's name came up. I grabbed a spoon from the soapy side of the sink and scrubbed it for all it was worth.

It wasn't too long ago that Glinda revealed she'd been

Melina Sawyer's best friend once upon a time. She attached herself to Mimi under the guise of helping Mimi learn more about her mother.

On the surface, it seemed like a nice gesture.

Beneath the surface, I smelled a rat.

I'd been seven when my mother was killed and understood Mimi's grief at the loss of her mom to cancer two years ago—and her desire to learn as much about her mom as she could.

I just wished that it wasn't Glinda who held the information. "She's a friend of the family and works for them, too? Isn't that a conflict of interest?"

In the reflection of the now-sparkling spoon, I could see anger flashing in my golden blue eyes. Glinda hadn't really disguised the fact that she wanted Nick for herself, and I couldn't help but suspect she was using Mimi to make that happen. She even went out of her way to be nice to me.

The woman wasn't stupid.

"Ordinarily, yes," Nick said. "But not in this case."

"Why not?"

"Because I asked her to take the job."

I looked over my shoulder at him. "You did what? Why?"

"Undercover mission to discover where Kyle's been living while on the lam. When I heard the rumors about Kyle's family harboring him, I hoped Glinda would overhear something while working at the studio. . . ."

I couldn't keep the doubt out of my voice as I said, "And she agreed to go undercover?"

"Why wouldn't she?"

"Being a family friend and all . . ."

"Her first priority is being a police officer. Kyle's case remains unsolved and is a stain on the department, seeing as how he broke out of our jail. If anyone can learn where Kyle is, it's Glinda."

With more force than necessary, I tossed the spoon into the drying rack and pulled the plug in the sink. The *glug glug* of the water draining echoed through the kitchen.

Nick came up behind me at the sink and slid his arms

around my waist and dropped his cheek onto my shoulder. "Are you okay?"

"I don't like that Glinda Hansel."

His laughter vibrated against my neck, tickling the sensitive skin there. "No, really? I guess I shouldn't invite her to your birthday party then."

I gave him a playful jab to his stomach. "Don't even joke. And I told you, no parties. Let's just treat it like any other day." My birthday was next weekend, and I was already dreading it.

"Not a chance."

"No parties," I warned.

Smiling, he said, "All right, all right. I won't plan one." He crossed his heart and planted a kiss on my nose. "And I know Glinda's not your favorite, Darcy, but she is Mimi's friend," he said reluctantly. "It would be best if we can all get along."

Hmm. Glinda may be Mimi's friend, but was Mimi a friend of Glinda's? Or a means to an end? "I suppose."

His warm lips kissed a spot behind my ear, and I tipped my head to the side, giving him better access.

"You're cute when you're jealous."

"I'm not jealous," I argued, resting my hands on his chest. "I just don't trust her."

Okay, I was a smidge jealous. But that smidge wasn't over Nick. It was over Mimi. I trusted Nick enough to know Glinda had no power over him. But Mimi . . . she was young. Naive. Defenseless against Glinda's guile.

"Do you like her? Trust her?" I asked.

"I like her just fine, and I trust very few," he said.

I knew. I sighed.

Warmth filled his brown eyes and he laughed. "Let's not talk about Glinda. How about you come over tonight after dinner? I'll make you dessert and show you just how much I like *you*. Mimi's been invited to a slumber party, so I have the house to myself. Well, Higgins will be there, too."

I smiled grudgingly. "You know I can't resist his drool." Higgins was the Saint Bernard Nick and Mimi had adopted last summer.

"It's a date then?" Nick asked.

"It's a date."

He was giving me a preview of just how much he liked me when the back door burst open, slamming against the wall.

Nick and I jumped apart as though we were two teens being busted by our parents.

Harper stomped into the kitchen carrying Starla's camera. She took one look at the two of us, rolled her eyes, and said, "Starla spotted me following her, so she let me walk her home. And she let me have this." She held up the Nikon, and then shoved it at Nick. "I don't want to tell you how to do your job, *Chief*, but I'd think you'd want to check that for prints, no?"

Spinning, she stormed out as fast as she came in and slammed the door again.

Nick looked at me.

"I'll talk to her," I said.

"I'm going to go interview people at the ice skating rink." He smiled and held up the camera. "And get this checked for prints."

Chapter Three

There were some days I was beyond grateful that my work hours were so flexible. Yes, it helped that I worked for my aunt, and she gave me a lot of leeway, but because As You Wish wasn't a retail store it was easier to slip out when I needed to run an errand . . . or a background check on a best friend's crazy ex-husband.

At As You Wish, our services ranged from the fantastical (one client wanted a carnival complete with elephants set up for a weekend party—on two days' notice) to the sweet (an impromptu getaway to an exotic locale) to the practical (help with cleaning a hoarder's house). Calls came in at all hours of the day from clients who usually desired something on short notice. They wanted, needed, *wished* for something impossible. Or at least impossible to them.

Not for us.

With Ve gone for the day, off to the Cape to manage a midwinter clambake, I made sure the voice mail system was switched on as I got ready to head out. Truthfully, our voice mail was probably the hardest worker at As

You Wish. Today it would be working overtime as I prepared to seek the counsel of the village's resident historian—I needed to talk to someone who knew exactly what had gone down two years ago between Starla and Kyle.

I'd just slipped on my snow boots when the doorbell rang. Missy went running toward the front door, and I hurried down the hallway behind her.

A shadowy figure stood just beyond the glass door, and as I looked out the window, I saw it was our usual package deliveryman.

"Down!" I said to Missy, who miraculously settled as I opened the door. "Hi, Sam."

Sam was mid- to late fifties, with kind eyes and silver-streaked dark hair. "Good afternoon, Darcy," he said as he handed me a clipboard, then bent to pet Missy's head. Standing, he smiled kindly and hefted a big box. "Where do you want it?"

I pointed at the coffee table. "There's good. Thanks, Sam."

Missy sniffed his feet as he put the package on the table. "Tell your aunt I said hello."

"I will," I promised, trying not to roll my eyes. These two had been flirting for as long as I'd known them.

I locked the door behind him and eyed the large box, wondering what it was. I found a utility knife and carefully sliced the tape along the top of the box. Lifting the flaps, I peeked inside and found hundreds and hundreds of teardrop crystals. They were beautiful but I had no idea what they were for. I racked my brain, trying to think if any clients had requested something to do with crystals and couldn't think of a single one.

Strange. I made a mental note to ask Ve about it when she returned and left the box on the table. Back in the mudroom, I quickly bundled up in a down coat and thick scarf, clipped on Missy's leash, and headed out the back door.

Salt crystals crackled beneath my rubber soles as I carefully navigated the snow-crusted back steps. In the hour since Starla had left, thick clouds had moved in and delicate snowflakes floated gracefully to the ground, mesmerizing in their elegance.

The yard, the whole village really, looked like a winter wonderland. What should have seemed stark—dark outlines of bare trees and shrubs against the crisp whiteness of the snow—was instead breathtaking in its simplistic beauty.

My eye immediately went to the brightest spot in the landscape, my scarlet macaw neighbor, Archie.

It was impossible to miss him with his vibrant plumage, the stunning red, blue, and yellow jolting against the pristine background.

Scooping up Missy, I followed a shoveled path over to Archie's cage.

He said, "'Who told you to walk on my side of the block, who told you to be in my neighborhood?'"

Archie and I were in constant competition to best each other with our movie quote knowledge. Trying my hardest to place the quote, I bit my lip and searched far-reaching corners of my mind. Finally, I just had to admit defeat. "I'm stumped."

"*Do the Right Thing*," he said with more than a touch of hauteur. His voice was James Earl Jones deep but infused with an authentic British accent.

"Show-off."

"Do not be envious, Darcy, of my considerable skills. You are but a novice, and I have, as they say, been around the block a time or two."

"That's because you're old." I brushed snowflakes from Missy's fur. "Didn't you come over on the Mayflower?"

I was only half kidding. He was old, *centuries* old, but not quite Mayflower vintage. In his human form, he'd once been a theater actor in merry old England. Currently, he was an outgoing familiar who reveled in all things cinematic. His form allowed him to captivate tourists with his theatrical abilities, them being none the wiser. They simply believed he was a "parrot" with a good memory.

He was also the Elder's right-hand bird, her majordomo, her eyes and ears. Her spy, though I wasn't sure why she needed one since she seemed to know most everything that went on in the village. The Elder, the ruler of all the Crafts, ran the village with an iron fist. I'd once been extremely terrified of her, but now I was only slightly terrified of her. She governed from a magical meadow in the forest, and her identity was kept an utmost secret. Very few were clued in as to who she truly was.

I was one of the clueless.

"Ha-ha!" he laughed in exaggeration and flapped his wings. "The Mayflower. Aren't you quaint?"

"The quaintest." Smiling at his dramatics, I felt the heavy weight of the afternoon shift from my shoulders the tiniest bit.

An outdoor heater stood near his cage, an elaborate iron masterpiece that had its own version of a doggy door so Archie could come and go. The main house, owned by Numbercrafter Terry Goodwin, had icicles hanging from the eaves and every shade drawn. Terry was a reclusive accountant, a dead ringer for Elvis, and except for seeing clients, he often kept to himself. He was also one of Aunt Ve's (many) ex-husbands and was trying his best to get her to take another trip down the aisle with him.

So far his best wasn't good enough, but not for lack of trying. The problem was that Ve seemed to be seduced by falling in love—but not staying in love. Which wasn't the least bit conducive to a long-term relationship.

Ve had been on the lookout for her next boyfriend for months now, but she refused to simply cut Terry loose. She liked having a bird in hand, as she often told me.

Terry had fashioned a lean-to around Archie's cage to protect it from the elements, and as Missy snuggled into my chest, I had the feeling she wished she shared the shelter.

Not me. I found the snow magical, and I loved being caught up in its whimsy.

Archie hopped along his perch closer to me and dropped his voice to not be overheard by any passing tourists. "I hear Kyle Chadwick has returned to the village."

"Did you see him?" If he could verify Starla's account . . .

"No, not I. Only Miss Starla as far as I've ascertained."

Missy stiffened in my arms, and I didn't know whether she was reacting to my uneasiness or if she had picked up something on her own. I rubbed her ears and said, "Nick's looking into it."

Terry opened the back door and called out to Archie to come inside. They did this several times a day during the winter so Archie wouldn't get too cold. Macaws were naturally tropical birds, but magical macaws could tolerate much more than their mortal counterparts.

"A moment," he said to Terry.

I waved but wasn't sure Terry had seen me before he ducked backed inside the house.

Archie's feathers fluffed out, then settled back down. "I feared Kyle's return one day."

"Well, cross your ancient toes that he hasn't."

"You, Darcy Merriweather, are a sore loser."

I cleared my throat. "'Being a true loser takes years of ineptitude.'"

Archie twisted his head upside down and peered at me with his small beady eyes. Finally, he cried, "Curses!" In a flutter, he pushed open his cage door and flew out.

"*Father's Day!*" I called after him, laughing.

Pulling Missy closer up to my face, I could feel a smile stretch my cheeks. Snow crunched beneath my feet as I pushed open the gate and headed toward the village square. But soon my humor at Archie's antics faded, and the weight of Starla's plight returned to my shoulders.

I had to find out as much as I could about Kyle Chadwick.

And I knew just the mouse who could tell me.

As I crossed the village green, I searched every face I came across as Missy happily examined the snowbanks along the path.

Young, old, tall, small. It didn't matter. So intent was I

on my task that I nearly jumped out of my skin when someone came up beside me, bumped my shoulder, and said, "Hey, doll."

"Mrs. Pennywhistle!" I pressed a hand to my chest and tried to calm the rush of adrenaline coursing through my body.

Tilting her head back, she laughed, a loud effervescent cackle. At eighty-plus, she was a firecracker of a woman, a Vaporcrafter who had the ability to disappear in the blink of an eye.

Today, the hood of Mrs. P's pink track jacket was pulled up over her spiky white hair to protect it from the elements. Red blusher heightened the natural flush on her cheeks from the cold and matched the artificial color on her lips. There was nothing Mrs. P liked more than her makeup—except maybe her love of velour. "Sorry! I didn't mean to frighten you. I thought you heard me calling your name."

My pulse still throbbed in my ears. "I was a little distracted."

"I can see why."

Fanning her face with one hand, she motioned to Nick with the other. He stood near the ice rink, speaking with the young woman working at the skate rental booth.

"He's a dreamboat. If I were but ten years younger, I'd steal him away from you."

Smiling, I eyed her. "You hussy."

She laughed again, the distinctive sound carrying in the chilly air. "If the strumpet fits . . ."

I'd met Mrs. Pennywhistle, fondly known as Mrs. P, just after I moved to the village. We'd been entangled in a murder case and had come out of it with a solid friendship.

"What's he doing?" she asked, snowflakes catching on her false eyelashes. "Did someone rob the rink?"

The news was bound to reach her before long, so I quickly told Mrs. P what had happened to Starla.

The sparkle in her eyes dimmed. "I'd known Kyle as a kind young man, but I heard he did have a bit of a temper, so I wasn't completely shocked when I heard what he did to Starla."

"A temper? He did?"

"Sure enough. At one of his art exhibitions he confronted a critic who was panning a painting in front of the whole gallery. There was a fistfight, and Kyle was charged with assault."

My eyes widened. "Get out."

"It's as true as I'm standing here. The assault charge was reduced to disorderly conduct, and Kyle was sentenced to community service and an anger management class."

I'd never heard any of this. It was the kind of information I needed. I wanted the whole picture of Kyle Chadwick.

"Does Vince know Kyle is back?" she asked.

Mrs. P worked for Vince a few days a week at his shop, Lotions and Potions. Mostly she was in charge of making sure he didn't put anything into his concoctions that would hurt someone, and of keeping an eye on the Seeker. She made a great spy. "Not that I know of."

"I should let him know. He cares for Starla a great deal." She wrung her hands. "This is so upsetting."

I agreed. "Do you have a few minutes, Mrs. P? I'm on my way to see Pepe to get a better idea of what transpired two years ago. I'd like your input too."

The light came back into her eyes, and she gleefully rubbed her hands together. "Darcy Merriweather, on the case!"

I glanced at Nick. "*Shhh.* Let's keep this on the down low, okay?"

"Right, right. Gotcha, doll. Let's go. I have all the time you need. Plus, I love that little Pepe. He's a charmer."

I laughed. "Maybe it's time we find you a date. As You Wish has done matchmaking before, so I'm sure we can find someone suitable."

A mourning dove cooed from a nearby branch as Missy led the way to the Bewitching Boutique, where Pepe worked as a master tailor—and lived in the shop's walls.

"Let's not get carried away." Mrs. P thumped her chest. "I'm not sure this old ticker can handle falling in love again."

"Who said anything about love? It would just be a date. A good time with a man. A little something hot and heavy to keep that blood pumping."

Looking off in the distance, she said, "It's a nice thought and all, but like I said, this ticker . . ."

I tugged Missy to a stop, and took hold of Mrs. P's arm. "Are you okay?" One mention of her "ticker" was a joke. Two mentions was cause for concern. And now that I was looking, I saw she looked a little paler than usual (aside from the blush), and that she was moving slower, too. Usually she operated at one speed only: fast-forward. Not today.

Her eyes softened, and she patted my hand. "I'm old, Darcy. Nothing lasts forever."

Unexpectedly, tears sprang to my eyes. "You're not that old. Eighty is the new sixty, haven't you heard?"

"Put those tears away, doll," she said softly. "The heart doctor tells me I'm too stubborn to let anything keep me down."

My breath caught. "You've been to a doctor?" This was news. Big news. Serious news. The "ticker" thing hadn't been a joke at all.

Giving my hand a squeeze, she said, "Nothing to worry about. Now, let's go. I'm freezing my wrinkles off out here."

But her saying there was nothing to worry about made me worry.

A lot.

Chapter Four

The Bewitching Boutique was a magical place where even the least fashionable witch (like me) could find an outfit that made her feel amazing. That was due to the talents of Cloakcrafters Godfrey Baleaux and of course, Pepe, who'd retained his Cloaking skills even as a familiar. It was quite the sight to see him wield a tiny needle.

Godfrey poked his head out from behind velvet curtains as Mrs. P, Missy, and I came in. He jumped forward and quickly closed the draperies behind him, holding on to the fabric behind his back. Laughing nervously, his chubby cheeks jiggled. "Three of my favorite ladies!"

He still hadn't let go of the velvet curtains. "Are you okay, Godfrey?"

"Me? Fine! Fit as a fiddle! Why do you ask?"

I motioned to his hands.

He chuckled and finally released the fabric. "I do love velvet."

Tipping my head, I studied him. He seemed . . . flustered.

"To what do I owe the pleasure of your visit?" he said

enthusiastically. "Have you finally decided to give up your obsession with velour, Eugenia?"

His tone was light, but his eyes were quite serious.

Shrugging off her winter coat, she handed it over to him and said, "Never, Godfrey. Never."

Holding Mrs. P's coat with two fingers (it was a polyester blend), Godfrey chuckled under his breath. "Never say never, my dear."

Godfrey was perfectly groomed as usual. His beard was kept clipped short, his skin glowed with good health. The only hint of his age (early sixties) came in the silver-gray of his hair, which had been tamed into gentle waves by some type of hair product. He was family—of a sort. He was Aunt Ve's third husband, the one she once referred to as a Rat Toad Bottom-dweller. They were on much better terms now, however. Friends, even.

Mrs. P arched a penciled eyebrow. "You will have to strip my velour from my cold dead body, Godfrey Baleaux." Gently, she slapped his cheek as she headed for the settee.

"Promise?" he asked.

"That's enough talk of dead bodies," I said, interrupting them. Especially of Mrs. P's body. I didn't want to even think about that.

Godfrey helped me out of my coat and hung both on fancy hooks at the back of the shop. Mrs. P lowered the hood of her track jacket, and white spikes of hair sprang forth as though they'd never been covered.

Godfrey and I stared. I swear, Mrs. P's hair was the eighth wonder of the world.

She patted her head, seemingly oblivious to the awe her jack-in-the-box styling had caused.

I unclipped Missy's leash, and she immediately went over to an arched door in the baseboard molding and let out a bark—her version of ringing Pepe's doorbell, I assumed.

As I straightened, I noticed something sparkly on Godfrey's shoulder. I leaned in and picked off a sequin. I handed it to him.

Smiling brightly, he said, "Hazard of the job."

Missy barked again, and the tiny door in the base-board flew open. Pepe rubbed his eyes and said, *"Ferme la bouche!"*

Shut your mouth. It was the classy French way of say-ing shut up.

Missy stopped barking and slurped his face, upsetting the glasses from his long nose. He righted the specs, twirled his whiskered mustache, and patted Missy's nose with his tiny fingers.

His daily outfit usually consisted of a red vest decked out with three gold buttons. Today he wore a tiny silk smoking jacket, tied around his chubby waist.

"Did we wake you?" I asked, eyeing the clock. It was almost three in the afternoon.

Missy sniffed his tail as he trudged toward us. *"Non.* I was merely resting."

"Are you well?" I glanced between him and Mrs. P. What was going on around here?

"I am not *unwell*," Pepe said dramatically, pressing his hand to his forehead.

He'd been chumming with Archie far too often, if his theatrics were any indication.

I shot a glance to Godfrey for an explanation. Thick silver-threaded eyebrows dipped as he said, "This is the week of Pepe's discontent. I'm surprised you managed to root him from his bed at all."

"Ah, yes," Mrs. P said. "I'd forgotten."

"His what?" I asked.

Pepe sighed.

I reached down, scooped him up, and set him on the arm of my chair. "What's going on?"

Buttons strained on Godfrey's suit as he sat next to Mrs. P. "This week marks the anniversary of Pepe's death. He's always a wee bit melancholy this time of year. He drinks too much and spends his days and nights in bed."

Wonderful. Another dismal anniversary.

"That explains the smell," Mrs. P said.

"Madame, I beg your pardon!" Pepe protested, then surreptitiously sniffed his armpits.

"How long has it been, Pepe, since you bit the dust, so to speak?" Mrs. P asked.

"I've lost count of the years," he murmured. "They tumble by, one after the other, blending together like the pastel hues of an Impressionist painting."

Yep, too much time with Archie.

"Two hundred and sixteen years," Godfrey provided, relieving the buttons of their pressure by opening his coat. His big belly spilled out over his lap.

I could practically hear the buttons' sigh of relief.

Pepe threw him a disgusted glance, but didn't threaten to nip an ankle. Depression had definitely set in.

"Do you regret it?" I asked. "Becoming a familiar?"

"At times," he said. "It can be lonely."

"Hey," Godfrey protested. "I'm offended!"

"*That* cheers me immensely," Pepe said.

I never really thought about this aspect of being a familiar. They often lived long lives, yes, but solitary lives. "There are no other mice familiars in the village?" I asked. "One you could . . ."

"Hook up with," Mrs. P said, finishing my sentence.

"*Non.*" He shook his head, his ears flopping. "Not many choose to become a mouse. Swayed by thoughts of carrying the plague, I'm certain."

I made a face. "Do you carry the plague?"

Giving me a frazzled look, he said, "*Non*, familiars cannot carry the plague." He said it as though I were a few apples short of a bushel. "But there is a reputation . . ."

"How old were you when you died?" Mrs. P asked.

I looked at her.

"What?" she said. "I'm curious."

"I was a mere youth," Pepe said.

"Ha!" Godfrey snorted. "You were older than I am now."

"Perhaps when you've lived for more than two hundred years as a familiar, then you will reevaluate your definition of youth," Pepe snapped, gnashing his teeth.

That was more like the feisty Pepe I knew.

"Now, *excusez-moi*. I must return to my bed. There is

a marathon of *Downton Abbey* calling my name." In a graceful leap, he hopped to the ground.

"Wait!" I cried.

Slowly, he turned back toward us, the extent of his displeasure at his grand exit being interrupted etched into his narrowed eyes. "You need something, *ma chère*?"

Suddenly the endearment didn't sound so . . . dear.

"You're not the only one experiencing an annual week of discontent, my little friend," Mrs. P said. "There's Starla."

Godfrey *tsk*ed thoughtfully. "Ah, yes. It's been two years now, hasn't it? I remember clearly the day she came in, a week after the attack, her graceful neck still black and blue." His voice tightened. "She was looking for turtlenecks to cover the bruising."

A shiver slid down my spine, one vertebra at a time. My hands began to ache, and I realized I was clenching them into fists. Fists of anger. Of helplessness. Slowly I unfurled my fingers.

Some of the attitude left Pepe's eyes, replaced with suspicion as he watched my hands. "What's brought you here? Has something happened to her?"

He was an intuitive little mouse.

Sensing the shift in the air, Godfrey straightened. "*Has* something happened?"

"There's been an incident," I said and quickly explained.

Pepe walked back to us. "We'll do whatever is needed to help."

"Absolutely," Godfrey agreed.

"Until we find out for certain that Kyle Chadwick is back in the village, what I need is information. Starla doesn't talk much about her past with him, and if I've learned anything from moving here it's that the past sometimes comes back to haunt the present."

"Sometimes literally," Mrs. P said.

She referred to the time I was imprinted upon—a spirit attached to me until I solved his murder. "Do any of you know how they met?"

Mrs. P cupped her hands and held them out to Pepe.

He climbed in and she gently placed him onto the coffee table. While sitting, his little legs and long tail dangled over the edge.

Pepe said, "I believe it was at the Firelight Gala, three years ago. It was love at first sight. They were engaged after two months, married after four more."

Six months after that, he'd tried to kill her.

Godfrey said, "Starla was the most striking bride I've ever seen. She wore an ivory dress, with a sweetheart neckline, fitted through the waist and hips and flared at the bottom. Stunning. Simply stunning. But it wasn't the dress that made her so memorable. It was the glow in her eyes. The love shining through."

"They made a beautiful couple," Mrs. P said. "The quintessential perfect couple. As all-American as apple pie."

"Kyle adored her," Pepe said. "His family adored her. His family even helped them buy a perfect little house and everyone in the village hoped they'd soon have beautiful babies."

A lump lodged in my throat at the picture the three of them painted. "How did it go so horribly wrong?"

They all stayed silent. I looked from face to face.

Finally Pepe said, "No one knows."

"Starla began to withdraw," Godfrey said. "She stopped dropping by as often."

"She turned down job offers," Mrs. P said.

"She even shut out her brother, Evan," Pepe added.

"Kyle stopped seeing as much of his family. His paintings took a dark turn and didn't sell as well. They stopped appearing so much in public."

"Then one day," Mrs. P explained, "Starla dialed nine-one-one. Kyle was arrested. The village was torn apart."

"Somehow," Pepe said, "Kyle escaped from jail."

"Somehow?" I asked.

"Everyone believes his family helped him." Mrs. P leaned back on the couch. "They denied it, of course, and began a campaign to redeem his reputation, claiming Starla made much ado about nothing."

"Nothing? He tried to kill her!" I said, shocked.

Godfrey stroked his chin. "They believed it to be a fit of temper, a crime of passion, and that everyone makes mistakes. Most of the village sided with Kyle."

"How is that even possible?" I asked, my heart breaking for Starla. It had to have been a horrible time for her—not only because of the attack, but the aftermath as well. "Were people so blinded by Kyle's golden boy charm?"

"You must remember, doll," Mrs. P said, "that Starla had only been a villager for a couple of years at that point. She didn't grow up here as Kyle did."

"The village tends to protect its own," Godfrey added. "Even when it's not justified."

"By all appearances Kyle adored Starla. Doted on her," Pepe said. "No one could imagine he would harm her. And because they couldn't imagine it, they couldn't believe it."

"Do you believe it?" I asked him and Godfrey. After all, they were longtime villagers.

"I saw the wounds," Pepe said, twirling his whiskers. "And witnessed Starla's heartbreak. I believed her."

"As did I," Godfrey said.

I looked from face to face. "Do any of you know why Kyle might have returned?"

"I can think of only one reason," Godfrey said, his tone dark and ominous.

"What's that?" Mrs. P asked.

His eyes flashed. "He has returned to seek revenge."

Chapter Five

Darkness fell early this time of year, and at a little past four p.m. evening shadows already stretched across the village square as Missy and I walked along the sidewalk on our way to Harper's bookstore, Spellbound. Information about Kyle and Starla whirled through my head, clouding out almost everything else.

Revenge.

Deep down, I feared it was true.

It seemed unlikely that Kyle had returned to make amends or to turn himself in. Or else he would have done those things by now and wouldn't have stalked Starla at the ice rink.

I'd left Mrs. P with Pepe and Godfrey at the boutique and excused myself with a vague explanation about having to run errands.

The truth was that my brain was on overload. I needed time to process the information the three had shared with me. The mother hen in me wanted to fix this problem as soon as possible. The wait-and-see approach was driving me crazy.

If Kyle were back in town, I wanted to know why he was here. I wanted to know what he had planned. And I wanted to make sure Starla was safe.

If.

If he were back.

My cell phone rang, and I pulled it out of my tote bag, glanced at the ID screen, and quickly answered. "Starla? Is everything okay?"

Her voice was but a whisper. "He's outside my house."

"Did you call the police?"

"They're on the way."

"I'll be right there," I said, scooping up Missy and breaking into a jog.

"Hurry," she said, and hung up.

I kept Missy pressed close to my chest to limit the jostling. I ducked into the back alley behind Harper's shop—it was a shortcut to the row of brownstones where Starla and Evan lived in a corner unit. I thanked my lucky stars that I was in decent shape, due to my morning runs, and made it to Starla's doorstep just as a village police car—a light pink MINI Cooper—pulled up at the curb. Glinda's car.

I beat her up the walkway and banged on Starla's door. "It's me, Starla!"

Inside, I heard Twink barking and then the metal clank of a deadbolt turning.

Footsteps clumped up the steps, and Glinda Hansel bumped me from behind, shoving me against the door.

"Oh, sorry." Her hand rested on her gun. "I slipped."

"Right."

She blinked innocently.

As usual, she was gorgeous. Her beautiful blue eyes were alert, intelligent. Her strikingly pale blond hair was pulled back into a twist, and her skin flawless.

Starla pulled open the door just enough to peek out. Tears stained her face, the moisture tracking down her cheeks. "Why aren't you going after him?" she asked Glinda.

Glinda's head whipped around, her keen gaze searching the area. "Where is he?"

Slowly, Starla's eyes widened. "What do you mean, where is he? He's right there!" she pointed to a lamppost across the street.

Glinda glanced at me.

"Darcy, tell her!" Starla implored.

I stared at the lamppost.

There was no one there.

No one at all.

"Where is she?" Evan asked, storming into the kitchen at As You Wish much like his sister had done hours ago. He'd just returned from delivering a cake to a party on the South Shore.

His cheeks were flushed red, and his ginger blond hair stuck up in fluffs—as though he'd been running his hands through it over and over again. Panic laced his blue eyes. With rush hour traffic and also an accident on the expressway it had taken him two hours to get here.

"She's upstairs sleeping," I said, putting the kettle on the back burner of the stove. I'd managed to talk Starla into staying here for the time being. I'd quickly thrown some clothes, her laptop, her toothbrush, and her makeup into a tote bag and brought her and Twink home with me. "I had Cherise Goodwin stop by, and Starla agreed to a sleeping spell. She should be out for a while. Maybe all night." Cherise was a Curecrafter, a healing witch. She'd also been married to Terry once upon a time—she and Ve had a lot in common.

Cherise had quickly pulled me aside to tell me she suspected what ailed Starla wasn't likely something she could cure. Emotional pain and anxiety disorders were beyond the scope of her magic. She could, however, treat the symptoms, and said that for now the best thing for Starla was sleep.

Starla hadn't spoken much after realizing that only she could see Kyle. Just trembled and stared blankly.

He said, "I'm going to run up and check on her."

"Top of the stairs to the right."

He took the steps two at a time.

After feeding Missy, I washed my hands, put two

mugs and the tea caddy on the counter, and contemplated what to have for dinner. It was after seven and I realized I hadn't eaten since breakfast. Suddenly, I was famished. I finally decided to order in Chinese food and placed a quick call.

I hung up and sat on the bottom step of the back staircase, watching Missy pick at her food.

Tea, dinner plans . . . It was so *ordinary* that it felt wrong.

This was not an ordinary day.

Far from it.

The kettle whistled, and I jumped up to shut it off before the noise disturbed Starla. I poured steaming water into the mugs as Evan slowly came down the steps.

"She was sound asleep with her laptop balanced on her lap." He stirred sugar into his tea and flicked me a troubled glance. "She had a search engine called up with Kyle's name typed in."

I didn't know what she hoped to find. I doubted there was anything online that would explain Kyle's sudden resurfacing in her life.

I held the tea caddy out to Evan and he plucked a bag from the selection. I chose a spice blend and dropped it into my mug, dunking it with more force than it needed.

"Tilda gave me a dirty look when I moved the laptop. She and Twink are keeping a close watch over Starla," Evan said, then absently added, "I'm glad she's not alone up there."

"I don't think she should be alone until this mess is sorted out. You're both more than welcome to stay here until this is all settled."

He nodded. "Did Cherise have any explanation? Is this all in Starla's head?"

"Cherise isn't sure, but she is leaning that way."

Evan drew in a long breath, then blew it out. "I don't want to believe that's true, but I don't know of an invisibility spell, do you?"

I shook my head. I wasn't even sure one existed. Invisibility was frowned upon in the Craft world, except in extreme situations. There was an invisibility cloak I knew about, but when it was no longer needed it had been destroyed at the Elder's command.

Mrs. P could vaporize, but even she had limitations. There was a narrow time frame for her invisibility—only minutes before she regained her human form.

"There is a vanishing spell," I said. "But that's just for inanimate objects. Not people."

Violating Craft Law, Melina Sawyer, Nick's ex and Mimi's mom, had kept an impeccable journal that detailed some of the Craft's secrets, spells, and inner workings. Afraid of it falling into the wrong hands, I ultimately had to cast the vanishing spell on the diary itself. It was safe from those who'd use it for harm, but still accessible to Mimi and me. Once in a while we plucked it out of the ether to read more about our heritage.

Evan sipped his tea. "I don't know what to do."

"I'm not sure, either." I cupped my mug, letting the warmth seep into my hands. "Waiting makes me feel helpless."

"I just wish I knew if she was really seeing him, or if her mind's playing tricks on her. The physical wounds she suffered have long healed, Darcy, but the ones on the inside, the damage done to her emotionally . . . I've always been concerned that would never quite go away."

My nerves tingled at the word "wish" but then I relaxed. Evan was part Wishcrafter—I couldn't grant his wish even if I wanted to. And I really wanted to.

I easily conjured the image of Starla's terrified face when she opened her front door earlier. I shivered and gripped my mug harder. "I've known Starla for a while now, and I've never seen her this way. My gut instinct says that she sees him. I don't know how or why but he's here in the village."

Rubbing his eyes, he said, "I don't know whether to hope you're right or to hope you're wrong."

Whether Kyle had returned or her mind was playing tricks . . . both were abysmal scenarios. Except Starla's mind didn't have the ability to kill her. Kyle did.

"I'll talk to Will, Kyle's younger brother," Evan said. "And try to find out if he's heard anything about Kyle's return. He's the only one in the family who still speaks to us."

"Really?"

"The Chadwicks are tight-knit. Family is everything to them, and protecting one of their own is simply second nature. And if you don't side with them, you're against them. It's sad," Evan said. "Starla didn't just lose Kyle in their divorce, but a whole other family, who she loved dearly. And who supposedly loved her as well." He shook his head.

What a horrible situation. The aromatic scent of my tea usually soothed me. The allspice, cinnamon, orange . . . but not tonight. My nerves were shot.

Evan drew his tea bag from the cup and wrapped the string around the dripping bag. Wrapping, wrapping until the bag looked ready to split from the pressure.

I reached over and took it out of his hands.

"The thing is, Darcy, none of what happened made sense. Kyle adored Starla. He was kind and generous. He was that charming, that likable. His whole family was."

Sometimes life didn't make sense.

Bad things happened. Good people got hurt. Families were destroyed. "I heard Kyle had a temper. Did you ever witness it?"

"I wouldn't call it a temper, necessarily." He slid his mug back and forth between his hands. "He had passion, Darcy. About a lot of things. He'd get heated during talks of politics, of Red Sox games, his art . . . anything that he cared a lot about. He'd get loud and all puffed up the way guys do sometimes. It never led to anything physical, except that one time with the art critic."

"And when he tried to kill Starla," I added softly. I recalled what Mrs. P had said about Starla withdrawing. It sounded like classic domestic abuse behavior, and I had to wonder if it had been the first time he'd laid hands on her.

Shoving a hand through his hair, Evan looked like he was in pain. Furrowed forehead, eyes winced, tight lips. Quietly, as though afraid to say the words aloud, he whispered, "She would tell me, wouldn't she, if he'd hurt her before that?"

Ah, he'd been thinking the same thing. My heart squeezed. "I don't know."

There was a knock on the front door—probably dinner. Missy barked and took off to greet the guest, and I grabbed my wallet from my tote bag and turned on lights as I walked down the hallway. The front room where Ve and I met clients was filled with rich blues and greens, and light glinted off the silver curlicues on the wallpaper. My gaze settled on the painting above the mantel, a large watercolor of a golden magic wand, whimsical and ethereal. It spoke volumes about this house and the people who lived here.

Missy sniffed the bottom of the door, but her tail didn't wag as it usually did when greeting someone delivering food. Apprehension filled me as I peeked out the window, and I became even more concerned at the sight of the two men who stood on the front porch.

Missy slipped out the door as I reluctantly pulled it open.

The two men stood side by side, oblivious to the weather as snow swirled around them.

The taller of the two gave me a nod and lowered his hand for Missy to sniff. "We heard Starla was here, and we were hoping to have a word with her."

Missy apparently approved of our visitor, because she allowed her head to be scratched.

The slightly shorter one said, "We don't mean her any harm."

I didn't know what to do as I looked at their faces. Will and Liam Chadwick were the last people I'd expected to find on my doorstep. "I'm not sure—"

"Let them in, Darcy," Evan said from behind me. "It's okay."

I wasn't the least bit sure about that but held open the door, my curiosity piqued. "Come back to the family room," I said, letting Evan lead the way. Missy looked up at me, blinked, then trotted after the men. Letting out a sigh, I followed.

The family room was separated from the kitchen by a wide but short hallway that had the laundry room on one side and a powder room on the other. Light spilled across the dark hardwood floors as we made our way into what I considered the heart of the home.

With its overstuffed sofa, love seat, and chairs, thick area rug, bookcases stacked every-which-way with books, and the walls filled with artwork, this room had captured Aunt Ve's personality perfectly. It was a mix of warmth and comfort and crazy.

"Would you like some tea or coffee?" I offered.

Will Chadwick, the taller of the two, shook his head. "No, thanks."

I glanced at Liam. He shook his head as well.

They were handsome—very. But instead of their good looks being intimidating, there was a quirkiness about the two as well that made them approachable. Both had incredibly blue eyes—light as a noontime sky on a cloudless day. Liam's were framed in a pair of thick-rimmed glasses. His dark hair was combed into a messy pompadour, and he wore a wool pea coat, knit sweater, and tight jeans with loafers. Will's wavy dark blond hair hung to his shoulders. He wore a tweed coat, black jeans, a white T-shirt, and had a thin cashmere scarf wrapped around his neck.

Artsy. That's what they were—appropriately.

The fireplace filled the space with warmth, and I switched on another lamp to give us more light as they sat on the couch. I sat next to Evan on the love seat.

Will leaned forward, his hands clasped together. "The police came to speak with us today about an incident that happened with Starla. We just want to try and figure out what's going on. Can we talk to her?"

The police. Meaning Glinda. I wondered exactly what she'd said and if the family had any idea she was working undercover.

"She's sleeping right now," Evan said. "It's been a long day."

"What happened?" Will asked. "Exactly?"

I explained both incidents to them, and was struck by how well they listened without interrupting, without being defensive. It seemed as though they, like us, truly wanted to figure out this situation.

Will said, "This is a tough time of year for everyone involved."

Evan leaned forward. "Clearly tougher for Starla."

Annoyance flared in Liam's eyes before he hid it. "Our family is aware of Starla's plight, but it's unacceptable for her to drag Kyle's name through the mud once again."

I felt Evan stiffen so I reached out and put my hand on his arm. I said, "If the mud fits . . ."

"Kyle is not here in the village tormenting Starla," Liam argued.

Clearly, their silence a few moments ago while I was explaining had been the calm before the storm. Because they were certainly defensive now.

"You can't know that for sure," I said, my voice tight with growing anger.

"Unless you know where Kyle is," Evan added. "In which case you're harboring a fugitive."

Both sat silent as statues, their silence speaking volumes.

Oh, they knew where Kyle was.

"It's not Kyle who Starla is seeing," Will finally said, his serious tone emphasizing the statement. "It's . . . impossible. Listen, our family wants to nip this in the bud. It's not fair to any of us. If Starla needs psychological help, see that she gets it instead of raking Kyle over the coals when he's not here to defend himself."

Sheesh. And he was the brother who was still nice to Starla and Evan? What were the others like?

"And whose choice is that?" Evan snapped, half rising off the couch.

I pulled him down just as the back door opened and Nick's voice floated in from the mudroom. "I ran into the delivery guy in the driveway. Good timing. I'm starving. By the way, I got the fingerprint report on Starla's camera: It had been wiped clean." There was a pause. "Darcy?"

Springing off the couch, Missy went off to greet him.

I wasn't as eager. He wasn't going to like what he saw in here. "In the family room."

Footfalls echoed down the wooden hallway, and I

held my breath as he appeared under the arch that led into the family room, Missy in his arms.

Nick froze as he took in the occupants of the room. "What's going on here?"

I opened my mouth to answer just as a bloodcurdling scream split the air.

Jumping off the couch, I ran for the stairs. "Starla!"

Chapter Six

I barely noticed Harper coming in the back door as I raced up the staircase. I threw open the door to the guest bedroom and found Starla sitting up in bed, her eyes slammed shut, her arms flailing.

"I'll kill you! Don't touch me! I swear I'll kill you!" she screamed.

I ran for the bed as everyone else rushed into the room behind me. "Starla!" I grabbed her arms so she wouldn't hit me. "Starla! It's me, Darcy. Open your eyes!"

Harper dropped down next to the bed. "What happened?"

"I don't know," I said. "Call Cherise, okay?"

She nodded and shoved aside the four males crowding the doorway.

Starla slowly opened her eyes, but her pupils remained unfocused. Letting out a heart-wrenching sob, she crumpled against me. I wrapped my arms around her. Evan came and sat next to her as I rubbed her back and smoothed her hair.

"Make him go away," she mumbled into my chest.

Nick immediately checked the closet and under the bed—where I heard a loud hiss followed by a high-pitched bark. Tilda and Twink must have been hiding under there.

Nick stood up and shook his head. The room was clear.

I glanced around. Everything seemed in its place. There was nothing overturned, no sign of a struggle. No sign at all that someone had broken in.

"Kyle was here?" I asked for confirmation.

"You must have been dreaming," Will said.

I hated to think that he might be right.

She straightened and wiped her eyes. Her whole body trembled. I draped a quilt over her shoulders as she tried to focus on the faces in the room. "No, he was here, whispering my name. He . . ."

"What?" Nick asked, checking the windows. They were locked tight.

Her voice shook. "He told me he was sorry, that he loved me."

The Chadwick brothers exchanged a glance I couldn't quite decipher.

Harper edged her way back into the room.

"He . . . touched me. I freaked out and started screaming. He grabbed my wrist." She held it up, and I gasped at the redness blooming on her skin.

Nick took a closer look and whistled low.

Liam said, "Could have been self-inflicted."

Harper jabbed him in the chest with her finger. "Don't make me kick your ass."

His eyes widened behind his glasses, and she cocked her head, daring him to say something else. He pressed his lips together.

"He was here," Starla cried. "I tell you, he was here."

"Tilda *is* freaked out under the bed," Nick pointed out. "Her fur's on end."

That was very telling—Tilda wouldn't have left Starla's side unless she'd been spooked.

"It's impossible," Will asserted. "Impossible!"

Starla leveled a stare on him. "He was here."

Evan rubbed her arm. "We believe you, Starla."

Liam, I noticed, took a step back into the hallway, and a moment later he came back in, slipping his cell phone in his pocket as he did so. I guessed he'd just texted someone. Most likely his parents. Or perhaps Kyle himself, to see if Starla's story was true. Nick could easily check his phone records.

"Did you see him come in?" Nick asked Starla. "Did he use the door? The window?"

She shook her head. "I don't know. I heard him saying my name—it's what woke me up."

"Even if he'd somehow gotten inside without us noticing," Will said, "we would have seen him leaving."

I hated that he was right. "Did he go out the door, Starla? Or the window?"

Tears spilled down her face. "I don't know. I closed my eyes, heard him say good-bye, and then you were in the room."

"This is crazy," Liam said. "She's crazy. You need to get professional help, Starla." He sidestepped away from Harper as she swung her leg to kick him.

"If you touch me," he warned her, "I will press assault charges."

"It will be worth it," Harper seethed.

"Enough," Nick said sternly.

Starla lifted her chin and drew in a deep breath. "If I'm crazy, how did I get these?" She opened her trembling palm, revealing two golden bands. Wedding bands.

Evan gasped.

Will's eyes widened. "Where'd you get those?"

"Kyle gave them to me," Starla said. "Just now. He pushed them into my hand."

Starla closed her eyes, then opened them again. "I don't know how he had both of them. Mine was in a jewelry box in my bedroom. I took it off after the divorce was finalized. He must have broken into my place to take it. His . . . He always had his."

Nick shot me a look, then quickly glanced away. Something about what Starla had said struck him as odd.

Liam's voice cracked a little as he said, "I don't know

how you did this, but it's not right, Starla. There's something seriously wrong with you. This . . . this is wrong."

Such strong emotion that I truly believed *he* believed what he was saying. Why couldn't he accept that his brother had been here? Those rings all but proved it.

Fresh tears filled Starla's eyes. "Get out!" she shouted to the brothers.

Harper was already herding them to the door. "It's time for you two to go."

Nick nodded. "I agree."

Both left without another word, and Harper followed them out, probably to slam the door behind them. Missy followed the trio.

A few seconds later, we looked up as we heard footsteps outside the doorway. Will Chadwick stuck his head in the room.

We all stared at him. Finally, Nick said, "Yes?"

Will cleared his throat. "What was he wearing, Starla?"

"Wearing?" she asked, her pale brows furrowed. She shrugged. "A white T-shirt and flannel pajama pants. Blue ones." She glanced at me. "Why is he out in this weather in a T-shirt? He'll freeze."

My heart squeezed. Even after everything, she still cared about him. Cared that he might get *cold*.

Will gave a quick nod and backed out of the doorway. His footsteps echoed on the wooden stairs.

I glanced at Nick. "They obviously know where Kyle is."

"It seems that way," Nick conceded.

So much for Glinda getting any information from the family.

He swiped a hand down his face. "How did Kyle get in and out without any of us seeing him?"

There was only one way. "It has to be some sort of invisibility spell."

Evan hugged his sister a little tighter. "We need to ask the Elder. Some spells have a recantation spell that will counteract it," he explained to Nick. "If we know which one Kyle is casting, then Starla might be able to get Kyle to appear to all of us."

I'd learned all about recantation spells this past summer. It was exactly what we needed. "I'll have Archie relay a message to the Elder that I'd like to see her," I said. It was the fastest way to get a meeting with her.

Starla started crying again. "Why is he doing this? Why?" She sucked in deep gulps of air.

My heart broke for her as she dissolved into sobs once again. I hesitated to leave, but Evan waved me off. Nick followed me out.

We'd just left the room as Cherise Goodwin appeared at the top of the stairs. Short and plump with beautiful shoulder-length white hair, she reminded me of Cinderella's godmother, only hipper with her teased hair and love of chunky jewelry. Kindness emanated from her eyes as she reached a hand out to me. "The sleeping spell didn't work?"

"It's a long story. She's not doing well. Evan's in with her, and he can explain everything. I need to see Archie to get a message to the Elder."

"Don't worry, Darcy. I'll take care of Starla." She gave my hand a squeeze, then rushed into the guest room, her gray woolen cape flying out behind her dramatically.

"How long do you think it will take for the Elder to get back to you?" Nick asked as we headed downstairs.

I peeked out the back door. Archie's cage was empty. "I'm not sure. Sometimes it's minutes. Sometimes it's days."

"And you still don't know who she is?"

"Not a clue." I glanced around. "Where'd Harper go?"

Nick's gaze fell on the hooks by the door. "Her coat is gone."

I held in a groan. If I knew my sister well—and I did— she was following the Chadwick brothers. "Missy's leash is missing, too. She probably took her for a walk." As a ruse . . .

"She's following them, isn't she?" Nick asked, his brown eyes full of incredulity.

Apparently, he knew Harper well, too. I scrunched up my nose. "That would be my guess."

I braced myself for a lecture from him, but instead he pulled me against his chest and kissed me.

I let myself get lost in his touch, wanting to forget—for only a moment—the chaos of this day. I wasn't one who let my emotions run wild or free. But I'd fallen hard for this man and couldn't help but feel the splinter of discontent that had pierced our lives. Our hearts.

Glinda had wedged herself in there but good. I needed to find a pair of tweezers to pluck her right back out again, because there was no way I was going to let her keep dividing us.

"Let me know what she learns, okay?" he finally said.

I smiled against his neck. It seemed he was ready to do a little tweezing as well. "While we were upstairs, I saw Liam duck out to the hallway to send a text message to someone. . . ."

"I saw that, too. I'll see about getting his phone records."

Snow fell gently, backlit by the porch light. I hoped those records led him straight to Kyle. "Do you want to come with me to see Archie?"

Slowly, he shook his head. "I'll stay and call in the incident to the station. Just in case Kyle somehow slipped past us. Then I'll see if Starla remembers anything else before Cherise knocks her out again."

I grabbed his hand, holding it tightly. I loved the roughness of his fingers as they curved around my own. "She's not crazy. This isn't in her mind. I think those wedding bands prove that."

He said quietly, "I don't know what to think."

"Do you trust me?" I asked him.

"It's not about trust. It's about evidence. How can you—"

And just like that the splinter doubled in size.

No, no, no. I willed it to shrink back down.

I pressed my fingers to his lips to cut him off. "It's not always about tangible evidence. Sometimes it's gut instinct. Sometimes it's a honed judgment. Sometimes it's only a *feeling*. One you have to trust. Especially here in this village. With our kind of magic. Do you trust me?"

Tension tightened the muscles of his body as his eyelids drifted closed. He'd come from a mortal world, where seeing was believing. Even though he knew of the Craft he still didn't fully understand it.

Even though I'd also come from a mortal world, I could feel the magic within me. It was easier for me to embrace what that meant along with all the quirks of the Craft. I *understood*. All he had to do was trust me.

Slowly, his eyes opened and focused on me with such intensity that I wanted to look away. He was searching my face for something—some sort of answer to an internal question.

I refused to blink or even breathe. I tried to tell him with my eyes all he needed to know. All he already knew and was either too blind or too stubborn to have seen before.

Cupping my face, he lowered his head and kissed me again. Slowly. Deeply. The kiss was an allegiance. A promise. He pulled back just a little, his lips still touching mine. "I trust you."

I bit my bottom lip, trying to keep from smiling too broadly. Those words meant a lot to him. Melina had broken his confidence, and I knew how difficult it was for him to open up his trust to another woman.

Almost as hard as it had been for me to open my heart to him.

I wanted to do a little happy dance right there in the mudroom as that splinter shrank right down to a tiny speck. But with the creak of footsteps overhead, the seriousness of the day practically smacked me upside the head.

I said, "I need to find Archie."

He said, "I need to get back upstairs."

Yet, neither of us moved.

I love you. My heart clutched just thinking the words, and couldn't imagine saying them aloud. But if ever there were a time, this was it. Our hearts pounding against each other. That look in his eyes . . . The realization that we were almost splinter-free.

"I . . . I—" I gurgled, the words stuck in my throat.

He smiled, encouraging me.

Just do it, Darcy. Say it! "I—"

A sudden knocking on the back door made me jump, and I banged my head against his chin.

He grunted as I groaned. "Ow!"

His eyes glinted mischievously in the light. "Funny, that's not what I thought you were going to say."

I smiled, but the spell had been broken. He rubbed his chin as I rubbed my forehead and reached for the door-knob as the visitor knocked again.

Pulling open the door, my breath caught at the man standing there, a wild look in his eyes and a disk in his hand. "Vince?"

"Mrs. P told me what was going on with Starla's ex. I've been worried sick since she's not at home and not answering calls, but I just saw Harper on the green and she said Starla was here. . . . Can I see her?"

"She's upstairs with Evan and Cherise Goodwin right now," I said. "Maybe in a little bit?"

"Is she okay? I mean, why is Cherise here?"

Although Vince was a Seeker, he knew of Cherise's medical abilities. Around the village she was a well-known naturopath but he didn't know about her *magical* heal-ing gift.

Trying to comfort him, I put my hand on his arm in hopes of stemming his panic. It was obvious how much he cared for Starla, and that made me feel guilty for not fully trusting him. "She's okay. Just a little stressed out. Cherise is giving her something to help her sleep."

I didn't mention that "something" was a spell.

He sagged in relief. "I can't tell you how worried I was. *Am.* If her ex is back . . . Did you find him yet?" he asked Nick.

Nick motioned him inside and closed the door. "We're looking for him."

I motioned to Vince's hand. "What's that?"

"Something I thought might help the investigation, but it only confused me. . . . I thought Starla should see it. Well, all of you should see it, I guess."

I led the way into the kitchen. The Chinese food bags were still sitting on the counter. "What is it?"

"My shop's surveillance footage from this afternoon. When Mrs. P told me about the incident from the skating rink, I realized my outside camera would have caught it." He kept throwing glances up the back staircase as though longing to go up there and see for himself that Starla was okay. "I thought the police might want verification that Kyle Chadwick was back in the village."

I heard a "but" in his voice. A big one.

"But . . ." he said, "well, you need to see it for yourself. Do you have a DVD player?"

"In the family room," I said, feeling uneasy. "Did you see Kyle on the footage?"

Vince looked at me, his big puppy dog eyes filled with confusion. "I'm not sure, Darcy."

"Why aren't you sure?" Nick asked.

Vince's Adam's apple bobbed. "Because whoever was at the rink today was invisible."

Chapter Seven

Invisible. I bit my lip and tried not to appear unnerved. "Really?" I asked, trying to inject levity into the two syllables.

"I know it doesn't make sense," Vince said. "But there's no denying what's on the footage."

"Maybe we should take a look." Nick took the disk into the family room and popped it into the DVD player.

Cherise and Evan came down the back stairs just as Vince was saying, "For some reason, Starla's image never comes up on film. She's just this strange bright blur, see?" He pointed at the screen.

Evan held Twink in the crook of his arm. "What's going on?" He scrutinized the TV.

"Vince brought surveillance footage of the green this afternoon," Nick explained.

"Starla doesn't have a metal plate or something, does she, that would interfere with signals?" he asked Evan.

Evan tried to look innocent as he said, "Not that I know of."

"Strange," Vince murmured. "It happens with you and Darcy and Ve and Harper, too. . . ." His gaze narrowed.

Cherise busied herself with a loose thread on her cape.

How long had he been watching us? "Maybe there's something wrong with your camera," I said quickly.

"Maybe," he murmured. "Anyway, you can see the camera clearly next to the white blur." We watched as the blur set the camera on the bench, then took off toward As You Wish.

"Is Kyle on the video?" Evan asked, setting Twink on the sofa. The tiny dog turned three times and settled into the corner of the couch.

"We haven't gotten that far yet," I said.

Cherise stepped up next to me and said, "Starla's out like a light, so I'm going to go home now. Call me if there's any change with her. I can be over in a jiff."

"Thanks, Cherise. I'll walk you out," I said, needing to speak to her without being overheard by Vince.

Her eyes filled with understanding.

"Can you pause that?" I asked Vince.

He nodded.

As Cherise and I headed into the kitchen, I heard Vince peppering Evan with questions about Starla's well-being, and Nick making a call to the police station.

At the back door, Cherise said, "What's going on with Vince, Darcy?"

I didn't mince words as I dropped my voice. "It looks like he has footage of an invisible Kyle tampering with Starla's camera. Can you do me a favor and find Archie? Let him know what's going on?" I didn't want to leave what was happening in the family room. "I think the Elder needs to get involved with this Vince situation."

A Seeker was bound to question the whole invisibility thing—and was more likely to tie it to Wishcraft than the average mortal.

"I'm on it." She pulled the hood of her cape over her head. "And call if Starla needs anything."

"Thanks, Cherise."

She patted my cheek, then disappeared into the swirling snow.

Nick had finished his call and when he spotted me heading back to the family room he unpaused the video. Vince sat on the arm of the sofa, his leg jiggling at a furious pace. Evan stood next to Nick, his gaze glued to the TV.

Vince said, "So you can see that Kyle's not in the shot, right?"

A *visible* Kyle wasn't at least.

Nick said, "This is some high-resolution video. You must have quite the surveillance system."

Fidgeting, Vince shrugged. "What's the point of having grainy images if there's a break-in? They won't be any help in making an identification."

I watched him closely. He wasn't telling the whole truth—I could tell by the way his gaze jumped around. Holding in a sigh, I hoped Cherise had luck finding Archie. I had a feeling Vince's high-quality video had more to do with keeping an eye on the village than potentially catching a would-be criminal. Once a Seeker, always a Seeker. How his relationship with Starla factored into his obsession with the Craft remained to be seen.

"It's coming up," Vince said, pointing at the screen. "You'll see Starla's camera clearly on the bench then . . . wait for it . . . there! Did you see it?"

I swallowed hard. It was impossible to miss the way the camera levitated.

Nick rewound, then replayed the footage as though not believing what he'd seen the first time.

Evan and I shared a worried glance as Vince jumped off the couch and went to stand a foot from the TV. By his look, he didn't know how to explain this away, either.

"It's clear as day," he said, pointing. "The camera lifts off the bench by itself, then lowers back down."

Nick glanced at me. "It's quite something," he murmured.

Vince spun around, his eyebrows furrowed. He looked from face to face. "Why don't any of you seem surprised?"

I gulped and stammered. "It's . . . it's just impossible, isn't it? It has to be a glitch in the video."

"Right," Evan said. "A glitch."

Vince's eyes narrowed. "There's no glitch. This is a state-of-the-art system. What's going on?"

I was saved from answering by the sound of a rooster crowing at the back door. Only it wasn't a rooster at all—the noise was Archie's calling card. He'd arrived.

"Is that a *rooster*?" Vince asked.

"I, ah . . . I'll check," I said, as though that were the most rational thing to do at that moment. "I'll be right back." I dashed to the back door, yanked it open, and slipped outside.

Archie hovered under the porch roof, his wings flapping loudly in the quiet night. A small plastic baggie dangled from his claws. "Here, take this, Darcy," he said, dropping the bag into my hands. "It's the memory cleanse. Blow some into Vince's face, and then come back and let me in."

I opened the bag, shook some of the fine sparkly powder into my hand, and then headed back into the house. My heart thumped loudly in my ear as I tried to appear calm.

As I came into the family room, I let out a forced laugh. "Not a rooster. Just the bird next door making noises."

Vince peered around me. "That's one strange bird."

"Oh, I know." I peered at him as though inspecting his nose. "What's that on your face?" I leaned in, lifted my hand, and blew the sparkly powder his way.

He coughed, waving away the pluming cloud. Then his eyes slammed shut and he crumpled to the ground as glitter rained down around him.

Nick's jaw dropped. "Is he dead?"

"Of course not," I said. "Craft motto is 'Do no harm,' remember? It's a memory cleanse. After he wakes up Vince won't remember a thing about his time here. Or the video."

Evan knelt next to Vince and said, "Perfect timing. I couldn't think of one thing to explain that footage."

I rushed back to the door and let Archie inside. He

flew past me and landed on the floor next to Vince's prone body. He poked him with his wing, leaned in close to Vince's nose as though checking for breathing, and then said, "'Good night and sweet dreams . . . which we'll analyze at breakfast.'"

I smiled and said, "*Spellbound.*"

Archie bowed. "Ah, how I adore Ingrid Bergman, and Gregory Peck can pluck me any day."

Evan stared at Archie, one eyebrow raised. "Vince is right. You *are* one strange bird."

Evan and Archie had never really gotten along. Evan thought Archie too melodramatic, and Archie thought Evan too starchy.

"You're a fine one to talk," Archie countered. "You know you'd let Gregory Peck pluck your feathers, too. And if I had my guess, you need a good plucking."

Apparently contemplating the scenario, Evan tipped his head and said, "You're right, I would." He smiled. "And I do."

"I might know of someone. . . ." Archie began.

"Um, hello," I said. "This isn't *The Dating Game*. We have an issue here." I gestured to Vince. I squinted. "Is the glitter dissolving?"

"It is. When it's completely gone, he will awaken." Archie prodded him again and said, "He will be out for an hour or so. Enough time to concoct a story as to why he passed out here."

"That's easy," I said. "He came over to see Starla, slipped in the icy street in front of the house, and hit his head. Evan carried him inside. Vince won't remember having the disk, so we'll just let Nick keep that for potential evidence."

"Better make it that Nick helped him inside," Evan said. "I haven't been to the gym in a while."

Archie coughed. "You mean ever?"

"I have two words for you: deep fryer," Evan threatened.

"I dare you." Archie puffed out his chest and opened and closed his beak like he was planning to bite something off Evan. A finger or nose or whatever he could get his beak on.

"That's enough, you two," I said. "You can save your whole Jets versus Sharks thing for later."

Nick rubbed his eyes but still looked stunned. "Should I be alarmed at how easily you came up with that lie about Vince?" he asked me.

"Impressed is a better word choice," I said. "When you're in the business of magic, being able to think on your feet is always a good thing."

Archie flew onto the arm of the couch. "Now I can't get 'I Feel Pretty' out of my head. Thanks a lot, Darcy."

"Ugh," Evan groaned. "Now it's in mine, too."

"I feel pretty," Archie sang.

"And witty and bright," Evan added.

Nick looked at me. "Where the hell am I?"

I stood up, gave his cheek a quick kiss, and said, "Welcome to the Enchanted Village."

I was about to join in the songfest (because, dammit, now the song was stuck in my head, too), when the back door flew open. We all froze, and I tried to quickly come up with a lie about why a glittery Vince Paxton was passed out on the family room floor.

But I'd apparently used up my ability to think on my feet.

We'd been caught in the act.

Fortunately, I realized quickly that we'd been busted by Aunt Ve, and I let out the breath I was holding.

At first Ve didn't notice us. She came sailing into the kitchen, whipping off her coat, and *oohing* over the Chinese food on the counter. "Darcy! I'm home and I'm starving! You wouldn't believe the traffic coming back from the Cape. And was that Cherise Goodwin's car I saw out front? Darcy?"

"In here," I said.

She spun around, took two steps toward the family room—just enough to see inside the space—and came to an abrupt stop at the sight before her: Nick and me standing side by side wearing guilty expressions. Evan kneeling next to a crumpled, glitter-covered Vince, and Archie softly whistling "I Feel Pretty."

She blinked once, twice, and then said, "Oh, I see.

Have all the fun when I'm not here. Let me get the food
and the plates, and then you delinquents can tell me all
about this." She waved her hand over Vince's body. "And
don't leave out a single glittery detail."

Later that night, Aunt Ve and I sat on the sofa in the
family room, sharing a blanket and a pot of herbal tea. It
was well past both our bedtimes—we were normally
early-to-bed kind of witches but this day had been far
from normal.

We were staying up until midnight, the witching hour.
There was a protection spell to be cast and that was the
time to do it.

Tilda lay on the back of the sofa, her tail flicking every
few seconds. Twink was upstairs, tucked into bed with
Starla, and Evan slept on a blow-up mattress on the floor
next to his sister.

Vince had awoken never the wiser as to what had
happened. He sat with Starla for a while, then went
home. Nick had gone home, too, without me. In light of
all that happened, our date night had been postponed.

Ve hadn't been able to explain Kyle's invisibility, either. His ability to travel freely about the village was disconcerting to say the least. When Archie left he had
promised to contact the Elder right away, but we hadn't
yet heard back from her. I had to wonder at the delay.
This situation seemed fairly dire to me.

The only light in the room came from the glow of the
flames dancing in the fireplace. A muted orange light illuminated Ve's face, highlighting drowsy eyes and the
coppery strands of her hair pulled into a high bun atop
her head.

"Maybe you should see if Harper made it home safe
and sound," she suggested. "I don't like her out and
about alone this late at night."

"Missy's with her."

Ve crooked an eyebrow.

Truth be told, I wasn't all that pleased about Harper's
excursion, either, but I was trying not to fly into mother
hen mode. Harper had finally texted me a couple of

hours ago, saying that she'd followed the Chadwick brothers into the Enchanted Forest—acres and acres of dense woods that surrounded the village—and would check in later.

The more I thought about Harper being in the woods on a moonless night, the more worried I became. I reached for my phone. "Fine. But if she lectures me about her being a grown woman and not needing someone to look after her, I'm giving you the phone."

Aunt Ve sipped her tea, her short fingers barely encircling the delicate teacup. "I'm not scared of her."

It was my turn to lift an eyebrow.

"Not much," Ve added, smiling.

I was punching in Harper's number when my phone vibrated with an incoming text message. It was from Harper.

I'm home. I'll keep Missy tonight. Will see you in the morning. Do you have snowshoes?

I loved how my sister used proper grammar and punctuation in text messages. I'd yet to see an LOL out of her and doubted I ever would.

"She wants to know if I have snowshoes," I said to Ve.

"Have mercy," my aunt said. "I can only imagine why she wants to know."

I typed back.

Me: No, why?

Harper: You'll need some.

Me: Whaaat?

Harper: He's in those woods. We need to find him.

We. I loved that there was no question as to whether I'd help her. She knew she didn't even have to ask.

Me: No, I don't have snowshoes.

Harper: We'll have to go shopping first then. Be ready first thing tomorrow morning.

She loved nothing better than to boss me around.

Me: Good night, Harper.

Harper: There's nothing good about it.

I could easily hear my sister's voice grumpily saying

those words, and I smiled as I ended the call. "She's on a mission."

Ve said, "I'm not sure it's wise to go back into the woods. The police are bound to be searching them as well, and if Glinda catches the two of you . . . don't make that face at me, Darcy Merriweather. You know it's true."

"I'm just so sick of Glinda." To my own ears I sounded as grumpy as I imagined Harper a few moments ago.

"Well then, let's change the subject to a happier topic," Ve said.

"Like?" Tilda's tail flicked me in the head, and I brushed it aside.

"Your birthday, my dear."

Happy. Ha. I thought not. The dreaded day was next Saturday.

"How would you like to celebrate your big day?" Ve asked with a gleam in her eye.

"Forget it?" I suggested.

"Not a chance. There have been enough memory cleanses here tonight," she said. "I was thinking a small party, next Saturday night. I can't do Sunday, as I have a prior commitment. We'll invite friends and family. Mrs. Pennywhistle, Godfrey, Pepe . . ."

"Have you seen Mrs. P lately?" I interrupted.

Firelight flickered in the pupils of her eyes. "Are you now changing the subject, dear?"

"Yes, but for good reason." I explained about my worrisome encounter with Mrs. P that morning and her potential heart troubles.

"I had no idea she's been feeling ill," Ve said, topping off her cup from the teapot on the coffee table. Thin wisps of steam rose from the dark liquid. "Has she been to see Cherise or Dennis?"

Dennis was Cherise and Terry Goodwin's son, a Curecrafter as well as a doctor with a proper M.D. He wasn't my favorite person in the village, but he was talented at his job and proving to be a stand-up kind of guy. "I'm not sure. She said she'd seen a heart doctor."

"I'll ask Cherise when I see her next. See if she has any scoop for us."

There was no right to privacy among Crafters, which accounted for our tendency to be secretive with just about everything.

"Now back to your party," she said. "We can hold it here, or at the Cauldron. Pepe can make you something lovely to wear. . . ."

"No party," I insisted. "Besides, Pepe's busy this week."

"With what?"

"It's the week of his discontent."

"Yes, yes. I'd forgotten." She sipped her tea. "Poor little man."

"Should we do something to cheer him up?"

"Like throw a birthday party for you? What a lovely idea! Everyone loves a party!"

Not everyone. Not at all. "You're relentless."

"Tenacious is more like it."

"I don't need a party. I like quiet birthdays."

"Phooey," Aunt Ve said.

I didn't want to explain to her that for most of my life my birthdays were simply another day on the calendar. Early on, after my mother died, I would get my hopes up about my birthday, creating fantasies of my father surprising me with a party or even a quiet family dinner out (so I didn't have to cook) or receiving a meaningful gift from him. And every year I was disappointed. My father rarely remembered my birthday at all and when he did, he usually gave me only a card with cash stuffed inside. When Harper was old enough, she tried to pick up his slack, and I treasured her little handmade gifts and lopsided cakes more than I could ever say. But really, birthdays dredged up all kinds of emotions I'd rather have left buried, exposed wounds best left hiding under a thick bandage.

I suppose my birthday was the day of *my* discontent.

"Pepe will be fine," Ve said after studying me for a long moment. "A little wallowing does no harm once in a while. He always snaps to once the week is up."

"I just feel like we should make him soup or something."

"Ah, Darcy. Such a tender heart you have."

"You say that like it's a bad thing." This wasn't the first time I'd uttered those words after she made such sweeping comments. Usually a life lesson for me followed soon thereafter.

"No, it's not a bad thing," she said softly. "Tender hearts are loving . . . yet often naive and can break easily. One must be very careful."

Thinking of Nick and Mimi, I bit my lip.

She watched me carefully for a few moments, then said, "I suppose a little soup couldn't hurt Pepe, and I know it will make you feel better at any rate."

It would make me feel better. I didn't like seeing my friends hurting. Doing something, anything, even making soup, would make me feel less useless. With that thought in mind, I also planned to make soup for Starla as well. Or perhaps a stew . . .

We sat in silence for a few minutes before I suddenly sat up straight. "Oh!" I said. "I forgot in the midst of all the chaos that a package arrived today. Crystals?"

Ve's eyes lit. She rubbed her hands together. "Good, good!"

"What're they for?"

"The Swing and Sway dance competition. I'm on the decoration committee."

"The what?"

"The Swing and Sway." She smiled. "It's held every January at the Will-o'-the-Wisp."

The Will-o'-the-Wisp was a local venue that often held wedding receptions and the like, so it was entirely plausible that a dance competition would be hosted there. "When is it?"

There was a twinkle in her eyes as she said, "This coming weekend. Sunday—it's the commitment I just mentioned."

"Why haven't I heard about it before now?" A dance competition would be highly publicized around the village.

"It's very exclusive. Invitation only."

"Why is it exclusive? Is it for swingers or something?" I mean, it was called the Swing and Sway after all.

"I wish."

I rolled my eyes.

"But, if you must know, Darcy dear, the dance . . ." Aunt Ve tipped her head as though searching for just the right explanation. "It's very secretive because there might be a few state ordinances being broken," she said. Then she giggled. "The competitors dance naked except for bow ties for the men and silk gloves for the women."

My jaw dropped. "You're joking."

"Nope."

Images rushed at me. I squeezed my eyes shut. I was going to have to wash my imagination out with soap. "I didn't need to know that."

She patted my hand and laughed. "You asked."

"I wish I hadn't." Wished it with all my might.

"Does that mean you don't want an invitation?"

I popped open an eye. "No, thanks."

Still laughing, she glanced at the clock, and drew back the blanket we shared. "Come on, my sweet little witch, it's time."

The minute hand on the mantel clock was about to sweep toward the number twelve. Midnight. It was time to cast the protection spell for Starla.

As I followed Ve into the kitchen, I couldn't help but wish she didn't need it.

But I feared she did.

Kyle Chadwick was back in the village.

And being invisible made him that much more dangerous.

Chapter Eight

The snowshoe idea had been abandoned when Harper showed up in my bedroom at six thirty the next morning. Missy leapt onto the bed, her tail wagging, her doggy breath fogging up my glasses as I settled them on my nose.

"Why aren't you awake?" Harper asked in a loud whisper. "We have things to do, places to see, a sociopath to track down. Let's go, let's go." She bent over and clapped in my face.

Yawning, I smacked her hands away. Usually I was up by now—I was an early bird—but I'd been up late with Aunt Ve casting the protection spell and was in no mood for my sister's enthusiasm.

"*Shh,*" I said. "Starla and Evan are probably still sleeping."

They were in the room next door, and the walls were quite thin. As far as I knew, Starla had slept through the night. I hoped she'd awaken today feeling less anxious. I hoped Evan slept in as well—Saturdays were the only mornings he wasn't at the bakery first thing in the morning.

He worked too hard, in my opinion, going to work in the wee hours and getting home late. I knew he loved his bakery and didn't mind the crazy-long workweeks, but I thought he could delegate a little more. It would allow him to have more of a social life as well. I'd love to see him fall for someone, settle down.

"They are. I just checked," Harper said. "All the better for us to go now so we'll get back before they wake up."

Outside, I heard a mourning dove cooing, its gentle song a direct contrast to Harper's animated voice. I squinted toward the window. "It's not even light out."

"It will be in"—she looked at her watch—"forty-five minutes. Just enough time for you to get up, get dressed, get caffeinated, get bundled, and hit the Enchanted Trail with me."

Missy bounded off the bed and out the door, probably anticipating her breakfast. I tossed my covers aside. "You're entirely too bright-eyed right now."

Rubbing her hands together, Harper smiled. "We're going to find him today, I just know it. I think I know where I lost the brothers' tracks last night. I went left when I should have gone right."

"You're lucky they didn't realize you were following them."

"What would they have done?"

I trudged to my dresser and pulled out a T-shirt, sweatshirt, a pair of thermal leggings and a pair of wind-resistant running pants I used for jogging this time of year. No jogging today, however. This trek through the forest would be exercise enough. "I'm not sure. Desperate people do desperate things, and if they know where their brother is hiding—and haven't turned him in yet—then they're both probably desperate to keep his location a secret."

She smirked. "That's a lot of desperation."

I threw a pair of rolled-up socks at her. "You joke, but I'm serious."

"Come on, Darcy. I could probably take both of them down. Did you see how skinny they were?"

I glanced at my tiny sister, all five feet (barely) of her,

and rolled my eyes before heading into the bathroom to brush my teeth and do something with my hair.

The thing was, she probably could take both of them down. People often underestimated her because of her diminutive size, but she was a ferocious opponent who had no qualms about fighting dirty.

However, I'd rather her not be placed in a situation where she had to fight at all.

When I came out of the bathroom, she was gone. I headed toward the stairs but stopped in front of the guest room, pressing my ear to the door. Evan's soft snores carried easily. Across the hall, Aunt Ve's bedroom door was open wide and Tilda sat on the already-made bed giving me the kitty equivalent of the evil eye. "Good morning to you, too," I said to her.

She turned around, giving me a good view of her tail.

Tilda spent every other weekend with an Emoticrafter friend of ours, Lew—the result of a strange shared-custody agreement concocted after she involuntarily spent some time with him last year (what an ordeal that was). He wanted to keep her; she wanted to stay with him; but Ve and I weren't ready to let her go. This wasn't one of her visitation weekends, and she was letting me know how unhappy she was to be stuck here with us.

The poor thing had such a rough life.

I crept down the back stairs, trying to be as quiet as possible as I descended into the kitchen. Harper sat at a counter stool and Ve was already showered and dressed and had a cup of coffee waiting for me. Missy and Twink stood side by side eating breakfast from twin bowls set on the floor. Missy was a small dog, but Twink was absolutely tiny next to her.

"You girls are flat-out crazy," Ve said as I sat next to my sister.

"Harper's the crazy one," I said, taking the mug. "I'm just enabling her insanity."

"Hey," Harper objected pitifully.

Really, she had no argument.

Humor filled Ve's eyes. "Just be careful. If you find

Kyle's hideout, do not approach him. Do you hear? Get out of there and call the police."

"I promise," I said. The last thing I wanted was a run-in with crazy Kyle.

Ve stared at Harper.

"Yeah, yeah," my sister grumbled.

"Does Marcus know what you're up to this morning?" Ve asked her.

Marcus Debrowski was a Lawcrafter and Harper's boyfriend. She liked to play coy about how deep her feelings ran for him, but I could see she was head over heels.

"He doesn't need to know what I'm doing every second of every day," she said in a tone that made me think she hadn't clued him in on her plans.

"The real question," I asked, "is whether he'd bail us out of jail if we get caught by Glinda, because you know she's itching to slap a pair of cuffs on us."

"Ooh, that Glinda," Harper seethed.

Sisterly solidarity.

"Have no fear, girls. I shall bail you out should you get locked up. Now go on with the two of you. Starla and Evan will be awake soon, and I don't want to explain where you're off to."

Harper didn't need to be told twice. She headed into the mudroom and started bundling up.

Reluctantly, I placed my coffee mug on the counter and put on my coat and pulled a stocking hat over my head. Missy ran into the mudroom, her tail wagging, and I leaned down and picked her up. "You stay here with Aunt Ve."

Missy growled a little, clearly displeased with having to stay home.

"Sorry," I said to her, "but you'll only slow us down." I handed her off to Ve. "We have our cell phones and will call if we'll be any later than an hour."

"I'll stay by the phone," she said, worry in her eyes.

Slipping into my boots, I just hoped I wouldn't be calling from the police station.

The town square was fairly empty this early on a Saturday morning. The foot traffic mostly belonged to locals heading toward the Witch's Brew coffee shop for their morning cuppa and a scone.

Honestly, I wanted to veer off in that direction myself. Only my innate nosiness and Harper's determination had me staying the course.

My breath puffed out in white clouds as I said, "Have you heard about the Swing and Sway dance competition?"

She tipped her head back and laughed. "Yes! I can't believe Aunt Ve is doing it. Is it wrong that I kind of want to go?"

I stared at her.

"What?" she asked innocently. "It sounds like it'd be fun. Once you overlook all the body parts that are literally swinging and swaying."

I squished my eyes closed.

She bumped me with her elbow. "Do you want to come with me? You know you do."

Opening my eyes to glare at her, I said, "I'm not getting naked in front of the whole village."

"Clothing is optional for the spectators. Just not the dancers."

"I think I'll be watching a movie that day."

She laughed and trudged ahead of me.

This village, its secrets, its charms, its quirks, never ceased to amaze me. A nude dance. Who on earth thought of such a thing in the first place? Magic might live here in this town, but eccentricity did, too. I kept forgetting that.

Morning light flickered across the snowy village as I glanced toward Bewitching Boutique and wondered how Pepe was faring. Overnight, I'd decided against making him soup and opted instead to bring him a slice of cheesecake—one of Pepe's favorite treats. I'd have liked to do more for him, but I recognized that Ve was probably right. Sometimes it was okay to wallow for a bit. I could simply be a friend offering support and comfort during this difficult week. It was a strange notion for sure, that I didn't have to fix *everything*, to realize that some things simply didn't need fixing.

I just needed to remember that. Better yet, adopt it and make it my new personal motto.

Snow crunched beneath my feet as we cut our own path through the village. In the distance I could hear the loud *whirr* of snowblowers, and I knew that village maintenance crews would soon be hard at work clearing sidewalks and roadways so the tourists could move freely about the dozens of stores that lined the square.

To my right, the road leading into the village looked like something out of a Currier and Ives winter print. Sunlight filtered through the canopy of dark bare branches that arched over the narrow snow-covered roadway, making the snow crystals sparkle.

It felt magical.

It *was* magical.

Inhaling deeply, I breathed in the crisp, cool air.

"Darcy, come on!" Harper snapped.

I'd stopped to admire the sheer beauty around me. "But look."

"At what?" she said on a loud sigh, clearly exasperated with my dawdling.

I grabbed her arm. "Look," I implored. She rolled her eyes so hard, I thought for sure they'd get stuck in the back of her head.

Letting out a huff, she crossed her arms and looked around. "What am I looking at? We have things to do, Darcy."

I gave her my sternest look, the one I saved for her most outrageous behavior. Like the time she'd been arrested. "Even in the darkest of times, it's important to notice the beauty around you. To realize that there's more good than bad in the world. In this village."

White wisps of steam puffed out of her mouth as she took a better look around. I felt some of the tension ease out of her as her gaze swept in the little details. The delicate prints left in the snow as a squirrel scampered about, pines trees that appeared to be frosted in vanilla icing. The take-your-breath-away loveliness of the glittering snow.

"It's pretty," she grumbled.

It was the most I was going to get out of her. It was enough.

Tapping her foot, she asked, "Ready now?"

I laughed. "What are you waiting for? *Sheesh.*"

A smile tipped the corners of her lips as she marched off. There were many paths leading into the Enchanted Forest from around the village and Harper led the way toward the one farthest from As You Wish.

"This is where Will and Liam entered the forest last night, after spending a good hour at the Cauldron. A stall tactic on their part, but I wasn't falling for it. I knew they'd lead me to Kyle eventually. They grossly underestimated my stubbornness."

The Cauldron was the local pub. "Or maybe they just needed a drink after a rough day?"

She squinted at me. "They were stalling."

I smiled, and she forged ahead.

Ten minutes later, we found ourselves deep in the woods. It amazed me how utterly silent—except for our footfalls—it was in here. The path itself was covered in a thick layer of snow, and our prints and those of small critters were the only ones visible. Following the trail was made easier by the blue blazes marked on the trees— and I was grateful for them. With the snow and the light and the tall trees it would be easy to become disoriented and get lost.

However, I didn't think Harper believed the same. She seemed to have some sort of internal GPS because she walked calmly and assuredly as though knowing exactly where she was headed.

Fifteen minutes in and I had to unzip my coat. Trudging through the deep snow was quite the workout. I was beginning to think that Harper was leading me on a wild goose chase when she slowed to a stop at a barely noticeable fork in the path.

"This is where I went left last night. I think the boys went right."

I looked to the left. It was bright and sunny. To the right, it was dark and foreboding, the trail not even a true trail but more like a bushwhacked footpath for a troll. Drooping branches didn't leave much headroom and spindly shrubs stuck out every-which-way promising to grab hold of anyone who dared trespass.

"Are you sure?" I whispered, preferring the bright and sunny route.

She gave a quick nod. Though she seemed determined, I spotted a flicker of uneasiness in her eyes.

"Do you really think he lives here in the woods? I mean, who does that?" I asked, trying to talk us out of this foolish endeavor.

"The Elder?" she returned.

Touché. "But, we don't really know if she resides in the forest. She could just visit that tree."

Harper said, "Semantics."

"Not really. There is a difference between visiting and residing. And anyone who wants to live in there"—I pointed toward the sinister gloominess—"is crazy."

"Exactly, Darcy."

Damn. She was right. Taking a deep breath, I said, "Okay then, let's go."

Without a word, she plunged forward, dipping under branches and pushing against the reaching shrubs. Clouds moved in front of the sun, making the path even darker, scarier. Thinking of Starla, I resolutely pushed forward.

In here, the snow wasn't as deep because the overhead branches had blocked most of the precipitation from hitting the ground. It soon became clear we weren't the only ones who'd been back here recently.

Footprints half filled with snow led the way to a shady clearing. Mossy patches poked through a thin layer of snow and the small area was completely surrounded by tall trees, both evergreens and deciduous. The clearing was actually a small canyon with rocky hills on three sides that were barely visible through the trees.

There was no way in and no way out other than the path we'd taken. It was a hidden little hollow, the perfect place to build a hideout. Except there was nothing here but what belonged in the natural space. Nothing visible at least.

"A dead end," Harper said. "I can't believe it. I'd been so sure."

I walked around, my footsteps unnaturally loud in the clearing. There was a feeling in here I couldn't shake. A dark cloud. A depression. This was not a happy place, and I had the eerie feeling this was exactly where Kyle had been hiding. "He's here."

"What?" She whipped her head around, searching to and fro. "Where?"

"I don't know. I can only feel it."

Slowly, she nodded. "You're right. I feel it as well."

Trying to calm my anxiety, I kept walking, circling the clearing looking for anything out of place. That's when I noticed the footprints in the muck near a stand of trees. "Over here."

Harper was at my elbow in a flash.

I pointed. "There are footprints."

My gaze followed their path to the trunk of a large tree. Harper edged closer. "There's a door cut into the bark."

As I looked more closely, I also saw there was a window disguised by a tree hollow.

I gulped. "We promised Ve we wouldn't go in."

"*You* promised," she said, pulling the door open. I held my breath as she stuck her head inside, and then quickly popped it back out again. "No one's home that I can see, which doesn't mean much, considering he's *invisible*. You have got to see this place."

I rushed over and stepped inside, my eyes widening in wonder. Not only at the design of the hiding place, the elaborate indoor tree house, which was essentially a studio apartment with its window, octagonal skylight, small kitchen, wooden floors, tiny bathroom. I couldn't even imagine how there was water and electrical out here and figured they'd come by some sort of magic.

The strong scent of lemon cleanser filled the air. The place had been recently scrubbed immaculately clean.

"My God," I breathed as I took in the room. Art supplies filled a table, and an easel had been folded up and tucked into a nook. Almost every other available surface was filled with artwork. Small canvases, large canvases. Sketch paper tacked to the walls, hung on the small fridge.

Each picture had the same subject.

Starla.

I walked over to the bed. The nightstand had nothing on it but a thick volume of Shakespeare's works. On the floor, something long and shiny glinted from the shadows near the headboard, but as I bent to pick it up, it squirted out of my fingers, farther under the bed. Then, Harper turned my attention back to her by saying, "Looks like he packed and left in a hurry."

I stood up and saw what she meant. Dresser drawers had been emptied, only a few straggler socks and T-shirts left behind. The bathroom had been cleaned out as well.

Damn.

Kyle Chadwick had escaped again.

Chapter Nine

An hour later I was back in As You Wish's kitchen, warming up with a steaming cup of coffee. Harper and I had waited in the forest for Nick and other officers to show up, then skedaddled before they asked too many questions. Nick had said he'd call later to check in.

Harper had to leave to open the bookshop but promised she'd be back as soon as she let her employees in and got everything set up for the day. Twink was asleep in Missy's doggy bed, and Missy was sprawled under my stool. Evan had already left to go to the bakery and Starla, just out of the shower, was upstairs getting dressed — we hadn't yet told her what was found. I dreaded the thought of that conversation.

Ve leaned on the counter as I finished telling the tale of finding Kyle's hideout.

She refilled my mug and said, "Did it appear as though he'd lived there long?"

"It looked well lived-in," I said. "So my guess is yes."

"Unbelievable," she said.

We fell silent at the sound of footsteps coming down the stairs.

"Good morning," Starla said sheepishly, giving Twink's head a pat as she passed. "I can't believe how long I slept in."

She appeared well rested. Gone was the anxiety from her eyes, replaced with the usual brightness I knew and loved. It did my heart good to see her looking so refreshed.

"Well"—Ve grabbed another mug and filled it with coffee—"you had a little help."

"Cherise works wonders," Starla said, sitting on the stool next to me.

"Are you hungry?" Ve asked. "I can make some eggs or pancakes or an omelet?"

Starla held up her hand. "Maybe just some toast, please? My stomach's a little unsettled."

"You're not planning to go in to work, are you?" I asked.

She covered her mouth as she yawned. "I'm not on the schedule at the paper today, and I think I'll keep Hocus-Pocus closed. Take a personal day and spend it on the couch at home."

"Do you want some company?" I asked. "We can watch a movie marathon. Musicals, maybe. Just not *West Side Story* . . ."

Ve winked at me.

"And we can stop at the market," I rambled on, "and pick up ingredients to make stew, maybe something chocolate for dess—"

I abruptly cut myself off. *Some things simply didn't need fixing.*

"Only if, you know," I added lamely, "you want company. No pressure."

Starla smiled sweetly. "Musicals sound great. A little *My Fair Lady*, *The Phantom of the Opera*, or *Seven Brides for Seven Brothers*. And you know I can't resist a good stew. Or chocolate."

"And you know I can't resist *My Fair Lady*," I said. "It's my favorite."

Ve and Starla shared a smile. "We know," Starla said.
I rolled my eyes. "I don't watch it *that* often."

Only every other week. No big deal.

Ve dropped two pieces of bread into the toaster. "I
don't happen to be doing anything today . . ." She batted
her eyes at us.

Starla laughed. "Ve, would you like to join us?"

Clapping her hands, she said, "What a lovely idea! I'd
be happy to."

"I suppose Harper will want to come as well," Starla
added.

Ve set out the butter dish and a jar of jam. "I don't
believe there is a way to stop her."

"The more the merrier. It'll be a regular girls' day in."
She yawned again. "That spell certainly wiped me out.
How long did I sleep through? Sixteen hours? I can't
remember ever sleeping that long before."

Ve and I exchanged a glance. "Well, not quite straight
through," I said slowly, testing these uncertain waters.
Why did she think she had slept through the whole night?

Starla tipped her head. "What do you mean? I slept
like the dead."

A shiver slid down my spine at the description.

Ve said, "You were up for a little bit last night, about
an hour or so. Don't you remember?"

Blue eyes opened wide as she shook her head. "Not
at all. Is that strange? Is it a side effect of the spell?"

I bit the inside of my cheek. How in the world could
she not remember Kyle's visit? The wedding rings? But
she certainly seemed oblivious to it all.

"It could be." Ve opened the silverware drawer and
pulled out a butter knife as the toast popped up.

Starla laughed. "I hope I didn't do anything embarrassing."

Ve slid the plate of toast over to Starla, but when neither of us replied to her question, she searched our faces.
"*Did* I do something embarrassing?"

"Do you recall Liam and Will Chadwick stopping
by?" I asked.

Her back straightened. "They were here? Why?"

"Oh dear," Ve murmured.

Starla reached out and grabbed my arm. "What happened? What's going on?"

Not sure how to even begin, I took a deep breath. I was just about to launch into an explanation when a knock sounded on the back door, and it swung inward.

Mimi called out, "It's so pretty outside!" She slipped out of her boots but left her coat on as she came into the kitchen.

Twink barked and Missy scrambled to her feet and launched herself at the girl, bouncing on her two hind legs until Mimi lifted her up and let the chin-licking commence.

"Hey Starla!" Mimi said. "I didn't know you'd be here."

"Sleepover," Starla said numbly.

"Oh, I had one, too. At a friend's house." She yawned, her long dark lashes brushing against her rosy cheeks. "I hardly got any sleep at all."

"Starla didn't have such a problem," Ve said with a smile. "Hot chocolate, Mimi, dear?"

"No, thanks. I just came by to ask Darcy a favor."

"Oh?" I asked.

"And you can't say no, because I came all the way over here and didn't text just so you could see my eyes and I could blink at you like this"—she blinked innocently— "and who can say no to my face when I look like that?"

Smiling, I said, "What's the favor?"

"Remember you can't say no." Missy lay happily in Mimi's arms. It even looked like she wore a smile.

"I'll remember."

"So it's like this," she began.

For having had little sleep, she was unusually animated. One hand held Missy tightly, and the other waved about. Her brown eyes lit from within, and her long dark curly hair sprung about her head in unruly waves. At almost thirteen she was growing up so fast, and I loved watching her go from little girl to young woman.

"Glinda was supposed to take me to my art lesson today, but she got called in to work, and Dad's at work, and I can't go alone because it's jewelry-making day, and I need to use a soldering torch, and in order to do that I need an adult's permission because of the whole flame thing. Will you take me?" She blinked at me again.

I couldn't believe she spewed out all that information in one breath. My skin had tightened at hearing Glinda's name, and I tried to play it cool. "Art lessons? I didn't know you were taking lessons."

Mimi's cheeks brightened even more. I fully expected her to launch into an explanation about how she didn't want to tell me about taking them because of Glinda's involvement, so I was completely unprepared when she said, "I know, I didn't want to tell you. It was supposed to be a surprise."

"A surprise?" I asked.

"For your birthday," she said bashfully. "You're so good at art, and I wanted to be just as good as you, so I started taking these lessons, and for your birthday I was going to make you something from what I learned."

Ve tipped her head and smiled at me, and Starla poked me with her elbow.

I stood up and went over and gave Mimi a big squish. "You didn't ruin anything, Mimi."

"So then you'll take me? I mean, I know I could have asked Aunt Ve or Mrs. P, but I really want you to see the studio. I think you'd like it there. Just as long as you don't peek at what I'm working on."

"When is it?"

"In fifteen minutes at Wickedly Creative."

I looked between Starla and Ve. I didn't want Starla to feel uncomfortable with me fraternizing with the enemy's family. "But . . ."

"But nothing," Starla said, reaching over to squeeze my hand. "Go, have fun. I'll wait here for you to get back, and then we'll have our girls' day in."

"And while you're gone," Ve said, "Starla and I will occupy ourselves with chitchat."

Ah. I got her message. She'd fill in Starla about what had happened last night. "Okay, then, let's go, Mimi."

Mimi jumped up and down. "We'd better hurry. I don't

like to be late." She gave Missy a kiss on the top of her head and gently put her back on the floor.

I gave Starla a hug. "Everything will be okay," I whispered.

"I know," she said. "Well, I hope."

Ve followed us into the mudroom and watched over us as we bundled up. Mimi headed out the door, and Ve said, "Don't worry about us here. But, Darcy, dear?"

"Yes?"

"While you're at Wickedly Creative . . . you may want to snoop around a little, if you know what I mean."

I looked at my aunt, at the glimmer in her eye. I winked. "It had already crossed my mind."

"That's my nosy little witch. Have fun, girls!" Ve called after us.

We waved, and as we headed for the art studio, Mimi linked her arm through mine, giving me a little pep in my step and a fullness in my heart.

A couple of blocks from the town square, Wickedly Creative art studio was housed in a renovated two-story dairy barn located behind the beautiful Chadwick family farmhouse. The land felt more like a compound, with all its outbuildings, ranging from stables to an outdoor amphitheater to a kiln building to a garage apartment Kyle's brothers shared.

The studio's renovation was spectacular, mixing rustic with modern. The outside of the barn still held its inherent charm with weathered clapboards and shake-shingled roofing, but the big barn doors had been replaced with glass doors flanked with tall windows.

The path to the entryway had been shoveled and salted, and I followed behind Mimi as she went inside.

I wasn't entirely sure what to expect . . . or how I would be received. After all, I was Starla's best friend, and she certainly was no longer welcome in this family.

"Mimi, right on time! Who's your friend?" A beautiful older woman with silver-streaked dark hair, troubled blue eyes, and a friendly smile walked over to us. The smile, I noticed, didn't reach her eyes.

I glanced around at the half-dozen tables dotting the main floor of the barn, almost all occupied by artists engrossed in their projects. Murmured voices carried from a far corner, where a glassed-off room revealed artists standing by easels painting still lifes of a black stiletto, a red rose, and a human skull. Will Chadwick walked about the room, murmuring to his students.

Mimi shrugged out of her coat and hung it on a sculptural metal coatrack. I did the same as she said, "Glinda and my dad had to work, so I brought my friend Darcy Merriweather."

Recognition fluttered in her gaze; then the corners crinkled as she smiled more broadly. A genuine smile this time. "Lovely to meet you, Darcy. I'm Cora Chadwick. I've heard much about you from Mimi."

I relaxed a little as she added the part about Mimi. If she'd heard things about me from Glinda, I might still be worried.

Warmth flowed from her hand as she shook mine. Strong fingers grasped firmly, and she rested her other hand atop our adjoined ones and said, "Welcome. And thank you for bringing Mimi. We require our younger students to have a guardian here when working with some of our more dangerous tools."

I sensed no animosity, yet her gaze remained troubled. Whatever was bothering her, I gathered, didn't have anything to do with me. I suspected it had to do with Kyle and Starla, and I wondered what it was like for a mother to realize her son was capable of such violence. The thought alone sent a surge of sympathy toward this woman, but then I recalled how the family had treated Starla in the aftermath of the attack and I took back my pity.

"I'm actually glad she asked. This place is amazing." It was, too. Octagonal skylights flooded the space with natural light and dark beams crisscrossed the ceiling. The barn had more of an industrial feeling inside, especially with its airy loftlike second floor, which allowed the center of the building to remain open to the ceiling. To my right, a curved staircase led upstairs to the upper level, and its twisted iron balustrades and railing continued up there, running along the perimeter of the loft as a safety measure.

Upstairs, there were many at work—young, old, and in-between. A watercolor group, a pottery class, and someone working on a loom. I also saw the glow of a blowtorch and sparks—someone was welding a metal sculpture. Everywhere I looked there was something to see, an object to admire, but my gaze kept going back to the skylights, six in all.

And how they certainly looked like the one in Kyle Chadwick's hideout. Though, really, that shouldn't be such a surprise to me. If his brothers were able to lead Harper to the tree house, then obviously some—if not all—of Kyle's family knew about the place. And, if those skylights were any indication, they'd helped him build it as well.

Anger started to simmer within me. How could this family have been so negligent to harbor a fugitive, family or not? With Kyle being in such close proximity, Starla had been at risk this whole time.

That train of thought led me to another—if Kyle had been living here in the village, why was he making his presence known to Starla only now, after all this time? Simply because of the upcoming macabre anniversary?

"We certainly love it here. There are chairs and magazines over there if you want to sit and wait, but feel free to wander around." With a wink, Cora added, "Everything with a price tag is for sale."

"Thanks, I will."

Mimi said, "Remember, no peeking on what I'm working on."

"I promise." I crossed my heart and everything.

Cora draped an arm over Mimi's shoulder and led her to a table with three other students, ranging in age from teens to baby boomer. Mimi slipped on a pair of protective goggles and picked up a small propane torch with more than a hint of excitement in her features. She caught me looking and gave me a shooing motion.

Smiling, I turned and looked at a group of paintings near the waiting area. They were well done, serene depictions of the village square. Tourists probably loved them. I moved along, following the perimeter of the room, stopping here and there to admire a glazed pot or a handbag made out of white duct tape. Near the rear wall, I purposely lingered near the oil painting studio in hopes that Will Chadwick would come out and see me.

I was admiring a gorgeous hanging quilt when he stepped out of his studio. "Darcy? What're you doing here?"

Success!

"This is stunning," I said, fingering the material. In dark blues and golds and charcoal, it reminded me of Harper's bookshop, which had been decorated in a *Starry Night* theme.

"My mother will be happy to hear that," he said. "It's one of hers."

"She's very talented." I caught a glimpse of the price tag. Six hundred dollars. "And out of my budget."

Dark brows pulled down in a frown. "Did you come here to shop?"

"No, I came to chaperone." I pointed toward Mimi. Her face was alight as she aimed her torch at a thin strip of metal.

He drew a hand over his hair. His eyes, I noticed, were just as troubled as his mother's.

"I'm glad you're here," he said. "I was wondering how Starla was faring."

I studied him carefully. "Do you really care?"

He winced. "I suppose I deserve that."

More, if you asked me. But I wasn't one to pick fights. Well . . . not often.

"But, yes, I care. I've never held ill will toward Starla. I was worrying about her all night."

Was he simply saying what I wanted to hear? Or did he mean it? I searched for telltale signs of dishonesty and found none. "She's okay. Drained. Confused. We all are."

"As are we," he murmured.

I tipped my head. "Why is that?"

"It's impossible for what has happened to happen.

And now he's disappeared. . . . Where could he have gone?"

"What do you mean? Who's disappeared? Kyle, because he escaped the tree house? And are you really asking *me* where he went?"

Will glanced around and suddenly froze. I followed his gaze and found his mother Cora giving him a stern look. After a second, she turned her attention back to her students.

"I should be getting back," he said, caution slipping into his blue eyes.

I grabbed his arm. "Before you go, do you know why Kyle has started bothering Starla? Obviously he's been a fugitive for a while, so why now? Is it because of the date? Is he just trying to mess with her mind? What? And you keep saying it was impossible. . . . Why?"

Will's face paled, and his eyes narrowed. He pushed a hand through his long hair. "It's not like that. Kyle's not a bad person, Darcy. That's what you don't understand."

"How can you say that? He tried to kill—"

A voice interrupted. "Will, you should probably be getting back to your class."

I turned and found a man standing behind me. Tall and thick-waisted, he had ice blue eyes, rosy cheeks, and a grizzled beard. He wore a thick leather welding apron and a disapproving look aimed at Will.

Will gave a sharp nod, glanced at me as though he regretted speaking to me at all, then ducked back into his studio.

As soon as Will left, the man's countenance shifted immediately. Gone was the disapproval, replaced now with hospitableness. He stuck out his hand and said, "I'm George Chadwick, Darcy."

Ah, so he already knew who I was.

"Can I offer you some coffee or tea?" he asked, gently shaking my hand. Like his wife's, his fingers were also strong but thick and callused as well.

"How about some answers?" I said.

His eyes softened. "How about we start with some coffee?"

I bit my lip. "Coffee would be nice," I said grudgingly, thinking of the mug I'd left behind at home.

"Come along with me." I followed as he said, "Did I see you eyeing Cora's quilt?"

He led me behind Will's studio to a small kitchen. An assortment of morning treats were laid out, from doughnuts to Danish. "The quilt is beautiful."

A Keurig machine sat on the counter alongside a stack of cardboard cups. He shook one loose and motioned to a turnstile filled with coffee options. I chose a bold roast and he dropped the cup into the machine.

The back wall was filled with family photos. I stepped closer, my gaze zipping from picture to picture. School photos, prom photos, Christmas. In each, Kyle's smile stole the scene. It was clear that he was the light of the family. My gaze lingered on one of the prom photos.

"Cora's passion is for fiber art," George said, "going so far as to have a few sheep grazing out back so she can make her own yarn."

"She has quite the talent. Did you make the coatrack near the front door?"

George said, "It's a dandy, isn't it? But no, that's Liam's handiwork. He has a way with a blowtorch. And a paintbrush. And even knitting needles."

"Don't you all?" I asked.

He chuckled, getting my drift. As Manicrafters, they could pretty much do it all.

"Some of us are better than others. For example, you do not want to see my oil paintings. Hideous."

I turned. "Don't you mean 'abstract'?"

"You should join our marketing team."

"Is this . . . ?" I tapped the prom picture.

"Glinda, yes." The coffee finished brewing and he motioned to the tray of goodies and said, "Would you care for something sweet?"

"No, thanks."

He patted his stomach. "I suppose one doughnut for me won't hurt anything."

I'd lost my appetite, but took the coffee from his out-

stretched hand. "Glinda and Will went to prom together?"

As he scratched his chin, his eyes glazed a bit as he
tried to remember details. "As I recall they both broke
up with someone a week before prom so they went together . . . as friends." His eyebrow twitched as he winked
at me. "They're really not each other's type." He sighed.
"Such a simpler time."

I turned back to the pictures. There were none of
Starla, of course, because of her starburst, but there were
some from their wedding. Kyle in his tux looking handsome and happy—and in love. What had gone wrong?
"Now about those answers . . ."

"How about a tour of the place?" George asked.

I recognized what he was doing—trying to distract
me. "Sounds good, as long as you can walk and talk at
the same time."

He wiped powdered doughnut from his face. "I'm not
sure I have any answers, Darcy."

"Will said Kyle's disappeared."

His eyes widened. "Did he? Well, I suppose that's ac-
curate. He vanished two years ago."

"I don't think that's what he meant. I think he meant
after he left his tree house last night."

George shrugged. "I can't speak for the boy. Come on
now, let's take that tour." He led me from the break
room.

Not giving up, I said, "Why is Kyle bothering Starla
now? Why did he give her their wedding rings?"

Pain flitted across his face. "I'm afraid we may never
know."

"Because he disappeared?"

Taking hold of my arm, he tugged me along. "Mimi's
a joy," he said, leading me out of the kitchen.

"I couldn't agree more, but you're changing the subject."

"Yes, I am."

"But Starla . . ."

He stopped and looked at me, holding my gaze.

"Darcy, please, if you have any mercy on this father's soul, please let it go for now."

I looked deep into his eyes, saw heart-wrenching pain. I bit my lip. Why was there so much agony? Because his son was charged with a crime? Because he was a fugitive? I didn't buy it. Those things didn't add up to the devastation in this man's gaze. Something else was going on. But as much as I wanted answers for Starla, I couldn't keep poking this man's wounds.

"Your coffee's getting cold," he said. "Why don't you drink it while I finish your tour?"

I let out a breath. "Okay, I'll stop asking about Kyle. For now," I added.

He acceded with a nod. After a long minute, he started walking again, leading me through the studio. "I'm glad Glinda brought Mimi here—she's a talented young lady."

"How long has Glinda worked here?" I asked, playing dumb about Nick's plan.

"Off and on since her teens. With her natural skill set, she fits right in. Her basket-weaving class is one of our most popular."

I tried not to grit my teeth. "How lovely."

As we climbed, I spotted Liam Chadwick walking around a table filled with students working on a mosaic pattern. Everyone was smiling and laughing—except Liam. His eyes were as troubled as the rest of his family.

"I hear you have some artistic talent as well," George said.

"I dabble with drawing and painting."

"More than dabble I hear told."

I glanced over the railing at the jewelry-making table. "Mimi's my biggest cheerleader."

"I heard it not only from her but Glinda as well. It's your artwork at Spellbound bookshop, is it not?"

Why was Glinda speaking of me at all? "It is," I admitted. "A favor to my sister who owns the shop."

"It's good work. Our doors are always open if you're looking for studio space." He motioned across the second floor to a section set up with six long tables. "We keep an open area for local artists."

"That's very nice of you, thank—"

I was cut off by the look on his face. I followed his gaze downward, to the group of people who'd just come in the front door. Nick Sawyer, Glinda Hansel, and two other village police officers.

"Excuse me, Darcy." George brushed past me and headed back down the stairs.

Cora abandoned her group as well and approached the officers.

Everyone in the studio had stopped working.

I started down the steps, and didn't miss the glaring gaze Glinda cast toward me. Mimi slowly pulled off her goggles and looked around, confusion darkening her eyes.

Keeping their voices low, George and Cora stood shoulder to shoulder while in deep discussion with Nick. Cora had her shoulders pulled back and stood ramrod straight, but her I've-got-this-under-control posture, however, was betrayed by the tears shimmering in her eyes.

I didn't need to hear their whispered conversation to know why Nick had arrived. He was looking for Kyle Chadwick. So it was no surprise when one of his sentences floated through the air, loud and clear.

"I'm sorry, but everyone needs to leave," he said. "We have a search warrant."

Chapter Ten

"Then we're in agreement?" Starla asked. "Raoul is an infinitely better choice for Christine than the Phantom."

"Definitely," I said.

Harper's jaw dropped. "I disagree."

"Me, too," Mimi added. "The Phantom rocks."

We were deep in a discussion of *The Phantom of the Opera* as I stopped in the middle of the aisle at the Crone's Cupboard. "That disturbs me on so many levels."

"Let me count the ways why Phantom should be Christine's choice. One, the Phantom loves her," Harper said. "He's just misunderstood."

"And two"—Mimi stuck a bag of chocolate chips in the carriage—"the Phantom is played by Gerard Butler. Gerard. Butler."

Harper stuck her head next to Mimi's. "We rest our case."

Starla laughed and headed toward the frozen food aisle.

I poked a finger at Harper and Mimi. "You two are incorrigible. Do I need to remind you that the Phantom is a psychopath? Cuckoo crazy." I was glad Starla had wandered off. She didn't need to be reminded about psychopaths. And even though *The Phantom of the Opera* was one of Starla's favorite movie musicals, I crossed it off the list to watch this afternoon. We needed to keep this day light and bright.

Harper laughed. "You do know he's a fictional character, right?"

"Why don't you two go find some heavy whipping cream?" I said sweetly before spinning toward the produce section.

"Raoul," I heard Mimi say as they walked away, then giggled. "As if."

"Seriously," Harper murmured.

I couldn't help but smile. As much as Harper might like the Phantom, in Marcus she'd chosen the ultimate boy-next-door type. Hopefully I had a few years to sway Mimi that way, too.

As I picked over carrots, Starla appeared at my elbow and dropped three pints of ice cream into the carriage.

"But what will you eat?" I asked her, blinking innocently.

She laughed. I took a moment to simply enjoy the sound. She'd had a couple of rough days but was handling it much better than I would have. Ve had filled Starla in on everything that had gone on last night and this morning. According to my aunt, Starla hadn't said much when she heard all the news, and I could see that even now a part of her was holding back from fully enjoying herself. Which was completely understandable.

She rooted through the potato bin and pulled out several for the beef stew we were going to make for dinner. "Any news from Nick?"

"Not yet," I said. "They'll find him."

"How? He's visible only to me. And how's he doing that, by the way?"

"Some kind of spell," I said softly. "I'm waiting to hear from the Elder about what kind."

Drawing in a deep breath, she said, "Let's not talk any more about it today."

"Deal," I agreed.

Harper and Mimi came strolling back, arms laden with all kinds of junk food we didn't need but couldn't wait to eat. Mimi, I noticed, topped Harper by a good three inches, and was looking more mature by the day. We'd told her only the bare minimum about what was going on with Starla, however. No matter how mature she was, there were some images a girl her age didn't need imprinted in her head.

I glanced at my watch. "We should get going. Ve and Mrs. P are going to meet us at your place in ten minutes, and I still want to stop by the bakery and get a piece of cheesecake for Pepe."

Mimi said, "And I need to run home and pick up *Beauty and the Beast*, *The Little Mermaid*, and *Tangled*."

We looked at her.

"What? They're musicals. And they have happy endings."

"Sounds perfect," Starla said, smiling. "Though I cry at the end of *Tangled* every time."

"I can leave that one," Mimi said, looking like she'd done something wrong.

"No, no!" Starla insisted as we turned toward the cash registers. "They're happy tears. The ending is so swe—"

Her voice dropped off as Cora Chadwick entered the store, along with Liam.

My pulse kicked up a notch as Starla gripped the carriage. Harper threw me a glance and Mimi smiled brightly. "Hi!"

Cora's gaze swiftly turned to Mimi. "Hello, Mimi. Long time no see." She looked at the rest of us and gave a quick nod. "Ladies."

"Hello," I murmured.

"Hi," Harper added.

Starla said nothing, only stared at the ground.

Liam kept quiet as well. His mother gave him a sideways glance.

"What?" he said. "I can't stand here pretending."

We stood in awkward silence for so long that Mimi

began looking from face to face. She finally asked, "Is something wrong?"

Liam said, "Ask Starla about that."

Puffed up, Harper took a step toward him. "How about you ask Kyle about that?"

"How about you stay out of things you know nothing about, Harper?" Liam returned.

I grabbed Harper's arm and said loudly, "We should get going."

"Us, too," Cora said, giving her son a small push.

Liam huffed and stormed off.

Harper forged ahead toward the registers while Mimi reached out and took Starla's hand, pulling her along. She said softly, "I don't know what's going on, but I'm on your side."

Starla put an arm around her. "Thanks, Mimi."

I followed behind them, hating that any equilibrium Starla had found today had just been crushed.

"Starla?" Cora said from behind us.

Starla stopped and turned around, and my heart just about shattered at the broken look in her eyes.

I was surprised to see the same look in Cora's eyes when I glanced her way.

What was that all about? It was the same look that had been in George's eyes earlier, too.

Cora said, "I . . . I mean . . ." She wrung her hands. "Have you seen him today?"

Him. Kyle.

Looking perplexed, Starla shook her head. "Not today."

Tears sprang to Cora's eyes. "Oh. Okay. Thank you. Take care of yourself." Abruptly, she turned and jogged to catch up with Liam.

Starla faced me. "What was that about?"

I hadn't told her that Will said Kyle had disappeared, and I didn't think now was the right time to do it. I shrugged. "Not sure."

I pondered why Kyle's family seemed so concerned that he had disappeared. It seemed to me that they should want him to go. After all, being caught by the police at this time would mean a very long prison sentence. Something felt so off-kilter about this family and their relationship with their fugitive.

Mimi said, "Seriously, you have to tell me what's going on. I'm not some dumb little kid, you know."

"That's the last thing we'd think," I said, tossing items onto the conveyer belt. "And I'll tell you all about it later."

"Are you okay, Starla?" Harper asked.

"I'm fine," she said steadily. "I just want to go home."

Mimi tossed me another look, her eyes full of curiosity.

"Later," I mouthed.

I mentally urged the cashier to hurry up. The sooner we left, the better.

Harper helped bag the groceries, and as soon as we were outside, Mimi headed left toward her house while the three of us turned right toward Starla's. My trip to see Pepe was going to have to wait a little bit. I wanted to get Starla settled in with a nice cup of tea. And I also wanted to check in with Nick to see if he had any news.

We were almost at Starla's when she said, "I should probably pop into Hocus-Pocus and check messages and pick up the mail, and go see Vince at Lotions and Potions to let him know I'm okay. I won't be but a minute. You two go on ahead, and I'll meet you there."

"We can come with you." I hated the thought of her being alone.

Starla smiled a smile that didn't quite reach her eyes. "That's okay. Ve and Mrs. P will be at my house soon, and I don't want to keep them waiting outside. It's cold out here."

Harper said, "How about I go with Starla and you go ahead, Darcy?"

"Perfect," I said before Starla could object.

"Fine, fine," she said, shaking her head. Giving me her house keys, she added, "And don't eat all the ice cream before we get back."

"I'm making no promises," I said as I walked off.

A mourning dove swooped by my head startling me as I walked up the steps to Starla and Evan's brownstone. It landed in a tree in front of the big picture window and tipped its head at me, blinking repeatedly, its gray feathers shimmering.

I tipped my head back and said, "Thanks for the heart attack."

It cooed, a peaceful yet sad sound.

Slipping the key into the lock, I hesitated, thinking maybe I'd wait for the others. I wondered why suddenly, after dozens of times of letting myself in and out of Starla's house, that I'd be filled with trepidation now. Because the bird had spooked me? Or was there another reason?

Feeling utterly paranoid, I turned the lock and opened the door. Sunshine spilled across the foyer, and I let out a breath thinking I'd been acting all kinds of a fool.

But then I turned around and saw the man lying on the couch, his eyes closed, a strip of duct tape over his mouth.

Despite never having met him before, I recognized him instantly.

Kyle Chadwick.

I dropped the grocery bags and was instantly torn—get the hell out of there or check to see if he was breathing. I dialed 9-1-1 on my cell phone as the mother hen in me won out. I had to see if he was okay. Because other than the duct tape, he looked like he was sleeping. Sure, he was a little pale, but other than that . . . he was fully clothed, had no visible injuries, and his arms rested on his chest as though he'd simply lain down for a nap.

If Snow White had been a man, it would have been Kyle, with his good looks, dark hair, pale skin. But I was certainly no Prince Charming and there were no cute little dwarves tending to him.

As I explained what was going on to the police dispatcher, I crept closer to him and noticed that there was writing on the silver duct tape over his lips. Spelled out in black block letters was FOUL IS FAIR.

I knew the quote—it was from Shakespeare's *Macbeth*: *Fair is foul and foul is fair*. However, I didn't have time to dissect why that was important right now. Swallowing hard, I reached toward his neck to feel for a pulse and suddenly jerked my hand back, afraid to touch him.

The mourning dove cooed.

I shuddered and forced myself to check for a pulse.

His skin was cool to the touch, and no life beat beneath it.

Kyle Chadwick was dead.

Chapter Eleven

"He was just lying there," I said for what felt like the hundredth time.

I sat with Harper, Aunt Ve, Mrs. P, and Mimi in Harper's bookstore. Harper had turned the sign on the door to CLOSED.

"He didn't, you know, attach to you," Harper said, shivering like she had a bad case of the willies. "Did he?"

The last time I'd found a dead body, the spirit of that Crafter had imprinted on me. This time I was lucky—Kyle's spirit had stayed far away. "No."

"Thank goodness for that," Ve said.

The store had undergone a drastic renovation since Harper took it over last summer. Gone were the plain neutral walls, replaced with a bold mural based on the *Starry Night* painting by van Gogh. Iron bookshelves in the shapes of trees and branches lined the walls and limbs climbed the ceiling as though reaching into the night sky. It was dramatic yet peaceful. Completely casual yet special. It was magical, and one of my favorite places to retreat.

Harper had added more seating to the floor plan for customers to linger over a cup of coffee or visit with friends. Mrs. P and Aunt Ve sat across from Harper, Mimi, and me.

Rubbing my temples, I kept going over it in my head. Kyle's peaceful face, the police cars, the chaos, Starla's reaction as she approached the house and was told what had happened . . .

Starla. My heart hurt for her, the pain in my chest tight and unyielding.

Aunt Ve whispered, "Have mercy."

"Was there any sign of forced entry?" Harper asked.

"Not that I saw," I said.

Sniffing contentedly, Missy and Twink wandered around the bookshop. Pie, Harper's cat, looked down on them disdainfully.

Mimi said, "If Kyle was invisible, could he walk through walls? Maybe he didn't need a key to get in."

Swimming with tears, Mrs. P's eyes were bright and shiny. "When I vaporize, I can slip under doors or through cracks. But Kyle wasn't a Vaporcrafter."

I glanced at Ve. "We need to figure out the spell he was using."

"It hardly matters now, Darcy," Ve said. "The focus now will be on his death. You said there were no visible wounds?"

Maybe she was right about the spell, but I couldn't help but feel that it was important. "Not that I saw. He looked peaceful . . . for a dead guy."

"Do you think he killed himself?" Mimi asked.

"I don't know," I said. "I don't know how he could have. He wouldn't have suffocated from that duct tape—it only covered his mouth."

"Maybe he had a big knife sticking out of his back and you just couldn't see it, Darcy," Harper speculated. "It would serve him right."

We all looked at her.

"What?" she said. "He did deserve it."

"Be that as it may," Ve said, "Starla is going to need a good lawyer."

She'd been immediately taken in for questioning; Evan had gone with her, but Nick wouldn't let anyone else accompany them.

"I've already called Marcus," Harper said. "He was going to meet Starla at the police station."

My head throbbed as I thought about the turn of events this afternoon. This was supposed to be a happy lighthearted day. I wanted to laugh at the absurdity of how it had truly ended up. I was beyond grateful that Starla hadn't been the one to find Kyle's body, though. I feared that might have been too much to handle, seeing him lying there in his jammies as though he was camped out to watch Sunday afternoon football.

Wait a sec. *In his jammies?*

Something Starla had said suddenly struck me as important. Very important. "You know what I just realized? That Kyle was dressed in pajamas. A white T-shirt and blue flannel pajama bottoms. Exactly like the ones Starla described him as wearing last night when he paid her a visit at our house."

"So he died not long after?" Harper surmised.

"I guess the autopsy will tell us for certain, but I'd say so," I said.

"Or maybe he died *before* he visited Starla," Mimi said excitedly, bouncing in her seat. "Maybe he's an imprinter! And he's stuck to Starla."

As the only one here who had firsthand experience with imprinters, I said, "Imprinters are invisible—to everyone. Starla wouldn't have been able to see him at all."

Mimi frowned. "Oh."

Harper went back to conjecturing. "So he saw Starla, then met his demise soon after."

"It's so strange," I said. "Where's all his stuff?"

"What stuff, dear?" Ve asked.

"From his tree house." I winced at the growing ache behind my eyes. "He cleared out of there in a hurry. Where are his clothes? His toothbrush?"

"With his family?" Harper said. "His brothers certainly knew where he was."

I bit my lip. "But his family didn't know where he

went." I explained how they all seemed worried by his disappearance.

"Is that why Cora asked if Starla had seen him to-day?" Mimi asked.

I nodded. "They're all extremely concerned. Overly concerned if you ask me." And now that Kyle was dead, I had to wonder if that was the source of their anxiety. "It's like they knew he was in danger."

"Or perhaps, doll face," Mrs. P said, "they were worried he'd attack Starla again."

Perhaps. They hadn't seemed concerned about Starla. Only Kyle. I hoped Nick was questioning the family. And that they actually told him everything they knew.

"She doesn't have to worry about an attack now," Ve said. "Plus, because she was knocked out after Cherise's sleeping spell, there's no way the police can say she had anything to do with his death."

Mrs. P said, "It's an ironclad alibi. She was at your place the whole night long."

"It's ridiculous that they're even questioning her," Harper grumped.

"She did threaten to kill him," I said, really wishing Nick hadn't overheard her say it. Everyone whipped their gazes to me. I held up my hands in surrender. "I don't think she did! But I think they have reason to question her. I'm sure she'll be let out in no time."

"I really want to know what happened to him," Mimi said. "What a strange way to be found. And stranger that he was going around town in his pajamas. Who does that, even invisibly?"

It was a good question, but one I didn't have an answer to.

"And what was with the words on the duct tape?" Aunt Ve asked, scooping up Twink and settling the tiny fluff ball on her lap.

"'Foul is fair,'" I said.

"From *Macbeth*," Harper added. "That's what I don't get. It should have been the other way around."

"What do you mean?" Mrs. P asked. "And tell me slowly, doll face. I'm old and don't follow along at quite your pace."

Harper rolled her eyes and explained. "The full phrase is 'Fair is foul, and foul is fair.' "

Missy trotted over and hopped up next to me on the couch. She bypassed my lap and settled into Mimi's.

"It's said by the witches near the beginning of the story and essentially means that what can appear as fair on the surface can be foul underneath," Harper explained, "and what appears foul on the surface could be fair underneath."

"Like how the witches are ugly, but actually give fair advice?" Mimi asked.

I nodded. "And how Macbeth was supposedly good but turned evil."

"I need to read more," Mrs. P said, laughing.

It was impossible not to share her humor. Her cackle was that infectious.

"So," Ve said, her eyebrows furrowed, "the duct tape on Kyle should have been 'fair is foul' because he was handsome and well liked, but he ended up rotten to the core."

"Right," Harper said. "Not this 'foul is fair' business because there was nothing fair about him."

"Who wrote the message?" Mimi asked. "Kyle himself?"

"Maybe," I said. "There was a Shakespeare book on the nightstand at the tree house. But no one knows yet. Hopefully your dad will have some answers for us soon. The autopsy should tell us a lot."

"Yes," Mrs. P said, "like exactly how Kyle died."

That would be nice to know.

"If he committed suicide, could the 'foul is fair' reference be some sort of message to Starla?" Aunt Ve absently rubbed Twink's ears. "Like he was still pleading his innocence?"

"If he did commit suicide," I echoed, "then he was obviously trying to send some sort of message. Why else would he be found in Starla's house?"

"But what if he didn't commit suicide?" Mimi asked.

"Murder," Harper mumbled, shaking her head.

I shuddered. "Who else besides Starla would have wanted him dead?"

Aunt Ve shook her head. "Kyle was much beloved around here, Darcy. Unless he's made some enemies while he was away, then no one."

Maybe it *was* suicide then. I was holding out hope.

Mrs. P said, "We need to look at the bigger picture. Though we may not like it, there are people who'd want him gone solely to protect someone they loved, namely Starla. Those people need to be considered as well."

"But that's everyone in this room, plus Evan, plus Vince," Harper said. "And I don't believe any of us are killers."

"There is nothing more dangerous than love, Harper," Mrs. P said, wagging a red-tipped finger. "Do not underestimate the lengths one would go to protect someone they care about. Kyle's death could have been a preemptive action taken on Starla's behalf."

Evan had been asleep at As You Wish the whole night long . . . but where had Vince been? Did he have an alibi?

"If that's the case," Mimi said, her eyebrows drawn together in concentration, "why would any of us leave the body at Starla's house? That just makes her look more guilty, doesn't it? Someone who loves Starla wouldn't do that. We'd dig a big hole in the Enchanted Forest, dump the body in there, and cast a Mirage Spell over it and no one would ever know. Ever."

Harper tipped her head, considering. "Mimi makes a good point."

Mrs. P smiled. "Yes, she certainly does. A vivid one, too."

"But, alas," Ve said, "it could eventually be uncovered. Mirage Spells last only seventy-two hours."

"Bummer," Mimi said.

"Wait, wait. A Mirage Spell? What's that?" I asked.

"I saw it in my mom's diary," Mimi said. "It's a spell that casts a mirage over something. Like, for example, if my room is a mess and my dad tells me to clean it up, then I can cast the spell on the room to make it appear clean—even though it's really not. It does have its downfalls, though. Like Dad could come in and trip over a shoe. Then he'd know something was up."

Missy made a funny noise, almost a gurgle. I rubbed her back and hoped she wasn't coming down with something.

Ve smiled. "Indeed. I've used it a time or two myself in the bedroom to, ah"—she glanced at Mimi and coughed—"keep a secret."

Undoubtedly to hide a dalliance . . . or two.

"Does the Mirage Spell work on people?" Harper asked. "Make someone ugly appear pretty?"

She was endlessly fascinated with spells and had accumulated dozens of spell books from the storage facility she'd inherited when she bought Spellbound and also bought some from other Crafters around the village.

Mrs. P cackled. "I believe that's called alcohol, Harper, sweetie."

I laughed as Harper said, "Ah, right, so silly of me." Then she whipped her gaze to Mimi. "But seriously, can it?"

"I don't know," Mimi said. "I've never tried it—on anything. I've only read about it."

"Oh, it works on people," Ve said. "I used it to cover pimples when I was a teenager."

"Cool!" Mimi said.

Ve smiled. "It'd probably work on these old wrinkles of mine, too."

"You're lovely the way you are," I said. I didn't like the idea of a spell messing with appearances.

Again, I thought about the vanishing spell and wondered if Kyle had somehow altered it to include people and not just inanimate objects. If that was even possible. When the Elder responded to my request for a meeting I'd ask her.

"With that in mind we're back to if Kyle was murdered, then it had to be by someone who wanted Starla to take the blame," Harper said.

The ache in my head was getting worse. "We should probably just wait to see what the autopsy determines," I said. "This speculation isn't getting us anywhere."

"How soon do autopsy reports usually come back?" Mimi asked.

"A few days," I said, rubbing my temples and wishing for some aspirin. "Sometimes longer."

It was going to feel like torture waiting for the results.

Mrs. P studied me. "Headache, doll?"

I nodded.

"You should take something," Harper said as though I were dense.

"Yes, I should. I wonder why I didn't think of that. Oh, that's right, I don't have anything on me to take. And neither do you. I already checked your break room when I got here."

"Cranky," Harper replied. "I have some upstairs in my apartment."

"I might have something in my purse," Ve said, digging into her enormous handbag. "Tissues, Tic Tacs, a notepad, a bottle of water, matches, pepper spray, a granola bar, some almonds, lipstick—"

"The Holy Grail," Harper intoned.

Mimi giggled and I smiled.

Mrs. P cackled, and said, "Save yourself the trouble, Velma. I wish that Darcy had some aspirin."

Mimi, Harper, Ve, and I looked at one another. Any one of us could cast the spell.

"Don't look at me," Harper said. "You know how I feel about that wishing stuff."

Harper hadn't quite come around to our culture.

"I'll do it," Mimi said. She cleared her throat. "Wish I might, wish I may, grant this wish without delay." Her left eye twitched twice, the telltale sign a spell had been cast.

I held my breath for a second—wishes made by other Crafters had to first go through Elder approval (apparently she used some sort of supernatural messaging system to know when a wish was made), and there was bound to be lag time while she pondered. If denied nothing would happen at all, except a summons to appear before the Elder for explanation would be sent to the Crafter who'd made the wish, kind of like court-ordered arbitration. If approved, the wish would be granted ASAP.

A bottle of extra-strength aspirin appeared in my

hand so suddenly that I almost dropped it. I bobbled it, finally gaining a good grasp.

"Even though it still freaks me out, magic is cool," Harper said.

"Way cool," Mimi agreed.

"Thanks, Mrs. P." I jumped up and headed for the refrigerated case next to the cash register that held bottles of water and soda. I slapped two dollars on the counter to pay for it before Harper could give me the business about freebies.

"No problem, doll face." After a moment, Mrs. P added, "We should look on the bright side of Starla's current situation. With Kyle's death there is no longer a threat on Starla's life, so for that we should be grateful. It's one hell of a silver lining."

"We'll have Starla and Evan move in with us for a little while," Ve said, adjusting her long scarf as she made the pronouncement. "No doubt the police will have the brownstone cordoned off until it can be fully processed. And though Starla is safe now, I would feel better knowing she is under our roof, with friends, until this is all sorted through."

"Me, too," I said.

"Me, three," added Mimi.

Missy barked.

Mrs. P said, "I'll run to the market and pick up duplicate ingredients for that stew we were going to make."

Disheartened, I thought of all the groceries left behind in Starla's foyer and hoped the melting ice cream wouldn't stain her carpet. It was such a trivial thing in light of all she had going on, but it was one more thing I hoped she didn't have to worry about.

"She will likely have little to no appetite when she gets back to As You Wish, but she'll need to eat something." Mrs. P patted her white spiky hair and stood up. Suddenly, her face drained of color, and she wobbled a little bit, holding out her arms for balance.

I jumped up and grabbed hold of her, easing her back onto the couch. "Mrs. P! Are you okay?"

She blinked, trying to reorient herself. "I'm fine, I'm fine. Just a little woozy. I skipped lunch. . . ."

Lunch, my foot. This wooziness had nothing to do with food. "I'll call Cherise."

"No, no," Mrs. P said, waving me away. "I'm fine. Good as new. Right as rain."

"Eugenia," Ve said, "let us call Cherise."

"Yes," Mimi said, her brown eyes wide with fear.

Missy barked as though offering her agreement.

"I'm already dialing," Harper said in a singsong.

"Have her meet us at As You Wish, Harper," Aunt Ve said. "Eugenia, you're coming home with us."

Mrs. P laughed. "You're all a bunch of thugs."

"Well-meaning thugs," I said.

She patted my face and narrowed her gaze on me. "Well, someone had better make another trip to the market."

Someone. Meaning me. I smiled. "I'll go."

"I'll go with Darcy," Mimi said.

"And who," Ve asked, motioning toward the front door, "is going to deal with him?"

Vince Paxton had his hand up over his eyes as he tried to peer into the shop.

Chapter Twelve

Melting snow left small rivers along the sidewalk as Mimi, Vince, and I splish-splashed our way toward the market.

Vince said, "We have to do something. We can't let the police railroad her."

He looked none the worse for wear after last night's memory cleanse. A dark stocking hat covered most of his floppy brown hair—only a few strands stuck out around his ears, curling under his lobes. He was bundled in a thick barn coat and his boots were covered in a thin film of salt. His eyes . . . well, they looked tortured. Despair crowded his pupils and anguish creased the corners of his eyes behind his glasses.

"No one's railroading her," I said, trying to reassure him. "Nick would never let that happen."

Squeals of laughter floated through the air. The village ice skating rink was packed with tourists enjoying the beautiful afternoon. It seemed so odd how life went on as normal for many when for some life was falling apart.

Kyle's death hadn't seemed to upset the village's equilibrium. Tourists strolled the sidewalks, the shops were busy, and no one appeared to have a care in the world other than enjoying the day.

Of course, right now, Kyle's death was unexplained and not a grisly murder—as had happened in the past. For that I was grateful.

"Darcy, how can you say that?" Vince asked. "Why would they be questioning her?"

"Because his body was in her house," Mimi said, shrugging. "It's protocol."

I glanced at her. Not many twelve-year-olds would know the word, let alone use it in a sentence.

He eyed her as though he'd forgotten she was there. "I don't like it."

"You don't have to like it," I said, edging out of the way as a couple passed in the opposite direction, "but you do have to accept it. I predict she'll be back at my place in time for dinner."

"This whole situation stinks to high heaven. I can't help but think that this is some elaborate plan to frame Starla for his death. Someone's gone to a lot of trouble to make it seem like she's guilty, starting with those weird sightings of him, and then putting his body in her house."

It was an interesting theory. But the only person I could think of who'd want to frame Starla was Kyle himself. And I wouldn't put it past him to try. One last twist of the knife in her heart.

I needed more time to think about it, to talk it over with Nick.

But I also recalled Mrs. P's theory that someone may have killed Kyle on Starla's behalf. "I'm sure we're all going to be questioned," I said, casting the first line as I fished for information.

A cloud moved across the sun, throwing Vince's frown into shadow. "Why would we?"

"Because we all didn't like Kyle," I explained. "I'd get your alibi ready if I were you."

He paled. "Me?"

"Of course. You're dating Starla. It only makes sense that you'd be questioned, too."

Mimi nodded. "You're probably going to be at the top of the suspect list. Rival love interests and all that. You could have acted in a jealous rage and killed your girlfriend's ex-husband."

His eyes widened as he glanced at me. "She's kidding, right?"

She wasn't. Love interests were usually the first suspects. I didn't really think Vince had it in him to kill Kyle, but I wanted him to squirm a bit. "It seems plausible to me."

"Look, Darcy," he said, "I know we've had our differences, but I'd never do anything to hurt Starla. If I had killed Kyle, I certainly wouldn't have left him in Starla's living room."

"Would you have put him in a big hole in the Enchanted Forest?" Mimi asked.

I shot her a look. She raised her eyebrows, widened her eyes innocently, and shrugged.

Vince stared at her as though she had three heads. "Big hole?"

"Never mind her—she just has a good imagination. Do you have a good alibi?" I asked, still wanting the information.

"I . . . No, not really. After I left your house I came straight home. I . . . read for a while, then went to bed."

There was a hitch in his voice, a stammer that told me he wasn't being altogether truthful. My instincts were usually right, but I couldn't be sure about which part of his alibi was a lie. The going straight home or the reading.

"No one to vouch for you?" I asked.

He jammed his hands into his pockets. "I did order pizza around nine thirty. The delivery guy can back me up. But after that, no. Do you think the police are really going to question me?"

I didn't hesitate to answer. "Yes."

He let out a breath and a cloud of white steam puffed from his lips. "I've been down this road before, as you know. I don't really want to go down it again. But for

Starla, I will. I'll do anything I can to help her." His eyes softened, glistening. "She's everything to me. It's killing me that she has to go through this and I can't help—not even a little."

Mimi sighed.

He *had* been down this road before, as a murder suspect in a local woman's death. He'd been cleared of that charge, but some big character flaws had been revealed. I didn't want to like Vince, I really didn't. But there was no denying his feelings for my best friend. And because of that, I liked him a little. Only a little.

As we neared Lotions and Potions, his shop, I thought it was a good time to ditch him. "You should go back to work and try not to think about it too much. I'll have Starla call you as soon as she gets back."

He nodded. "If you talk with her before then, tell her I'm thinking about her, okay?"

"I will," I reluctantly agreed. I wasn't keen on sharing his lovey-doveyness.

After ducking into his shop, he turned and gave us a quick wave.

I thought again of the possibility that someone had killed Kyle to protect Starla. I didn't want to believe that Vince could have done it. I really didn't—for Starla's sake.

But it would be foolish of me not to consider it a possibility.

The second trip to the Crone's Cupboard proved uneventful, and afterward Mimi and I decided to make a quick pit stop at the Bewitching Boutique to visit Pepe before heading home.

There were several customers in the store, and Godfrey was in his glory as he helped them shop.

We smiled and waved and headed straight into the sewing room at the back of the shop. This room was one of my favorites in the village. It was warm and cozy and filled with clutter—which should have driven me crazy, but didn't. Two sewing machines sat side by side on a long table and everywhere I looked there was fabric of all colors, patterns, and textures. Bright hues, pale pastels. Swirls, florals, plaids. Silk, cotton, taffeta, tulle. It was easy to get caught up in it all—and I normally would have, but I'd been distracted by a stunning gown displayed on a dress form in the middle of the room. The white silk charmeuse column dress was breathtaking with its sheer overlay embellished (especially at the neckline) with pearls, iridescent sequins, and crystals. The design looked so familiar, yet I couldn't quite place it.

I fingered the intricately beaded sheer cap sleeve and wondered why Godfrey and Pepe were working on such an old-fashioned dress. Someone's wedding gown, perhaps? I felt a twinge of envy, simply because the dress was so beautiful.

Mimi bent down and knocked on an arched door cut into the baseboard as Godfrey came rushing into the room, pulling up short when he spotted me standing next to the gown. Swiping at his brow with a handkerchief, he stammered, "L-lovely to see you ladies."

"Is something wrong?" I asked him, concerned with his red cheeks. "Are you feeling all right?"

"Me? Oh, I'm quite well," he said, glancing at Mimi as though looking for inspiration. "I just, ah, wanted to say hello."

I looked between the two of them. As I did the color on Mimi's cheeks rose to match that of Godfrey's. "Why are you two acting so strangely?"

"*Pshaw,*" Godfrey said. "Strange is as strange does in this village."

Tipping my head, I studied him. "What does that even mean?"

Uncomfortable, he laughed somewhat maniacally. "Pepe! Remove your rodent self from your slumber and say hello to your guests!"

Pepe's door flew open, banging against the white baseboard. He stomped out, dressed in a full-length cotton gown like something out of a Dickens novel. "Need I remind you, this is the week of my discontent? Did no one notice the DO NOT DISTURB sign on my door?"

Sure enough, a small sign hung from the door's door-knob. I would have needed a magnifying glass to read it, though. "Sorry to disturb you, Pepe."

"Darcy!" His little mouse cheeks turned rosy as well. He glanced at Godfrey, then Mimi, then me again, then gulped.

"Look who dropped in!" Godfrey said brightly.

I searched each of their faces. Something was up. Way up.

"I'm sorry, too, Pepe," Mimi said. "I didn't see the sign when I knocked."

"*Non*, it is all right." He waved away our apologies. "I have already watched all the seasons of *Downton Abbey* available, and doing so has left me no more cheerful, but only instilled within me a fervent desire to employ a houseful of servants." He eyed Godfrey as though sizing him up for a butler's uniform.

"Your discontent is why we stopped by," I said, rooting through grocery bags. "My apologies that it is not from the Gingerbread Shack, but desperate times and all." I produced a small container with a perfect sliver of cheesecake visible through the clear plastic. "What is discontent without calorie-laden treats?"

"*Ma chère,*" Pepe bowed, "you indubitably know the way to this mouse's heart. *Merci.*"

"You're welcome," I said as I set the plastic container on the floor and patted his head.

"But what is this business about desperate times?" he asked, blinking slowly behind round glasses set high on his nose.

"I haven't yet told him what has happened," Godfrey acknowledged. "*I* heeded the Do Not Disturb sign because the instances in which I have infringed upon the request my ankles have been nipped."

Pepe was a biter. Especially where Godfrey was concerned. The two were like bickering siblings—always ready to spar but the love was always there behind the jabs thrown. Pepe had lived with the Baleaux family since becoming a familiar so I suppose Godfrey was like a brother. In a weird, magical kind of way.

Although Pepe was the village historian, he had revealed little about himself to me. Learning about the week of his discontent—and his loneliness—was the most I'd discovered about him since I moved to the village.

I wanted to know more. About Godfrey, too. He was a Cloakcrafter, yes, and one of Aunt Ve's exes, but was he as lonely as Pepe?

Would he, perhaps, be looking to date?

"What has happened?" Pepe said, motioning for Mimi to pick him up. Bending over, she cupped her hands, and he jumped into them.

Placing him on the edge of the sewing table, she giggled. "Your feet tickle."

Twirling his whiskered mustache, he said, "Most have ticklish feet. My feet tickle. It is a talent few possess. Now tell me what I have missed in the village."

Mimi and I took turns telling the story of how Kyle had been found dead in Starla's brownstone. And then we rehashed the conversation that had taken place at Spellbound.

There were still no answers. We all had to wait to see what the autopsy would reveal.

"I'll take a stroll over to Wickedly Creative," Pepe said. "To see what I can overhear."

"You can't do that," I said. "It's the week of your discontent. You're in lockdown mode, right?"

He fussed with the hem of his dressing gown. "Truthfully, I have grown tired of my discontent."

"Should I take back the cheesecake, then?" I asked with a smile.

"Do and I shall bite your hand." He leapt off the table and pushed the plastic container through the opening in the baseboard.

Godfrey chuckled.

Mimi said, "We probably should have bought him a whole cake instead of a slice."

Pepe's voice carried from his hole. "She is a wise girl."

I eyed Godfrey. "This may seem like it's out of the blue, but I'm wondering if you're seeing anyone right now."

Grabbing my hand, he twirled me around. "I thought you'd never come around, Darcy. Dating that," he rolled his eyes, "stodgy policeman."

"Hey!" Mimi protested.

I laughed. "You know as well as I do that he's not stodgy. And I'm still dating him."

Godfrey dropped my hand. "There goes my grand plan for a trophy wife."

Pepe appeared in his doorway dressed in his little red vest. The fur between his ears was damp, combed back in a slick 'do. "You wish."

I tensed at the word "wish" but because Pepe's statement hadn't been phrased properly according to Wishcraft Law (*I wish that . . .*) I was under no obligation to grant the request.

"Indeed," Godfrey said on a sigh.

"Well, I don't know about a trophy wife, except that the woman I have in mind is truly a prize, but how do you feel about older women?" I asked.

Godfrey caressed his beard. "How old? As old as Pepe? Because I do possess some standards."

Pepe gnashed his teeth, cleared his throat, and said, "'For age is opportunity no less than youth itself, though in another dress, and as the evening twilight fades away, the sky is filled with stars, invisible by day.'"

"Pretty," Mimi said.

He bowed. "Henry Wadsworth Longfellow."

"You've been hanging around with Archie too long," I said. I didn't know if I could handle dramatic readings from both of them.

"Blowhard," Godfrey said in a huff.

I wasn't sure if he referred to Longfellow, Pepe, or Archie.

Pepe, however, needed no clarification. He took immediate offense and charged at Godfrey while gnashing his teeth, but Godfrey quickly picked him up by the tail and held him at arm's length. As Pepe dangled, he swung little fists this way and that. Godfrey paid him no attention whatsoever. "Now who is it you have in mind, Darcy?"

"You'll get yours!" Pepe cried, still swinging away.

Mimi said, "Give him to me." She held out her hands and Godfrey dropped Pepe into them.

"Ruffian," Pepe mumbled as he straightened his vest and smoothed his hair back down.

"*Moi*?" Godfrey pressed his beefy hands to his chest. "You are the one who attacked me."

"Enough!" I said. "My head is aching and you two are making it worse."

Godfrey immediately said, "Do you need some aspirin?"

"No, thanks. I've got that covered, thanks to Mrs. Pennywhistle. Speaking of, she's who I'm referring to. You know, if you're interested in dating."

"Eugenia?" Godfrey said, his eyes growing wide. "I didn't know she was back on the market."

She'd been a widow for a while now and declared herself permanently single. It was a declaration I was ready to test.

"I'm not sure *she* knows." Mimi set Pepe on the sewing table.

I frowned at her. She shrugged at me.

Pepe said, "Is she lonely, too?"

"Well"—I fussed with the fringe on my scarf—"let's just say she's been a little blue. I thought a date might cheer her up."

"Blue, you say." Godfrey stroked his beard again. "I cannot foresee a love connection, but a dinner with Eugenia would be lovely."

Pepe made a throaty disgusted sound. "*Non.* Eugenia's wit and wisdom would be wasted on a toad such as yourself. *I* shall take Eugenia out to dinner. Or rather, we shall order in."

"Darcy asked *me*," Godfrey said, thumping his chest.

"Because she believed me to be preoccupied with my week of discontent. However, now that I've cut short my discontentment, I am available to be of service as Eugenia's companion."

"First come, first served!" Godfrey said, drawing his shoulders back.

Watching their eyes flare with agitation, I sighed and picked up the grocery bags. "Not this again. Come on, Mimi, let's head back to As You Wish before these two come to blows. You know how I feel about the sight of blood. Good-bye, you two. Pepe, let me know if you learn anything at Wickedly Creative and also what you two decide about Mrs. P."

Ignoring me, he seethed to Godfrey, "It was an oversight I plan to rectify!"

As Mimi and I went back out into the cold, she said, "They both need hobbies."

"Or separate houses."

"That would work, too."

She smiled. "Is it wrong that I think it's adorable when Pepe gets worked up and starts swinging his little fists?"

I put an arm around her. "If so, then I'm guilty, too. So cute."

With mitten-covered hands, she made little punching motions. "Adorable."

With that amusing image in my head, I smiled, glad for a break from the day's weighty events. It wasn't until I was pushing through the side gate at As You Wish that I remembered that I never asked about the fancy dress in the sewing room and who it had been for.

Maybe I didn't ask because subconsciously I wished it was mine.

Curse that rule about not granting my own wishes. . . .

Chapter Thirteen

We certainly had a very full house, I reflected as I chopped carrots for the stew. Ve stood at the stove browning the meat, and Mrs. P and Mimi sat at the counter making a batch of double fudge brownies.

Cherise had been here and gone. She'd cast a spell over Mrs. P to prevent dizziness, but warned that the underlying ailment was beyond her scope. Her heart was old and failing—there was nothing a Curecrafter could do to change that. She also prescribed a lot of rest, which Mrs. P had immediately scoffed at. We, however, had promised to do our best to make Mrs. P slow down.

Cherise had pulled me aside on her way out and shared that Mrs. P was more ill than she let on. Her heart wasn't just failing—it was failing fast.

The news had left me stunned, and I didn't quite know how to deal with it, because curling up in a ball under my covers wouldn't cut it with all that was going on around here.

Harper had just taken Twink and Missy for a walk

when the back door opened and Starla and Evan came inside.

"Have mercy! Just look at you," Ve said, abandoning the stovetop and rushing over to Starla. She wrapped her in a big hug, enveloping her with warmth and understanding and love.

It was clear from Starla's puffy eyes that she'd been crying.

Evan hung his coat on the overflowing hooks, kicked off his wet shoes, and came into the kitchen shaking his head.

I immediately went to the liquor cabinet and pulled down a bottle of whiskey—Ve's good stuff.

"You must have been reading my mind," he said, reaching for a tumbler. "Fill 'er up."

Ve still clutched Starla like a long-lost child. Starla pointed at the whiskey and said, "Pour one for me, too."

"That bad?" Mrs. P asked.

Starla finally wiggled out of Ve's grasp and took off her coat. "I suppose it could have been worse. They could have arrested me."

Ve whispered, "Have *mercy*."

I pushed a glass toward Starla. She eyed the amber liquid, chugged it all down, then winced and coughed. I patted her on the back.

Making a sour face, she said, "I don't suppose you have any margarita mix, do you? This stuff is way too strong."

Ve shook her head.

"I can run to the store," I offered. Third time was a charm?

Mrs. P waved a hand. "No, no, no more running errands. I wish we had a big batch of margaritas, some salt-rimmed glasses, and plenty of limes."

Nerves tingling, I held up a hand. "I've got this one. Wish I might, wish I may, grant this wish without delay."

"Oh, no way the Elder grants that wish," Mimi said, taking Starla's coat and hanging it up for her.

"It is rather indulgent," Ve murmured.

"What's a wish for if not indulgency?" Mrs. P asked.

Mimi sat back down and stirred the brownie batter. "Is indulgency even a word?"

I shrugged. "I think so?"

Evan stared into the bowl in horror. "Is that a *boxed* brownie mix you're using?"

"Sorry," I said. "You were preoccupied."

Suddenly a big pitcher of margaritas appeared on the counter, along with six glasses rimmed in salt and a plate of lime slices.

"Hot damn!" Mrs. P shouted, whooping like she'd just won the lottery.

Ve rubbed her hands together. "Eugenia is handy to have around."

Starla climbed onto the empty stool next to Mimi and pulled the pitcher toward her. "What will the rest of you drink?" she said, echoing my earlier sentiments about the ice cream.

Mrs. P laughed, her cackle bouncing off the kitchen's high ceilings. "Do I need to wish for more?"

It was so hard to believe she was ill at all.

"No, no," Starla smiled wanly. "I'll share."

"And I'll throw this out," Evan said, reaching for the brownie batter, "and start fresh."

"Hey!" Mimi reached for the bowl. "At least let me lick the spoon."

"Fine," he said, handing it to her, "but if you get salmonella don't come crying to me."

Mrs. P coughed. "Can I get a spoon, too?"

Evan rolled his baby blues, stuck a spoon into the batter and swirled it around. He pulled it out and handed it over. "The salmonella thing goes for you, too."

I glanced around at everyone and despite the dramatic events of the day, suddenly my heart filled with happiness. I'd grown up in a teeny tiny family, in peace and quiet. It hadn't been an easy life, not hardly, but it hadn't been bad. Then my father had died and Ve had come to Ohio, told Harper and me of our witchy backgrounds, and bing, bang, boom my whole life had changed in an instant.

But what had changed most was *me*.

I'd never realized the happiness that could be found if I just opened my heart to it. It was a lesson I'd learned here, in the village. And I also learned that a family could be more than just blood relatives. It could be a best friend. An old woman. A girl on the verge of becoming a teenager. An outraged baker. It was the people who loved me. And I honestly didn't know what I'd do without any of them.

Ve walked back to the stovetop to her sizzling pan. "Let's get this stew going to counterbalance all that hooch," she said. "Or we'll all be falling-down drunk in no time."

"I'm okay with that." Starla sipped her drink and let out an *"Ahhhhh."*

Evan rifled through cabinets, pulling out baking chocolate, flour, and sugar. He grabbed eggs from the fridge and snagged a corner of the kitchen to work his magic.

Mimi gave Starla a sideways glance. "Soooo, how'd it go?"

Starla laughed and kissed the top of Mimi's head. "Honestly, it sucked. They want me to take a polygraph."

"Why? Was he . . . murdered?" Mrs. P asked.

It was a question we all wanted an answer to, but to hear it spoken aloud felt like a kick in the gut.

"They don't know yet," Starla said. "The police wanted Evan's and my alibis for last night between eight and midnight. Nick vouched for us between eight and ten, and when we told them we were sleeping after that, that's when a polygraph was suggested."

Eight and midnight—the ME must have narrowed Kyle's time of death.

"Did you take it?" Mimi asked, as she licked every speck of chocolate from her spoon.

"No. Marcus said not to. Not yet." She looked around. "Where's Harper? I wanted to thank her for sending Marcus over so quickly."

"Out walking the dogs," Ve said, "and probably meeting up with Marcus to get the lowdown."

Why hadn't I thought of that? She *had* been gone a long time. It was probably exactly what she was doing.

"Unfortunately," Evan said as he cracked eggs into his mixture, "neither of us can prove we were sleeping. Glinda Hansel hinted that one of us may have slipped out without the other noticing, especially since I'm a heavy sleeper and Starla was under the influence of a sleeping 'pill.'" He used air quotes on the pill part.

Setting aside the chopped carrots, I moved on to peeling potatoes. I bit my lip from saying something snide about Glinda in front of Mimi. I bit it so hard that I could taste the coppery hint of blood in my mouth. Grabbing my margarita, I took a sip, letting the limey flavor sit for a moment before swallowing.

"By the way," Starla said, "when Glinda says 'one of us' she means me. She was ready to arrest me this afternoon, but Nick overruled her."

I bit my lip again. More blood. More margarita.

Starla pushed her glass back and forth between her hands. "I'm not sure I'd pass a polygraph."

We all turned and stared at her.

Her shoulders lifted as she shrugged. "I don't remember. I have zero memories of last night at all. I mean, I can't even recall what happened with Kyle visiting me upstairs. I did threaten to kill him, or so I'm told. So . . ."

"So *nothing*," I snapped. "You did not leave this house."

"You don't know that, Darcy," she said softly.

"I do know that." I waved the potato peeler as I spoke. "Because you're not someone who goes around killing people."

Her eyes were awash in tears. "*People*, no. Kyle, possibly."

"No." I shook my head. "No, no, no."

"I agree with Darcy," Mrs. P said.

"Me, too," Ve echoed.

"Me three," Mimi said.

Evan waved a chocolate-covered spoon. "Me four."

"So *enough*," I said, using my sternest voice. "No more about that, okay?"

Her watery gaze met mine. And though she nodded, I could see the doubt in her eyes. That was fine—for now.

I'd have faith enough for us both until I could prove she had nothing to do with what happened to Kyle.

After a short stretch of tense silence, Mrs. P said, "Evan, my spoon is empty."

"Mine, too." Mimi held hers out as well.

Evan shook his head and singsonged, "Salmonella."

"Spoilsport," Mrs. P muttered.

"Yeah," Mimi said.

A rooster crowed at the back door and I said, "Mimi, can you let Archie in?" as I walked over to Evan's batter and dunked two spoons.

"Hey!" he said.

"You didn't see anything." For crying out loud, if Mrs. P was dying, then she could damn well have whatever salmonella-laced treat she wanted. I handed one spoon to her and waited for Mimi to return to give her the other. In a flash Archie stood at the end of the counter, eyeing the lot of us.

He didn't crack any jokes about the margaritas or the brownies or my cooking, which made me instantly suspicious that he wasn't here on a social visit.

Puffing out his chest, he said, "You've been summoned, Darcy. The Elder will see you now. Right now. Go quickly, go alone, and do not dillydally."

I wanted to tease him about using the word "dillydally" but by the look on his face, I could tell the reason I was being summoned was quite a serious one.

Glancing at Starla, I had a feeling I knew what this meeting was about.

Bold blue and deep orange hues colored the sky as dusk settled over the woods. A biting cold wind nipped at my cheeks as I made my way through the Enchanted Forest to see the Elder. Drawing the hood of my cloak tighter, I forged ahead, trying to ignore just how cold I was.

The cloak I wore was truly special, designed for Crafters to use when visiting the Elder. With the hood up, the cloak made Crafters invisible to mortals, which came in quite handy when a witch was traipsing through a magical forest.

A witch like me.

And the forest was magical, not only because it housed the Elder's meadow, but as I glanced behind me I noticed that my footsteps in the snow disappeared almost as quickly as they formed. I left no trail as I trudged to the Elder's secret domain. No path that might lead others—mortals—to one of the most cherished places in the entire village.

With the sun going down the woods appeared dark and ominous. The wind howled through the bare trees, and my footsteps echoed loudly on the snow. I clicked on the flashlight I'd brought with me and swept it side to side, up and down.

I knew this path well from the many times I'd been called before the Elder. I'd had more than a few infractions of the Wishcraft Law while learning the ins and outs of my Craft. Fortunately, the Elder had been patient with me, knowing I was a novice to my new culture.

In the distance, a mourning dove cooed, that soulful heartbreaking call that seemed to match my mood right now so well. The look in Starla's eyes before I'd left the house was haunting me.

She truly believed she may have killed Kyle.

I couldn't stop thinking about the way I'd found him. Whether suicide or murder, his death had been premeditated. That was obvious by the way he'd been lain out on Starla's couch with the duct tape over his mouth. Someone had taken the time to craft his reposing scene. And that's what it felt like. A scene from a play.

Foul is fair.

If Harper's supposition was true, the message was meant to convey that Kyle had been unjustly seen as foul but was really fair. That he was good and not evil.

Who'd want that message to get across most? The answer was obvious to me: Kyle and his family. Even though his family never denied he attacked Starla, they stood behind him. They were willing to overlook Starla's bruises, her pain. They were stalwart in their belief that Kyle had made a *mistake*. That he was still a good person who had had a bad moment.

Foul is fair.

Ha! I didn't think so. Not for a moment. Maybe that was stubborn of me, and if so, then so be it.

Shivering, I huddled deeper into my cloak and really wished that the mourning dove would go coo somewhere else—like New Hampshire. Its melancholy song was starting to wear on me.

The farther into the forest I wandered, the darker it became. The orange tint to the sky had faded, replaced now with a blend of navy blue and deep purple. I picked up my pace, hoping to reach the Elder's meadow before the sun completely disappeared.

Before I knew it, I was practically jogging. I had never been a graceful runner to begin with, but in the heavy cape and high snow, I was positively comedic. Flailing and stumbling, I bore right at a familiar landmark and bent to catch my breath and soak in the wondrous scene that appeared before my eyes.

Sunshine beamed down, setting a desolate meadow aglow. Before my eyes, snow melted, green grass grew, and wildflowers bloomed. In an instant, the expanse was transformed from a winter wonderland to a summer oasis. At the heart of it all rose a weeping tree—I didn't know what variety other than *magical*. It stood majestically, its branches bare and heavy with snow, so considerable the limbs almost touched the ground. The Elder's tree. In a blink, the snowy limbs perked up, shed their winter coat, and small green buds unfolded into beautiful leaflets.

"Come in, come in, Darcy," a female voice said.

Warmth cast over me as I approached the glen, and I tugged off my gloves and turned off the flashlight. I lifted my face to the sunshine, allowing the heat to chase away the chill in my cheeks, my bones.

"Have a seat," the Elder said, and as I'd become accustomed to, a tree stump appeared behind me.

I sat, soaking in the warmth, the beauty, the *magic* of this moment. "I need to visit you more often during the winter. Wait. No, I'm just kidding." Seeing the Elder more often? Had I lost my mind? "But this place is a little slice of heaven right now. It's already been a long winter."

There was a hint of humor in her voice as she said, "Ah yes, it may well be the winter of all our discontent. There seems to be a lot of that happening recently. Pepe, you, Starla . . ."

I didn't even ask aloud how she knew of my internal discontent, the tinge of depression that accompanied my birthday. The Elder just knew these things. It was more than a little disconcerting.

"Starla is why you've summoned me, yes?" I asked.

"Is she? I believe you summoned me. Something about an invisibility spell?"

In the chaos of finding Kyle's body, I'd forgotten I'd asked Archie to contact the Elder about that spell. "Do you know of it? How does it work? Isn't it against general Craft Law? How did Kyle get away with using it? Did he alter the Vanishing Spell? Is that even possible?"

She *tsk*ed. "Such questions when you already hold all the answers. Have you learned nothing, Darcy Merriweather?"

I really hated when she took that tone with me. I let out a frustrated breath. "How do I hold the answ—" I broke off, recalling another conversation I'd had with the Elder months ago.

"I'm waiting," she said.

"Melina's diary."

"You have come a long way for a novice Crafter, Darcy, but you've yet to fully learn to think like a Crafter. Your first thought shouldn't be to seek help from others. But to seek help from within. If that fails, that is when you ask for guidance. Not before."

Feeling duly chastised, I remained silent. As I always did when I visited the Elder, I couldn't help but wonder about her true identity. Did she truly live here, in that tree? Or did she have a home in the village? Had I sipped coffee while sitting across from her at the Witch's Brew? Bumped into her at the Crone's Cupboard? Who was she? And when would her real identity be revealed to me?

Would it *ever* be revealed to me?

"Now that we have gotten that out of the way," she said, "it is my turn to seek your help."

"Did you already look within?" There was nothing but stone-cold silence in reply to my question. And despite the warmth of the meadow, I felt a chill. "Sorry," I mumbled.

"Apology accepted. There are many things as Elder that I can do. However, there are some I cannot without revealing my identity. This is when I need help from a trusted few. You, Darcy, are one of the few."

Now I felt really bad about my sarcastic comment. "What do you need?"

"During the past year several criminal investigations have taken place in the village, most involving the Craft in one form or another."

I knew. I'd been part of most of them.

"In light of those cases, I have come to the conclusion the Craft needs its own investigative presence. A presence that would work independently of the village police and whose mission is to look into these cases with an eye on the magical details."

"A presence?"

"More precisely, a snoop. That snoop is you, Darcy."

"Me?"

"You have proven yourself a worthy sleuth, Darcy, and that is exactly what I need."

"But . . . why?"

"Why not?" she countered.

"What about Glinda?" She was, as far as I knew, the only full Crafter on the village police force. "She already has access to crime scenes and techniques that I'll never be able to get."

"You've done quite well on your own so far."

"I know, but—"

"What is your hesitance? I believe this is nothing you aren't already doing on your own. Now, however, you'll be doing it in an unofficially official Craft capacity."

"Unofficially official?" I asked.

"It is not technically a job. Merely a . . ." She trailed off, clearly looking for the right word.

"Presence?" I provided.

"Precisely."

What *was* my hesitance? Because she was right—it was a job I'd been doing since I first moved to the village. Then I realized the reason why I was balking. Or rather, *who*.

Nick. There was already tension between us related to my snooping. If I were *officially* snooping, that might cause a real divide.

"Why not Glinda?" I asked again.

There were a few seconds of silence before the Elder said, "Snooping for me might eventually put her in a position to choose between her Craft and her mortal badge. And that would be unfair to her."

"She's not going to like this."

"She doesn't have to. I will speak to her about my plan of action. If she has cause for concern, she can take it up with me."

I rubbed my temples. It was a lot to think about. The ramifications, especially.

"Well?" the Elder asked.

Sighing, I quipped, "Does this nonjob come with a 401K plan?"

"No."

I knew I couldn't refuse her, even if I wanted to. The Elder didn't ask favors. She made commands disguised as favors. "I'll do it."

"Wonderful. Your first task is to continue to nose around the death of Kyle Chadwick. I do not like the direction it is heading."

"That makes two of us. Did you know he was living in that tree house?"

"No."

"Why not? He was here in the forest, how could you have not known?"

"I am not omniscient, Darcy. He violated no Craft Laws."

The "Do no harm" motto of our magic pertained only to magic. Not attempted murders. I wasn't sure I believed her about the omniscient part, though. She seemed to be able to read my mind often enough.

"Do you know if he was murdered or committed suicide?" I asked.

"No."

"You're not a big help," I said.

"That's why I hired you."

"Unofficially."

"Yes. Now, good-bye, Darcy. You'll be hearing from me again soon."

With that, the sunshine faded to darkness, the flowers disappeared, and the Elder's tree shriveled into dormancy. I stood up and the tree-stump stool turned into sparkling glittery snowflakes that fluttered elegantly to the ground. I suddenly found myself knee-high in snow and chilled to the bone as the winter wind whistled through the meadow.

With a lot on my mind, I pulled my cloak tightly around me and headed for the trail. The mourning dove's soulful coo kept me company the whole way home.

Chapter Fourteen

"So, you're what? The Craft snooper?" Harper asked.

Aunt Ve's eyes twinkled. "Is that anything like a court jester?"

"Or the class clown?" Starla giggled.

Flames danced in the family room's fireplace as I looked at each of them. "I'm not finding this amusing."

"Well, you should be," Harper said, adjusting the blanket we shared on the sofa. "Did you at least hold out for a retirement plan and good benefits?"

I flipped a page in Melina's diary. "Not funny," I sang, keeping it to myself that I'd joked to the Elder about a 401K, too. Sometimes, Harper and I were more alike than I realized.

Starla was snuggled on the love seat, her laptop balanced on her lap. She was fighting off yawns every couple of seconds.

Evan, Mimi, Missy, and Twink were walking Mrs. Pennywhistle back to the Pixie Cottage, a local B and B, where Mrs. Pennywhistle, as the former owner of the place, was a permanent guest with her own suite. It was a deal she'd worked out with Harmony Atchison, the cottage's current proprietor and the village's resident Dumpster diver. Even though I still wasn't sure if Harmony was mortal or Crafter, I considered her—and her life partner, Angela—friends.

"What do you think Nick will say about this new job?" Harper asked, watching me closely.

I skimmed and flipped another page. Melina's handwriting was small and cramped, and so many words were crammed onto a page that it was turning into a painstaking process to find the invisibility spell. "I'm not sure."

"You'll tell him?" Ve asked, her thin eyebrows lifting in surprise.

"I have to," I said. "I don't want that kind of secret between us."

Ve sat in an armchair with her slippered feet up on an ottoman. She whistled low. "Sometimes things are better off left unsaid."

Said the witch who'd been married four times.

"Not in this case," I said.

"Maybe he won't care," Harper said in a whisper.

I glanced at her to see why she'd dropped her voice and she motioned toward Starla. Asleep, with her head lifted back, her breathing was slow and steady, and finally, after a couple of days of turmoil, she looked at peace.

Ve crept over and lifted Starla's laptop and drew a blanket up to her chin. Starla shifted a little, then settled back into a deep sleep. Ve *tsk*ed as she looked at the computer screen. "She's been Googling him again." She turned the laptop toward us, and images of Kyle's paintings appeared.

"Can I see that?" I asked, reaching out.

Ve handed it over, then dropped back into her chair. "What do you think she's looking for?"

Harper said, "An explanation."

Sadly, that was probably true. The Internet page Starla had opened belonged to a Boston gallery that featured Kyle's artwork.

"The prices on those paintings are going to skyrocket," Harper said, leaning over my shoulder.

Undoubtedly. It happened often—an artist becoming more famous after death. And a fugitive artist at that? The sky was the limit.

I glanced at the thumbnail images. As with the paintings of Starla in the tree house, the ones on the Web site could be divided into two categories. Realism and surrealism. "Why do you think he changed his painting technique?" I asked, keeping my voice low.

Aunt Ve whispered, "The change began shortly after Kyle married Starla. Gossip around the village was that marriage wasn't agreeing with him, and he was taking it out on the canvas."

"So the pretty pictures are from before he married Starla?" Harper asked.

Ve nodded. "And the ugly ones came after."

I glanced at her.

"What?" she said. "I'm just saying what we were all thinking."

"You're not wrong, Aunt Ve," Harper said, pushing back the blanket. "They're hideous. Anyone want some tea?"

Ve and I both nodded.

"Art is subjective," I said to both of them, though silently I agreed with their assessment. The "after" paintings were horrid with a strong leaning toward macabre, especially with all the red that looked like blood.

"Well, in my subjective opinion, Kyle was seriously disturbed when he did those later paintings." Harper headed off to the kitchen.

Before and after. Had marriage really been the thing that flipped the creative switch in Kyle's head?

"Did you know Starla well back then?" I asked my aunt in a whisper. "Were they having trouble adjusting to the new marriage?" It had been a whirlwind courtship after all. Maybe they realized they'd made a mistake in rushing to the altar and took it out on each other.

"Not as well as I do now," Aunt Ve said. "But we were friends. We Wishcrafters tend to stick together." Her eyes glazed a bit as she looked out the window, as if remembering a specific moment in time. "I have never seen Starla happier than when she was with Kyle, at least in the beginning and right on up through about three months of marriage. Then things started changing."

I glanced at Starla, who still slept peacefully. "Did she say why they were changing?"

"She never said anything was wrong at all. But I could see it. The strain in her smile. The bags under her eyes. She denied anything was wrong. If only I'd pushed for answers . . ."

If only . . .

I took another look at Kyle's paintings. The befores. The afters. The fair. The foul. "Unfortunately, we can't change what happened in the past."

"Sadly, no," Ve said. "But I'll be damned if I'll let her get hurt again."

That made two of us.

Slowly, I lowered the laptop screen and a blinking light flashed, catching my attention, but when I opened the screen again, the light had disappeared. Strange.

Teacups clattered in the kitchen as I set the laptop on the coffee table and went back to looking at Melina's journal.

Ve nodded toward the leather-bound book. "Are you sure the Elder said the answer was in there?"

"Not in so many words, but, yes. Does she make everyone figure things out for themselves or is it just me?" I asked.

The teakettle whistled as Ve smiled. "You and Harper are not precisely the norm around these parts. You came into the Craft later in life, so there is a bigger learning curve. It's important to learn things on your own."

Flickering flames cast dancing shadows on her face as I studied her. "Sometimes it's easier to be taught by others."

"But it's not always as rewarding," Ve said.

I frowned and Ve chuckled.

As I turned another page in the diary, I noticed something I hadn't before. A page was missing—neatly cut from the binding, leaving a few centimeters of margin near the spine. Odd. Had it always been this way and I simply hadn't noticed the doctoring? Or was this excision new?

But most important . . . what spell had been removed from the diary? And why?

Harper brought in a tray laden down with a teapot and cups. Muted laughter carried in from outside just before the back door swung open. Mimi was still giggling when she came inside, Evan behind her. Twink and Missy's nails clattered on the wooden floor as they raced into the family room to greet us.

Sleepily, Starla sat up, rubbed her eyes, and yawned. She glanced around. "How long was I asleep?"

"Not long," I said.

"Tea?" Harper asked, already pouring.

Starla nodded and stretched.

Mimi came into the family room, all smiles. "Did you find anything?" she asked, pointing to the journal.

"Not yet."

She let out a sigh as she sat on the arm of the couch. "Mom could have organized that thing better. An index or something."

I opened my mouth to ask Mimi about the missing page when suddenly Missy barked sharply, then hopped up on the couch next to me and shook her fur. Bits of moisture flew everywhere—snow drops.

Mimi ducked for cover as I let out a cry and jumped up to grab a towel from the laundry room.

I spotted Evan at the back door, peering out. "What're you doing, Evan?"

"He's spying," Mimi said.

"On what?" Harper asked.

"Dad and Glinda are out there," Mimi said. "They ran into us on the way back from Mrs. P.'s."

I brought the towel back to the couch and grabbed Missy just as she was about to run off. Gently, I rubbed her paws, drying them off. "Did you and Evan get Mrs. Pennywhistle settled?"

Mimi nodded. "Harmony said she'd check on her throughout the night."

"Evan, are you overhearing anything good?" Ve asked. "Are they talking about the case?"

"They're talking to Archie right now," Evan said. "I can't hear much. They're too far way. Oh! They're coming in!" He dashed away from the door, sprinting into the family room.

He dove onto the love seat next to Starla and reached for a teacup, trying to appear as though he hadn't been doing anything suspicious.

Missy barked as Nick and Glinda came inside the house. She danced around Glinda's feet nipping and growling.

"Missy!" Mimi said, picking her up. "That's enough of that!"

Not nearly enough, I thought.

Glinda laughed, a pretty tinkly sound, and patted Missy on the head. "She's not bothering me." Glinda looked around. "Full house." Her gaze settled on Starla; then she abruptly looked away.

"Starla and Evan are staying with us for a little while. Tea, Glinda?" Ve offered.

"No, thanks, Ms. Devaney," she said. "I'm actually just waiting for Archie. Nick suggested I wait inside to keep warm. I hope you don't mind."

Missy growled low in her throat.

I agreed with the dog.

"Of course we don't mind," Ve said without the slightest hitch in her voice that would indicate otherwise.

She was a good actress.

"Sit down, sit down, Glinda." Ve leaned forward. "Why are you waiting for Archie?"

Leave it to Aunt Ve to get right to the heart of the matter.

Glinda walked toward a chair, and I noticed she limped a little. "Did Missy get a piece of you?" I asked, nodding to her leg. Mentally, I praised the little dog, but if she had really bitten Glinda, it could be a problem.

"No, no," she said. "I twisted my ankle in the woods yesterday. Tripped on a tree root."

"Oh my," Ve said. "Have you seen Cherise? She can probably fix that right up."

As she shook her head, Glinda's blond hair glistened in the firelight like spun gold. I reached for the teapot, gripping its handle a little too tightly.

"It's no big deal," she said. "Just aches a bit."

Ve nodded, took a sip of her tea. "Those trails in the forest can be quite treacherous."

Almost as much as the fugitives hiding in there.

"Now what's this about Archie?" Ve asked.

"He said it's something to do with the Elder. He asked me to wait for him while he consults with her."

"You don't say," Ve said.

Nick sat on the sofa arm and gave me a warm smile. I was glad to see him—and couldn't wait to quiz him about what he'd learned today about Kyle's death. We were supposed to have our dinner date tonight, but I was still full from a late lunch of stew and brownies. The date would be postponed again. Nick would understand.

"Maybe it has something to do with your newest case?" Ve added innocuously.

Glinda stiffened and slid a glance toward Starla. "I doubt that."

Starla rolled her eyes and reached for the towel to dry off Twink. In a matter of seconds, he looked like a puffy white cotton ball.

Evan gripped his teacup as though he was imagining his fingers around Glinda's neck.

"Why doubt it?" Harper asked. "If there's a chance the Craft is involved . . ."

Glinda looked between all of us, shrugged, and said, "I just do. We'll see." She glanced around at each of us, then blinked innocently. "I wish I had brought my Crafter cloak. I wasn't planning an impromptu trip to see the Elder."

All of us were obligated by Wishcraft Law to grant the wish, even though doing a favor for Glinda grated my last nerve.

Fortunately, I was spared from casting the spell myself

when Mimi volunteered to do it. The cloak appeared on Glinda's lap a moment later.

Nick shook his head in wonder.

A rooster crowed at the back door and I said, "There's Archie."

Saved by the bird.

Glinda slowly rose and said, "Thanks for letting me stay warm—and for the cloak."

"I'll see you out," Nick said.

As Glinda passed the coffee table, her eyes widened as she spotted Melina's journal. "Is that—" She bent to pick it up and Missy lunged, her teeth poised to take a nip out of Glinda's hand.

Glinda yanked her fingers back, and I grabbed both the journal and Missy. "I don't know what's gotten into her tonight." I wished I knew—so I could encourage it.

Archie crowed again.

"You shouldn't keep him waiting, Glinda," Ve said. "You know how he gets."

"Yes, well." Glinda looked around, gave Mimi's arm a squeeze, then said nothing else as she hobbled to the back door.

"Bye!" Mimi called out.

Glinda smiled and waved before heading out.

I watched her walk away and couldn't help but wish for her to keep walking . . . and never come back.

Chapter Fifteen

The moon played peekaboo behind high thin clouds as Nick and I sat on the porch swing. Cold air nipped at my cheeks, my nose. I tugged the edge of my stocking cap lower onto my forehead and burrowed more deeply under the thick blanket Nick and I shared. It was dark — we'd kept the porch light off — and the wind whistled through the quiet evening.

I snuggled closer to him to share his body heat. "I heard you saved Starla from being arrested this afternoon." I gave the swing a good push with my foot and sent us swaying.

"There wasn't enough evidence to support the suggestion."

"Glinda's suggestion?"

"I don't think I can deny that it seems as though she has it out for Starla."

"Because of me?"

He hesitated only slightly before saying, "That's my guess."

I said, "I figured as much. She knows how to hurt me most." By hurting those I loved.

He nudged my chin upward. Looking straight into my eyes, he said, "I'm sorry about all this."

"All what?"

He ran a hand down his face. "I brought this on. Instead of distancing myself and my family from Glinda, I allowed her to get close to Mimi. I thought it was a good idea. A way for Mimi to connect with Melina. But now Glinda's *too* involved in our lives, and I don't know how to *uninvolve* her without hurting Mimi. What a mess."

This probably wasn't an appropriate time to say "I told you so." I bit the inside of my cheek instead. He had a point about hurting Mimi that I hadn't thought of. Mimi considered Glinda a friend—to ban the woman from her life now would only confuse her.

"You can say I told you so," he said. "It's all right. I deserve it."

"Nah. I said it in my head—that was enough."

He laughed softly, leaned in, and kissed me. After a few seconds, I barely even noticed the cold anymore. In fact, it was feeling downright toasty beneath the blanket.

The sound of flapping broke through my warm and fuzzy fog, and I forced myself away from Nick just as Archie landed on the porch railing.

He eyed the two of us and fanned himself with his wing. Clearing his throat, he said, "'You shouldn't kiss a girl when you're wearing that gun . . . leaves a bruise!'"

I narrowed my gaze on my feathered friend. "You've just been dying to use that quote, haven't you?"

He wagged his wing at me. "Months! The two of you aren't exactly known for public displays of affection. Do you have an answer for me?"

I gritted my teeth and looked to Nick for help. There was humor in his eyes as he shrugged.

Archie laughed, a loud booming noise that sounded a little like thunder. "Give up?"

I rolled my eyes. "Yes."

"Murder, My Sweet."

"Of course!" I said. "It was on the tip of my tongue."

"Sure it was." Smugly, he puffed out. He was a cocky bird. "My apologies at the interruption of your little rendezvous, but I wanted to give you fair warning," he said, his tone turning serious.

"Warning about what?" Nick asked.

Just as the words left his mouth, noise came from the trailhead behind the house, and Glinda appeared, angrily muttering and stomping through the snow. Adrenaline must have softened the ache of her twisted ankle, because her limp was all but gone. She spotted us and headed our way.

"That," Archie said before giving us a slight bow. "It is time for me to bid you a good eve." He flew off.

Nick glanced at me. "There's never a dull moment with you around."

"Would you want it any other way?"

His gaze softened. "Never."

Glinda pushed open the back gate and stormed along the shoveled pathway toward us. Her cape flew out behind her dramatically.

I summoned some faux concern. "Glinda, what's wrong? Did it not go well with the Elder?"

Steam practically blew from her ears. "You know how it went with the Elder. I don't know how you tricked her into getting your way, but I shouldn't be surprised. Everyone around here seems to have fallen under your spell." Her tone shifted to mocking. "*Darcy this and Darcy that.* Yuck! You don't fool me, Darcy Merriweather!"

I tipped my head and kept my voice calm. "Well, you don't fool me, either, Glinda Hansel, so I guess we're even."

"Ugh!" she cried, then turned sharply and angrily hobbled off, slamming the gate behind her.

Nick slid a questioning glance my way. "What was that about?"

"She's mad."

He laughed, and I loved the way the sound washed over me, flooding me with warmth. "No kidding."

"It's about the Elder," I explained. "She summoned me earlier. She wants me to be her eyes and ears on Starla's case."

"Because of Craft involvement?"

I nodded.

His forehead furrowed in confusion. "Why didn't she ask Glinda?"

I explained the Elder's reasoning. "Looks like Glinda didn't take the news so well." We swayed on the swing for a bit, and when he remained silent, I said, "I know this kind of throws a wrench in me staying out of your cases. . . ."

Smiling, he said, "Actually, it doesn't. Don't you see, Darcy? The Elder gave us a gift."

"I don't understand."

He shifted on the swing to face me head-on. "It's why Glinda is so mad. It's not because the Elder asked you and not her. It's because you can now interfere with this case as much as you want and Glinda can't object at all because as much as I'm her supervisor on the force, the Elder is her boss where the Craft is concerned, and around here Craft Law trumps mortal protocols. By asking you to look into Starla's case, the Elder just neutralized any threat Glinda held over us."

I perked up. A gift, indeed. "We can work together now? Share information?"

He nodded, then lifted an eyebrow. "Do you have any information?"

"Not really. I just . . ." I faced him. "Did you question Kyle's family?"

"I tried, but they clammed up and asked for a lawyer. Is there something in particular I should ask them?"

I gave him a quick rundown of my visit to Wickedly Creative. "They seemed really concerned that he had disappeared. I suspect they knew he was in danger. Now that Kyle is dead I have to wonder if he willingly left his tree house or if he was forced out by someone. But another question is what happened to his belongings? Did you find any fingerprints other than Kyle's at the tree house?"

"The tree house had been wiped clean of most fingerprints—a nearly impossible task. Only yours, Harper's, and a few of Kyle's remained. Someone went through a lot of trouble."

"But who? His killer? Or his family trying to cover up their presence there?"

"Good question."

But one we didn't have an answer to yet.

"Any idea what killed him?" I asked.

"No, but there was a puncture wound in his thigh."

"Puncture?" I had visions of ice picks and really long daggers.

"An injection site. He also had a sizable wound on his calf, but it wasn't serious enough to cause a fatality."

"An injection site? You think he might have been poisoned?"

"It looks that way. The ME promised a preliminary report in the next day or two. We'll know more then."

I whistled. Poisoned.

"It would be a good idea for Starla and Evan to take the polygraph," he said. "The sooner we can rule them out, the better."

I fussed with the blanket and said, "Doesn't it make more sense to wait to find out for certain how Kyle died in the first place? That injection site could have been . . . recreational."

He rested his forehead against mine. "I'd just like to rule them out once and for all."

In my mind it still didn't make sense for Starla to take that polygraph—especially when she wasn't sure she'd pass it. I changed the subject. "Are you sure you're okay with me nosing around?" I asked, still not wanting to step on his investigative toes. He cupped my face and kissed me. I lost myself in the moment for a bit before saying, "I take that as a yes?"

"I guess that means I've fallen under your spell, too."

It was exactly where I planned to keep him.

Whether Glinda liked it or not.

Chapter Sixteen

Long after Nick, Mimi, and Harper left, I sat on the sofa in the family room with Missy and the flames in the fireplace keeping me company.

A lamp cast a soft glow over the pages of Melina's diary as I searched for an answer to how Kyle was able to be invisible. It was in these pages somewhere, and I was determined to find it.

I held the diary far from Missy, who seemed intent on pawing its pages, and rubbed her ears. Fighting back a yawn, I eyed the mantel clock. It was just before two in the morning. Long past my bedtime.

Resting the diary on my chest, I leaned my head back and closed my eyes, letting the events of the past couple of days swirl around my mind like a dust storm. Kyle's reappearance, his death . . .

As they often did when I was overtired, my thoughts wandered to another death, one that happened a long time ago.

My mom.

There were times when I missed her so much my

chest ached. This was one of them—it always happened with an approaching birthday. I could easily recall the last birthday I shared with her. I'd turned seven, and there hadn't been a big party at all, just my parents and me and cake and balloons . . . and love. So much love.

I could picture the lopsided homemade chocolate cake she'd made, and see the love-struck look in my father's eyes as he gazed at her, but try as I might, I couldn't recall her whole face. It swam in and out of focus, even as I could hear her singing an off-key, high-pitched version of "Happy Birthday" to me. The voice was there, imprinted perfectly in my mind, but not what she looked like.

I'd catch a glimpse of one of her eyes, rimmed in the metallic blue eyeliner from Avon she loved so much, or the delicate freckles that dotted her skin, or the way the corner of her lips curled when she smiled. . . . But I couldn't ever quite put it together to make one solid picture of her in my mind.

Not too long ago, I'd shown my sketchbooks to Mimi with all the images of my mother I'd drawn over the years. The bits. The pieces. She'd asked me why I hadn't drawn a whole picture and it hurt to tell her that it was because *I couldn't remember what she looked like.*

I'd do just about anything to remember.

Tears leaked from the corners of my eyes as I let the memory of my mother's voice singing "Happy Birthday" to me play over and over in my head, and sat up with a start when I heard a noise—footsteps.

"I'm sorry," Starla said as she sat next to me on the couch. "I didn't mean to wake you up."

I was about to say I hadn't been sleeping, but when I glanced at the clock again I saw it was nearly four in the morning. I must have drifted off.

"Have you been crying?" Starla asked, leaning in to get a good look at my face. "What's wrong?"

"Nothing's wrong." I rubbed my eyes and felt the salty residue left behind by my tears.

"Oh, right, because crying in your sleep is normal," she said.

I smiled at her sarcastic tone. "I'd been thinking about my mom. That's all. Not a bad thing, just missing her."

Starla nodded. "Grief is tricky like that, sneaking up on you when you're least expecting it."

Only, I did expect it this time of year—because of my birthday. But I didn't want to talk about it, so I said, "Did you get any sleep?"

"A little."

She'd refused another visit from Cherise, and I couldn't say I blamed her. It had to be disconcerting to lose a half day of your life like that.

Missy lifted her head and blinked sleepy eyes. Starla ran a hand down the dog's back and Missy put her head back down. "I can't seem to turn off my thoughts."

"About Kyle?" I asked softly.

Nodding, her eyes drifted closed. I had the feeling she wanted to talk, but I didn't want to push her to open up. She'd get there in her own time.

The mama hen in me just wanted to pull her in my arms and hold her for a little while—here, in her froggy-printed pajamas with her hair pulled back and not a speck of makeup, she looked like a lost little girl.

You can't fix everything, I had to remind myself.

Despite those words echoing in my head, I couldn't quite help myself from reaching over and taking her hand in mine. I gave it a squeeze. I might not be able to fix what ailed her, but I could make sure she knew I was there for her.

Her eyes fluttered open and she turned her head to look at me and offered a small smile. She squeezed my hand back.

She adjusted the blanket and drew her legs onto the couch, tucking them beneath her. "It wasn't supposed to be like this. We were supposed to live happily ever after. I loved him so much. He loved me. I know he did," she said fiercely, as though I was going to debate it.

Arguing was the farthest thought from my mind. "How could he not?"

"Exactly," she said, her voice cracking. "Exactly. If he loved me, how could he have . . ." She shook her head.

"I don't know." I wish I did, so I could label it. *This is why.* It would be closure for her, and she desperately needed an explanation.

Unfortunately, with his death it wasn't likely she was ever going to get a reason.

"It was so perfect for a while," she said with a smile on her face. "He was . . . perfect. Truly, he was. Handsome and funny and smart. He was kind and attentive. Doting. We'd cook dinner together every night because we worked such different hours and wanted to make sure to share at least one meal together. He was a night owl who usually stayed up late painting while I got up early, so he'd leave me a little love note every morning next to my coffee cup complete with a cute little drawing so I'd see it right off. . . ."

My heart thumped hard in my chest as I listened to her. Heard the love in her voice. Heard the loss.

"The change in him was subtle at first," she said. "Skipping dinner and going to his studio earlier at night. A harsh comment here and there. No more love notes in the morning. Then out of the blue he'd return to his normal self. Laughing, playful, loving, and I'd start to believe I was crazy for thinking anything was wrong in the first place. But then the harsh comments became commonplace, and the playful side of him began disappearing altogether. He became angry all the time. Withdrawn. He would hardly look at me, and when he did, there was nothing in his eyes but uncertainty, like he didn't know why he was behaving that way." She looked me straight in the eye. "I was scared at the change, but I didn't want to tell anyone."

"Why?" I asked.

She pulled her bottom lip into her mouth, and I could see her chin quivering. Finally, she said, "I—I felt like a failure."

I squeezed her hand harder. "Oh, Starla."

"Our marriage was supposed to be . . . perfect; everyone said so. And it wasn't. I wasn't. Obviously."

"It wasn't you," I said. "It was him. . . ."

"Was it?" she asked me. "I probably could have been a better wife. . . ."

My tone was firm. "Stop it. It was him. There is no excuse for what he did."

"I know," she whispered. "He was just so unhappy. I wanted him to be happy, Darcy. Why wasn't he?"

Tears filled my eyes. "I don't know." I gathered up what courage I had and said softly, "The day you called the police . . . was that the first time he'd hurt you?"

A teardrop tracked down her cheek as she shook her head. "There were other times."

My heart cracked straight in half.

"Not as badly as that day," she went on. "A push here, a shove there. I let it go because he never slapped or actually hit me. Wrote it off as his temper. I shouldn't have done that."

No, but saying so now wouldn't help any.

"He'd just get so worked up about something. Trivial things, too—the cap left off the toothpaste or it being too cold in the house—and suddenly one of the traits I loved about him most—his fiery passion—I didn't like so much. My gut instinct said that something was wrong. Inside here." She tapped her head. "So I suggested he see Cherise."

"Did he go?" I wondered about a mental disorder. Depression or schizophrenia. Or maybe I was just grasping at straws, looking for a *reason*. An excuse for the inexcusable.

"My suggestion just made him angrier. He didn't think there was anything wrong with him. The more he objected, the more I began to think that I was the one with the issue, and that I'd been unfairly blaming him. I let it go."

She said nothing for a long time, then whispered, "I don't know how to feel right now, with him gone. . . . On one hand, I'm relieved because I'd been so scared of him. On the other, I'm really sad. How twisted is that? To be sad?"

"I don't think it's twisted at all. At one point, you loved him very much."

"Maybe I still do. Maybe that's why I haven't been able to fully commit to Vince, holding myself back a little. Maybe that's why I feel this crushing weight on my chest."

Maybe that was why she couldn't forgive herself for staying in a destructive marriage for so long. I hoped one day she would forgive herself. One day soon. I squeezed her hand tighter.

"Why did it have to be this way? Why?"

Tears leaked from my eyes just from the sheer agony I heard straining her voice. There was nothing I could say to that. No amount of soothing that could console her at this point. Maybe ever.

Missy clambered into Starla's lap and gave her chin a lick. With watery eyes, Starla said to the dog, "It's okay, I'm okay."

If only that were true.

If only.

Even though I was sleep deprived, I took an hour the next morning to go for my morning jog. I needed the time to clear my mind. So much had happened over the past two days that I could barely keep it straight.

Early on a Sunday morning was probably the quietest time in the village. I spotted only a few hearty souls out walking their dogs as I jogged along. Even though another snowstorm was supposed to hit later on today, right now temperatures hovered above freezing. Everything was perfectly still, peaceful. And for a change lately, I didn't hear the cooing of the mourning dove.

I kept running, unzipping my thermal jacket as I warmed from exertion. The cold air I breathed in felt both soothing and painful—a strange combination to be sure—but one I'd become accustomed to during my winter runs.

As I Looped around the square, the scent of vanilla filled the air—Evan putting the day's cakes in the ovens at the Gingerbread Shack. I hoped baking would calm him a little bit—he'd been up early today and hadn't been able to sit still. Like me, he was full of nervous energy. Wondering what would happen with this case. With Starla.

There was a light on in Harper's apartment above the bookshop, and I noticed Pie sitting on one of the windowsills, watching birds fly about. I glanced down the street, at the center of town, then back over my shoulder, toward a trailhead that led into the Enchanted Forest. In a snap, I made a decision and headed for the woods.

I couldn't deny the sudden urge to take another look at Kyle's tree house.

Despite the snow it didn't take long to reach the path that led there. The snow had been trampled down, undoubtedly by investigators, and was dirty and slushy. Sunbeams poked through the canopy, spotlighting the overgrown path.

All around me was still and silent as I slowed to a walk, the only noise coming from my breathing and the crunch of my sneakers on the snow. There was no birdsong, no village noise. It was eerie but oddly peaceful. The trail abruptly ended, and I stepped into the glen.

Light spilled into the open clearing, highlighting frosted shrubs and making tree branches sparkle. It was a tranquil place, and if I were a Realtor pitching hideouts to fugitives, this place would be at the top of my list.

My gaze shifted to the tree house. I fully expected to see police tape and warning signs not to trespass. What I hadn't expected to see was Liam Chadwick sitting in the tree's doorway.

He held up a beer bottle to me in greeting. "Seems I'm not the only curiosity seeker around here."

I walked over to him. His dark hair had been left loose instead of being slicked back and his glasses only seemed to highlight the dark circles discoloring the skin beneath his grief-stricken eyes. He wore the same coat as when he'd stopped by As You Wish with Will, and had on a black sweater, worn jeans, and a weathered pair of zippered leather ankle boots.

I said, "Seems to me *I'm* the only curiosity seeker here." My guess was he had known of this place for a long, long while.

"Touché," he said, reaching behind him for another bottle of beer. He offered it to me.

"Thanks, but it's a little early for me."

He shrugged and scooted over, creating a seat next to him on the threshold. "If we're being completely truthful, neither of us are curiosity seekers, are we?" He blinked those impossibly blue eyes. "I heard a rumor that you're snooping around on behalf of the Elder."

News sure traveled fast in this village. I sat. "*Are* we being completely truthful?"

Thin shoulders lifted in a shrug. "What is the truth, really? Everyone's perceptions of it are different. And don't you know the saying about the truth hurting?"

"And lies don't?"

He drained his beer, then reached for another. "Sometimes it's better not to know the whole truth."

I had the feeling he was trying to warn me, but I couldn't fathom why. "Not when Starla's freedom is at stake."

He lips curved wryly. "Right. The truth shall set her free."

"You're mocking."

"Darcy, the truth won't set her free. Like I said, truth hurts."

Biting my lip, I wondered at what he wasn't saying. Because even if he wasn't saying why the truth would hurt, I fully believed him that it did. "I'm confident she'll be cleared," I said, trying to wrap my head around his riddles. "It's just a matter of time."

"Will she be cleared?" he asked, his eyes challenging me from behind his glasses. "She certainly had motive. And a whole roomful of people heard her threaten to kill him."

My temper rose. "Starla wouldn't hurt anyone. She's not that kind of person, as you should know."

"Kyle wasn't that kind of person, either."

Nearby, a squirrel scampered from branch to branch. "So I've heard. Foul is fair." When he didn't react to my barb, I added, "But it doesn't change the fact that he tried to kill her."

"Or change that Starla threatened to kill him," he countered.

We could go round and round on this and never agree.

"Starla has been under some stress lately," he hypothesized. "Extenuating circumstances can make someone snap."

Was he serious? "Extenuating, like your brother stalking her?"

He gripped his beer bottle tightly—I wasn't the only one trying to keep a temper in check. "If she's guilty," he said, "she'll go to jail. It's as simple as that."

He was trying to get a rise out of me, and it was working. I could feel the heat in my cheeks as I said, "She was at my house the whole night."

"Allegedly."

"You know differently?" I asked tightly.

"Just speculating," he said with a fake smile.

"Well, I speculate that if she does get arrested, she should consider breaking out of jail and being kept hidden by her family."

A flicker of real amusement flashed across his face. "I'm not sure what you're inferring."

"Everyone knows your family hid Kyle. Built him this tree house, too, I bet."

Trying to look innocent, he blinked. "Did we?"

Frustrated, I said, "Do you deny your family has known where Kyle has been this whole time?"

He full-out grinned. "Completely."

Shaking my head, I fought the urge to slap the smile from his face. "Does anyone in your family take responsibility for wrongdoing?"

"Who's to say what's wrong?"

"The law?"

He shrugged. "Who's to say laws are always right?"

I stuffed my hands in my pockets to keep from acting on my urge to hit him. "You're just full of double-talk, aren't you?"

Stretching his legs, he said, "Perhaps, but I'm not wrong."

Once upon a time I would have argued that point, but these days I didn't necessarily disagree with his statement. Some laws were meant to be broken. But not in this case. Kyle should have been in jail.

When I said nothing, he looked at me, and my anger instantly dissipated at the sadness I saw in his eyes. I'd almost forgotten in the midst of all this that his twin brother had died. No matter what I thought of Kyle, I couldn't imagine what it was like to lose a sibling. Just the thought of something happening to Harper made my chest hurt.

"You're a good friend to Starla," he finally said, "and that's admirable, but you don't understand the situation."

"Enlighten me."

He took another swallow of his beer and said nothing.

Cold air stung my nose as I took in a deep breath. "Starla said Kyle's personality began changing a few months into their marriage. Did you notice that, too?"

"No." He looked off in the distance. "If only I had . . ."

His voice rang with echoes of regret. I studied him. "And if you had?"

Long lashes brushed his glasses as he closed his eyes. When he opened them again, light shimmered off the moisture. "Maybe everything would have been different."

I recalled Starla's regrets at not telling anyone of her troubles. Hindsight was excruciating.

He finished his beer and dropped the empty bottle back in its cardboard container. Giving me a withering glance, he said, "I think it's time for you to go."

It was clear I wasn't going to get anything more out of him. "Fine, I'm going."

"Don't let me stop you."

I stood, took a few steps, then turned around to tell him off. But when he looked at me, all I could see was his grief shimmering in his eyes. I bit back my angry tirade and said, "I'm really sorry you lost your brother."

His anguished gaze searched my face. "Go away, Darcy, and save your pity for someone who wants it."

Chapter Seventeen

With Liam's rebuke still ringing in my ears, I headed for the Witch's Brew, in need of strong coffee and something sweet.

Pulling open the door made a bell jangle as I breathed in all delicious scents. Coffee and cinnamon and chocolate and vanilla and something citrusy, maybe orange or lemon. It took some of the edge off my bad mood.

The cashier behind the counter greeted me by name and we chitchatted while I picked out baked goods to take home for breakfast and to take to Mrs. P and also to Nick and Mimi later on. It would be nice to spend part of the day with them. Right now, with my temper still flaring, I needed a big dose of *normal*.

"Great minds," a voice said from behind me.

I turned and found Vince with his hands stuffed in his pockets, his damp hair curling about his forehead, and his brown puppy dog eyes watching me carefully behind his glasses.

"I was just going to take some pastries and coffee

over to your house," he said. In a rush he added, "Starla said it was okay if I stop by."

I recalled what Starla had said last night, wondering if she was holding back from Vince because she still loved Kyle. . . . That could be true, but, I'd seen how happy she was with Vince. And I saw how he looked at her when he thought no one was watching. Maybe it was time I let my guard down around him. Because I had the feeling he wasn't going anywhere anytime soon.

"Well, I'm not going to object to more pastries," I said.

He smiled that lopsided boyish grin of his and nodded. "The doughnuts here are great."

"My favorites are the lemon tarts."

"Too sour," he said, making a face.

"Your palate is clearly lacking." I forced myself to joke with him. It was more difficult to befriend him than I'd imagined.

He smiled as I passed the cashier my credit card and my customer reward card (buy eight cups of coffee and get one free!). As she handed my bag to me, she wished me a happy early birthday.

Confused, I tipped my head. "How'd you know my birthday was coming up?"

Her eyes grew wide and in my peripheral vision, I could see Vince making some sort of movement, but when I looked back at him, he just shrugged.

The cashier said, "I—I . . ." She tapped the computer screen. "It's right here in our system on your customer reward information. Don't forget you get a free coffee on the big day."

"Ooh, free coffee," I said. "I'll be back, then."

I waited for Vince to order and started walking back to As You Wish with him.

He said, "Has there been any news on the case yet?"

"Not really." I didn't want to mention the possibility that Kyle had been poisoned. Not until we knew for sure. "Nick's still waiting on the medical examiner."

Vince stopped walking, and when I turned to see why, his troubled gaze locked on mine. He said, "Is Starla okay? I mean really okay? She says she is, but I hear something in her voice. . . ."

I bit the inside of my cheek and finally said, "I think she'll be okay. In time. It's been a rough two days."

"More like it's been a rough couple of years."

"That's true." We started walking again, and just the sight of As You Wish cheered me up a bit with its purple paint and Victorian charm.

"I went to school with the Chadwick twins, you know. The same graduating class."

"No, I didn't know."

"They were . . ." His brow furrowed.

"What?"

"What I wanted to be."

I thought about the handsome and popular Chadwick brothers and could imagine how shy Vince had been in high school, undoubtedly with his nose buried in a witch-craft book. "The grass isn't always greener. And sometimes nice guys do get the girl in the end."

I spotted Archie watching us from inside his cage as Vince held open the back gate for me. "Thanks for saying that. And just . . . thanks."

"For what?" I asked.

"Not hating my guts."

My stomach twisted. I didn't *hate* him, that was true. But I didn't exactly like him. Yet. I nodded. "Go on in. I've got a croissant here for Archie, and I know how you two get along."

"Crazy bird," Vince mumbled as he headed for the back door.

Archie let out a loud caw, then said, "'I'm not crazy. I'm just colorful.'"

Vince gave him a perplexed look as Archie repeated the phrase over and over in increasingly louder and more angry tones. Vince glanced at me. "What's with him?"

I shrugged. "It's a quote from *Butch Cassidy and the Sundance Kid*. He must have heard it on TV or something."

"I'm not crazy!" Archie shouted, sounding absolutely off his rocker.

Vince's eyes widened and he scurried off into the house.

I smiled as I approached his cage. "Subtle."

Agitated, Archie scooted side to side on his wooden perch. "Calling *me* crazy. At least I'm not a moron."

"Now, now. There's a difference between intelligence and wisdom," I said.

Archie stilled and gave me a withering glance. "Then he's not *wise*," he said scathingly. "He is, in fact, a dunderhead."

It was a point that was hard to argue against. To distract him from his hissy fit, I singsonged, "I brought you a croissant."

Still miffed, he turned his back to me.

"It's warm from the oven."

He casually looked over his shoulder. "Leave the croissant and go. *Crazy*," he muttered under his breath. "I'll give him crazy."

Smiling, I gingerly slipped the croissant into his food dish and noticed Lawcrafter Marcus Debrowski coming up the driveway. I met him at the gate.

"What's with Archie?" Marcus asked. "Why's he talking to himself like that?"

"He has a 'crazy' complex." I gave Marcus a long once-over. "You're out early." It was only a little past nine. By the look on his face, this wasn't a social visit.

In his late twenties, dark-haired, green-eyed Marcus Debrowski looked every bit a young professional with his spiffy wool peacoat, trendy trousers and shoes, and the dark-rimmed glasses that made him seem that much more intelligent.

He and Harper had been dating for a while now, and she was completely smitten. The feeling was mutual—he adored her—and I really hoped the two of them worked out. Some couples just fit. They were one of them.

"I need to pick up Starla," Marcus said. "She didn't tell you?"

"I just got home. What happened?" Because it was obvious something had.

"Glinda Hansel called an hour ago. Some new evidence was found, and the police want to question Starla again."

Glinda. I bet she loved making that phone call.

We walked toward the back door. "What kind of evidence? Does it implicate Starla? Is that why they want to talk to her again?"

Marcus shrugged and held the door open for me. "I don't know yet."

I wanted to call Nick and find out, but if new evidence had been found, he would be too busy to answer. Which also meant that my afternoon of *normal* was out the window.

The strong scent of coffee hung in the air as Marcus and I came into the kitchen. We were met by three grim faces. Ve's, Starla's and Vince's. Vince sat next to Starla at the counter, and she gripped his hand.

Twink and Missy shared the dog bed by the back door, and Tilda watched us from the top step of the back staircase.

Ve gave Marcus a kiss on the cheek. "Coffee?"

He shook his head. "If only I had time. We really should go, Starla. They're waiting for us."

"Isn't this harassment?" Vince asked. "She didn't have anything to do with Kyle's death."

Marcus said, "They're investigating. Questions come up that need answers."

"It's okay," Starla said, patting Vince's hand. "Maybe this will be the end of it."

"Well, I'm coming with you," Vince declared. "Moral support."

Marcus said, "We could be there a while, and you won't be allowed in the interview room."

"I don't care about that." He glanced at Starla and there was such tenderness in his eyes that I felt myself liking him just a little bit more. "I just want to be there if Starla needs me."

Moisture filled Starla's eyes as she looked at him.

Ve slid me a look. I let out a resigned sigh. Starla might not be able to admit it to herself yet, but it was obvious she'd fallen for this Seeker.

Vince helped her with her coat, and she promised to fill us in when she returned.

Marcus was the last one out the door, and when he turned back, my stomach sank at the apprehensive look on his face. "Wish us luck."

Both Ve and I did, and as soon as the door closed, Ve said, "Why do I have the feeling he'll need it?"

I didn't want to think about it. My stomach churned as I unpacked the treats I'd brought home.

Ve eyed the plate. "Between you and Vince, we have enough to feed the whole village."

"Some are for Mrs. P, Nick, and Mimi," I said. "I'm going to shower, and then head out."

"Mrs. P will enjoy the visit."

"I'm worried about her."

Ve draped an arm around me, giving me a quick squeeze. "You've a kind heart, Darcy. It gets hurt easily only because of how full it is." She took a sip of coffee. "Starla mentioned you had a dream about your mother last night. . . . There were tears?"

I leaned against the counter and unexpectedly tears filled my eyes again. "I think I'm just overly emotional this week. Nervous for Starla, for Mrs. P . . ."

"And, of course, your birthday is coming up."

I rolled my eyes. "I wish people would stop mentioning it."

"Ah, but I can't grant that wish, now, can I?"

I drew a circle on the countertop with my fingertip. "I don't know what the big deal is. It's just another day."

"Is it, dear?" She danced her way to the sink to soak dishes. "I don't think so."

"What was that?" I asked, pointing to her feet. Distraction at its finest. I didn't want to talk about my birthday anymore.

"A grapevine." Her eyes twinkled. "I'm practicing for next Sunday."

The Swing and Sway dance. Dear heavens. "I can't believe Terry agreed to this." He was a private man, and a nudie dance competition didn't seem his kind of thing.

Her cheeks flushed, and she tittered. "Well, ah, you

know men. They'll do anything for the women they love."

I eyed her. "Terry is your partner, isn't he?"

"I'm working on it," she said dully.

I laughed, and then nearly jumped out of my skin when a tile suddenly popped out of the backsplash, landing with a clatter on the counter. But I quickly realized this was no random tile. It was a doorway.

Pepe stuck his little brown head out of the wall. "Oh, *mon Dieu*, I thought Vince would never leave!" Pepe hopped onto the counter and dusted off his vest and adjusted his glasses.

"He wasn't here very long," Ve said.

"It was an *eternity*," Pepe said. "Your walls . . . they are not the cleanest."

Ve tucked a strand of hair back into her twist. "*Hmmph.*"

Pepe eyed the plate of goodies. "Is that a cheese Danish I spy?"

I broke off a chunk and handed it to him. He sat, his chubby belly straining the buttons on his vest, and nibbled. "My apologies for the early-morning visit, but I had the most interesting night."

"Ooh," Ve said. "Do tell. Did your week of discontent turn into a night of debauchery?"

Pepe blinked at her. "If only . . ."

I smiled at his earnestness.

"It was not *I* enjoying the debauchery," he said, "but someone in the village had quite the evening."

I said, "I'm not sure I want to know" at the same time Ve said, "Who was it?"

I gave her a look.

"What?" she asked innocently. "A little gossip never hurt anyone."

Pepe said, "I was snooping around Wickedly Creative and the Chadwick homestead, on an eavesdropping mission. . . ."

In the craziness of the past day, I'd completely forgotten he was going to do that.

His beady eyes grew wide. "And what to my wondering ears did I hear but quite the tryst and pillow talk."

Ve fairly danced with joy and rubbed her hands together. "Who? Who?"

"None other than our good fellow Will Chadwick."

"Well, I suppose," I said, "that's one way to deal with grief."

Copper eyebrows nearly hit Ve's hairline as she said, "I bet he's good in bed. Don't you think?" she asked me.

"Ve!"

"Oh, come on. Surely I'm not the only one who wonders these types of things."

"Yes," I said. "Yes, you are."

"His partner had no complaints," Pepe said.

Ve winked. "You little voyeur, you."

With cheeks growing redder by the minute, he said, "*Au contraire.* When I realized what was going on, I left, and then came back an acceptable amount of time later in time to hear the pillow talk. That's when things became really interesting."

"I doubt that," Ve said, setting her mug in the sink.

I could only shake my head at her. Out of the corner of my eye, I spotted Tilda creeping down the steps. She liked to "play" with Pepe. He was convinced she was trying to eat him. I wouldn't put it past her. "What kind of pillow talk?"

Pepe rested his hands on his tummy. "They were speaking about Starla."

"Who was Will speaking to?" Ve asked. "Who's his partner?"

"Alas, I do not know. I tried to uncover her identity, but there was an enormous yellow beast with big brown eyes and sharp teeth watching me watch the room . . . he was plotting my demise. Much like Tilda is doing now. Go away!" he shooed her.

She sat on the fourth stair, and her gaze zeroed in on him. Her tail flicked.

"I like her better when she stays with Lew," Pepe bemoaned.

If it were up to Pepe, she'd live with Lew, the Emoticrafter, permanently.

"Aw," Ve said, picking up Tilda and rubbing her chin. "She's just a love bug. Aren't you?"

Tilda hissed.

Quite the love bug. Ha.

I sat on a stool. "Back to the pillow talk. What were they saying about Starla?"

"It was quite strange," Pepe said, eyeing Tilda cautiously. "They were speculating what could have happened to Kyle, and how long it would take before it was revealed that his death could not have been a suicide." He tipped his head. "That theory is bothering the Chadwick family quite a bit."

I guessed that Nick hadn't yet shared the information about a possible poisoning with Kyle's family. "Why are they so certain it wasn't suicide?"

"Because apparently there was no way Kyle could have transported himself to Starla's home."

"He couldn't? Why not?" Ve asked.

I added, "He seemed to be getting around the village just fine to see Starla. Invisibly, yes, but still."

Pepe twirled his whiskers. "Because according to what I overheard . . . Kyle Chadwick's legs were paralyzed."

Chapter Eighteen

Pepe decided to tag along with me to visit Mrs. P, and we found her easily enough in the dining room of the Pixie Cottage, draped in a hot pink caftan, sipping tea near the bed and breakfast's stone fireplace.

I'd tried to get in touch with Nick to tell him about Kyle supposedly being paralyzed, but he wasn't answering his cell phone. I left him a message to call me as soon as possible.

Paralyzed. It was hard to believe, but I immediately knew it had to be true. It made perfect sense now why Kyle's family was so concerned he'd disappeared—because he couldn't just walk away on his own.

But knowing that he had been paralyzed opened new questions. How was he getting around town just fine in order to see Starla? Was he killed at his tree house and moved to Starla's place? It wouldn't have been easy carrying his body through those woods—or town—without being seen by someone. . . .

Oh! Especially someone who had a fascination with video surveillance. I made a mental note to ask Vince if he had footage from Friday night. Maybe he had evidence and didn't realize it.

High arched windows let in plenty of light, brightening the cottage's dining room, which was filled with nature-inspired decor. Lots of heavy wooden pieces, twig tables and chairs. Harmony had truly brought the outdoors inside with her interior designing.

I skirted a pale purple armchair and Mrs. P looked up. She brightened when she saw me and positively lit up when Pepe peeked out from behind the curtain of my hair—he'd been sitting on my shoulder.

"A stowaway!" she cackled, then looked around. "Let's go back to my quarters, shall we?"

The other guests in the dining room of the charming little B and B barely paid us any attention, but a talking mouse would surely catch them off guard.

I followed Mrs. P down a short hallway to her suite. Once upon a time, she'd owned the inn, but when she had financial troubles a few years ago, she sold it to Harmony with the promise that she could live out the rest of her days here.

My chest ached when I realized that the end might be sooner than any of us thought.

At room number four, Mrs. P slipped a key in the lock and turned the handle. The space was as whimsical as the woman who lived there. A huge canopy bed made of branches took up a good portion of the room and two mirrored nightstands flanked the bed. There were a couple of upholstered arm chairs, a small dining table, and a tiny kitchenette.

As she entered, Mrs. P nudged the thermostat in the room and the heat came on. I thought it was plenty warm in the room already. Tropics warm. I set Pepe on the table and began to unwrap my scarf and unzip my coat.

"I can't seem to chase away this chill," she said, pulling a throw blanket onto her lap as she sat in one of the upholstered chairs. "Sit, sit. To what do I owe the pleasure?"

I wished I'd worn a T-shirt instead of a sweater as I handed her a plate of pastries. "We brought you some goodies."

A penciled eyebrow shot up. "These are merely a tasty ruse; you're checking up on me."

"Guilty," I said, studying her. The spikes of her hair were wilted, and her black eyeliner had smudged beneath her eyes. False eyelashes were coming unglued and stuck out a bit, giving her a somewhat crazed look. "We're worried about you."

"How are you feeling?" Pepe asked, sitting on the edge of the table.

"You two are dears but I'm fine. Just fine. A tiny dizzy spell isn't going to keep me down for long. I'm simply placating Cherise by taking it easy today. Otherwise, I'd be getting Lotions and Potions ready to open instead of sitting here whiling away my time. Now tell me all the news. What's the latest with Starla?"

Pepe and I filled her in on all the latest developments.

"That's all we know," I said as we finished telling her about Kyle's paralysis. "And we only know that thanks to Pepe overhearing a conversation between Will and a lady friend."

"Way to bury the lead, Darcy," Mrs. P said, her eyes lighting. Bright red lipstick had seeped beyond her lips, giving her a Joker-ish appearance. "Lady friend? Who's this lady friend?"

"A mystery lady friend," I said. "Pepe didn't see a face."

"Not for lack of trying. There was a beast," he explained. "A big one. With sharp teeth."

Mrs. P said, "And you probably looked pretty tasty."

He nodded. "A midnight snack of the highest caliber."

Mrs. P cackled. "The absolute highest. Now, if Kyle was paralyzed, how did he get to Starla's town house?"

"That's the million dollar question right now."

"Surely the police don't believe Starla brought him there?" she said. "That's ludicrous."

"I'm not sure they're aware he was paralyzed." I glanced at my watch. "I'm curious about this new evidence the police supposedly have. I'm waiting for Nick to call me back."

"I can't imagine Mademoiselle Starla will be at the police station much longer," Pepe said.

Mrs. P shrugged. "Unless they've arrested her."

"Bite your tongue!" I cried.

She tipped her head. "It's best to be prepared for the worst."

I had the sinking feeling she was right. I just didn't want to believe it. Standing, I said, "I should get going. Mrs. P, you'll call if you need anything."

She waved a hand. "I'll be fine."

"You'll call?" I pressed.

She sighed. "I'll call."

Pepe hopped to his feet and bowed. "Perhaps you'd do me the honor of dinner tomorrow night?"

Aha. So Pepe had won the battle with Godfrey for the date with Mrs. P.

Mrs. P straightened, a pleased smile plumping her hollow cheeks. "I'm the one who will be honored to join you. But perhaps . . ."

"Oui?"

"Perhaps," she said, "if you have some free time now you'd like to stay and play an old lady in a game of poker?"

Pepe smiled and glanced at me. "*Ma chère*, I do believe I'll find my own way home later. I'll be staying with my friend Eugenia a little while longer."

I glanced between the two of them. "You two stay out of trouble."

Mrs. P laughed, her cackle reverberating off the walls. "Just try to stop us."

As I walked out, I glanced back as Mrs. P pulled out a deck of cards. Pepe was already boasting his superior playing skills and she promised to test him sorely.

Seeing them together gave me a warm and fuzzy feeling, even as I headed back into the cold.

Head down against the suddenly gusting wind, I turned toward Old Forest Lane—Nick and Mimi's street. Even though Nick was working, I could still get a small dose of normal by spending some time with Mimi. She was sure to love the box of pastries I had with me. No one had a sweet tooth like she did.

Deep snowbanks bracketed the cobblestoned street, but the twisting sidewalk had been shoveled. I passed by Glinda Hansel's cottage and had to admit it looked charming with its snow-covered eaves and bluish purple paint. Windows were dark with shades drawn and the garage door was closed, which made sense since she was probably at the police station grilling my best friend.

The farther I walked down the street, the more the houses spread out. At the end of the lane, I spotted Nick and Mimi's place, a quaint yellow farmhouse with a wide front porch, a picket fence, and an oversized workshop garage behind the house.

I pushed open the front gate and was surprised to see Nick's police car in the driveway. It was hard to miss, being that it was a black-and-yellow MINI Cooper. I called it the Bumblebeemobile and thought it was about as intimidating as a frosted cupcake. Maybe Nick had walked to work today? Or taken a ride from Glinda?

That latter thought had me gritting my teeth. Okay, so maybe I was a little jealous of her feelings for Nick. A teeny tiny bit. Even though I was confident Nick had zero feelings for her, I couldn't help but want her out of his life. I didn't much like this about myself, so I took a few deep breaths, told myself to let it go, wished it were that easy.

The stone walkway had been shoveled and sanded, and I carefully navigated the porch steps before knocking on the front door. Higgins, a Saint Bernard, immediately started barking. If I were a burglar, his sonorous *woofs* would have me scurrying off as fast as my feet could carry me. Mimi swished aside the sidelight curtain and peeked out. When she spotted me, her eyes widened and a smile stretched her cheeks to their limit.

My heart swelled at her reaction as I heard locks tumbling.

"Higgins, back! Back!" I heard her say as the door cracked open. She wedged her body into the opening and said to me, "Hurry!"

I pushed inside, and quickly closed the door behind me, leaning against it. "Come here, Higgins," I said, patting my chest. It was better to get the licking over with right off the bat.

Tongue lolling, Higgins propped his giant paws on my shoulders and commenced bathing my face with his slobbery tongue.

"All right, all right," I cried after a few seconds, shoving him backward. "That's enough, or we're going to have to get married."

Mimi giggled as Higgins' tail slashed the air as he pranced around my feet.

"Yuck!" I wiped my face with my scarf.

Mimi said, "There's no getting used to the drool."

She looked sleep-rumpled and adorable in a pair of sweatpants, a long-sleeved T-shirt, and fuzzy socks. Her hair stuck out every-which-way.

I said, "I didn't wake you up, did I?" She was almost a full-fledged teenager, so it wasn't out of the question for her to sleep past eleven in the morning.

She waved me into the family room. "Just watching TV. There's a *Gilmore Girls* marathon on, and you know I can't resist that."

The show was one of her favorites. I also noticed she had a paperback of *The Hobbit* on the coffee table along with an empty cereal bowl and a spoon.

I dangled the pastry box. "I hope you saved some room."

Her eyes widened. "Please tell me there's a chocolate croissant in there. Pleasepleaseplease."

"There is."

She squealed and reached for the box before flopping back onto the sofa. "I didn't know you were coming over."

I sat next to her on the sofa.

Higgins tried to join me, but Mimi snapped her fingers and said, "Bed!" in a stern voice. "Are you here for Dad because he's— Bed, Higgins!" She pointed.

Higgins lumbered over to his bed and lay down with a huff.

I laughed. "He knows who's boss. I hope you don't mind that I dropped by. I just needed . . . some normal."

She smiled around the croissant in her mouth. "We're your normal?" Her hand shot up to catch falling crumbs, but her eyes were wide with hope.

She wore her heart on her sleeve, this girl. I tugged her into a hug. "Absolutely."

Footsteps sounded on the wooden stairs and I twisted around to see who else was here, surprised we weren't alone.

Nick rubbed a towel over his wet hair and said, "I thought I heard voices."

"What are you doing here?" I asked.

He laughed and gave me a kiss. "I live here? Are you okay? Are those croissants?"

I stood up. "I know you live here, but right now Starla is at the police station being questioned about some new evidence that was found. Why aren't you *there*?"

Color drained from his face. "She's what?"

I repeated myself, adding more details about the phone call Marcus had received and how long Starla had been at the station.

Angrily striding into the kitchen, he grabbed his cell phone off the counter. "The battery's dead." Letting out a deep breath laced with an undercurrent of curse words, he said, "I need to go." He dashed up the stairs.

Mimi hung over the back of the couch. "He's mad."

An understatement, if the throbbing vein in his forehead was any indication. I walked into the kitchen and picked up the landline phone and heard the dial tone. Even if the station hadn't been able to reach Nick on his cell, he could have been reached this way.

Someone had purposefully left him out of the loop.

Not someone. Glinda. I'd bet my Craft on it.

Nick came dashing down the steps in his uniform. He tucked in his shirt and said, "Preliminary autopsy came in this morning on Kyle Chadwick. Something interesting showed up."

"That he was paralyzed?" I asked.

Nick's eyes widened. "He was what?"

"Paralyzed?"

"Wow," Mimi said.

"You didn't know?" I asked him. I thought for sure it was what he'd been about to tell me.

"No."

"What were you going to say?"

"Prelim tests on the injection site came up positive for extremely high levels of morphine."

"Is it what killed him?" I asked.

"It was certainly a fatal dosage, but everything is inconclusive right now until more tests are done. *Paralyzed*?"

I explained what Pepe had overheard. "Could Kyle have administered the fatal dose himself?" Maybe this was a suicide after all.

"No. With a dose like that there would have been no time to clean up the scene. We would have found the syringe still in his thigh. We didn't find anything other than his body at Starla's."

"So he was . . . murdered?"

"That's our working theory. Again, we need to—"

"Wait for the ME I know. Are these early autopsy results why Starla's being questioned right now?"

Dark eyes blazed with fury. "Darcy, I have no idea why she's being questioned. But I'm going to find out."

Chapter Nineteen

Late that afternoon, I was in the kitchen at As You Wish with Ve and Harper and Marcus, watching Starla's misery play out. She'd just returned from her day-long interrogation and it hadn't gone too well.

I couldn't help but wonder at Glinda's motives for excluding Nick from Starla's interrogation. Was there a power struggle going on within the force? Or was Glinda simply putting my friend through the wringer to hurt me? If that was the case, she had just declared all-out war.

Starla dropped her head into her hands. "I wish I were in the Bahamas. On a beach. With a pitcher of frozen margaritas. And not a care in the whole wide world."

She could wish all she wanted—none of us could grant it.

I rubbed Starla's back as Ve said, "The margaritas I can handle—the rest of it, though, not so much."

"That's okay, Ve," Starla said. "I should probably keep a clear head. I feel like the police are going to be here any second now to arrest me." She frowned. "On second thought, go ahead and whip up a batch. Who wants to be sober when arrested?"

"They're not going to arrest you," Harper said, helping Ve round up the margarita fixings.

There was a noise on the back porch and we all froze.

"See?" Starla said. "Here they are. At least there will be some humor when the photographer tries to get my mug shot and it comes out as nothing but white light."

I smiled at the thought. When Harper had been arrested back in Ohio, the police eventually gave up on photographing her and brought in an artist to do a mug shot rendering. I shoved off the stool to see who was at the door. "It's probably Nick and Mimi." They were going to meet us here after Nick finished up at the station. It had been a long day for everyone.

I stepped down into the mudroom when suddenly there was a brisk knock and the back door flung open. Mimi came rushing in. "It's snowing like crazy out there!" she said, doing a full body shiver to shake loose the snow that had accumulated on her hood and shoulders.

I glanced out the door, into the whiteout. A few inches had already settled on the pathways. "Where's your dad?"

"He got a call on the way inside. I don't know who it is, but" — she dropped her voice to a manly monotone — "he got very serious all of a sudden."

"He's probably rounding up the troops." Starla glanced at Marcus. "Does the village police have troops?"

The corner of his mouth twitched. "No."

Missy danced around Mimi's feet until she picked up the dog.

"Why do you keep saying they're coming for you, Starla?" I asked, helping Mimi wiggle out of her coat. "What evidence do they have?"

"Yes," Ve said, "spill!"

Starla groaned and dropped her head in her hands again.

We all looked at Marcus.

He said, "The police found a roll of duct tape in the Dumpster behind Starla's brownstone. It was the same tape used on Kyle's mouth. A strand of Starla's hair was stuck to the adhesive."

Starla moaned again. "Margarita?"

"I'm working on it, honey. Hold on," Ve said, pouring tequila into the blender as fast as her fingers would go.

"Starla's fingerprints were on the duct tape," Marcus said, "but for good reason. The roll had probably originated from her house."

"If that's true," Harper argued, "it's entirely plausible her hair might be on it. Transference. They don't know *who* threw the roll away."

He smiled at her, and his eyes twinkled with love and affection. "Exactly. This so-called evidence is circumstantial at best."

"Were there any other prints on the roll of duct tape?" I asked, hanging Mimi's coat.

"No others," he said. "Glinda jumped the gun a bit, pulling Starla in for questioning. But it's the polygraph that didn't go as well as planned."

Starla groaned. "Don't remind me."

"Polygraph?" I asked. "I thought you said no to that."

"In light of the new evidence," Marcus said, "and with Glinda Hansel eager to arrest Starla, we agreed to take one. Evan and Vince took one, too."

"What were the results?" Mimi asked.

"We don't know yet," Marcus said.

Starla lifted her head. "But I know I didn't do well. I couldn't remember anything. It was embarrassing. Stupid sleeping spell. They're going to be here any minute," Starla said. "I'm telling you."

"They wouldn't arrest you. They don't have conclusive evidence," Ve said.

Marcus loosened his tie. "They might not need it if the prosecutor thinks there's a case. Plus, Glinda seems to have a grudge against Starla."

"Why?" Mimi asked, looking completely confused.

"The grudge isn't with Starla," I said. "It's with me." I explained about the Elder's new mission for me and how it had upset Glinda.

Mimi frowned. She was a smart girl—she knew there was more to my rift with Glinda than met the eye.

"If only I could remember that night," Starla moaned, gently thunking her head on the counter.

Rubbing her back, I glanced over my shoulder at the back door. Where was Nick? I wanted to know how Glinda explained not telling him about questioning Starla. Mimi wrung her hands. "What if you could . . . remember?"

Ve said, "Time out, everybody!" and pressed the blender's button. Ice cubes loudly turned to slush as the blades whirred. She pushed the STOP button and said, "Okay, go ahead."

"What do you mean, Mimi?" Starla asked.

Color flooded Mimi's cheeks. She glanced at me, then away. "What if there was a spell that makes you remember something? Would you use it?"

"Of course!" Starla said.

"Is there a memory spell?" Harper asked, looking between Mimi and Aunt Ve.

"I seem to recall there is," Ve said, pouring drinks. "However, I don't know it. I'm trying my best to forget my younger years."

Mimi gulped, set Missy on the floor, and pulled a piece of paper out of her front pocket and smoothed it on the countertop.

I immediately recognized the writing on the sheet of paper as Melina's and noted that the page had been neatly cut along its edge. I suddenly realized what it was. "Is this the missing page from your mom's journal?"

Mimi pressed her lips together and nodded.

Harper picked up the page. "Yep, there's a memory spell."

"Why, Mimi?" I asked. "Why'd you take this out of the journal?"

Tears filled her brown eyes as she said, "I'm sorry! I know it was wrong to cut it out, but I didn't want you to see it."

"Why?" I asked.

Her voice clogged with emotion as she said, "Do you

remember a few months ago when you drew my mom's picture from my memories?"

I recalled. In a box in the garage I'd found an old sketchbook filled with uncompleted drawings of my mother. As Wishcrafters who couldn't be photographed, drawings and paintings were the only visual images we had of one another. But Mimi had asked why none of my drawings were finished. I'd had to confess it was because I couldn't remember my mother's entire face. Just bits and pieces. When Mimi worried that the same would happen to her, that her memories of her mother would fade, I'd offered to draw Melina Sawyer. Mimi had sat next to me, her eyes bright with tears, while I sketched.

"How can you draw her when you never met her?"

Dust mites floated on the weak light coming through the window. "I don't need to meet her. I've met you. You're all I need."

"Really?"

"It may take some trial and error, but I'm willing to put the effort in if you're willing."

"I'm willing!"

Time was lost as we sat together, piecing together an image of a woman I would never know, but to whom I'd always feel grateful. If not for her, her life, her Craft, Nick and Mimi would not be in my life.

The tears in Mimi's eyes spilled over, and she suddenly bounded out of her chair and threw her arms around me. I set the pad down, settled her on my lap, and held her close.

"Thank you," she said into my ear.

"You're welcome," I whispered.

"You . . . gave me back my mom."

I could feel her tears seeping into the back of my shirt.

"No," I said, rubbing her back. "I didn't. Your mom's always been with you, Mimi. You just shared her with me, that's all."

The memory brought tears to my eyes, even now. "I remember very well."

"When I saw the spell in my mom's diary and realized

what it was, I decided I wanted to give it to you on your birthday. So you could finally remember your mom's face. And draw her picture like you drew my mom's picture. So you can see her every day and remember how much she loves you. I wanted the spell to be a surprise." Taking a deep breath, she swallowed hard. "But . . . but right now I think Starla needs it more than you. I'm so sorry."

I felt every eye in the kitchen looking at me. A tear slipped down my cheek as I pulled Mimi into a hug.

"You're not mad?" Mimi asked softly.

"Not mad," I murmured into her hair.

"A little tape," Harper sniffled, "and this page will go back into the journal, no problem." She joined in the hug.

Before I knew it, Ve and Starla had joined in as well, and Marcus stood off to the side until I pulled him in as well. Undoubtedly, he'd be family soon, too.

After a long minute, Starla said, "Can we try the spell now?"

Ve laughed. "Yes, let's! And the margaritas are ready."

"Okay," Harper said. "It says here that the person without the memory needs to close their eyes and recite the spell three times while thinking about the time period you can't remember." She slid the journal entry toward Starla.

Starla's hand shook as she picked it up and read silently for a moment. Her eyelids fluttered closed. Her voice was strong as she said, *"Mind blank; Conscious spark; Lost memories; Return to me."* She repeated it twice more and went dead silent.

After a long moment, a teardrop slid down her cheek and dripped off her chin.

We all stood silently, waiting for her to say something. Finally, she blinked open her eyes and shook her head. In a coarse whisper, she said, "I saw him."

"Kyle?" I asked.

"When he came into my room." Another tear dropped. "Oh God."

"What?" I asked.

Horrified, she looked at me. "I . . . I overreacted."

"What do you mean?" Harper asked. "Overreacted about what?"

She shook her head. "I . . ." Her voice dropped away and she breathed deeply as though unable to pull in enough oxygen.

"It's okay, dearie," Ve said, rubbing her back. "Take your time with it."

"Skip ahead, Starla. What about after the meeting in the bedroom?" Marcus asked. "Later that night? What did you see?"

"There's nothing," Starla said. "I was sleeping."

I watched my friend carefully, wondering what she had seen in that memory of Kyle. I hoped she'd tell me when she was ready.

Starla sighed. "It was worth a try. Thanks, Mimi."

Mimi reached for the journal page and glanced up at me. "Can you just pretend you never saw this?"

I smiled. "Deal."

"Good," she said, scooping up Missy again.

We all turned as the back door opened. Vince came in, followed closely by a grim-looking Nick.

Uh-oh.

"What's wrong?" Mimi asked after one look at her dad's face.

He stepped up beside me and took my hand. His gaze, however, turned to Starla.

"What is it?" Marcus asked.

Vince went and stood behind Starla, placing his hands on her shoulders. Her hands immediately came up to grip his, and I saw how his presence brought her comfort.

Nick squeezed my hand. "I just got off the phone with the prosecutor's office. They think they have a strong enough case against Starla for us to arrest her."

Starla asked, "You're here to take me to jail, aren't you?"

"You can't!" Mimi cried.

Nick let go of my fingers and dragged his hand down his face.

"The evidence is circumstantial," Marcus said sternly.

Vince's voice cracked. "She's innocent." He'd gone deathly pale.

"I believe that," Nick said. "I truly do. That's why I talked the prosecutor into giving me a few more days to investigate."

There was a collective exhale in the room.

Starla reached over and squeezed Nick's hand. "Thank you."

Nick said, "Don't thank me yet. The prosecutor doesn't just think that Starla is guilty. He thinks she colluded with Vince to kill Kyle. The theory is that Starla discovered Kyle's hideout, made up the story about Kyle stalking her, and then killed him or had Vince kill him and carry him to her town house."

"Why on earth would she put him in her own house?" Ve asked, her voice incredulous.

"Yes, why?" Starla cried.

"To throw off suspicion," Nick said.

"What a bunch of bul—" Harper's voice dropped off as she looked at Mimi. "That's ridiculous. What evidence do they have of this so-called collusion?"

"The polygraph tests," Nick said. "Evan passed. . . ." His voice trailed off, yet his message was loud and clear.

Vince and Starla had not passed.

As if in slow motion, each of us turned to look at Vince. We knew why Starla hadn't passed. Why hadn't he?

He stammered, "I didn't do it!"

Harper's brown eyes narrowed. She looked like a beautiful angry elf. "Then why didn't you pass the polygraph?"

A guilty flush crept up his neck. "I don't know."

Instantly, I knew he was lying. But why—and about what?

"Unfortunately," Nick said. "I need Vince to come back with me to the station so I can ask him a few more questions to get his alibi straightened out. As for the prosecutor, I may have bought you two a couple of days," Nick said to Starla and Vince, "but we're running out of time. We need to figure out what happened to Kyle, and we need to do it soon."

Chapter Twenty

"You okay?" Nick asked me later that night as we sat side by side on his sofa. "This movie usually makes you smile, not frown."

We were trying our best to enjoy our date—the one that had already been postponed twice.

"I'm sorry," I said. "I'm distracted."

He pressed his lips to my temple. "Starla?"

"Yes. And Kyle. And Vince. And Glinda."

After being questioned, Vince returned to As You Wish and swept Starla off to a late dinner in the city. Ve had volunteered to keep Missy for me and entertain Evan, and Nick had arranged for Harper to watch both Mimi *and* Higgins for the night. Snow fell heavily— school had already been called off for the next day—and neither Nick nor I had anywhere to go.

We were blissfully alone.

I should have been smiling. The evening he'd planned, by any standards, had been just about perfect.

Nick had made a wonderful candlelit dinner for two.

Dessert had been amazing. And Nick, who wasn't all that fond of musicals, had *volunteered* to watch *My Fair Lady*.

That's what we were doing now—watching the movie, our bodies pressed tightly against each other, our legs tangled, our hands clasped together.

It should have been more than perfect. It should have been heaven. Except . . .

We hadn't talked about the case yet, declaring it off-limits during dinner. But now . . . I wanted answers. "Did Glinda ever explain her behavior this morning?"

He smiled. "I'm surprised you held off this long from asking."

I nudged him. "Only because you're so distracting."

"You tease, but I'm glad we had a little bit of normalcy for a while."

I tugged at the fringe on the lap blanket. "Normal is nice."

"Mimi told me what you said, about us being your normal. I'm glad, Darcy."

My heart thumped erratically. "Me, too." I basked in the moment for a few seconds before saying, "Now what about Glinda?"

Nick tipped his head back and laughed.

I gave him a playful shove. He caught my hand and kissed it before saying, "Glinda claims she tried calling me on my cell."

"But not your landline?"

"She said it slipped her mind."

I scoffed.

"The situation with her might get worse before it gets better. I suspended her today."

"Not fired?"

"Unfortunately, that's not my call. It has to go through the village council review committee. My guess is that she'll get another slap on the wrist."

She'd been reprimanded last year. "How many chances will the council give?"

"Usually three."

I bit my lip. "How will this affect Mimi?"

"I don't know, Darcy. Mimi cares about her a lot."

I knew. Glinda had completely wormed her way into Mimi's heart.

"I'm planning to talk with Mimi tomorrow morning. She needs to be aware of what's going on. She might not be able to fully understand the dynamics—"

"I wouldn't underestimate what she comprehends. She's a smart girl."

"It won't make her hurt any less if her friendship with Glinda dissolves because of what's going on with the police force."

"No." A lump wedged in my throat. "It won't."

"Needless to say, Glinda is irate and taking no responsibility for her actions. Her behavior can go either way right now. She'll either fall in line or become a loose cannon."

Why did I have the feeling that it was going to be the latter option? Not wanting to think about it, I said, "How'd the interview with Vince go?"

"He's definitely hiding something, but he clammed up and asked for a lawyer."

As a former murder suspect, he'd know not to say anything incriminating. "You don't really think he killed Kyle, do you?"

"No, but he does have a good motive. I mean, if I were in his shoes, and your ex was harassing you . . ." His eyes flashed.

"Luckily for my ex, he's happily married with a brand-new family." I'd tried to keep my tone light, but even I could hear the tiny bit of bitterness that had seeped into my words.

Nick nudged my chin. "Do you want me to hunt him down and kick his ass?"

I smiled. "Sure."

Nick pulled me into his arms and said, "I would, you know, but while I'm there I might have to thank him. His loss was my gain. I know how lucky I am to have you in my life."

"Nick Sawyer, are you getting sappy on me?"

"It happens once in a while."

I tucked my head into the curve of his neck and breathed in his scent. "I like it."

I tried to just enjoy the moment, the happiness, the *love*. But I couldn't keep thoughts of the case from intruding on my warm and fuzzy haze.

Finally giving in to my persistent curiosity, I said, "Did you ask the medical examiner's office about Kyle's paralysis?"

"I called, and the ME said she'd try to move up the autopsy on her schedule, but she said she didn't see any outward signs of muscle atrophy on his legs. Only that wound on his calf—which turned out to be some sort of burn."

"That's just bizarre. Why would Will Chadwick think his brother was paralyzed if he wasn't?"

"The ME said she'd know for sure once she performs the postmortem exam and can take muscle samples."

On the screen, Eliza's father was singing and dancing his way to his wedding—one of my favorite scenes, but tonight I found no entertainment in the movie. "It just doesn't make sense. And the morphine? Was it Kyle's? I mean, it would make sense that it was if he'd been in some sort of accident that paralyzed him. But otherwise, where did it come from?"

"We're looking into it, but it's not easy. He could have had a fake ID for any kind of medical treatment, but with all his personal belongings missing . . . and morphine is not uncommon; it could have come from anywhere. I'm bringing Kyle's whole family in for questioning again tomorrow. Maybe one of them will crack."

"I doubt it. If they admit to knowing about Kyle's recent medical history, that's pretty much confessing to harboring a fugitive. Isn't that a felony?"

"I spoke to the DA earlier, and he agreed to drop any charges against the family in exchange for information."

"Really?"

"I think it's our only hope to figuring this out. His family wants to know what happened to him as much as we do."

I recalled the worry I'd seen in his parents' eyes, his brothers'. There was no denying their love for Kyle.

I tried to put myself in their shoes. If Harper, in a fit

of temper, attempted to kill Marcus . . . would I help her hide from the law?

I bit the inside of my cheek. I wanted to believe I'd do the right thing, but . . . it was Harper. My baby sister. My heart. I'd stash her in a secluded tree house in a hot second. I sighed.

"What?" Nick asked.

"I'm just realizing yet again that sometimes life isn't black and white."

He pulled me closer, resting his head atop mine.

"But," I said, "there may be another way to crack this case."

"Oh?"

"I've been thinking about Vince and his high-tech surveillance equipment. I have a feeling his cameras have nothing to do with catching robbers and everything to do with catching Crafters."

"It wouldn't surprise me. He's a Seeker, after all."

"If you were a Seeker on a quest," I hypothesized, "would you have only one camera in the village?"

Nick stiffened, pulling his shoulders back. "No. I'd have hidden cameras everywhere."

"Right," I said. "And if you're especially concerned about your girlfriend . . ."

"I'd have one near her house." His eyes grew wide. "I need to talk to Vince again."

"You might need a warrant. He's not going to willingly admit that he has cameras around the village."

"It might be why he failed the lie detector."

"Wouldn't surprise me," I said, echoing his earlier words.

He pulled me closer. "You're pretty good at this snooping stuff."

"You flatterer."

He kissed my temple and I snuggled in closer to him and tried to focus on the TV. To let Audrey Hepburn and Rex Harrison distract me.

It worked a little, but I could still feel the anxiety inside me, waiting to pounce as soon as I allowed thoughts of Starla's situation to intrude on my conscious. She'd been on an emotional roller coaster and I felt as though I was along for the ride.

As the credits rolled, Nick said, "As hard as I try, I'm not sure what you see in this movie."

I yawned and stretched. "It's romantic. Plus the costumes and the music . . ."

"Professor Higgins is kind of a jerk."

I smiled. "I know, but that's his charm. The jerk was able to fall in love. I admit the ending would have been better if he showed more of a transformation, but I think Eliza knew what she was getting into."

He frowned at the TV.

I laughed and said, "Not everyone needs grand gestures. Sometimes it's the little things that show someone how much they're loved."

Dark eyes searched my face. "I agree, but don't you think he should have, I don't know, said 'I love you' or at least brought *her* a pair of slippers?"

I gripped the front of his shirt and pulled him in closer. "Slippers?"

Leaning in, he smiled. "Like you said, it's the little things."

"I'll remember that."

As his lips settled on mine, I thought his kiss was a much better form of distraction than I had ever dreamed. Except for thoughts of him and me and an empty house for the whole night, pretty much everything else flew out of my head. We should have started the night off with this.

I was happily lost in just *feeling* when my brain finally registered an odd sound. A cell phone. Reluctantly, I pushed Nick away.

"What?" he asked.

"Listen."

He tipped his head, and then groaned as he heard the sound, too. Mumbling something about bad timing, he reached behind the sofa for his phone on the console table. Gruffly, he answered the call. "Sawyer here."

I sat up, readjusted my sweater, and tried my best to

make out the words of the caller. A flustered voice was talking a mile a minute.

"Slow down," Nick said, his tone hardening. "Say that again."

His gaze zipped to mine, then away again. I didn't like what I'd seen in his eyes, the apprehension. The regret.

Dragging a hand down his face, he said, "I understand."

Hanging up, he looked my way, a strange look on his face.

"What's going on?" I asked.

"I have to go. I'll drive you home."

"Why?"

"One of my officers has been painstakingly going through the trash from the Dumpster that was behind Starla's house. When he unwrapped what looked like a wad of duct tape, he found . . ."

I didn't like his tone. "What?"

"A syringe."

Chapter Twenty-one

Sometime in the middle of the night, I bolted upright in bed and looked around, my eyes trying to focus in the dark.

I reached over and flipped on the light, wincing at the sudden brightness.

Slipping on my glasses, I took a longer look around the room now that I could fully see. There was no one here but Missy and me. I narrowed my gaze on her, and she blinked sleepily at me.

Looking around the room, I said, "Did you hear something?"

She wagged her tail. I didn't know whether that meant yes or no.

Turning, I glanced at the bedside clock. It was a little past three in the morning.

Since I'd been home, I'd done my best to forget about the syringe and how it was another piece of circumstantial evidence that Starla had killed Kyle. I hadn't had a chance to tell her about it, either. She'd still been out with Vince when I arrived home. I'd stayed up, trying to wait for her, passing the time by searching Melina's diary for the invisibility spell, but at some point I had fallen asleep. I realized my eyes still ached from squinting at the journal's small print. I made a mental note to stop by Spellbound tomorrow and pick up some reader cheater glasses to make the task a little less painful.

Still reeling from the adrenaline rush of being woken out of a sound sleep, I flopped back onto my pillow and dragged the blankets up to my chin. My heartbeat still throbbed in my ears, pulsing loudly, a rhythmic *thump-thump-thump*. Drawing in a deep breath, I let it out slowly, and rubbed Missy's head until she settled back to sleep.

I set my glasses back on the nightstand and turned off the light. Shadows played on the walls, cast by the moonbeams slipping in under the edges of the window shades.

My thoughts felt like they were caught in a tornado, twisting round and round.

Missy shifted, adjusting to my fidgeting. I couldn't quite see the look in her eyes because of the darkness and my poor vision, but I had the feeling she was giving me the evil eye for disrupting her beauty sleep.

"Sorry," I mumbled.

I squeezed my eyes shut, trying to force out any thoughts of this case. I wanted peace. For me, yes, but more for Starla. I hated seeing her suffering.

Flipping to my other side, I pounded my pillow again. *Let it go*, I willed myself. Right now, my focus should be squarely on Starla. Making sure she was okay. The mother hen in me was already plotting a girls' weekend away. Somewhere warm and sunny, just like she wanted. I wondered if there was a memory cleanse I could use on her to erase this week from her memory. To erase the heartache. The anguish.

You can't fix everything.

The reminder flitted through my head, irritating me. Huffing, I flopped onto my back and stared at the ceiling. I wanted to fix this. I wanted it more than anything.

I willed myself to think of other things, to clear my head of all despairing thoughts. I mentally rearranged As

You Wish's office, organizing to my heart's content. Slowly, I felt myself relaxing. So much so that I added cleaning up the space tomorrow morning to my morning to-do list. If I attempted it a little at a time, then Ve might not even notice the change.

Soon, my thoughts started to drift to another subject that made my heart ache—in a good way this time.

Mind blank; Conscious spark; Lost memories; Return to me.

As much as I wanted to, I didn't repeat the memory spell three times to cast it. I'd wait until my birthday, as Mimi had planned. But even the thought of seeing my mother's face again filled me with such happiness that I almost felt guilty about it in light of Starla's predicament.

I swiped at the moisture in my eyes. For the first time in a long time, I was looking forward to my birthday—and I had Mimi to thank for it.

I snuggled more deeply into the cocoon of my blankets. Slowly, I let the stress of the week go. But just as I was drifting off, I jumped at the sound of something hitting my window.

Missy sat up, her ears perked—she heard the sound, too, and was quicker than I was to react. She leapt off the bed and dashed to the window, growling at the pane.

What on earth? Throwing back the covers, I grabbed my glasses but kept the light off as I lifted the window shade to peek out.

Snow fell heavily, coating everything in sight in white, including the shadowy figure of a man on the sidewalk. He reared back and hurled something upward. A second later, the object *pinged* against the windowpane. A pebble.

Missy let out a bark.

"Shh!" I whispered, not wanting her to wake everyone in the house.

My heart pounding, I cracked open the window. Snowflakes rushed inside and melted immediately on my skin. "Who's there?"

"You don't recognize my manly silhouette?" Nick's voice floated upward.

I smiled. "My apologies, but from up here you look like the Abominable Snowman. Plus, my glasses are fogging from the cold. Is everything okay? Why are you here?"

Please not to arrest Starla . . .

"I forgot something earlier. Can you come down?"

"Give me a minute. I'll meet you by the back door."

Quickly, I grabbed my robe and slipped into it. I stuck my feet into my raggedy slippers. Missy raced ahead of me to the bedroom door and nudged it fully open with her paw and dashed out. I flipped on the hallway light and quietly headed toward the stairs, wondering what Nick had forgotten. I didn't recall seeing anything he'd left behind.

Aunt Ve's door was firmly closed, but the guest room door was open a crack. I gently pushed it open and peeked inside. The bed was empty, but Evan was asleep, snoring softly on the air mattress on the floor.

My gaze zipped to the bathroom door. It was open wide and the room was dark—Starla wasn't in there. Had she not come home yet?

I had irrational visions of her and Vince skipping town, but as soon as I reached the top of the steps, I noticed flickering light filtering into the kitchen from the family room. Trying to be as quiet as I could, I carefully navigated the stairs and saw that the light was coming from the TV set. *The Phantom of the Opera* was playing, the volume low. Starla sat tucked into the corner of the sofa, with a sleepy Tilda snuggled on her lap. There was a stack of silver wrappers piled high on the coffee table. I smiled. She'd found my stash of frozen Peppermint Patties.

She glanced over her shoulder as the floor creaked. Using the back of her hand, she wiped away chocolate remnants from her mouth, and then said, "Did I wake you?"

Tilda lifted an eyelid to give me a dirty look.

"Not at all. Nick did. He's waiting for me to open the back door."

Her eyes went wide. "Is he here to arrest me?"

"I don't think so."

She slumped in relief and in the depths of her eyes I saw just how worried she was about the prospect.

"Booty call?" she asked with a twinkle in her eye.

I smiled. "I don't think so."

"Then why's he here?"

"He said he forgot something earlier. How long have you been awake?"

"I haven't gone to bed yet. Too much going through my head."

I could understand that.

"Seemed like a good time to watch a movie to get my mind to concentrate on something else—anything else." She smiled. "Wouldn't you just love to dress up and go to a fancy dance?"

"As long as the chandelier doesn't crash down on me."

Laughing, she reached for another chocolate. "Yeah, that might put a damper on things."

"I'll be right back," I said. "I need to let Nick in."

She nodded and turned up the volume on the TV another click.

Missy was sitting in the mudroom, glaring at the closed doggy door. She hated being locked inside. I peeked out the curtain and saw Nick pacing the porch. I released the deadbolt, and the noise turned his head.

Missy raced out the door and danced around his feet. He bent and rubbed her head. "I was beginning to think you forgot about me," he said, a smile tugging on his lips as he pulled off his hat and brushed snow from his shoulders.

"Sorry." My breath transformed into a white cloud of steam. "I was distracted by Starla—she's in the family room watching a movie. Come inside. The snow's really coming down."

Missy raced ahead of him and perched on the step leading into the kitchen as he came into the mudroom, stomping his feet on the doormat. I closed the door quickly.

"I was just on my way home from work," he said.

"Anything I need to know?"

He glanced over my shoulder and dropped his voice. "Early tests on the syringe came back."

My pulse kicked up a notch. "Was there morphine in it?"

He nodded. "And also Kyle's blood type on the needle."

"So it's probably the murder weapon."

"Probably," he acknowledged.

"Were there any fingerprints on it?" Dare I hope there were? Someone other than Starla?

"There's a smudged set that we're having trouble identifying. The duct tape did a number on them. I've called in an expert."

"When should you know?"

"Later today or tomorrow."

More waiting. More worrying.

"There's something else," he said, "and I'm hoping you can help me with it."

"What?"

"While I was at the station earlier, something Starla said the other night about Kyle's ring came back to me and had me doing a little digging."

I recalled his odd look while she talked about the rings. "Digging?"

"In the evidence locker. Kyle escaped jail, so his personal belongings still should have been at the station, including his ring."

My pulse kicked up. If it should have been in the evidence locker, how did Kyle get it? "What did you find?"

"This is the strange part. The ring was in a sealed bag with his watch, his shoes, his clothing, but when I reached in to pull it out, there was nothing in the bag at all." He dragged a hand down his face. "Literally nothing there, Darcy. Nothing but air. It was like a hallucination."

Adrenaline flooded through me. "Not a hallucination. A mirage." I quickly explained about the Mirage Spell. "But it works only for seventy-two hours, which means that whoever broke in to steal his things had to cast the spell on Thursday or Friday." If we could catch who cast the spell, it might be the break we needed.

"I'll check the cameras at the station. Do you think I'll ever get used to this magic stuff?"

"You don't need to. That's why you have me."

Smiling, he said, "Lucky me."

My heart went to mush.

Glancing at his watch, he said, "I should go. I probably shouldn't have come by," he said, "but I couldn't resist the temptation."

I was slightly mesmerized by the way snowflakes clung to his eyelashes. "You said you forgot something? I looked around but didn't see anything. . . ."

"That's because what I forgot isn't something you can see."

I tipped my head. "You lost me."

He pulled me in close again. "When I dropped you off earlier, I forgot to kiss you good night, Darcy."

I couldn't help my smile as I saw the tenderness in his eyes. "Sappy," I accused in a whisper.

"You should probably get used to it," he said, leaning in.

Oh, that wasn't going to be a problem.

At all.

"He's a keeper," Starla said after I saw Nick off.

The movie still played—it was the big scene with the masquerade ball. Missy hopped up alongside her as I sat on the arm of the sofa. "I think so."

Sadly, she smiled up at me. "You're lucky."

I thought of all she'd been through. "I know."

"You deserve it, Darcy."

"You deserve it, too." I just wished I knew for sure that Vince would make her happy.

Absently, she nodded, and picked up another Peppermint Pattie to unwrap.

"Want some company?" I asked.

"Sure."

I sat next to her, clapped twice, and Melina's diary appeared in my lap. Tilda hissed and turned her back to me.

"Find anything yet?"

"No. But it has to be in here somewhere."

Starla lifted the edge of her throw blanket and tossed it over my lap. She placed the Peppermint Patties in a small pile between us. "You'll find it."

I was beginning to have my doubts.

Missy pawed the diary, and I lifted it up so she could settle on my lap. Only she didn't budge—just kept pawing the diary.

"Looks like she wants to help you," Starla said.

I laughed. "She might have better luck."

Starla pointed at the screen. "Did you know Kyle and I met at a ball?"

"The Firelight Gala, right?"

"It was the most amazing night," she said. "I was fairly new to the village and had, of course, signed up as a volunteer." She glanced at me. "I was in charge of the lighting, and in a complete panic when several strings of my party lanterns wouldn't work. There I was in this ethereal gold ball gown, trying to splice wires together without pliers and having no luck whatsoever when this man, the most amazing man I'd ever seen, steps in and with a few flicks of his fingers has everything fixed. Then he held out his hand to me and nodded to the dance floor."

I closed the diary and set it aside. "Magical hands," I murmured.

She nodded and flexed her fingers as though reliving that exact moment.

"You must have looked so beautiful." It wasn't hard at all to imagine Starla in a gold gown, her blue eyes shining, her blond hair shimmering.

"He said so." She smiled. "And he . . . he was breathtaking. Dressed in a tux, his dark hair combed back, his blue eyes sparkling with . . . life. With animation. He had the most amazing way of telling a story with just his eyes."

Foul is fair.

"We danced the whole night long, never leaving each other's side for even a moment. By the end of the night, it felt like we'd known each other forever. I saw him the next day, and the day after, and when he asked me to marry him a couple of months later, I didn't even hesitate. Not in the slightest. I loved him." She sucked in a deep breath. "Oh God, how I loved him. With every beat of my heart, every breath I drew in. He was . . . he was my soul."

My throat ached with the lump lodged there, and as I listened to her talk about him, I could only grieve the love my friend had lost.

"Like I said, it was so perfect, those early months of marriage. Just like while we were dating. Then things began changing."

On the screen, the chandelier came crashing down, and Starla winced as though it had physically landed atop of her.

Tears shimmered in her eyes. "And then one day he woke up, went into his studio, and accused me of hiding his paints." Shaking her head, she added, "He just wouldn't listen to reason, even when I kept telling him that I'd never do such a thing. He had this look in his eyes—such rage, such confusion. I told him I was leaving until he calmed down. . . . He grabbed me—my throat."

Fair is foul. I placed my hand on her arm, and tried to keep tears from falling.

Her voice crackled as she said, "He wouldn't let go. And"—she inhaled—"I've never told anyone at this, but I didn't fight back."

I couldn't keep the tears in. They fell from my eyes, dripping onto the blanket. "Why, Starla?"

"Because I knew. In that moment I knew he wasn't the man I had married—that man had vanished months before. It was the first time I saw it clearly. If I couldn't have the man I loved, the old Kyle . . . he was the reason for living. My breath. My soul. But he was gone, and that realization was so painful that I didn't want to go on. I wanted to die."

I swiped my eyes with my sleeve. "But you did go on. You broke loose, called the police. . . ."

"No," she said. "I didn't. He let go. Almost as abruptly as his rage started, it stopped. His eyes . . . the regret, the pain. He ran off. I called the police, because I hoped—

prayed—he could get the help he needed. But then he escaped, and I never saw him again until this week. I was so scared of him that I didn't realize it was the old Kyle visiting me."

"What do you mean?"

"I remembered his visit here Friday night clearly when I used that memory spell. The spell is strange, because it's like you're looking at the scene as a viewer—not a participant. I didn't see it through my eyes—I was observing. He was being kind and gentle and trying to explain something. His eyes, the way he looked at me, were just like that night at the Firelight Gala. But I didn't notice. I yelled and screamed at him. . . . All he knew was how much I wanted him to leave. The bruises on my wrist were from me pulling away from him, not from him holding me too hard. If only I'd listened instead of *reacting* . . . maybe I'd know why he had treated me like he did."

The pain in her eyes nearly did me in. "You were scared. You didn't know."

"But if I had just listened . . . then that meeting might have been so different. I might have been able to tell him . . . that I never stopped loving him. Never stopped wishing that the Kyle I knew and loved would come back to me. Now, he'll never know. And we may never know the truth of where he'd been and what happened to him."

My throat swelled with emotion, making it hard to swallow. I ached for my friend, but all I could do was put my arms around her and hold her tight.

After a long minute Missy barked and pawed my lap as though trying to offer her consolation, too. I reluctantly let go of Starla. After wiping my eyes, I spotted what Missy had been up to when I was engrossed in Starla's story. "Oh no!" I cried. "Ohnoohnoohno," I repeated as I grabbed the open journal and eyed the damage. Most of the pages were damp from drool or torn along the edges.

"What?" Starla asked; then her eyes widened.

Holding up the journal, I sighed. The Elder had entrusted this diary to me to keep it safe. And now this.

"It's not so bad," Starla said, her voice still hoarse

with raw emotion. "Most of the rips are along the edges, and the drool will dry."

"I guess," I said, feeling a knot forming in my stomach. I dragged the hem of my shirt along the page that had received the worst drool.

As I furiously rubbed, trying to dry the page, one of the headings caught my attention. THE GOOD-BYE SPELL.

The Good-bye Spell? I skimmed the spell and felt the hair on my arms stand on end. I glanced at Starla.

She tipped her head, giving me a curious look. "What is it, Darcy?"

"I think it's what I've been looking for."

Scooting closer, Starla looked over my shoulder as I read aloud,

> *"Body weak, spirit fly,*
> *With death near,*
> *Hold no fear,*
> *Fly, fly to say good-bye."*

Chills swept down my spine.

"What's that even mean?" Starla asked.

I read Melina's fine print. My breath caught. "It's a spell for Crafters who are bedridden and near death like from a terminal illness. It's a way for them to visit loved ones to say good-bye before they die. Their spirits retain mortal traits like speech and touch but are visible only to those chosen to be visited."

Eyebrows furrowed, Starla looked pensive. "But that means . . ."

The spell was still sinking in. I bit my lip, then whispered, "It means that if Kyle used this spell . . . Kyle was dying."

Chapter Twenty-two

The next morning, I found myself in As You Wish's office, trying to wrangle our billing statements into an organized system. I'd have loved to switch to computerized files, but Ve was old-fashioned and still liked to use paper. I did manage to persuade her to start using an electronic appointment system, so there was hope for more change. I'd just have to keep pestering her.

The snowplows had already been by, and because New Englanders were a hardy lot, it would take much more than a measly eight inches of snow to shut down the village. There was work still to be done. For most of us at least—Missy and Twink were asleep in front of the desk, Tilda was hiding out somewhere, and Starla was still asleep upstairs.

She hadn't said too much after we'd found the Goodbye Spell. I'd called Nick right off, and he promised to put some pressure on the ME's office first thing in the morning.

Body weak, spirit fly,
With death near,
Hold no fear,
Fly, fly to say good-bye.

Dying.

I couldn't even wrap my head around it. First the paralysis, now this. Was either true? We knew he couldn't have committed suicide, so what really happened to Kyle? Would we ever know?

I thought about Liam's strange riddles the day before, and how I felt as though he was warning me about learning the truth. Was this why? Because Kyle had been dying? I just didn't know and wished Liam had just told me what was going on.

Evan had left already for the bakery, and Ve was out of the house for an early-morning meeting with a client. But before she went, she shared the morning's gossip: Kyle's funeral was being planned for Wednesday, on the assumption that his body would be released by then, and his family had made it clear that all who had cared for him were invited to attend.

After last night I had such mixed emotions toward Kyle. It was hard to hate him knowing how much Starla had loved him. But I still couldn't understand how he could have hurt her the way he had. She sounded so ready to forgive him because he had somehow morphed back into the "old" Kyle, yet I still wanted him to pay for what he had done to her.

He'd not only attacked her that day, but he had killed part of her spirit. A part, I feared, that could never be brought back.

I wanted to die.

Tears brimmed in my eyes, and I blinked them away.

Sighing, I shoved a pile of papers into a folder and rubbed my temples, trying to assuage another headache. My first appointment wasn't until early this afternoon, which left me plenty of time to sneak in some organization and drop by Mrs. P's in a little bit to check on her.

I was still filing papers when the doorbell rang. Missy

and Twink went scurrying down the hall, with me on their heels. Sam the deliveryman smiled when I pulled open the door.

I wasn't expecting a delivery and figured this was more decorations for the Swing and Sway dance.

"New dog, Darcy?" he asked as he bent to pet the dogs' heads.

"Not quite. It's a long story."

"A good one, too, I bet. I'll have to get Ve to tell me about it sometime." He winked.

I sized him up. "You don't dance, do you?"

"Two left feet, why?"

"No reason," I said, smiling. "You can put the box over there."

He set it on the table, tipped his hat, and walked out. I glanced down at the dogs. "Do I dare?"

Missy barked and Twink twirled in circles.

I made quick work of the packaging and lifted the box flaps. I shoved aside Styrofoam popcorn and pulled out a pair of individually wrapped long white satin gloves. I rummaged in the box. There were dozens of pairs.

I recalled what Ve had said. *The competitors dance naked except for bow ties for the men and silk gloves for the women.*

Amused, I could only shake my head. I went back to organizing, trying my best not to be intrigued by this dance. Maybe I'd check it out. After all this talk of death and dying, I needed a good laugh.

An hour later, bells chimed as I sailed through the doors at Spellbound. Harper looked startled when she spotted me. "What're you doing here?"

"Good morning to you, too."

"Hi. But seriously, what're you doing here?"

Smiling at her, I said, "I need some reading glasses. Melina's diary is going to make me go blind otherwise." Even though I'd found the Good-bye Spell, I knew there would be other times I'd have to read the journal. It would be nice having a pair of reading glasses on hand.

I wanted to tell Harper about the syringe and spell,

but when I called Nick this morning he had asked me to keep it quiet for now. I said I would, but it was going to be hard to keep anything from Harper for long.

I strode over to the reading glasses display and pulled a pair of bright pink polka-dotted frames. I peered at myself in the mirror and laughed.

"They're perfect," Harper said. "Take them and go. On the house."

"You're the blind one, if you think they're perfect." I tried another pair. "Why do I feel like you're not happy to see me?"

Her eyes went wide. "What? No. Ah . . ."

I stared at her.

She smiled brightly. Too brightly. *Hmm.*

"Do you want some coffee?" she asked.

"No, thanks." I was overcaffeinated as it was, which probably didn't help my aching head. I watched the snow fall outside. Gentle flurries looked like they were waltzing in the wind, and oddly, it was quite peaceful watching the dance.

A lone customer browsed the fiction section as Harper came over and pulled out a pair of glasses, handing them to me. "Try these."

They were purple with white swirls and oddly reminded me of the magic wand painting in the front room of As You Wish. "I like them."

"Me, too."

I bumped her with my elbow. "Are they still on the house?"

"No, that was a limited-time offer."

"Of what, twenty seconds?"

"That's right."

"You're acting strangely today."

"More than usual?" She grinned.

"It's making my headache worse. I need aspirin."

"You've had a lot of headaches lately," she said, eyeing me. "Maybe it's time you make an appointment with Cherise."

"I've been under some stress, and the teeny tiny print of Melina's diary makes my eyes ache."

She tapped her foot.

I sighed. I couldn't blame her for worrying—she always did about my health. I was the only immediate family she had left. "If they keep up I'll make an appointment."

"Thank you."

"You're welcome. Now, some aspirin. You have some upstairs, right?"

"What?"

"Aspirin. Upstairs?" I headed for the back hallway.

"Yeah, in the medicine cabinet in the bathr— No! No, I don't have any." She sprinted in front of me and held out her arms to the side to block my way.

I arched an eyebrow. "What is going on with you?"

"Sorry," she said brightly. "I forgot I was out."

Rubbing my temples, I said, "So you don't have aspirin?"

"Nope. Nonc."

I studied her closely. "You don't have someone up there, do you? Marcus, maybe?" I waggled my eyebrows.

Her cheeks flamed. "Marcus! Yes, yes. He's up there. Naked as a jaybird." She smiled brightly and shrugged. "You caught me. Busted."

My eyes opened wide, I backed up and said, "Too much information, Harper. Too much information."

She started humming "Afternoon Delight."

Hmm. Years of experience told me that she was lying, but I didn't know why. As I walked back to the eyeglass display I was about to prod and pry when I caught a glimpse of a man striding along one of the village green's pathways. Will Chadwick.

I made a sudden decision and grabbed my coat. "I'm leaving. I'll talk to you later!"

"Wait!"

"What?" I turned and caught the glasses she'd thrown at me.

"I extended the limited-time-only offer."

"Thanks." I tucked the glasses in my pocket.

"Why are you rushing off? What did you see?" She peered around me.

"I figured I'd leave you to your delight. Three's a crowd, right?"

She flushed again. "Oh. Right."

I laughed. "Actually, I need to see a man about a tree house."

"And you call me the strange one?" she mumbled.

"That's right." Bells jangled as I headed out the door and across the street. Over my shoulder I looked back at Spellbound, then upward toward the twin windows of Harper's apartment.

Huh. The flurries weren't the only things dancing.

Aunt Ve and Godfrey were locked in an embrace, tangoing across the apartment, back and forth, back and forth.

Looked like Ve had found her dance partner. Terry wasn't going to be happy with this turn of events.

There was no sign of Marcus at all.

Next thing I knew, Harper suddenly appeared, peering out at me. She smiled and waved and quickly pulled down each and every window shade.

Strange.

As a cold wind gusted, I suddenly remembered why I was out here in the first place.

Will Chadwick.

His long-legged gait was easy to spot on the opposite end of the green, and I set off at a run to catch up with him.

I dodged tourists and snowbanks, slowing briefly at the ice skating rink. Where this Kyle madness had begun.

My head pounded as I pressed on, determined to catch Will and ask him point-blank about Kyle's supposed paralysis and if he'd been ill. My hope was that Will could fill in some blanks. A doctor's name or something.

Cold stung my nose and fat snowflakes smacked me in the face as I followed the path. I could barely see Will ahead, crossing the street at the far end of the green. Drawing in a deep breath, I picked up my pace, breaking into a sprint.

I threw a glance left and right before I crossed the street and hurried down the shoveled sidewalk that led into one of the residential streets that surrounded the green.

Ahead, Will dashed up a set of stone steps, slipped a key into the lock on a brownstone, and went inside, closing the door firmly behind him. With a start, I realized the home wasn't that far from Starla and Evan's place, which was just around the corner.

When I finally made it to the walkway leading to the door, I bit my lip, wondering what to do. It was one thing to "accidentally" bump into Will on the green and ask him a question. Quite another to knock on the door and pepper him with questions.

I hemmed. I hawed. I wondered what the Elder would do. I mused about that for a second, and realized she wouldn't be chasing him at all. She would have beckoned him to her.

Well, I didn't quite have that power, so I finally worked up enough nerve to knock on the door, the hollow sound echoing down the quiet street.

No one answered.

Hmmph. I knew he was in there.

Was this his girlfriend's house? The woman Pepe had heard him with? If he was trying to keep that relationship secret it might explain why he didn't want to open the door.

I knocked harder, and after a long minute of staring at the closed door, I decided to just go. I couldn't very well force Will to speak with me, and I couldn't very well stand there all day. It was getting colder and the snow was starting to accumulate again. Abruptly, I turned and carefully navigated the steps, wondering if Will was watching me leave.

Let him.

He wasn't the only brother I could pester for answers about Kyle.

Mr. Truthful himself, Liam Chadwick, owed me some explanations.

Chapter Twenty-three

I was debating when to track down Liam as I walked into the Gingerbread Shack. I still needed to check on Mrs. P. After that, though, I was going to find Liam and make him answer some questions.

Bells quieted as the door closed behind me, but no one was manning the front counter. The place appeared empty, but I could hear a muted conversation coming from the kitchen.

"I'll be right with you," Evan shouted just as a loud crash rang out. It sounded like a pan had fallen to the floor.

"It's just me," I called as I unwound my scarf and followed the delicious scent of chocolate and the sound of his voice. "Is everything okay back here?"

Suddenly, a flour-covered Evan appeared in the doorway separating the kitchen from the front of the shop. He set his arms on each side of the doorframe, much like Harper had done earlier. In a faux cheery voice, he said, "Darcy, I didn't know you'd be stopping by!"

I put my hands on my hips. "What is going on?"

"What do you mean?" A flush crept up his throat. Naturally fair, his blush turned him beet red.

"First Harper, now you." I peeked around him. "Who were you talking to? Don't tell me you've got a naked Marcus in here, too." I used air quotes around "naked Marcus."

Confusion flashed across his eyes; then he smiled. "No, but I wouldn't mind if I did. He's kind of cute, don't you think?"

He was trying to distract me. "Seriously, what's going on? Who were you talking to?"

Suddenly a voice rose from near my feet. "It is just *moi, ma chère.*"

Pepe peered up at me, then motioned for me to follow him to a table. I glanced between him and Evan and reluctantly followed my familiar friend.

Pepe easily scrambled onto a chair, then leapt from its back to the tabletop. If a mortal customer ever saw him sitting there . . .

Evan disappeared back into the kitchen, and I heard a lot of slamming and cursing. "What's he doing back there?" I asked Pepe.

"One of his cakes did not turn out so well," he said, fussing with his vest. "Then, alas, it fell to the floor in a heap of chocolate and failure. I do believe he's currently disposing of the remains."

I wrinkled my nose. "A mishap like that isn't supposed to happen to a Bakecrafter, is it?"

"Our friend," Pepe said, twirling his whiskers, "is not quite himself these days."

Leaning down, I looked straight into Pepe's dark eyes. Blinking innocently, he smiled, his long front teeth sticking out from his mouth, which never failed to amuse me—and he knew it.

"Spill," I said.

Letting out a sigh, he said, "I was instructing Evan on the fine art of the foxtrot. He's a bit clumsy, hence the cake avalanche."

I groaned. "Don't tell me he's participating in this silly dance competition."

"I've been thinking about it," Evan said, coming out of the kitchen. He sat next to me. "But only if this business with Starla is settled by then. How is she this morning?"

I refused to even think about Evan doing a naked foxtrot. "Still sleeping."

"I didn't even hear her come in last night."

"It was late," I murmured, biting my tongue to keep from telling him about the spell. Hopefully Nick would call soon to give me an update on the case—and the okay to reveal the secrets I'd been keeping.

"I just saw Will Chadwick and was going to ask him about Kyle's . . . paralysis, but he slipped into a brownstone and wouldn't answer the door when I knocked. He had a key to the house," I went on. "I was wondering if it's his girlfriend's place." I rattled off the address. "It's not that far from your place, Evan. Do you know who lives there?"

Evan looked confused again as he stood up. "It's Will's house."

I tipped my head. "Will's house? I thought he lived with Liam in the garage apartment at Wickedly Creative."

"He used to. He moved about six months ago."

"If he lives in the brownstone . . ." I glanced at Pepe. "Are you sure it was Will you heard with the woman at the apartment?"

Pepe rocked on his feet. "It was dark . . . I may have been mistaken. It may have been Liam."

"Undoubtedly it was Liam," Evan said with a smile.

"You're so sure?" I asked.

"One hundred percent. Will wouldn't be with a woman. He's gay."

Ha! No wonder George Chadwick had said that Will and Glinda weren't each other's type. Leaning down, I glared at Pepe.

Pepe shrugged. "I forgot. I'm old. Practically an antique."

"Yeah, yeah." I drew circles on the tabletop with the pads of my fingertips. So it had been *Liam* talking about

Starla. . . . *Hmm*. This knowledge might help me question him. And so help me if he riddled his way out of answering.

I stood. "I should get going. Mrs. P is expecting me soon. Could I get a few treats to go?"

Evan nodded and headed for the display case filled with miniature desserts of every kind.

"I must go as well." Pepe hopped down from the table and went to a certain floorboard. He lifted it and faced us. His voice turned somber. "I have much work to be done at the boutique before I conquer Eugenia in checkers this evening. Please tell her I look forward to the visit."

I smiled. "I will."

He bowed and hopped down the hole.

While Evan was distracted with filling my order, I hot-footed it to the kitchen and peeked inside. I wasn't sure I completely bought Pepe's foxtrot explanation, but nothing looked amiss back here except . . . something sparkled on the floor. I bent down and picked up a shiny clear crystal.

Evan came up behind me, plucked it out of my hand, and tossed it in his mouth. "Edible cake crystals. It's amazing what can be made nowadays, isn't it?"

My mouth dropped open. "Ew. That was on the *floor*."

"*My* floor. It's impeccable." He quickly boxed up an assortment of Mrs. P's favorite mini desserts.

"Hello," I said. "Pepe was walking all over this floor. Haven't you ever heard of the plague?"

"Are you inferring that Pepe carries the plague?" He laughed. "I can't wait to tell him."

"You wouldn't."

"I would. Just to see Pepe's face. No one emotes indignation like Pepe."

That was true. I headed for the door. Snow swirled. It should have been so peaceful, but instead I couldn't quite shake the feeling that the storm was just beginning.

I was on my way to the Pixie Cottage and not too far from Nick and Mimi's house when a golden retriever puppy bounded down the sidewalk, galloping toward me on paws too big for its small frame.

Quickly, I glanced around for its owner before I bent and scooped it up. I didn't see anyone around, but as the dog bathed my chin in sloppy kisses, I noticed a tag hanging from a loose blue collar.

His name was Clarence, and there was a phone number listed as well.

"Aren't you the cutest thing I've seen all day," I cooed to him. "Don't tell my cat Tilda that, though. She might go back to upchucking on my bed every day." He continued to lick my face. "Where do you live, hmm? Someone's probably missing you right about now." The streets weren't too busy today, but it was still dangerous for a puppy to be running loose. "Are you an escape artist like Missy?"

He didn't answer. Just kept licking my face.

Smiling, I juggled Clarence with one arm and fumbled for my cell phone to dial his owner. Just as I'd punched in the number and listened to the first ring, I heard a woman call out, "Clarence!"

Looking around, I groaned. "Say it isn't so."

Glinda half jogged, half limped toward us, not seeming to care that she was wearing slippers and not proper shoes on the snow. Bunny slippers at that.

"Clarence!" she cried.

My stomach sank clear down to my toes as I looked into the pup's dewy eyes. "You belong to Glinda?"

His rear end swished as he wagged his tail.

"You're too cute to belong to her."

He didn't seem to agree as he kept wagging and trying to lick me.

Glinda's eyes zeroed in on me, and I wished more than anything that I could suddenly disappear. She slowly approached, a bathrobe tied tightly around her waist, her nightgown hanging just below the robe's hem.

Her gaze settled the squirming puppy in my arms, but I could practically feel the daggers being thrown my way. I wanted to take the puppy and run, but, resolved, I walked toward her, a bit like a felon being led to the gallows.

"What are you doing with my dog?" she asked as she limped toward me.

"When did you get a dog?"

"It's a friend's dog. Not that it's any of your business." She reached for him.

I couldn't help myself. "I'm pretty sure that as an officer of the village you know about the leash law."

Clarence went willingly into Glinda's arms—losing some of his cute factor in the process—and Glinda growled at me. "Go away."

"Gee," I said, trying to hide a smile. "You're welcome that I found the dog you lost and saved him before he got hit by a car."

"Thanks," she said through clenched teeth.

It was then—as she glared at me—that I noticed she'd been crying. Her eyes were red and swollen and the more I studied her the more I realized she looked horrible.

It was a first.

She must be taking her suspension hard. I felt a pang of sympathy for her, even though she didn't deserve it. "You're welcome."

With a huff, she turned and hobbled away.

I watched her go for a moment before continuing on to the Pixie Cottage. A few minutes later, I was stomping my feet on the welcome mat, trying to shake loose clinging snow.

At the registration desk, Harmony gave me a glum smile.

"How's Mrs. P holding up?" I asked.

"About the same." Harmony's long wild hair had been pulled back in a loose ponytail. "Except now she's not eating very much. A piece of toast is all she would take this morning."

My heart sank. It had been only a few days since I learned Mrs. P had heart trouble and now it seemed as though she was failing fast.

"I also think she's hallucinating. Whenever I pass her room, I hear her talking to herself. And once, she was playing a game of poker . . . alone."

I held back a smile. I didn't have one hundred percent confirmation, but I was pretty sure Harmony was a mortal. Undoubtedly Pepe would take cover whenever she was near. "I'm sure she's just amusing herself."

"Maybe," Harmony said, sounding like she didn't believe that theory for a moment. "Let me know if she needs anything. A snack, tea . . ."

"I will."

I headed down the hallway and gently knocked on the door to Mrs. P's room. I let out a breath of relief when I heard her shout out, "Come in!"

I opened the door and found her sitting at her dressing table carefully gluing on false eyelashes.

In awe, I sat on a velvet-tufted settee and watched the process.

"What is this nonsense," she said right off the bat, "about Vince being considered a murder suspect again? Despite his shortcomings, he is not the homicidal type."

Mrs. P appeared to be a bit more energetic than she had been yesterday, but despite the layers of blush artfully applied to her high cheekbones, she still looked pale. Her hair, usually sprayed into spiky points, had been tucked inside a satin turban and I had the feeling the style had more to do with Mrs. P not having the strength to do her hair than any kind of fashion statement.

"I don't think he is either." I adjusted a bolster pillow. "However, the prosecutor believes people can do crazy things in the name of love." Which was entirely true. I just didn't believe it was what was going on in this particular case.

I also had to wonder what the prosecutor thought of the new evidence. How long would it take Nick to call and give me an update? The waiting was starting to weigh on me.

Mrs. P spun around, her eyes bright. "Isn't it wonderful? He *is* in love, isn't he?"

She was a sucker for a good romance, and for some reason she had a soft spot for Vince. He'd certainly grown on her while she'd been working for him.

"I'd say so."

"And Starla? She feels the same?" Mrs. P asked. "Are there wedding bells in their future?"

I preferred that thought over jail cells. "I don't know. I think she's scared to love again. To openly love again." My heart ached as I recalled how she spoke about Kyle last night.

"I don't blame the girl." Mrs. P spun back to the mirror. "Not one little bit."

None of us did.

"She's not going to be able to move on," Mrs. P said, "until this Kyle business is wrapped up."

"Nick's going to be offering the Chadwick family immunity in exchange for information on Kyle."

"And?" she said, narrowing her eyes. "That bothers you?"

She knew me too well. "I just feel like someone needs to pay for putting Starla through hell these past two years."

Mrs. P tapped the mascara tube on the back of her hand as she nodded thoughtfully. "I see."

"The thing of it all is that I probably would do the same thing as they did. So I can't really blame them for harboring Kyle, but I just want . . . justice for Starla." I sighed.

She smiled, the bright red of her lipstick a sharp contrast to her teeth. "Lately I've come to look upon situations through a very different set of eyes. Understanding versus vengeance. Rebuilding rather than destruction. Sometimes there is an interesting shade of gray between black and white. Life's short, doll. Don't dwell on the past."

The black-and-white comment hit me hard, considering I'd just recently said something similar to Nick.

"Just something to think about," Mrs. P said, turning back to the mirror.

"You're telling me to let it go. To forgive and forget."

"I think the most important things to consider here, doll face, are that Kyle is gone and Starla is safe. Let the past remain there."

She was right. I knew it, but it was hard to let go.

We chatted for a while before she started yawning, looking in need of a long nap. It was my cue to go. I stood up and kissed her cheek. "I should get going, but I've brought you pastries from Evan, and Pepe said he'd be over later."

"That little mouse bluffed me out of all my Peanut M&M's last night during a round of poker." A guilty flush crept up her neck.

Seeing it, I said, "Are you sure you didn't let him win?"

"Maybe once," she admitted, "but then my competitive side kicked in. He swindled me but good."

I laughed.

"Tonight we'll stick to checkers or perhaps a nice thousand-piece puzzle. That way I won't be tempted to wring his little rodent neck by losing my midnight snack." She walked me to the door, and I couldn't help but feel a pang of sadness at how slowly she was moving.

I faced her. "Forgive and forget?"

"That's right." She patted my cheek.

"I'll try."

She smiled. "You can do it."

I nodded, but as I walked away I couldn't help but think it was easier said than done.

Chapter Twenty-four

As soon as I left Mrs. P, I headed out to find Liam Chadwick.

It was proving a futile task.

Wickedly Creative was closed up tight, and there wasn't even a car to be seen in the driveway of the main house. The studio would probably remain closed for a while as the family prepared to bury their loved one. I tried knocking on Liam's apartment door, but he didn't answer.

I checked around town with no luck before finally heading to the one place I'd found him before.

The tree house.

Snow was piled high on the path, but the blue blazes on the tree kept me on the right track. Wind whipped through the woods, giving me a case of the heebie-jeebies and making me wish I hadn't come alone.

Almost as soon as I had the thought, I heard the coo of the mourning dove somewhere nearby. It soothed my rising anxiety, but I quickened my pace, finally reaching the tree house a few minutes later.

Much to my dismay, Liam was not sitting on the threshold with a beer in hand. The crime scene tape had come loose and flapped in the wind, making eerie noises as it whipped about. The door to the tree house was open, and I could see that snow had blown inside.

I marched over, planning only to pull the door closed, but I couldn't help but take one last peek inside.

It looked much like it had the other morning when Harper and I were here, but the disarray was even more pronounced—the police had been thorough in searching the place. All the drawings of Starla had been taken away, and I wondered where they went. To an evidence locker or to Kyle's family?

The lemon scent had faded, and another smell dominated. I sniffed, trying to place it, and realized with a start that it reminded me of a hospital.

> *Body weak, spirit fly,*
> *With death near,*
> *Hold no fear,*
> *Fly, fly to say good-bye.*

Was this tree house more a hospice than an actual home? Biting my cheek, I wondered how long the full autopsy report would take.

And what it would show.

I let out a small cry when my cell phone buzzed, startling me. I laughed at myself as I fumbled to answer.

"Where have you been?" Harper asked in a frantic tone.

"Long story," I said. "What's wrong?"

"Marcus is in quite the tizzy after Nick called a few minutes ago."

Uh-oh.

"How soon can you get home?" Harper asked.

"Ten minutes." If I jogged . . .

"Good. We'll meet you there."

"What's this about?" I asked, fearing the answer.

"There's some sort of new development, and by the way Marcus is acting, my guess is that it's bad news for Starla. Very bad news."

With my stomach in knots, I said, "I'll be right there."
I hung up.

Wind ruffled my hair as I took another look around
the tree house, feeling a mix of sadness, anger, and heart-
felt wishes that things had been different for Starla and
Kyle.

"Forgive and forget," I murmured.

With a heavy sigh, I closed the door behind me. And
on the past.

As I jogged away, the mourning dove cooed.

It felt as though there was an electrical buzz in the air as
I rushed through the back door of As You Wish and
found Marcus, Harper, and Nick waiting in the kitchen.
To my surprise, Vince was there, too.

"Where's Starla?" I asked.

Marcus said, "We're waiting for her to return from
walking the dogs."

I slipped out of my coat and turned to Nick. "What's
going on? Did the autopsy report come in?"

Before he could answer, the back door opened and
the dogs raced in, covered in snow, and Starla took one
look at us and immediately froze.

Missy and Twink shook their fur as Starla calmly removed her coat and hung it on the pegs near the back
door and walked into the kitchen. She looked at each of
us. "Just spit it out. Don't beat around the bush. I've had
a long week and am not in the mood for sugarcoating."

Marcus pulled out a stool next to Vince and motioned
her to sit. She did.

By the way they were all acting, I decided I ought to
sit down, too. I opted for the third to last step on the
staircase. Tilda came down from her usual spot on the
landing and sat next to me, which clued me in that I'd
better brace myself for whatever Nick was about to say.

"Tell me," Starla said, a bit of fire in her voice.

"Nick wants you and Vince to turn yourselves in,"
Marcus said abruptly.

Starla reeled back as though the words had slapped
her in the face.

Nick flashed me a quick look before taking a deep breath. "The prosecutor thinks there's enough circumstantial evidence to file charges." He explained about the threat to Kyle's life, the failed lie detector tests, the duct tape, and finally the syringe that was found.

"Were the prints on the syringe identified?" I asked.

"Not yet," he said. "But I doubt an ID would change his mind at this point. I did my best to try and stall, but he's not biting. I'm sorry."

It felt as though his words echoed off the cabinets, the counters. Nobody spoke. It seemed like no one dared breathe as what he said sank in.

There was a tightness around Nick's mouth that hinted at his internal conflict. He was trying his best to hold it together while delivering this news. I wanted nothing more than to go to him, offer comfort, but I needed to let him do his job.

"You can't," Starla said, her voice breaking. "I didn't do it."

"I happen to agree," Nick said, "but my hands are tied."

"Untie them," Harper said fiercely.

Nick held his ground. "I'm sorry. Starla, Vince, you're going to have to come with me."

Vince jumped up. "You can't arrest her. She's innocent."

"I'm sorry, Vince. I have to," Nick said.

"No," Vince interrupted, his voice shaky, "you don't understand. She's innocent. I can prove it."

Chapter Twenty-five

"I'm confused," Starla said, her gaze searching Vince's face. "How can you prove it?"

"You didn't do it yourself, did you?" Harper asked.

His gaze whipped to her. "What? No! Of course not."

"Don't give me that look," she snapped. "You can't blame me for thinking that way."

I didn't blame her—it was a reasonable leap to make. Wryly, he frowned at her.

She shrugged but didn't apologize.

He was so ashen, I was afraid he was going to pass out as he turned his attention back to Starla and said, "I'm so sorry, Starla. So sorry. I was only trying to protect you, to watch over you. That's all. I swear. Please believe me."

"I'm still confused," she said. "And now you're scaring me."

"Maybe you should explain, Vince?" Nick suggested.

Vince pulled a disk from his coat pocket.

Not this again.

I wondered if Archie was nearby in case we needed more memory cleanse.

"Can I use your DVD player?" he asked.

"By all means," I said.

Thick tension filled the air as we trooped to the family room to watch the video. I glanced at Starla. She sat ramrod straight on the arm of the sofa, her gaze intent on the TV.

Vince still looked ill as Nick picked up the remote and hit PLAY.

My stomach knotted. A combination of anger and curiosity bubbled inside me as everyone focused on the TV.

I heard Vince gulp as the screen suddenly came into focus. It looked like a home movie, in a bedroom.

I gasped. It was footage taken upstairs, in the guest room.

The fact that there was footage upstairs wasn't the shocking part—it was the fact that Starla was *visible*. On film. Sleeping.

I glanced at Harper and her eyes were as wide as mine. Starla slowly turned and looked at me. I shrugged. I had no idea how that was possible.

Evan, on the floor, was a bright white blur.

Starla gripped the edge of the couch as she watched the screen.

Nick slid a questioning glance to me, and I could only shrug at him as well.

"This was taken Friday night," Vince said, his voice surprisingly strong. "You can see the date stamp just fine. If you watch all the footage, you'll see that Starla didn't leave. She was asleep the whole time. This footage is her alibi."

Harper was the first to say something. "You were *spying* on her?"

"No," Vince shook his head. "It's not like that. I was just watching over her. Protecting her."

Starla kept staring, unblinking.

I felt as though I might be sick.

Marcus said, "How'd you get this footage?"

"I'd like to know, too," Nick added. "Are there cameras in the house?"

Suddenly panicked at the thought, I glanced around.

"No, there are no cameras." Vince fidgeted. "I tapped into Starla's laptop from my computer."

Tapped. He meant hacked.

I'd heard about this before, on one of the morning news programs, warning people (mostly teens) to be careful leaving their laptops open because predators could watch you from afar.

"If her laptop was open, I could watch her through the webcam lens," Vince said. "It was my way of making sure she was okay."

"Your way is creepy," Harper said, giving Vince the evil eye. "Way creepy."

"I know, but it was the only way I could make sure she was okay." Vince pressed his lips together. Then, as though realizing there was nothing he could say to make this right, he said to Nick, "The disk is yours. If you need to check out my system to verify the times or whatever, just let me know. I'll gladly turn it all over to you. Everything you asked for."

Everything. He must have footage of Starla's house from Friday night as well. Have mercy, as Ve would say.

"I'll be in touch," Nick said, "but I think it's best if you go now."

By the look on Harper's face, I thought that was a good idea. I could practically see the plan to flog Vince forming in her eyes.

Vince gave a quick nod. "Starla, could I talk to you for a minute? Outside?"

I noticed she was trembling as she watched the footage of her sleeping. Her chin lifted, and she turned her head to look him in the eye. "I think I've heard enough of what you have to say."

"I—" He swallowed. "I'm sorry." Running for the door, he dashed out into the cold, leaving his coat hanging on the pegs near the door.

We all stood in silence for a moment, watching the screen as the white blur on the floor continued to toss and turn. Thankfully, Evan didn't need to prove his alibi or he'd be out of luck. At one point on the footage, Tilda came in, swatted Twink, and hopped onto the bed with Starla, snuggling in close.

Harper grabbed the remote and paused the video.

She gestured at the screen. "Wh— H—" she stammered. "I mean, what the hell is going on? Why can we see Starla?"

I'd already grabbed my cell phone, dialing Cherise. There had to be a reason for this. The only thing different about that night was the sleeping spell.

Cherise answered on the third ring and *hmmm*ed for a good ten seconds before saying, "Well, I've never heard of such a thing, but it makes sense, I suppose."

I had her on speakerphone. "How does it make sense?"

"The only time Wishcrafters are visible on film is when they're dead."

Nick's eyes widened in horror.

"Shut the front door," Harper said.

How did we not know this?

Starla said, "So you're saying I was dead?"

"No, no," Cherise said, chuckling. "But the sleeping spell, especially while in a deep sleep, slows regular breathing to an abnormally low level."

"Oh," Starla said blithely, "so I was *mostly* dead."

"Exactly! The spell must have tricked your body."

"Thanks, Cherise," I said. "We were freaking out."

"I'm still freaking out," Harper said.

"I can help you with that," Cherise said. "A nice sleeping spell . . ."

"No!" we all shouted.

She laughed and hung up.

Starla let out a sigh.

Harper stepped in to give her a hug. "I suppose the silver lining of this is that your name has been cleared."

Starla glanced around at us. "Then why does it feel like I've just lost everything all over again?"

Half an hour later, Nick and I sat in the family room, trying to make sense of this latest twist.

Not long after Vince left, Starla said she wanted to be alone and excused herself to the guest room. Marcus and Harper had left, too, leaving just Nick, me, the dogs, and Tilda, who'd scurried off somewhere.

"What now?" I dropped my head onto the back of the sofa and closed my eyes. If I was this exhausted, I couldn't imagine what Starla was feeling. This week had been emotionally draining.

What Vince had done was such a betrayal. Yet . . . he'd given Starla an alibi. It was hard to be mad at him because he'd saved her from being unjustly arrested. But I was truly disgusted with him and his behavior. I wasn't sure I trusted what he'd said about spying on Starla only as his way of protecting her. Once a Seeker, always a Seeker.

There was no need for a small-town bath and body shop owner to own such high-tech gadgets and surveillance equipment. I had no doubt all that fancy gear was being used solely to uncover magic within the village.

So that left me with the question of whether he'd truly been spying on Starla for her protection—or if it was because he suspected she was a witch.

Which led me to question whether his feelings for her were real at all or if he was using her.

I hated to think that he'd been using her, so I chose to believe, perhaps foolishly, that he *had* been looking out for her in his own misguided way.

After all, he apparently loved Starla so much that he had been willing to lose her to save her from going to jail. . . . It was the ultimate act of love.

"I'll check out Vince's surveillance equipment," Nick said, "to verify the footage, and I'd really like to see what he recorded in front of Starla's house on Friday night." He threaded his fingers through his hair. "Where were you off to this afternoon?"

"At the tree house, looking for Liam Chadwick."

"Find him?"

"No. But I know he has some answers we're looking for—it's just a matter of getting him to tell them." I explained about Pepe being mistaken about which brother he'd overheard. "Did you ever check to see who Liam texted Friday night while he was here? Maybe it's this mystery woman, and we can quiz her."

"Dead end," he said. "He dialed one of those pay-as-you-go cell phones. Untraceable."

"So, it was probably Kyle's."

"Yes."

I rubbed Missy's ears as she stretched out between Nick and me. "What if this wasn't some sort of regular murder? If Kyle really was dying, what if it was a mercy killing?"

Mercy killing, also known as euthanasia, made sense to me. It was logical that someone close to Kyle—very close—didn't want to see him suffer any longer.

"You think his family had something to do with it."

"Well, if Kyle used the Good-bye Spell, then he had to be terminally ill. . . . Mercy killing is considered homicide, right?"

"In this state at least."

My mind was making leaps. "So let's say one of the Chadwicks is guilty. They'd be charged with murder."

Dark eyes watched me carefully. "Yes."

"So it would behoove one of them to frame Starla for the crime, especially if they didn't like Starla much. Two birds with one stone kind of thing."

"Behoove?"

"Don't distract me."

He chuckled. "It would, in fact, behoove one of them, yes. But which one?"

"I don't suppose one of them popped up on the station's footage of the evidence locker?" Someone had cast that Mirage Spell.

"There's no footage. Apparently the camera to the evidence locker hasn't worked in months."

"You're kidding."

"I wish I were."

Tingling, but unable to grant that wish, I said, "No other cameras are nearby?"

"No. An oversight I plan on fixing immediately."

Great. Another dead end. "Well, I think any of the Chadwicks are capable of ending Kyle's life because they loved him and seeing him die a little more every day must have been truly heartbreaking." I was having a rough time seeing Mrs. P struggle and we weren't even family. Not by blood at least. "But we have the added factor of someone placing Kyle's body at Starla's house. Someone wanted Starla to take the blame. The message on the duct tape was clearly their way of defending Kyle's reputation."

"Someone like one of his parents? I'm not sure I could watch my child suffer like that."

The image of terminally ill Mimi flashed through my head and instantly made me queasy. I couldn't even imagine.

"Maybe." It was such a parental thing to do, to defend a child's reputation. I thought of George and Cora and how distraught they'd been Saturday morning when Kyle was "missing." I found it hard to believe they had known he was dead in Starla's brownstone. "I don't really know how to narrow it down. Did you already offer them immunity?"

"The offer was made through their attorney, but they haven't responded yet." He sighed. "I'll have to talk to the prosecutor again. If this is a mercy killing, it changes the rules of the deal."

"What about Vince?" I asked. "Will he face charges for computer hacking?"

"Possibly," Nick said, dragging a hand down his face. "Such a shame. I was rooting for those two."

I hadn't been and now felt guilty that my ill wishes had somehow doomed the relationship. "He was growing on me." I couldn't believe he'd thrown it all away.

"Like fungus?"

"Something like that," I mumbled. "It doesn't matter much now."

My heart ached for Starla. This week must have felt like pure hell to her. First Kyle, now Vince. She was betrayed by both of them, albeit in very different ways for very different reasons.

Nick said, "I need to get going. I have to speak to the prosecutor and explain why Starla and Vince aren't in jail." He caressed my cheek. "Are you going to be all right?"

I pushed my face into his hand and smiled. "I'll be fine."

It was Starla I was worried about.

Later that evening, I took Missy for a walk and tried to clear my head. Snow fell steadily, coating everything in sight in white—including Missy. I'd actually wiggled her into a doggy coat earlier, and she hadn't been pleased.

"I bet you're happy you have that coat now," I said to her as we crossed the street, headed toward the green.

Missy looked up at me, and I would have sworn she gave me the doggy equivalent of an evil eye.

I smiled, adjusted my scarf against the blowing snow and let Missy sniff around. My heart pinged when I saw Mrs. P's favorite bench, looking stark and lonely. I wished fervently that she'd come streaking out of no-where, a pink velour blur, hip bump me, and cackle as she said, "Hey, doll."

She was the closest thing I'd ever known to a grand-mother, and my heart ached thinking about not hearing her laugh or seeing her smile.

Missy whined and put her paws up on my legs. I wiped my eyes and said, "I'm all right. I'm just . . . not ready to let her go. I just found her, really." It hadn't even been a full year.

Taking a deep breath, I brushed the snow off Missy's head and said, "Let's finish our walk and get back."

We looped around the ice rink and were just about to head back to the house when I heard, "See, I told you she's been following us."

I turned and found Will and Liam Chadwick strolling toward me.

With a sneer, Liam said, "She is the Elder's snoop."

Great. Just what I needed. Tag-teamed by the Chad-wick brothers.

Immediately, my temper ignited. "How did I follow you? I was here first."

"Were you?" Liam asked, his eyebrow raised.

I wasn't in the mood for his riddles.

"Do you deny you chased me through the village earlier?" Will asked, his eyes looking even bluer than usual in the snowy landscape.

I couldn't, so I countered by saying, "Is there some reason you were evading me? I only wanted to ask you some questions." I narrowed my gaze. "There wouldn't be any particular reason why you wouldn't want to answer them, now would there?"

"What kind of questions?" Liam asked. Snow frosted his shoulders and the simple black hat he wore.

"Oh, the usual," I said, scooping up Missy to keep her warm. "Like, how did Kyle become paralyzed? How long had he been terminally ill? And did you know mercy killing was a felony?"

The brothers stood like stone statues. I'd definitely hit a nerve.

"We don't know what you're talking about," Liam said.

I rolled my eyes. "And more lies. I shouldn't be surprised. I know you two were together at the Cauldron until around nine on Friday night. Then you went to Kyle's tree house. Did you kill him there? Or carry him to Starla's and do it there? Nice touch, trying to frame her for the crime, but she's been completely cleared now. So, epic fail with that."

"Stop it," Will seethed. "You don't know what you're talking about."

"What do you mean, cleared?" Liam asked.

"Surveillance footage gives her an airtight alibi. Unlike for the two of you. Where were you two, exactly, between nine and midnight Friday night?"

"Together," Liam said automatically.

I glanced at Will. He looked pale. "I'm just curious . . . are you selling that same story?"

"I . . ." he stammered, then clamped his lips closed.

"Well, you know what they say about curiosity and the cat," a voice said behind me.

George Chadwick had come up without me noticing. When he stood next to his boys, he didn't look nearly as friendly as he had the other day in Wickedly Creative.

"It's a good thing I'm not a cat," I retorted, not liking his tone.

George glared at me, but said to Will and Liam, "I think it's time for us to leave. Your mother's waiting for us. We have a funeral to plan," he said bitingly.

Liam stepped toward me. "Just so you know, we were all together Friday night. Mom, Dad, me, Will. And we'll all vouch for each other. Got it?"

I got it, all right. They were willing to cover for one another. Never mind that Starla had almost gone to jail because one of them wanted retribution against her. I stepped toward him. "Someone once told me that the truth hurt. Well, I suspect when I figure out what happened Friday night, that those words will come back to haunt him."

Liam glared. I glared right back.

"Come on," George said, and they all turned their backs on me.

I held Missy closer and watched them go. "I will figure out what happened."

Missy barked, and I set her back on the ground. "Let's go home."

Chapter Twenty-six

The next morning, I slumped back onto my pillow, wishing I could sleep a few more hours.

But as I rolled onto my side, tucked under my covers, I listened as grief unfolded in the guest bath next door. Starla had been in the shower a while now, and though she was probably trying to muffle it with the sound of water, I could still hear her sobbing through the wall. It made me want to cry, too.

Missy lounged at my feet, her gaze firmly on me as though willing me to fix what ailed Starla. Only there was nothing I could do. There was no fixing her broken heart.

Bypassing Missy, Tilda hopped onto my bed. With her tail in the air, she tiptoed toward me and brazenly plopped onto my stomach.

Her fur was as light as fluff as I scratched her ears and under her chin. Her purrs filled the air and immediately made me feel a little better.

When the water cut off and the pipes—and Starla's cries—silenced, Tilda lifted her head and looked at me as if wondering why it was suddenly quiet. She put her head back on my sternum and resumed purring. Her tail swished back and forth across my thighs.

I eyed the clock and decided I should probably get up. Make some coffee. Pretend everything was normal. The only thing on my to-do was visit Mrs. P. Other than that, my day belonged to Starla.

The cell phone on my bedside table *aaaooo*ed—Harper's ringtone—and I reached over and grabbed it.

Tilda tensed. "Don't worry," I said to her. "I won't tell anyone you're being nice to me."

After narrowing her gaze, she let out a meow and hopped down, slinking out the narrow opening of the bedroom door.

Missy lifted her head, blinked at me.

"Cats," I said to her with a shrug, then answered the phone with a bleary, "Hi, Harper."

"Why do you sound sleepy? Are you still in bed?"

Her incredulity was well earned. It was now almost nine a.m. "Late night."

Abruptly, she said, "I saw Vince this morning."

"Oh?"

"He was packing his shop. There's a FOR SALE sign in the window. He's leaving town, Darcy. He said it was too hard living in the village alongside Starla without her in his life."

My chest ached. "Did he tell her he was moving?"

"I don't think so. Maybe someone should." Unsubtly, she coughed.

I sighed. "Fine, I'll tell her."

"You're the best. See you soon." She hung up.

I dropped my cell phone on the bed and glanced at Missy. "Sisters," I said, shaking my head. "I don't know how she ropes me into half the things she does."

Missy blinked.

A tap sounded on the door and Missy hopped to her feet, ready to leap off the bed at a moment's notice.

Starla stuck her head in the room. Her hair was wrapped in a towel, and although she was dressed in her froggy pj's, she'd already applied makeup. Unfortunately, there wasn't enough concealer in the world to cover the pain etched under her eyes. "Who are you talking to?"

"Just now? Missy. She's a good listener."

"Is it a private conversation or can I come in?" she asked, a teasing lilt to her voice.

I patted the empty side of my queen-sized bed. "There's plenty of room."

She rushed inside, pulled back the covers, and slipped in next to me.

I said, "Rough day yesterday."

"Rough week," she countered.

"The roughest."

"Pepe might be on the right track with his week of discontent," she said. "I could use a week away from reality with nothing but the TV, books, and my favorite foods and cocktails. Preferably somewhere warm."

"I was serious the other day when I said we can make that trip happen."

"We *should* make that happen. Soon."

"Where do you want to go? Florida? Bahamas? Mexico?" As much as I wanted Starla to get away for a while, a vacation sounded like heaven to me, too. It had been a hellacious week.

"Any of them. All of them. But we can't book it for this weekend, as much as I'd like to get out of here." She fluffed a pillow. "I'm taking pictures at the dance competition at the Will-o'-the-Wisp and it's too late to cancel."

I gaped at her. "They let you take pictures?"

"Head and shoulders only."

I laughed as the craziness of the event sank in. "Nothing in this village should surprise me anymore."

"I hear you." Her voice took a turn toward the somber.

I had the feeling she was suddenly thinking about Kyle again and was a little shocked when she said, "I can't believe Vince is leaving town."

"How did you know?"

"Ve and I saw the sign in his shop window this morning while we were walking the dogs."

I couldn't believe they'd already been out and about.

And no wonder she'd been sobbing in the shower. "I'm sorry."

"Me, too." She let out a weary sigh. "Is it bad that I don't want him to go?"

I rolled to face her. "Are you saying you've forgiven him for the hacking?"

"I . . . I don't know."

I had to ask. "Are you the least bit concerned about him being a Seeker and other possible motives of his surveillance, not just of you but of the whole village?"

"I've thought about it. How could I not? But Darcy, he's ready to leave the village because he doesn't want to live here if he can't be with me. He loved me enough to lose me in order to give me an alibi. That has to mean something, right?"

"It means a lot." After a stretch of silence, I said, "Are you going to talk with him, ask him to stay?"

"Maybe. He loved me enough to let me go, but I can't decide if I love him enough to fight for him. Maybe it's better for all of us if I just let him leave town. One less Seeker to worry about."

"Starla, your decision shouldn't have anything to do with all of us. It should have to do with how you feel and that's it."

"I don't know how I feel." She drew the covers up to her chin.

"Give it time," I said.

Flicking a glance at me, she said, "But with him leaving that's the one thing I don't have, isn't it?"

She had me there.

I took a quick shower, blow-dried my hair, and finally headed downstairs for a much-needed cup of coffee. At this point, a vat of coffee would be nice.

Humming, Aunt Ve stood at the sink doing dishes. Just beyond her, a mourning dove bobbed its way along the windowsill outside, the beautiful blue ring around its eye shining iridescent in the morning light.

"Where'd Starla go?" I asked, patting Tilda's head as she lounged atop the fridge.

"She and Twink went to visit Mrs. P and then to Hocus-Pocus. Said she felt like she was neglecting her job. Personally"—Ve tucked a loose strand of coppery hair behind her ear—"I'm glad. The sooner she gets back to a semblance of normal, the better."

Normal. It was sadly lacking these days.

As I stirred half-and-half into my coffee, I said, "Do you think there will ever be a semblance of normal again?"

She shut off the faucet, shook droplets from her hands, and then wiped them on a dish towel. "A new normal perhaps."

A new normal. One that included picking up the pieces of this past week.

"So you know about Vince?"

"Yeah." I didn't mention the sobbing I heard in the shower. His leaving seemed to have hit Starla harder than any of the other blows she'd suffered this week.

Ve *tsk*ed.

"What?" I asked.

"I thought he'd fight harder for her, that's all."

Surprise rippled through me. "You want them to get back together?"

"Perhaps it's the romantic in me," she said, twirling around, reminding me again—unfortunately—of the Swing and Sway dance.

"But he creepily stalked her online."

Ve draped the dish towel over the oven handle. "For good reason, no? I want Starla to be happy," she said. "Vince makes her happy. It's as simple as that. Is that your phone?" Ve asked, tipping her head, listening.

It was. I heard it buzzing upstairs and went running. I reached it just before it clicked over to voice mail. *Nick.*

"Have I got something to show you," he said, his voice filled with wonder. "Can you meet me at my house?"

"Now?" I asked.

"Can you? I think it's pretty important."

"Give me ten minutes."

"Hurry," he said.

Chapter Twenty-seven

Wondering what Nick had to show me, I hurried across the village green, practically jogging. I had just turned the corner onto his street when I was greeted by the sight of a galloping puppy being chased by none other than Glinda herself, who limped comically after him.

"Not again," I mumbled.

Clarence stumbled to a stop in front of me, and I reached down and scooped him up. He licked my chin.

"Some things never change," I said to him.

Glinda looked like she'd been put through the wringer and hung out to dry. I'd be surprised if she'd slept or eaten the past couple of days—she appeared almost zombielike, with dark circles beneath her eyes, her cheeks hollowed. She wore the same bathrobe, the same nightgown as yesterday. But at least she'd traded the bunny slippers for a pair of slip-on sneakers.

"This is becoming tiresome," she said.

"I can't help it if your dog likes me better than you."

Anger fired in her eyes, and I was almost glad to see it. It gave her life. Vitality.

"Fine," she snapped. "Keep him. Keep it all!" Spinning, she gimped back toward her house. "Beware, though. He's an escape artist."

I glanced at Clarence. "Where's she going?" I trotted after her. "Glinda, wait! I was kidding about the dog." I quickly caught up to her—she couldn't limp that fast. "Stop."

Turning to face me, she said, "Why, Darcy? Keep him. You get everything you want, so why shouldn't you keep the dog, too?"

Taken aback, I said, "What does that mean? I don't get everything I want."

"Please." She folded her arms over her chest. "You show up in this village all sweet and innocent and within days you have everyone eating out of your palm, including the Elder, who is notoriously picky. You've got a beautiful house, my dream job investigating for the Elder, a great family. You're beautiful, you're smart, you're fun. And you've got Nick and Mimi as a perfect ready-made family for you. You have everything I've ever wanted, and now you've got a cute dog, too. I hope you're happy."

"Don't you dump all that on me," I snapped. "Your insecurities aren't my fault."

"They're completely your fault. I was fine until you came here."

"Then you're delusional, too."

Letting out a sigh, she said, "Whatever. Look, I'm not in the mood to discuss my life with you. You're lucky I don't—" She cut herself off. "Just leave me alone. I already quit my job. The dog likes you better than me. There's not much left."

Shock rippled through me at the news. She quit?

"You've won, Darcy. You've won."

I handed Clarence back to her. "It was never a game, Glinda. It didn't have to be this way."

She cuddled the dog to her chest, gave me one last sour look and limped into her house, slamming the door behind her.

"That went well," I said sarcastically. I shook my head and headed for Nick's house at the end of the lane.

Higgins greeted me at the door with lots of slobber. I was going to need another shower. "Seriously," I said to him. "We need to stop meeting this way."

Nick tugged him off me, and gave me a kiss.

"I just had quite the conversation with Glinda." I said.

He put his arm around my shoulders, pulling me close to his chest. "Did she mention she quit?"

"It came up." I snuggled in, enjoying the warmth of his body heat.

"It's a bit of a relief," he said. "Saves the trouble of waiting for the council."

As I told him bits and pieces about the conversation I'd had, I realized that I felt sad for her. My mind began churning with ways to help her, but I realized what I was doing.

Fixing.

I had to let this go. I had no business trying to fix her issues. If there were ever a situation I needed to steer clear of, this was it. She wasn't my friend. She never had been.

"What did you have to show me?"

He took my hand and pulled me into the living room. "It's in here. Sit, sit," he said as he grabbed the DVD remote.

I settled in on the couch. Higgins came over and put his big head on my lap. I scratched his ears. He missed Mimi fiercely while she was at school.

"Vince came through for me this morning," Nick said. "He dropped off all the surveillance footage he had for Friday night, including video of Starla's town house. The front of it at least. He said there had been some sort of electrical malfunction at Starla's, but he didn't see how it would have helped her case," Nick said in a strange tone. "That's why he says he didn't turn the footage in before now."

Sure. It had nothing to do with him filming the whole village. "Electrical malfunction?"

"I don't know what to think. Here, watch." He sat next to me. "I've queued it up. This is a little after eight."

I stared at the TV, at the crystal clear image of Starla's

brownstone. A car drove past, a couple walked by with their dog. All was quiet.

Then suddenly, bright glittering light illuminated the windows of Starla's living room, shooting beams into the darkness. It disappeared as soon as it came.

"What was that?" I asked, staring.

"I was hoping you'd know. It looked . . . magical."

It did. "Probably some kind of spell." I took the remote and rewound the video again. "It might be how Kyle's body got into her house." It fit the window of his time of death.

"What kind of spell would do that?"

I racked my brain. I'd read so many spells these past couple of days that they jumbled together. "I'm not sure. I know I read one about transference in Melina's diary."

"This spell you recall . . . does it involve teleportation?"

Moving a *body* from one place to another, not just an object. "I just can't remember. I was so focused on finding an invisibility spell that I kind of skimmed everything else."

"We need to look at that diary."

I smiled. "That, I can do." I murmured the spell, clapped my hands twice, and the diary appeared on my lap.

Higgins let out a loud woof and went running to his doggy bed. He put a paw over his face.

"Aw, poor pup," I said.

Nick crouched next to Higgins and rubbed his head. "Welcome to my world, buddy."

"Hey!"

Nick smiled. "I'm getting used to it, and he will too."

I reached in my pocket and pulled out my new reading glasses. I started flipping through the diary.

Smiling, Nick said, "Cute."

I glanced at him and had to pull the glasses down my nose to see him clearly. "Too much eyestrain lately. Melina's handwriting . . ."

"It was always horrible."

I glanced at him. "It's kind of strange, isn't it? How much she's still a part of our lives?"

"Does it bother you?"

I shook my head and again thought about how much I owed to a woman I'd never met. "I actually feel . . . like she's a friend. I know that doesn't make sense."

"It actually does," Nick said, sitting next to me. "After all, you've gotten to know her through Mimi and this diary."

We'd never really discussed his divorce from Melina, but I knew it had wounded him deeply. They'd repaired some of the damage after she was diagnosed with cancer and had been friends by the time she died, but I saw some of the scars she'd left on Nick. His trust issues, mostly.

In time, those were scars I hoped I could heal.

I thumbed pages of the diary, skimming, skimming. Nick paced. Higgins snored. A half hour later, I finally found what I was looking for. "Yes! The Special Delivery Spell."

Nick leaned over my shoulder. "What's it do?"

"Conveys an object from one location to another."

"Can that object be a person?"

I eyed down the paragraph. "It doesn't say it *can't* be a person. Hmm."

"What?"

"It says 'Use with extreme caution' but doesn't say why. But look"—I pointed—"'Incandescence will occur upon delivery.'"

"The bright flash," Nick said.

"Right. And," I said, "incandescence usually comes from heat. It could probably cause a burn."

"Like the one on Kyle's calf."

I nodded.

Nick kissed me loudly on the lips. "I think you just uncovered how Kyle got into Starla's house."

"But," I said, hating to burst his bubble. "We still don't know who killed him."

"We're getting there," he said. "You solved one major piece of the puzzle, ruled out a major suspect, and uncovered more clues."

"What suspect, what clues?"

"This spell narrows Kyle's time of death to the eight o'clock hour and shows that he was probably killed elsewhere and transferred to Starla's. And though he didn't know it when he handed it over, the video also absolves Vince," he said. "That's the biggest clue of all here."

"The absolving of Vince? How?" He hadn't arrived at As You Wish until nine-ish.

"Because he's mortal."

I managed a wry smile. "If not for lack of sleep lately, I would have put that together sooner." It had to have been a Crafter who killed Kyle if a spell was used to move his body.

"That's why we make a good team."

I nudged him. "We do, don't we?"

"The best," he said softly. "Now we just have to figure out which Crafter is responsible. I'm still leaning toward someone in his family. A mercy killing, like we talked about."

"What did the prosecutor say about that? Because his family has already planned alibis for each other," I said, explaining my run-in with the Chadwick men last night.

"I figured they would. The prosecutor said he'd mull it over and get back to me. Because we ruled out Starla with that video of Vince's, the prosecutor wants to wait until the full autopsy results are in."

"Which will be when?"

"Any minute now."

That was good to know. I tapped the diary. "If a Crafter used a spell to move a body he or she just murdered, that has to be breaking Craft Law. The Elder is sure to know something—I'll make an appointment to see her." I tried to think if this was a problem I could solve on my own, but there was no way—she was the only one who knew when laws were violated. While I was there, I'd also ask about the warning on the Special Delivery Spell. I had a feeling it was important.

Very important.

Nick's cell phone rang as I sent the diary back into the ether.

He answered the call and said, "Can you repeat that?"

He listened for a sec, his incredulous gaze slowly pivoting to me. "You're sure? Okay, thanks."

He hung up and let out a whooshing breath.

"What?" I asked. Something was clearly wrong.

"The fingerprint expert finished his exam of the syringe and was able to ID the smudged prints."

I couldn't help but feel anxiety at the tone of his voice. "Whose prints were they? Kyle's?"

"No, Darcy," Nick said, his dark eyes troubled. "They were yours."

Chapter Twenty-eight

I was still reeling as I crossed the green, heading straight for Archie's cage. I needed to get a message to the Elder.

I couldn't figure out how my prints had been on that syringe, and could only assume someone had planted them on purpose. But I had to wonder why. Why my prints and not Starla's? Why implicate me?

I wasn't sure, but I was beyond grateful that Vince's video showing the Special Delivery Spell had also given me an alibi as well. I suppose I owed him for saving me a lot of stress about whether the DA would charge me with killing Kyle.

As I passed by the Bewitching Boutique, Godfrey looked up from the dress he was steaming—that gorgeous gown I'd seen in his back room the other day. I wanted to go inside and ask how Pepe was doing and also see that gown up close again, but I had things to do and wasn't sure I could face Godfrey so soon after learning that he was Ve's partner for the Swing and Sway.

He quickly spun the dress around, so its back was to

me, and gave me a tremulous smile and a cautious wave. Confused at his strange behavior, I smiled, waved back, and hurried along the sidewalk.

Archie was in his cage in Terry's yard, regaling a small crowd of tourists with an overly dramatic rendition of Bette Midler's "The Rose."

I was pretty sure Archie never did anything that wasn't overdramatic.

The tourists were enraptured by the performance, standing transfixed just beyond Terry's fence. I waited patiently while he finished belting out the ballad.

As the crowd cleared out, I approached his cage, applauding.

He bowed and fluffed his colorful feathers. "I admit, it's a favorite."

"I know," I deadpanned.

"You have your *My Fair Lady*, I have my Bette. I won't judge you if you don't judge me."

Smiling, I said, "Deal."

"What brings you by? I'm sure it wasn't just to ruffle my feathers."

I leaned on the fence. "I need to meet with the Elder."

Archie leaned closer to me. "Oh? Why?"

"Craft lawbreakers."

His beady eyes flared. "Do tell!"

"I don't have anything to tell." I laughed. "That's why I need to see the Elder."

"Curses."

"You'll send the message right away?"

He flew out his door. "I'll go now. I'll be in touch soon."

After watching him fly off, I then glanced at the house and recalled what Ve had said earlier about Starla.

Vince makes her happy. It's as simple as that.

It really was as simple as that. I'd do just about anything to see Starla happy again.

So I knew just what I needed to do.

If someone accused me of trying to fix someone else's problem again, I'd argue that it wasn't fixing.

It was being a friend.

*　　*　　*

While I waited to hear from the Elder, Missy and I, under the guise of going for a walk, headed out on a mission. I had her leash in one hand and Vince's coat in the other. It was only *neighborly* of me to return it to him. And if I could talk him into sticking around the village a little bit longer, all the better.

The snow squalls had passed, and the sun had come out and was shining bright, bringing much-needed warmth to a cold, dreary week. Melting snowbanks caused puddles on the pathways and streets. Tree branches and eaves dripped relentlessly, making me wish I'd brought an umbrella.

As I neared Lotions and Potions, I was hit with a sudden wave of sadness. Officially Mrs. P had worked for Vince part-time but she had been the heart and soul of the shop. It was impossible to go inside the store without seeing her in every display, every color choice, every jar and bottle. It hurt knowing that she'd probably never return to the shop.

As I stopped in front of the plate glass window, I was taken aback. Most of the inventory had already been packed away. Cardboard boxes were stacked high and Vince was busy wielding a tape gun like a pro. He'd been busy.

Taking a deep breath, I ignored the CLOSED sign and knocked on the door.

Vince's head snapped up. When he saw me, resolution flashed across his face. He waved me inside.

The sweet herbal smell of the shop hit me like a punch to the stomach. It reminded me so much of Mrs. P—she often carried the scent of the shop on her clothes, like a perfume—that I had to remind myself that she wasn't standing next to me.

Vince set down his tape gun. "Are you okay? You just went white."

"It's the smell," I said as Missy went over to sniff his feet. "It makes me think of Mrs. P."

Bending to pat Missy, he said, "It hit me, too, when I walked in this morning. It was strange at first, like she was in here with me, but the longer I've been here the more comforting it's become." He smiled. "Like she's really in here with me."

As soon as he said it, I felt myself relax a little bit. It was much better to focus on the scent being comforting rather than intensifying my sadness at my friend's decline. "I like that point of view."

He grabbed a Sharpie and wrote something on the top of a cardboard box. "It's helped me. Her illness came as such a shock. I knew she hadn't been feeling well, but she's gone downhill so quickly. I spent some time with her this morning, and despite being extremely tired, she was still cracking jokes as usual." His curls flopped as he shook his head. "It never ceases to amaze me how fast life can change."

By the tone of his voice I could tell he wasn't speaking about Mrs. P anymore.

I held up his coat. "You left this at my house."

He took it and set it on the counter next to the cash register. "Thanks."

Missy wandered back to me and sat. I tapped the top of a box. "So, you're moving."

"Not very far," he said. "I found a place in Beverly. I have to stick around a while to see if charges are going to be brought against me."

Beverly was just up the coast a bit. "Why not just stick around until you find out? I'm sure you'll know soon." I knew he would, though I wasn't sure how Nick was going to convince the prosecutor. He couldn't show him the Special Delivery video, but I had faith he'd think of something.

Vince grabbed another box and started packing it with lip balms and cold creams. "I can't. It . . . hurts too much. I truly meant her no harm, Darcy."

"I believe you."

"But I'd do it all over again," he said in a rush. "I don't regret it. Not when it proved her innocence. Honestly, I would have confessed to the crime myself if it would have saved her."

"Well, luckily, it didn't come to that."

Unhappiness clouded his eyes, and the corner of his mouth tipped downward into a frown. "How is she?"

I leaned against a box. "She's . . . confused. Sad. Missing you," I said, gauging his reaction to my words.

Slowly his head came up and his gaze bore into me. "Really?"

"I'm just saying that maybe you should postpone your move. Wait a week or two and see what shakes out."

Hope bloomed in his eyes, widening them. "You're serious?"

"I wouldn't joke about Starla's happiness."

In a rush, he came over and hugged me.

"*Oof*," I said as he crushed me.

"You've just made me the happiest man alive."

I backed away from him and poked his chest. "Don't get so excited just yet. All I said is she misses you. Now it's up to you. Talk to her."

"Missing me is enough for me to stay. I thought she hated me."

"And *if* she decides to forgive you, you'd better not hurt her again. Got it?"

"Got it."

He tossed his Sharpie in the air, but missed catching it as it came down. "She misses me!"

The phrase "crazy stupid love" flashed through my head as I bent to retrieve the pen that had rolled under the counter.

As I crouched and reached for it, it triggered a fuzzy memory, one that wouldn't quite come into focus. Odd.

"And no more cameras," I added as Missy and I headed for the door.

"Consider them gone." He held the door of the shop open for me. "I'll sell them right away. After I unpack a few boxes." He rocked on his heels, a smile stretching his face. "She misses me."

"Yeah, yeah," I said, rolling my eyes. "Don't forget what I said about hurting Starla."

"I won't. You have my word."

"I want your actions to speak louder than your words, Vince. Starla deserves the best."

He glanced downward, dragged his foot across the floor, then finally looked at me. "I'm not the best, Darcy.

Not hardly. Not yet. But every day that I'm with Starla, I become a better person. That has to count for something."

Emotion wedged in my throat. "It's not something. It's everything. I'll see you later."

As Missy and I headed home I couldn't help but feel that everything would work out between Vince and Starla.

It had to.

Her happiness was at stake.

Chapter Twenty-nine

Nick was waiting on the porch swing when Missy and I returned to As You Wish.

"I'm glad you came back in time. I only have a few minutes," he said, standing up.

I unclipped Missy's leash, but she didn't dash into the yard. Instead, she sat, looking at Nick intently. "What's wrong?"

The back door was locked and I figured Ve was out visiting Mrs. P, or perhaps prepping for Sunday's dance. Nick and Missy followed me inside.

He said, "I think the entire medical examiner's office needs the memory cleanse."

In the midst of taking off my coat, I stopped, pivoted, and looked at him. "You're serious?"

"I got a call a few minutes ago from one of the ME's assistants. They're freaking out over there."

"Why?"

"Sometime while waiting his turn for autopsy in the morgue's cooler, Kyle's body changed from a healthy-looking, albeit dead, guy to a thin, gaunt dead guy. He suddenly had multiple injection sites, and his muscles were visibly atrophied. The office had never seen anything like it."

My jaw dropped. I quickly did calculations in my head. Seventy-two hours. "He'd used a Mirage Spell before he died."

"It's the only thing I can think of."

I started shaking my head. "But no . . . he had that one injection site visible. Plus that burn on his leg. The Mirage Spell would have covered that."

"I have no explanation for that," he said. "This magic is way beyond my scope. As of this morning, he looked like someone who'd been terminally ill."

> *Body weak, spirit fly,*
> *With death near,*
> *Hold no fear,*
> *Fly, fly to say good-bye.*

"The assistant who called gave me a heads-up that the pathologist performing the autopsy quickly discovered why Kyle looked the way he did."

"Why?" I barely dared ask as I hung my coat on the peg.

"Widespread brain cancer."

Cancer. My pulse pounded in my ears. "Do we know the cause of death yet?"

"Not yet." Nick glanced at his watch. "Pathologist was finishing up and said he'd send the report immediately. I'll make you a copy."

"Will you send a copy to Cherise, too? As a Curecrafter, she might have insight I don't."

He nodded and pulled me into a hug. "I need to get back to the station. I'll call."

"I'm waiting on the Elder. If I see her, I'll ask about the memory cleanse for the medical examiner's office."

He gave me a kiss and strode out the door. I sighed and looked at Missy. "I guess I should get reading Melina's diary again." I needed to "look within" and find out what kind of spell Kyle had used to cover his illness.

But as I dried off Missy's paws, I couldn't help but shake the feeling that I already knew the answer.

Hours later, I gave up on the diary and headed over to the Pixie Cottage to visit Mrs. P. I hadn't found anything that would explain Kyle's appearance except for the Mirage Spell. There had to be something I was missing.

When I tapped softly on Mrs. P's door, Cherise opened it and motioned me inside the room. Mrs. P was sound asleep.

"What're you doing here?" I asked.

"Just keeping an eye on her. She collapsed last night while playing checkers with Pepe."

"Why isn't she at the hospital?"

"She's stubborn, that's why," Cherise whispered. "She'd rather stay in her home."

"I don't blame her." A lump had wedged in my throat.

"Me, either."

"Why didn't anyone tell me?"

Cherise reached over and squeezed my hand. "She didn't want you to know. She knew you wouldn't leave her side."

I wouldn't have. "She looks peaceful," I said as I sat next to Cherise on the settee.

"She is. She's not suffering."

I tried not to notice the medical bag at her feet. Even though she could heal using her Craft powers, she still carried around normal medical instruments. A stethoscope, a blood pressure cuff, thermometer, and other first aid paraphernalia. "Thank you for staying with her."

"She's an amazing woman."

She was.

Cherise said, "Tea?"

A tray sat on a large square coffee table that held a teapot and an assortment of miniature treats that I recognized as coming from the Gingerbread Shack.

I nodded.

"Nick e-mailed me an interesting report on Kyle."

My eyebrows went up. "Really?" I hadn't checked my e-mail before heading over here and wished I had. Undoubtedly, Kyle's autopsy report was in.

Cherise *tsk*ed as she poured steaming water into a mug. "Kyle truly suffered these past couple of years."

My first thought was *Good*, which made me feel slightly guilty. I took hold of the mug Cherise passed to me and voiced my second thought instead. "Past couple of years?"

Cherise drew her feet beneath her. She munched on a tiny lemon tartlet, and said, "His type of cancer undoubtedly began as a small tumor and grew into the monster it became. Even with treatment he had very little chance of survival beyond two to three years. Without treatment . . . he was lucky to have made it this long."

Lucky. My stomach churned.

"Do we know he had no treatment?" I asked. "Is the cancer what killed him? Or the morphine?"

"Nick only sent me the postmortem exam notes. The toxicology will probably come in later, as the results come in, so the cause of death is still pending." Cherise's eyes flashed with mischief. "I hope you don't mind, but I took it upon myself to make a few phone calls after I read the report. There are only a few specialists in this area who would treat such an advanced tumor."

Mind? She saved me from having to ask her to do it.

"I finally found one who treated a patient named Chadwick," she said, "and worked my magic to wheedle information from him."

"Magic? Literally or figuratively?" I asked, smiling.

She sipped her tea and grinned. "A little of both."

"Never underestimate the power of womanly wiles?" I surmised.

"Especially mine." Cherise waggled her eyebrows.

I swear she was as bad as Ve. Two peas in a pod.

"This particular oncologist had been treating the patient for eighteen months, after he was diagnosed by an emergency room physician with a stage four tumor that had originated in the frontal lobe and spread. It was inoperable but other treatments were offered, radiation and the like, but the prognosis was grim." Cherise topped off her mug. "The patient refused all treatment but accepted terminally ill palliative care, which basically means that he'd accept medication to make his remaining time more comfortable."

My mind reeled from all the information.

"It's a terrible fate he suffered, to be sure," Cherise added.

I held my mug tightly. "Karma, some would say. For what he did to Starla."

"Ah, but Darcy, I don't believe Kyle was responsible for his actions toward her."

"Why would you say that?"

"I believe it was the tumor." She dropped her feet to the floor and leaned forward, her eyes earnest as she studied me. "The tumor's location in his brain definitely would have produced personality changes. Confusion, lethargy, rage among other things. Cancer was literally destroying his brain. Looking back it's clear to me that Kyle's early symptoms presented not long after he and Starla married. He had absolutely no control over the things he said or did. Worse, he probably had no idea why he was behaving that way and possibly had no memory of it, either. The tumor could have affected that as well. It also explains the change in his paintings. He was probably seeing things very differently from what his brush was producing."

Her words sank in. I covered my mouth to hold in a cry as tears stung my eyes. Nausea rolled through my stomach. I recalled part of the conversation I'd had with Starla a couple of days ago.

He'd just get so worked up about something. Trivial things, too—the cap left off the toothpaste or it being too cold in the house—and suddenly one of the traits I loved about him most—his fiery passion—I didn't like so much. My gut instinct said that something was wrong. Inside here. She tapped her head.

Her gut instinct had been right. Dear Lord.

"What bothers me, as a healer," Cherise said, "is that he sought no treatment early on. He had to be experiencing terrible headaches. Dizzy spells. I see this a lot with younger men especially, who go into denial that there's anything wrong with them."

I bit my lip. "Could . . . could he have been cured if he'd come to you back then?"

"Possibly. It's hard to say. As you know, I cannot alter the course of a terminal or chronic illness, but that early on? I probably could have saved his life."

Ramifications of that statement exploded in my head, making me close my eyes against the sudden pain.

Kyle had never meant to hurt Starla. If only he'd seen Cherise, or any healer, then he would have been diagnosed, treated, possibly *saved*. Starla would still be living her fairy tale with her prince charming. Perhaps not as she originally planned, but still. *In sickness and in health. Till death do us part.* They would have been together. Fighting together to save him.

Instead he'd been cast as a villain, misunderstood. *Arrested.*

Liam's voice echoed in my head: *You're a good friend to Starla and that's admirable, but you don't understand the situation.*

I hadn't understood the situation. At all. "Foul is fair," I said, opening my eyes. "Kyle wasn't foul at all. He was ill. If not for that tumor, he would have still been the man Starla fell in love with."

Cherise leaned back. "Exactly."

"This changes everything."

She nodded.

My mind raced. "His family had to know. Why didn't they say anything?"

"I'm not sure, but they certainly were aware. The patient the oncologist treated wasn't named Kyle." Her eyebrow lifted. "His name was Liam." She used air quotes around the name. "And he was always accompanied to every appointment by his brother Will."

I rubbed the skin between my eyebrows to ease my headache as I put the pieces together. "Kyle used Liam's identity to get treatment."

"Yes," Cherise said. "It makes sense, I suppose, with Kyle being a fugitive. He couldn't very well get help on his own without the police finding out. And he looked enough like his brother to pass for him."

I glanced at Mrs. P and recalled what she had just said to me earlier: *Lately I've come to look upon situations through a very different set of eyes. Understanding versus vengeance. Rebuilding rather than destruction. Sometimes there is an interesting shade of gray between black and white.*

Cherise had just told me where I could locate the hard evidence to prove that the Chadwicks had harbored a fugitive—at that oncologist's office. But in light of Cherise's revelations about the cancer I didn't know what to do with the information. It really did change everything. If ever there was a shade of gray, this was it.

"Starla's going to be devastated," I said, my chest tightening just thinking about it.

"Yes, I imagine so. It's probably best if you let me tell her, in case I need to use my healing on her. Long term, I have a very close friend who's a therapist. I'll make sure Starla gives her a call."

Tears stung my eyes. "It could have all been so different."

So very different.

Liam Chadwick had been right: The truth hurt.

Chapter Thirty

Later that afternoon, I was back at As You Wish, my mind whirling with information. I'd left Cherise and Evan upstairs with Starla after sitting with her through the initial explanation of Kyle's illness. We'd simply let her feel what she was feeling. There had been tears. Many tears. But also anger and frustration and confusion. Before I finally came downstairs, there had been talk of another sleeping spell.

Despite the freakishness of being mostly dead, I gave a hearty stamp of approval on that. It was infinitely better than letting her thoughts run rampant and being unable to silence the voice in her head reminding her of the hell she'd lived through the past two years and how it could have been so different.

I'd just settled onto the sofa with a mug of coffee, the diary, and my reading glasses when I heard a rooster crowing at the back door.

Archie.

Missy followed me as I opened the door to Archie, who flew inside in a blurry colorful haze. He settled on the kitchen countertop and shuddered. "I've been flying here, there, everywhere this morning. I'm freezing my feathers off, I tell you."

"Sounds like you need a tropical vacation, too."

He closed his eyes and *hmmm*ed. "If only."

"Did you get in touch with the Elder?"

"Indeed," Archie said. "She will see you now."

I perked up. "Really?"

Clearing his throat, he said, "'*Really, really.*'"

I bit my cheek and absently said, "*Shrek.*"

"Drat. I'm leaving. Can you get the door?"

I obliged, and as he flew off I heard him mumble something about molting.

I glanced at Missy. "He really is a strange bird."

She barked.

Dashing around the house, I quickly prepped for my trek through the woods. Boots, scarf, gloves, cloak, fortitude.

Instead of bothering anyone, I left a note on the counter and left to see the Elder.

I hoped she'd have the answer that cracked this case wide open.

For the second time in a week, I made my way through the Enchanted Woods to the Elder's meadow. This time when I arrived, it was alive with the colors and warmth of spring. Wildflowers of every hue dotted the landscape and the mushroom-shaped tree had perked up, its silver-green leaves glistening in the sunshine.

A tree-trunk stool appeared in the clearing, and I made my way over to it and sat down.

"Good afternoon, Darcy," the Elder said.

"Is it?" I asked. "I don't think so."

"Ah, I see you're still in the midst of your birthday-week discontent."

Tears gathered in my eyes.

"Darcy?"

"Actually, my current discontent has nothing to do with my birthday. It's this case. I need your help."

"Do you?" she said in such a way that I began to doubt myself.

"I do. I can't quite put the pieces together."

"I heard you're handling everything quite well on your own."

I had a feeling I knew the feathered friend who'd been relaying the information. "I suspect that Kyle's body was moved from his tree house to Starla's by using the Special Delivery Spell."

"Interesting."

I explained about the video. "I'm hoping that a Crafter using magic to move a murder victim's body is an infraction of Craft Law."

"It would be, yes," she said.

"So then you know who used the spell?"

There was a long stretch of silence before she said, "There's been no infraction of the Special Delivery Spell."

"How is that possible?" I asked. "It's the only thing that makes sense. Unless he transported *himself* to Starla's town house . . ."

"Crafters cannot use that spell to teleport themselves, Darcy. Only objects."

Damn. So he hadn't moved himself. Maybe the Special Delivery Spell was a wild-goose chase. "There was a warning about the spell, but Melina's journal didn't say what it was. Does it have to do with burns? From the incandescence?"

"Good deduction, Darcy. Yes, burns are a side effect of the spell, which is why it's not commonly used. A burn results where the transfer object comes in contact with the skin."

"He had a burn on his leg . . . which also leads me to the Mirage Spell he cast over himself." I told her about the medical examiner's office. "Nick said it really freaked them out."

She laughed and the noise shook me to my core. I'd heard the melodic sound before. It was so . . . familiar, but I couldn't place it for the life of me. I wished she'd keep on laughing until my brain put it together. "I'll bet."

"Do we need to memory cleanse the lot of them?"

"I'll handle it," she said.

I'm not sure I wanted to know how.

"Anyway," I went on, "when Kyle was found, he had two visible wounds: an injection site and the burn. Why weren't they covered by the mirage?"

"If he was under the Mirage Spell, the only way those wounds would have been visible is if they were inflicted after the Mirage Spell had already been cast. He would have had to cast a new spell to cover those specific wounds."

After. I guessed that made sense. Whoever killed him might not have known about the Mirage Spell.

"Or," the Elder continued.

"What?" I asked.

"If the wounds were inflicted after he had already died."

Chapter Thirty-one

Late the next morning, the sun was trying to peek out from behind a layer of thin clouds as Starla and I sat in the car staring at the front entrance of a funeral home that was located a couple of miles outside the village, in Salem proper.

She'd come to me early this morning with the request to come here.

"There's something I need to do, and I don't want to go alone. I was hoping you'd come with me. I'd like to get there before his service, which is at noon. I don't really want to see anyone else. I just want some alone time with him. To"—her voice cracked—*"say good-bye."*

Which was why my car was currently the only vehicle in the lot besides the hearse that was parked in the carport next to the building. I adjusted the temperature down a notch as the car idled and surreptitiously looked at Starla. We'd been sitting here five minutes now and she hadn't said a word and hadn't made a move to go inside the building.

I fought off a yawn. I'd spent most of the night at the

Pixie Cottage, getting the pants beat off me in gin rummy. Mrs. P was . . . failing. It was the only way to describe it. I'd tried to focus all my attention on her, but I kept turning around and around my talk with the Elder. I was still confused why only two of Kyle's wounds were visible, and if they, like the duct tape, were some sort of message. But now I also wondered when he'd *received* the wounds. Before he died. Or after.

I glanced at Starla. I wasn't going to rush her, but I was very curious as to what was going through her mind. A few times I'd seen the funeral director peek out the door at us. I'd called him earlier to tell him we'd be stopping by. He promised to have everything ready for Starla to spend a few minutes with Kyle.

After a few more minutes, she finally said, "I'm sorry. I know we should go in, but I can't quite bring myself to."

Shifting to face her, I said, "Do you want to go home?"

Her lip quirked into what should have been a smile but looked slightly manic. "Where's that, Darcy? My home . . ." She shook her head. "I have to move. Evan's already started looking for new places for us. I can't live there knowing that's where Kyle died."

"That's understandable."

Her nose wrinkled. "Is it? Because it seems kind of foolish when I start thinking hard about it. Packing everything up, putting the house on the market, finding another place. We'll probably lose money on the deal because I'm ready to sell it to the first person who offers, no matter how low the bid, and that seems silly in light of all Evan's and my hard work to buy the house in the first place."

"If walking through that front door every day is going to bring back bad memories, then it's time to sell. Your peace of mind is too important."

A flush reddened her cheeks. "That's what Evan said, too." Letting out a frustrated huff, she added, "I don't know how to feel. Sadness, anger, confusion . . . all these emotions are just jumbled up inside."

"Oh, Starla. They'll unjumble over time."

Watery eyes glanced at me. "Is unjumble a word?"

"It is now."

Releasing a gusty exhale, she leaned back in her seat. After a few seconds, she said, "We should go inside before others start arriving."

I had to ask again. "Are you sure you want to do this?"

"I have to do it. I have some things I need to say, and I need to give these back to him." She unfurled her fist to reveal her and Kyle's gold wedding bands in the palm of her hand, glinting in the emerging sunlight.

"Both of them?" He'd gone to so much trouble to give them to her.

"I think they should be buried with him." Her voice was thick with emotion. "That way a little piece of me will always be with him. A good piece. The day he put that ring on my finger was the happiest of my whole life. That's what I want to remember. That's what I want for him to take with him. I think that's why he gave them to *me*. But I don't need these to remember that day. I have it here." She thumped her chest over her heart.

Unshed tears stung my eyes, my nose. "Okay."

"Let's go in." Pushing open the door, she quickly slammed it shut behind her and hustled to the front steps of the funeral home without waiting for me. It was as though once she finally made up her mind to go inside she didn't want to slow down for fear of having a change of heart.

I turned off the car and sprinted after her, catching up just as the funeral director came to a stop in front of one of the viewing rooms. He excused himself and quietly disappeared down the hallway, leaving us alone.

Well, mostly alone. I caught a glimpse of an open casket and touched Starla on the arm. "I'll wait out here for you," I said, wanting to give her privacy.

Looking as fragile as I'd ever seen her, she nodded and stepped into the room.

I pressed my back to the wall and stared down at the carpeting, my gaze tracing its intricate pattern. When I heard Starla's voice, I peeked into the room and saw her seated on a folding chair next to the casket. She looked to be having a conversation with Kyle while continually wiping tears from her eyes.

I bit my lip and decided pacing the halls would be a better use of my time.

I'd been pacing for a good fifteen minutes when I heard someone say my name.

"Darcy. What a surprise." Cora Chadwick approached me slowly.

Quickly, I explained about accompanying Starla.

Cora's hand flew to her mouth. "She came?"

I said, "She wanted to say good-bye."

Cora nodded. Grief had aged her these past few days, deepening the lines around her eyes, her mouth. "I'm glad. I feared she wouldn't."

I had so many questions to ask Cora, but I couldn't bring myself to voice them. Not here, not like this. Today she was a mother burying her son. There would be time enough for questions later.

"How long has she been with him?" Cora asked, glancing down the hallway.

I glanced at a wall clock. "About twenty minutes."

Looking over her shoulder at the parking lot, she said, "Others will be arriving soon."

"I'll let Starla know." I turned but stopped when I felt a hand on my arm.

Cora said, "Let me go. There're some things I want to speak to Starla about."

"I'm not sure this is the best time. . . ."

"It is," Cora said firmly, giving me a kind smile.

She walked down the hallway and stepped into the viewing room. As much as I wanted to eavesdrop, I refrained. As I passed a window, I noticed a car pull into the lot and park next to mine.

Liam, Will, and George.

Fabulous.

I tried to blend in with the striped wallpaper as the three entered. One by one, they noticed me, and one by one, each of their grim faces turned dark and stormy.

I silently hoped Starla would wrap up her visit soon, but I'd never actually ask her to. She needed this time, and if that meant that I had to tolerate the Chadwicks, then I would.

"What are you doing here?" Liam said.

"I came with Starla."

All three heads snapped toward the viewing room. They seemed to do everything in tandem.

"I'm surprised she came." Will tugged a cap off his head, releasing a plume of blond hair. It fluffed out around his face, making him look somewhat angelic.

False advertising, I decided.

I wasn't about to defend Starla's reasoning, so I shrugged and began to pace again.

When Liam stepped toward the viewing room, as though planning to interrupt Starla's time with Kyle, I reached out and grabbed his arm. "Leave her be."

He glared at my hand. "Let me go."

My temper spiked. "You all had your chance to say good-bye to him. Let her have hers." I let go of his arm.

"We don't know what you mean. Chief Sawyer only shared the autopsy results with us this morning," George said, rocking on his heels.

I could feel my face heating as I said, "Look, I don't know what happened to Kyle exactly—not yet at least—but I can't stand here while you pretend you didn't know he was ill." I pointed at Liam. "You let him use your ID for health insurance, and you"—I motioned to Will—"accompanied him to doctors' appointments. I'm sure the oncologist can ID you well enough. So just drop the act. I can't stomach it today. My best friend just learned that she's been living a lie for two years—a lie no one bothered to correct—and that the man who she loved more than life itself—" I broke off, too choked up to go on.

Anger darkened Liam's eyes. "She should have known something was wrong."

I gathered my composure as best I could. "Did *you* know something was wrong?"

"I wasn't married to him," he said.

"No, you were his brother. His flesh and blood. His twin."

He kept his voice low as he spat, "Don't try and turn this around on me, Darcy."

I put my hands on my hips. "Then don't try to act like this was Starla's fault. It only makes you look ignorant. You all may want to gloss over it, but the fact is he hurt her. Just because he had an excuse as to why it happened doesn't change the fact that he almost killed her. She's as much a victim in this as all of you are. Including Kyle."

"Stop it," George said, stepping between us. "This is not what Kyle would have wanted."

I stepped back, folding my arms over my chest.

George looked between his sons, then said, "About six months after Kyle broke out of jail, he had a seizure."

"Dad," Will began.

George held up his hand. "Enough is enough. I'm tired of the deception. Will took Kyle to the hospital, and Kyle received the devastating diagnosis. He didn't want Starla to know. He felt as though he'd hurt her enough—he didn't want her to have to watch him die. He thought it was best that way. We all took turns caring for him. He talked about seeing Starla one last time to give her back his wedding band, but we didn't know he actually had the ability to do it until all hell broke loose last Friday."

What he said rang true, especially the part about the spell. They'd all been so vehement that it was impossible for Kyle to have been stalking Starla.

"Which one of you broke into the police station to get the wedding band?" I asked.

None of them said anything.

"The same person who broke him out of jail in the first place?"

Still nothing.

"Fine, which one of you framed Starla for his death?" I asked, narrowing my gaze on Liam.

"None of us," George said. "We . . . we don't know what happened to him and don't know how he got to Starla's house."

What did I expect? Harboring a fugitive was far less a crime than a mercy killing. I shook my head. "Right."

I was saved from more lies by the sound of a car door slamming.

We all glanced out. Glinda Hansel had arrived.

My word. Could this day get any worse?

She'd managed to change out of her robe, opting for a tea-length black dress, black tights, and had swapped slippers for heels. Gripping the neckline of the capelet she wore, she limped her way up the steps of the funeral home.

As she walked into the lobby, she saw Will first and said, "I brought Kyle's watch." She held it out for him to take. Then she must have realized everyone was acting strangely, because she looked from face to face.

When she got to mine, I smiled and scrunched my nose. "Hello," I said cheerily.

Handing the watch to Will, she glared at me. She was back to looking gorgeous. Perfect hair, perfect makeup. I was actually glad to see her looking more herself, though I couldn't understand why I cared.

"What are you doing here?" she fumed.

"You all make me feel so welcome," I said. "Really, it's like a big hug."

Glinda opened her mouth, then suddenly snapped it closed again. She stared over my shoulder.

Cora and Starla stood in the hallway. Both had tear-streaked faces, and Cora had her arm around Starla as they came toward us.

Awkward, party of seven.

Cora finally broke the ice saying, "I think we all will live with regrets for what has happened these past couple of years and wonder what life would have been like had we known Kyle was so ill."

Ah, Starla must have been hearing the same speech George had just given me.

"No matter how much we'd like to, we cannot change what has been done," Cora said. "However, we can change how we go forward. Forgive and never forget that Kyle would want us all to be happy and move forward and mend what's been broken."

"Come on," Liam said angrily, grabbing Will's arm. "I've heard enough."

Glinda hobbled after them.

With a depth of sadness in her eyes, Cora stepped

next to her husband and watched her sons stride down the hallway toward the viewing room. She patted Starla's arm but didn't say anything about the brothers' behavior.

"We should go," Starla said to me.

Studying her, I saw that she looked a little bit . . . lighter. As though some sort of weight had been lifted off her shoulders. Apparently speaking to Kyle had been the best thing for her right now.

Cora gave her a gentle hug. "Don't be a stranger, okay?"

In the car, Starla slipped on a pair of sunglasses and looked out the side window. Her body language clearly said that she didn't want to talk, so I let her be.

I didn't need to fix everything.

I checked my phone for messages and saw that Nick had tried to call three times. A voice mail just told me to call him as soon as I could. My pulse kicked up a notch. He must have news.

"You know what's kind of ironic?" Starla asked.

"What's that?"

"Cora said Kyle didn't want me to see him ill. It's probably why he used the Mirage Spell when he visited me, to cover how his cancer had changed his looks." She shifted to face me. "Yet, the spell wore off, and in his casket he looked . . . ravaged."

I gripped my car keys so tightly they cut into the skin of my palm. I didn't know if that was irony or just some strange twist of fate.

"So basically," she said, "he put me through two years of misery for nothing."

And with that, she didn't say another word the whole way home.

Chapter Thirty-two

I dropped Starla at As You Wish and called Nick as I took a long, slow walk over to see Mrs. P.

"Sorry," I said when he answered. "I was at the funeral home with Starla."

"The funeral home?"

"Oh yeah," I said wryly. "It was all kinds of good times."

"I can imagine."

I wished there was something I could do for Starla, but at this point, I figured only time could help her heal. I needed to tell Nick about my conversation with the Chadwicks, but wanted to know why he needed to talk with me so badly. My curiosity was killing me. "You called?"

I heard him let out a sigh. "The ME's office called."

"And?"

"The cause of death is in. Darcy, Kyle died of natural causes. Basically, his tumor grew into the part of his brain that controlled respiration. He simply stopped breathing."

I leaned against a lamppost. "What? What about the injection?"

"It was determined that the injection was delivered postmortem. The morphine never made it into his bloodstream."

I let that sink in. "After death?"

The Elder had planted the seed that the injection could have been after Kyle died, but I still couldn't figure out why. "Why?"

"Someone obviously wanted us to believe he was murdered."

"Someone was trying to frame Starla, not to cover up a mercy killing, but out of . . . what? Spite?"

"It seems that way, yes."

My anger skipped simmer and went straight to boil. I could easily picture Liam earlier at the funeral home.

She should have known something was wrong.

Liam blamed Starla for his brother's death, so why wouldn't he take it a step forward and frame her?

Foul is fair.

"Liam," I bit out, explaining the confrontation in the funeral home.

"I'm going to wait until Kyle's funeral is over, then question his family again. And, yes, especially Liam."

"He can't get away with it, can he? Did he tamper with a body? Hinder an investigation? *Something?*"

His voice softened. "Yes, something. Don't worry, Darcy. I'll take care of it. You think you can stop by? I want to make sure I understand the Craft facets of this case before I talk to the family again."

I glanced at the Pixie Cottage. "I'm just about to check on Mrs. P, but as soon as I'm done there, I'll be over."

"I'll be waiting."

I hung up and slipped my phone in my pocket. All around me, I tried to take in the beauty of the village. To find the good in the bad.

But try as I might, right now all I could see was the bad.

A few minutes later, I stood in the hallway outside Mrs. P's room. I drew in a deep breath, gathered what little composure I had left, and knocked gently. "It's Darcy."

A soft "Come in" floated through the door.

I slipped inside and found Cherise sitting near the fireplace, glued to her smartphone. She gave me a sad smile as I came in.

My gaze zipped to the bed where I found Mrs. P with her eyes closed. Pepe sat next to her shoulder and was reading to her from *Alice's Adventures in Wonderland*, his French accent charmingly endearing.

He nodded at my presence and kept on reading.

I crept over to the bed and pressed a kiss to the top of Mrs. P's head, which was still covered in a pink turban wrap. She looked so frail that it nearly broke my heart straight in half. I was pleased to see she still wore her beloved makeup and had the feeling someone had helped her apply it — her fake eyelashes were on straight.

Cherise set her phone on the coffee table, and as she crossed her ankles, she kicked the medical bag on the floor. It toppled onto its side, the contents spilling out.

She laughed softly and said, "You can't take me anywhere. How is Starla?"

I helped her scoop items back into the bag. "I think she's going through emotional whiplash. She went from hating Kyle, fearing him, to being sad for him. Sad for herself. She's filled with regrets and just a touch of anger."

"Understandable, no?"

"Definitely." I handed her a blood pressure cuff. "On top of that, she's also dealing with her feelings for Vince."

Cherise *tsk*ed. "It seems too much for one to bear, but Starla is strong. She'll find her way."

I hoped she was right. I reached for an EpiPen, but it rolled out of my grasp, under the settee.

As I crouched to retrieve it, I had such a flash of déjà vu that I gasped.

"Darcy?"

"Do you have a syringe?" I asked in a rush.

Her eyebrows dipped. "Of course. Why?"

"Can I see it?"

She dug around the bag and came out with a syringe. I examined the clear plastic tube, the plunger, the needle protected by a long, thin cap.

Suddenly, I knew why my fingerprints had been on

the syringe that had been used on Kyle. I'd touched it. At his tree house, the morning I'd found his body. It had been the object on the floor near his nightstand, and as I'd gone to pick it up, it had rolled out of my grasp. Then I'd been distracted by Harper and forgotten all about it. Until now.

"My dear, what's wrong?" Cherise asked. "You've lost all color in your face."

My mind raced to connect the dots. If the syringe had been at the tree house, it should have been logged into the evidence locker by the police. How did it get into the Dumpster behind Starla's?

I could only come up with one conclusion that made sense, and it alternately made my blood boil and my heart ache from the fallout it would cause.

"Darcy?" Cherise gently tucked my hair behind my ear. "What's wrong? Did you jab yourself?"

I gave my head a shake. "No." I handed her the syringe. "Just feeling the sting of ultimate betrayal."

Pepe stopped reading and glanced at me over the top of his glasses. My heart thrummed with the theory my brain was piecing together. How oblivious I'd been to what was right in front of me this whole time! Only I hadn't been able to see it, but not because of a Mirage Spell. No, this was because I never dreamed a person could stoop so low. I'd been so naive. But how far did the betrayal go? And could I prove it?

"Maybe you should lie down," Cherise said.

"I'm all right. Really." I had to deal with this, but there was time for that.

Pepe went back to reading, managing to keep his voice mellow and melodious.

"How is she?" I asked, motioning to Mrs. P.

"Her heart is weakening quickly. She fainted earlier and gave Pepe quite the scare."

Cherise patted my hand, then squeezed it. Her gaze was soft, her tone gentle as she said, "Eugenia's time has almost come. It won't be long now."

Pepe stopped midsentence, glanced at us, then went back to reading, his voice cracking slightly.

"There's nothing you can do?"

She shook her head. "I'm very sorry."

Not as sorry as I was.

Cherise leaned in. "Pepe hasn't left her side."

Which meant it was going to be all that much harder for him to say good-bye when the time came. My chest ached. "He's a good friend."

Poor Pepe. It was unusual how close he'd grown to Mrs. P over these past few days, but there was no denying that he had. "Indeed."

"I'll stay with her tonight as well and try to make her as comfortable as possible, but Darcy, it's time to gather her loved ones to start saying good-bye."

It hurt to even contemplate.

"If you'd like, I can make some phone calls. . . ." Cherise offered.

Numbly, I nodded. "Thank you."

"Is that Darcy I hear?" Mrs. P murmured.

I popped off the couch and made it across the room in two long strides. The bed dipped as I sat on its edge. "I'm here."

Mrs. P smiled tremulously as I took hold of her hand. She said, "I'm glad I didn't miss your visit. I'm like Rip Van Winkle these days. *Zzzzzz.*"

"Better than Ichabod Crane," I said.

She laughed, but even her cackle had lost its luster. "Ain't that the truth."

"Do you need anything?" I asked. "Something to eat? To drink? A puzzle?"

Smiling, she patted my cheek. "I've got everything I need. But, doll?"

Worry had crept into her sleepy eyes.

"What?"

"I don't think I'll be able to make your birthday dinner."

I knelt next to the bed. "We'll bring it here. No problem."

With a tip of her head and a knowing look in her eyes, she said, "Just in case that doesn't work out, I just want you to know that I hope all your birthday wishes come true. They're magical you know, birthday wishes, so make sure you come up with some good ones."

"I will," I promised.

Tears pooled on my lashes as her eyelids fluttered closed again, and I glanced at her chest to make sure it still rose and fell. It did. She'd fallen back to sleep.

My gaze met Pepe's and I feared that what I saw in his eyes—the raw sorrow—was mirrored in my own gaze. There was nothing I could say to offer comfort. Not when my own heart hurt so much. I stood up and whispered, "There's something I have to do, but I'll be back in a little bit."

Mrs. P's eyes slowly opened. Her sleepy gaze fastened onto my face and she smiled again. "Leaving without saying good-bye, doll?"

"Never." I barely choked out the word.

"Good, good." She reached for my hand. "But instead of saying good-bye how about we say 'see you later' instead? Good-byes always seem so sad, and I don't want you to be sad."

Gently, I squeezed her gnarled fingers and forced the words from my parched throat. "I'll see you later, Mrs. P."

"Ain't that better?" she asked Pepe.

"*Oui,*" he murmured, polishing the lenses on his glasses with the hem of his vest. "Much better."

I bent and gave her velvety soft cheek a kiss, waved to Cherise, then turned and walked out of the room.

In the hallway, I leaned against the wall, took a deep shaky breath, and let the tears fall.

Chapter Thirty-three

With pieces of my heart breaking off with every breath I drew in, there was only one place I wanted to be. With Nick.

It was such a startling revelation that I stopped short and my feet nearly flew out from beneath me on the slippery sidewalk. I grabbed onto the Pixie Cottage's picket fence and held on much tighter than necessary for a simple stumble.

Because it was more than a tumble. My whole world had just shifted a bit.

I knew I cared for Nick—deeply. But I hadn't realize just how much I'd come to depend on him over the last few months for comfort, support . . . *love*. I was so used to being independent, not needing a man—not needing anyone, really—that I'd barely noticed how I had fallen head over heels in love with him.

I loved him.

"Love," I murmured, testing the word aloud.

It sounded right. It sounded better than right. It was perfect. And I had to tell him.

Shoving away from the fence, I started jogging toward Nick's house. I was halfway down his street when I noticed him running toward me. It was like something out of a Hollywood cliché, two lovers with outstretched arms racing in slow motion toward each other in a field of wildflowers, with orchestral music rising in crescendo. But right now, cliché or no, amid snowbanks instead of wildflowers, my broken heart fluttered, and grew full to bursting with each and every beat.

Until . . .

"Grab him!" Nick shouted.

Confused, I slowed to a stop. The crescendo faded away.

"Grab him!" Nick yelled again, motioning to something darting into the street.

My romantic vision evaporated as I saw what he was pointing to. Clarence was dodging between parked cars. "For the love," I cried, borrowing Harper's favorite phrase. I pivoted, leapt a puddle, and jumped in front of the dog.

He spotted me and started wagging his tail. Maybe he did like me better than Glinda. Smart little guy. But then he heard Nick's footsteps and scampered away again.

I gave chase, Nick hot on my heels. "Clarence!" I called.

The puppy stopped, turned, wagged. Snow covered his snout, making him look like he had a white mustache.

I held up a hand to Nick, motioning for him to stop so he wouldn't startle the dog again. I crouched down. "Here, Clarence. Come here, buddy."

More wagging, but he didn't move.

I duckwalked closer to him and held out my hand for him to sniff. His little nose shot into the air, nostrils flaring. His rear wiggled.

"It's okay, Clarence. Remember me?"

He took a step toward me, then looked back over his shoulder as though seeing his freedom slipping away. Just as he was about to dash off, I dove at him. I came up with a wiggly puppy and a face full of snow.

Nick leaned down and brushed snow off my cheeks.

Clarence licked my face.

I looked between the two of them and giggled. That giggle blossomed into a laugh. "Wildflowers!" I cried.

"Wildflowers?" Nick repeated, puzzled.

"And crescendos." And before I knew it, I was laughing so hard I couldn't catch my breath.

Suddenly, I found myself hiccupping. Then the tears came, and I couldn't stop them from falling. And just like that, my heart finally cracked.

"Darcy?" Nick gathered me into his arms, Clarence wedged between us. "What's wrong?"

I tried to talk, but I couldn't get the words out past the tightness in my throat. It had all come crashing down on me, the emotions from this week. Starla's devastation. Mrs. P's illness. My theory of what happened to Kyle . . .

Nick whisked tears from my face as fast as they fell. "Come on, shhh," he soothed, helping me to my feet.

Clarence licked my chin, Nick's hand, the snow from his nose.

I sniffled and snuffled as we walked back to his house, and I brokenly told him about Mrs. P.

"Is that why you were running just now? To tell me?"

"Kind of. I needed . . ."

He nudged my chin so I'd look at him. "Needed . . . ?"

I needed to tell you I love you.

"Darcy?"

I tried to look deep into his brown eyes, but moisture in my own made them blurry. *Say it. Just say it.* "I needed . . . you."

"Me?" He thumbed another tear from my cheek.

I nodded.

Taking deep breaths, I tried to pull myself together. Nick stared at me for a few seconds, then leaned in and kissed me. Which made me lose my breath all over again.

When he pulled away, I saw sadness had darkened his eyes.

"Mimi and I will go to see Mrs. P as soon as Mimi gets home from school."

"She'd like that," I said, stepping onto the porch. Loud

woofs echoed through the door, and Clarence instantly perked up and barked back, an adorable *arf*.

"These two are apparently BFFs now," Nick said, eyebrows raised.

"Mimi been teaching you teen lingo?"

"Always." He went in ahead of me to get Higgins under control, but as soon as I was inside, Clarence wiggled and squirmed until I set him down. He went straight to Higgins, and the two circled and sniffed.

Nick hung my coat on the newel post and ducked into the powder room. He came back with a handful of tissues. "I take it you and Clarence know each other?"

"We go way back," I said, wiping my eyes, my nose. I couldn't stop sniffling. "He's a licker."

He laughed. "There are worse things. Well, your old friend came to visit Higgins. He's not wearing a collar and took off when I tried to get him into the house."

"What happened to your collar, Clarence?" I asked him.

He stopped sniffing Higgins and glanced at me. After deciding Higgins was more interesting, he went back to his exploration.

"He had one," I said, shrugging. "It was blue. It was really loose, though, so it probably slipped off when he ran away. I heard he's an escape artist."

"Who does he belong to? I've never seen him around here."

"I'm not sure. I met him through Glinda." I bit my cheek at the name. "She said she was watching him for a friend."

"I'll call her," Nick said, picking up his cell phone from the console table by the door.

I sat on the sofa and dropped my head back on the cushion. Hellish day. Hellish, hellish day. I didn't quite know how to break my theory on Kyle's death to Nick.

"She's not answering her home line," he said. "I'll try her cell."

"Look." I nodded toward the dogs. They lay in a heap of gold and rust on Higgins' dog bed, plumb worn out.

"I'm not keeping him," Nick said, hanging up the phone. "She's not answering her cell, either."

"She's probably still with the Chadwicks. I saw her with them earlier at the funeral home."

He glanced at his watch. "It's a little after one. Kyle's service is probably just wrapping up."

"I called the number on Clarence's tag the other day, but hung up before anyone answered. It's still in here." I wiggled my cell from my pocket and eyed his watch. It had triggered another memory, another piece of the puzzle. I found the number in my log and handed him my phone.

Blowing out a breath, he glanced at my cell phone. Then looked back at me. "This is the number from Clarence's tag?"

"Yeah," I said, wondering at the strange tone in his voice. "Why?"

"I know this number. I've dialed it a million times over the last few days."

"You have?"

"Darcy, this is the number Liam dialed the other night while at As You Wish."

"Well," I said, shaking my head. "I wish that surprised me. It doesn't."

"Why's that? Because it's pretty shocking to me. That dog probably belonged to Kyle."

"Because," I said, "I think I was wrong about Liam. Glinda is the one who framed Starla."

"Why?" he asked. "Why do you think Glinda did it?"

"I realized today why my fingerprints were on the syringe." I walked him through how I'd found the syringe at Kyle's tree house. "I actually don't think she meant to incriminate me in any way. I just think she pocketed the syringe when the police arrived that morning—probably didn't realize she'd dropped it the night before. She didn't have any way to know my prints were on it."

"Why weren't her prints on it?"

"Probably wiped it clean after injecting Kyle, then accidentally dropped it in her hurry to empty the tree house."

He paced. "It seems like a stretch. Liam could have found the syringe, too, and taken it."

I understood his reluctance to accept my theory. As much as he didn't want to admit it—maybe even to himself—he'd trusted Glinda. Maybe not as a person, but as an officer. "When? I touched it. Then the police were there. . . ."

His jaw set.

"Plus, remember the other day, when you told me about Kyle's belongings in the evidence locker?"

"Yeah?"

"You said he had a watch. Did it have a silver face with a black leather strap? Big numbers on it, all jumbled instead of being clockwise?"

One of his eyebrows rose. "How'd you know that?"

I let out a breath. "Because Glinda brought it to the funeral home this afternoon."

His shoulders stiffened as I told him about the way she'd come in with it.

"Kyle really wanted his ring to give back to Starla," I said. "I guess Glinda decided to grant his dying wish. And while she was there, she took everything."

I bit my lip. "Do you know if Glinda was on duty the day Kyle escaped jail?"

His gaze whipped to me, and he muttered a string of curse words under his breath.

Wincing, I said, "I take that as a yes?"

"I only know this because I was just reviewing his file. She had nothing to do with his intake, but she was there, working a desk at the time. And, surprise, surprise, some of the video cameras in the station that day didn't work properly, so we never knew exactly how he got out."

The same way the camera didn't work the day someone cast the Mirage Spell in the evidence locker.

"She double-crossed me," he said, his voice full of disbelief.

"Yes."

His eyes drifted closed. "How'd she get Kyle to Starla's?"

It was the one piece I still wasn't sure about. "I'm still trying to figure that one out."

"We need to talk to her."

She wasn't going to like that. "When?"

Anger set his lips into a grim line. "Now."

Chapter Thirty-four

My mind still spun as Nick and I drove over to Wickedly Creative. Clarence bobbled on my lap, but I kept a tight hold on him as he pressed his nose to the Bumblebeemobile's window.

I was trying to figure out how Glinda had gotten Kyle to Starla's house and kept going back to Vince's video of the brownstone that suggested the Special Delivery Spell.

But that spell didn't transport people. Only objects.

I was missing something, I could just feel it. It was making me crazy. Maybe Liam helped her in some way. . . . I sighed. Clarence looked back at me and licked my face.

"If he was Kyle's dog, maybe he needs a new home. I've been thinking that Missy needed a playmate."

"What would Tilda think of that?" Nick asked.

"Maybe Higgins would like a new roommate. Seeing as how they're already BFFs."

He glanced over and humor took some of the edge off his anger. "I'm not keeping him."

"Maybe Harper would take him. . . ."

"Maybe he doesn't need a home. One of the Chadwicks would probably want him."

Cars lined the lane in front of the Chadwicks' farmhouse—where the postfuneral reception was probably being held—so Nick turned into the parking lot adjacent to the studio.

"If that was the case," I said, "then why did Glinda have him—"

"Well, well," Nick said, cutting me off. "Look at that. I think we've found your explanation."

Glinda and Liam were locked in a tight embrace. It wasn't just any ol' hug. It was a nose to toe, full body press. When they heard the crunch of tires on the gravel lot, they split apart.

Glinda, at least, had the grace to blush.

Liam just looked angry with the world.

She had to have been the woman sharing pillow talk with Liam the night Pepe was spying. Then something else he'd said nearly made me laugh out loud.

There was an enormous yellow beast with big brown eyes and sharp teeth watching me watch the room.

Clarence's tongue lolled. I couldn't wait to tease Pepe about the "beast" he'd encountered at Liam's apartment.

"Ready?" Nick asked, shutting off the car and opening his door.

"As I'll ever be."

Liam started toward us. "This isn't a great time."

"It never will be," Nick said.

"What's this about?" Glinda asked.

I lifted Clarence out of the car. "I think we have something that belongs to you. Or should I say Kyle?" Clarence slurped my cheek.

Liam glanced back at Glinda. She said, "I told you he's an escape artist."

He squirmed in my arms when he heard her voice. Maybe he wasn't as smart as I thought he was.

The back door to the farmhouse opened, and Cora and George came out. They headed toward us.

"What's this about?" George asked. "Couldn't it wait?"

"Not really," Nick said.

"Let's go in the studio then," Cora said. "It's warmer in there."

The older couple led the way, with Liam and a limping Glinda behind them. Nick put his arm around me as we followed them inside. I set Clarence down as soon as the door closed, and he rushed straight over to Liam.

Liam picked him up, and I admit I felt a pang as the dog licked Liam's chin.

"What's so important that it couldn't wait?" George asked as Will opened the studio's door and slipped inside.

"When you didn't come back," Will said, "I thought I'd join you." He stood next to his brother. Clarence tried to lick him, too.

Huh. It was probably for the best. Tilda would have been really put out if I'd brought him home with me.

"Just trying to tie up some loose ends," Nick said. "The final autopsy report came in. Kyle died of natural causes."

Cora slumped against her husband.

George looked confused and said, "The morphine?"

"Never reached his bloodstream," Nick answered. "It was administered after death."

I glanced around. All the Chadwicks looked genuinely shocked at this news. But not Glinda. She was busy with a loose string on her cuff.

"I don't understand," Will said, looking around.

I said, "I think Glinda might be able to help you with an explanation. Right, Glinda?"

She met curious looks with a defiant glare. "I don't know what you're talking about."

"I think you do," I said.

"Glinda?" George's gaze shifted between us. "I don't understand."

"She's the one who gave him the shot of morphine," I said. "She's the one who put him in Starla's apartment. She's the one who planted the syringe and duct tape to frame Starla."

"You're delusional," she said to me.

"We also suspect she's the one who helped him break out of jail and stole his belongings out of the evidence locker."

"Those are vastly different charges than framing Starla for murder," Cora said, her hand at her throat. "Glinda wouldn't do that."

"No, she wouldn't," Will said. "Besides, she didn't know where he was. She never knew his location. Only the family."

George put his arm around his wife. "You don't know what you're talking about, Darcy."

I lifted an eyebrow. "Maybe her boyfriend told her."

"Glinda didn't know about the tree house," Liam said.

"I think you all underestimate Glinda. She would have made it her business to know where Kyle was. And Will and Liam didn't exactly cover their tracks all that well. After all, Harper followed you fairly easily."

"This makes no sense," Will said. "Even if she knew where the tree house was, she certainly couldn't have known he had died that night." He glanced at Nick. "You did say it was natural causes?"

Nick nodded.

"Maybe not, but she was working the night Kyle visited Starla at As You Wish. Maybe Liam called her and told her about the incident. Or maybe she heard the news at the police station. It doesn't really matter. All that matters is that she went to check on Kyle. And when she found him already dead, she hatched a plan."

Liam's brow furrowed as though working through the plausibility of this scenario.

Will said to his brother, "You did call her from the Cauldron, after we left As You Wish."

"Leave Liam out of this," Glinda snapped. "He had nothing to do with it."

And right then something else Pepe said came back to me.

They were speculating what could have happened to Kyle and how long it would take before it was revealed that his death could not have been a suicide.

If they had been speculating about what happened,

then clearly Liam didn't know what had happened to Kyle's body. After all, they were in the privacy of a bedroom. There was no reason not to speak openly.

Nick stood at my shoulder, showing with his presence that he supported what I was saying, and let me go on. "It's interesting, Glinda, isn't it?"

"What?" she said through clenched teeth.

"Just the other day you were saying that I had a perfect ready-made family in Nick and Mimi—something you always wanted."

I felt Nick tense—I hadn't told him that part.

"But it seems to me that these people, George and Cora and Liam and Will and probably Kyle, were *your* ready-made family. I mean, look at the way they jumped to your defense."

Tears shimmered in her eyes. "What's your point?"

"So why," I said softly, "did you put them all through the misery of wondering what happened to Kyle? Unless . . . it wasn't about them. Or Kyle. Or even Starla. Was it about hurting me?"

She let out a strangled cry. "Why is everything always about you?"

"Because you made it that way."

"I despise you," she said, limping toward me to get into my face.

"Girls!" George said, stepping in between us. "Whoa now."

He was a brave man, because Glinda had her claws out.

It was then that I noticed she wore an ACE bandage under her black tights. But it wasn't wrapped around her ankle—it was around her lower leg.

"What are you staring at?" she hissed.

And now that I thought about it, the other day in her slippers . . . her ankle hadn't been the least bit bruised. The last piece of the puzzle clicked into place. "I thought you twisted your ankle?"

She said, "I did."

I lifted my eyebrows. "Then you need an anatomy lesson."

"And you need to go to hell, Darcy."

Nick tensed behind me as I glared. "I don't think there's room for both of us."

"Gah!" she cried. "You think you're so smart. *If* I was behind what happened to Kyle, it wouldn't have been to hurt you, though that is a fringe benefit, I admit."

"Glinda?" Liam asked.

She waved him off. "If I did it, it would be because I hated the way Starla had acted when she saw him. Like he was some sort of monster."

"To her he was," I said.

"But he wasn't," she said, her beautiful features twisted in pain. "It was only because he'd been sick. I thought Starla ought to see how it felt to be accused of something she didn't do. To feel the backlash. The shame. The confusion of realizing people actually believed she could do such a thing. And to realize that she wasn't perfect, either—I mean, how could she be? With you as a best friend?"

I let the comment slide, hoping she'd keep spewing information.

"Starla was fully prepared to kill him if she had to," Glinda said. "Which just proves that anyone can be pushed to the limit under certain circumstances."

"Fair is foul," I said, quoting the other part of the quote Glinda had left on the duct tape.

"Exactly," she said.

"Oh, Glinda," Cora said softly.

"How did you move him?" Will asked.

Liam kept silent, holding Clarence.

"I think you should go," Glinda said to Nick and me. "You've infringed enough. And you can't prove I did anything."

She was mostly right. There was no way to prove she was the one to break Kyle out of jail or steal his belongings. But . . . "I don't need to," I said. "Your limp is all the evidence I need that you moved Kyle."

A dash of fear flickered in her eyes. "You're crazy."

"Nick, which of Kyle's leg had a burn?"

"His right."

Everyone's gaze went to her right leg, where the ACE bandage was barely visible through her tights.

"We can let the Elder settle it. I'm sure she'd be very interested to take a look at the burn on your calf. One that matches Kyle's from when you used the Special Delivery Spell on his body."

George said, "That spell doesn't work on people."

"It does when the person is dead," I said softly. Because at that point, with their spirit gone, they become an object.

"Is that a burn on your leg, Glinda?" Cora asked.

Glinda looked from face to face, and abruptly broke into sobs. "I just wanted Starla to feel what Kyle had felt."

Liam passed off Clarence and took Glinda in his arms, holding her tightly.

I couldn't help but remember Glinda's meltdown in the street.

You show up in this village all sweet and innocent, and within days, you have everyone eating out of your palm, including the Elder, who is notoriously picky. You've got a beautiful house, my dream job investigating for the Elder, a great family. You're beautiful. You're smart. You're fun. And you've got Nick and Mimi as a perfect ready-made family for you. You have everything I've ever wanted, and now you've got a cute dog, too. I hope you're happy.

Only, I wasn't happy. At all. In fact, I felt myself actually understanding why she did what she did. The Chadwicks had become her family. And like a true Chadwick, family came first. Always, even if that meant trying to teach a misguided lesson that didn't need to be learned.

Black and white. And interesting shades of gray.

Foul is fair.

The more I thought about it, the more I wondered if Glinda's message hadn't been about Kyle at all.

But about herself.

I was still wondering when my cell phone rang.

I went to silence the sound but froze when I saw the Caller ID. I glanced at Nick. "It's Cherise."

"Go. Take it."

"Hello?" I answered, heading for the studio's front door.

"Darcy, it's Cherise."

Her voice chilled me to my bones.

"I'm sorry to call you like this. . . ."

I gripped the porch railing. "She's gone, isn't she?"

There was a beat of silence. "A few minutes ago."

Drawing in a gulp of icy air, I felt my legs wobble and crouched down before I fell. Tears spilled from my eyes.

Nick opened the front door, took one look at me, and immediately dropped and wrapped his arms around me.

See you later.

But I wouldn't.

I'd never see her again.

Chapter Thirty-five

"You don't look any older," Starla said early Saturday afternoon as we headed to the Witch's Brew to get my free cup of birthday coffee. I'd almost forgotten to claim it.

"I feel older." This past week seemed to have aged me. Missy tugged on her leash.

"Are you ready for your birthday dinner?" Starla asked. "Ve's given us all orders to be on time and look extra-special."

"Ve's gone a little birthday crazy with this dinner." She was holding it at home and it had blossomed from close friends and family to a big dinner party. We were all to be seated at precisely eight o'clock for the festivities to begin. I wasn't much in the mood to celebrate—not without Mrs. P.

We passed Mrs. P's bench on the green, and I slowed to a stop.

Starla put her hand on my arm. "Can't you practically see her sitting there?"

I could. And I could hear her laugh, too. "It's so strange not having her around."

"I know."

Mrs. P's funeral had been yesterday and was raw and fresh in my memory. She'd been cremated and wanted her ashes sprinkled in the Pixie Cottage gardens, so she'd always live on in her beloved flower beds. We'd have to wait till the spring thaw before doing the actual sprinkling, so until then Harmony was keeping Mrs. P's urn in a safe place.

"Did I tell you that she wanted me to forgive Vince?" Starla said, her voice quiet.

"You didn't tell me, but it doesn't surprise me that she tried to convince you. She's a romantic at heart, and she has a soft spot for Vince."

"She told me life was too short to be unhappy." Her gaze flitted across the green, toward Lotions and Potions.

Starla had yet to speak to Vince, and I was beginning to wonder if I'd made a mistake in asking him to stick around.

"If this past week proved anything, it's that we should appreciate each and every day we have with those we love. Forgiveness has to be a big part of that, I suppose."

"Mmm," she said noncommittally. "I think I met my forgiveness quota already."

She had met with Nick yesterday to express her desire that no charges be brought against Vince for the hacking or against Glinda for bringing Kyle's body to her home. She simply wanted closure and healing and thought that would be the best way to achieve it.

The village council urged Nick to let the whole matter go. With Glinda already off the police force they wanted to just sweep the whole matter under the rug. Nick hadn't been too happy about that, but with most of his evidence being related to the Craft, he swallowed the bitter pill and agreed.

I had mixed emotions about Glinda getting off so easily. But the more I thought about it, the more I realized that whatever internal battles she faced were probably enough punishment. The last I heard the Chadwicks had closed ranks around Glinda. Liam had moved in with her and Clarence was still sneaking out. I hadn't seen her since the big showdown and didn't care if I ever saw her again.

Mrs. P would want me to forgive and forget. I could forgive what she'd done, but I wasn't sure if I could forget. And I damn well wouldn't underestimate her ever again.

"You don't think you have a little forgiveness left? A teensy bit? This much." I held two fingers a smidge apart.

"Maybe," Starla said with a slight smile. "I don't know. But enough about that." She fished in her bag and came up with a wrapped flat box. "Here."

"What's this?"

"A present, silly. Open it."

"But the party's tonight. . . ."

"*Shh*. Open it."

I couldn't help the smile as I tore into the paper. I couldn't remember the last time a nonfamily member had gotten me a birthday present.

My life had changed so drastically in a year.

For the better.

I handed Starla the discarded paper. I couldn't even imagine what was inside the package. Though it looked like a bracelet box, it was light as a feather and nothing clinked around as I shook it.

"Just open it!" Starla said, bouncing on her toes.

I carefully lifted the top off the box and stared at the pieces of paper inside. Tickets for a three-day cruise in the Bahamas. The trip was dated for next weekend.

"What do you think?" she asked immediately, still bouncing. "I know, I know. You wanted to plan it. But I wanted to surprise you with it." Her voice caught. "You've done so much for me this week, and I wouldn't have gotten through it without your support. Your friendship. There're two tickets. One for you and one for me."

Tears sprang as I hugged her. "This is too much."

"You're worth it, Darcy Merriweather."

"Thank you," I managed to say. She had no idea the gift she'd just given me—and it had nothing to do with the trip.

She linked arms with me. "Yeah, well, don't thank me yet. We have to find bathing suits in the dead of winter."

I shuddered.

"Exactly," she said as we crossed the green.

I spotted Godfrey walking out of the Bewitching Boutique with a garment rack, see us, then turn around and walk back into his shop.

"I'll be glad when the Swing and Sway dance is over and done with." I pulled open the door to the Witch's Brew. "Everyone's been acting so strangely."

She laughed, but the sound abruptly faded away as Vince walked out of the coffee shop. Her cheeks flamed red, and he immediately started stammering.

"I, ah . . ." He gestured behind him. "I . . ."

Nearby, a rooster crowed. I glanced across the street and saw Archie land in a maple tree. He motioned to me with his wing.

Vince hadn't noticed—he had eyes only for Starla.

"Why don't you two, ah, go for a walk?" I suggested. "There's something I need to do."

Starla's eyes widened, but Vince said, "Yes! A walk."

He held out his hand for her to take, and I held my breath, wondering if she'd accept the gesture.

After a painful moment, she placed her hand in his, and I could breathe again. I crossed the street and met Archie under the tree. He was watching Starla and Vince walk down the sidewalk.

He cleared his throat. "'If you love a person, you can forgive anything.'"

"I have no idea what it's from, but it's perfect."

"*The Letter*," he said, fluffing his feathers. "And I have a knack for finding just the right words."

"You're modest, too."

He laughed. "As much as I enjoy our banter, I have summoned your attention for a purpose. The Elder would like to see you at six p.m. this evening. As they say, be there or be square."

"No one says that."

"Spoilsport," he accused.

"Just pointing out the obvious. Why does the Elder want to see me?" I had already given her the full report on Starla's case, and she had proclaimed mine a job well done.

"I do not profess to know."

"I'm shocked. There's something you don't know?"

"It's a rare occurrence to be sure." He launched into the air, and circled around my head. "I shall see you tonight, birthday girl."

I watched him fly away, then headed back to the coffee shop for my birthday brew. For the first time in forever, I was determined to enjoy every minute of this day. I just hoped the Elder didn't have bad news for me.

At six o'clock on the dot, I found myself in the Elder's meadow, sitting on a tree-stump stool, feeling a little like I'd been called to the principal's office, except I wasn't sure if I had done something good or something bad.

"I imagine you're wondering why you're here."

For what felt like the hundredth time, I wondered if she could read minds. "Yes."

"I have a quick job for you."

"Oh?"

"You've heard of this dance competition happening at the Will-o'-the-Wisp tomorrow?"

"I heard," I said, humor lacing my words.

"Well, I want you to do a bit of snooping for me. I'm not entirely sure this competition is something I want associated with the village."

"Whoa now! I'm not sure I—"

She cut me off. "No excuses."

I sighed and wondered if it was possible to wash eyeballs out with soap. "What do you want me to do?"

"There is a box here near the trunk of the tree. Take it immediately to the Will-o'-the-Wisp."

"Tonight?" I asked. Ve had given me strict orders about dinner and I didn't dare disobey.

"Do you have other plans?"

"Kind of." I was a little bit stung that she didn't remember what day it was.

"Your plans shall wait. This task shall not. The side entrance of the building is unlocked. Go into the lobby and near the top of the stairs you will see a potted palm— take the box to the tree. Do not open the box until you

are at the specified location. Directions on how to use
the device are included in the box."

"Is it a camera? This all seems very Double O Seven-
ish."

"You hardly look like Daniel Craig."

"Thank goodness. That would be a little strange with
the facial hair and all."

She laughed, and again I tried to place the sound.

"Hurry up with you now," she said. "The device must
be in place soon. We are under a time constraint."

"The contest isn't until tomorrow."

"Are you talking back?"

"No ma'am," I said, shaking my head and trying not
to grin.

"Come get the box and be on your way. I'll send Archie to fetch you tomorrow for a full report of your ef-
forts."

At the base of her tree I stooped and picked up the
box. It was small, maybe big enough to hold a mug or a
ball cap. It weighed next to nothing, and I couldn't begin
to imagine what was inside. Probably some sort of magical Crafter gadget I knew nothing about. I was actually
rather curious to see what it was.

As I headed back to the trail, her voice stopped me in
my tracks. "Oh, and Darcy?"

I turned. "Yes?"

Her voice softened. "Happy birthday."

I smiled the whole way back to the village.

Chapter Thirty-six

"What do you think I should do?" Starla asked as we made our way toward the Will-o'-the-Wisp. I'd stopped by home to tell Ve that I had to run an errand and Starla volunteered to come with me. "Should I give Vince a second chance?"

"What's your gut instinct say?" I asked.

"Once upon a time my gut told me something was seriously wrong with Kyle but I didn't listen. . . ."

"But what is it saying about Vince?"

Mist swirled around lampposts as we walked. "It told me to trust my heart."

"And what's your heart say?" I asked, smiling at her wry tone.

"I think I might love him."

She said it as though it were the worst affliction in the world.

"Then why are you hesitating?" Moonlight poked through high, thin clouds, highlighting her face.

"Just because my heart trusts him doesn't mean my head does." She scuffed her boot on the sidewalk. "There is always going to be worry in the back of my mind because he's a Seeker. I always need to be extra cautious around him, careful of what I say, do. It isn't natural. But . . ."

"What?" I asked, looking at her.

"I think I love him." She laughed.

"Oh, Starla." I put my arm around her.

"I don't know what to do."

There were no cars in the Will-o'-the-Wisp's parking lot as we approached. "I can't tell you what to do, but there's no harm in taking your time. You've only known each other a short while, and you've just been through the most emotional week someone has ever endured. Maybe he's the man for you, maybe he's not. Time will tell. And until then, just enjoy what the two of you have."

"Enjoy?"

"I know; seems like a foreign concept after the last week, doesn't it?"

Smiling, she hugged me. "But what about him being a Seeker?"

"He promised no more cameras," I said, and added with a wink, "And we have plenty of memory cleanse left."

"Time?"

"Time."

"Okay, then, I'll give him a second chance."

As I saw her smile, I had the feeling she wasn't just giving him a second chance—but herself, too. It did my heart good.

I tugged on the door and just as the Elder said, it was unlocked.

It was dark and spooky inside the building with only perimeter lighting casting a soft glow.

"Did you bring any Mace?" Starla whispered.

I kept my voice down, too. The situation seemed to call for it. "No jokes at a time like this."

"Who's joking? This place is scary-town."

Chills went up my arms. "Let's get this over with, the quicker, the better. Do you see a palm tree?"

"There," she said.

I should have spotted it myself—it was one of the only things around that had light shining on it. The fronds of the tree cast long shadows across the floor, looking like outstretched fingers. Completely creeped out, I hurried over to the tree.

Taking a deep breath, I opened the box. There was a note on top of a tissue-wrapped object.

"What is it?" Starla asked quietly.

"I don't know yet."

I opened the note and held it up to the light. It was written in sparkly curlicue letters.

I read it aloud. *"Unwrap object. Place on head."*

Thoroughly confused, I took the object out of the box and quickly unwrapped it.

"Nice," Starla said, oohing.

It was. The beautiful tiara sparkled in the ambient light.

"Put it on," Starla urged.

"I don't really understand. . . . What does this have to do with the Swing and Sway?"

"I don't know," Starla said, "but I wouldn't disobey something the Elder told me to do."

She had a point. I placed the tiara on my head. As I did so, the lights flashed on and a deafening shout of "Surprise!" nearly scared me to death.

I blinked at the sudden brightness and tried to focus on what I was seeing. I couldn't believe my eyes. At the bottom of a grand staircase stood a ballroom full of my family and friends.

At first I was so taken aback that I couldn't process what was going on. I was shaking from the sheer adrenaline and it wasn't until the group started singing "Happy Birthday" that I finally came to my senses.

This was a surprise party.

For me.

Tears welled and threatened to overflow.

I spotted Harper and Marcus; Evan, Mimi, and Cherise; I even saw the elusive Terry Goodwin along with dozens of other people I'd come to know over the past year. I didn't see Nick or Aunt Ve but knew they were here somewhere.

Everyone was dressed to the nines in their black-tie best, with the men in tuxedos with crisp white bow ties and fancy handkerchiefs. The women wore long satin gloves and were dripping in jewels and feathers. Crystals hung from the ceiling, and everything glittered and shone, from the fancy marble columns to the extravagant chandeliers to the tall decadent cake decorated in sparkling crystals—edible, I would bet (that sneaky Evan). Next to it sat a small lopsided chocolate cake, and I immediately recognized it as one of Harper's creations. She usually made my cake, and I was happy that this year was no different. My gaze found hers, and she blew me a kiss. I blew one back.

I blinked and realized I'd seen this all somewhere before. It all seemed so . . . familiar. It took me a moment, but it finally registered. I gasped.

The space had been decorated to replicate the ballroom scene in *My Fair Lady*. Trying to hold back floodgates of emotion, I couldn't believe this had all been done for *me*.

My gaze swung to Starla. She was bouncing up and down, her eyes shimmering. "Surprise!"

"You knew!"

"Of course. Ve was the mastermind, but the whole village knew."

She gave me a noisy kiss on my cheek. "I've got to run back and change. Don't have too much fun without me."

And suddenly the tiara made sense. But the rest of my outfit made me feel woefully underdressed. Almost as soon as I had the thought, Godfrey stepped out of the shadows and came over to me. I was glad to see he was fully clothed in an impeccable tuxedo. He gave me a grand bow, and boomed to the crowd below, "We shall return in a moment."

Clapping filled the air as Godfrey whisked me away to a private room. And as soon as I opened the door and saw Aunt Ve standing there, I burst into tears.

"Now now," she said, pulling me into her arms. "Are these happy tears or sad tears?"

"H-happy," I stuttered. "How did you . . . Why?"

Aunt Ve held me tight, smoothing my hair and rubbing my back. "Everyone deserves a happy birthday, Darcy dear. And there are many bad ones to make up for. This party is a start."

"You didn't have to—"

She cupped my face with her hands. "Hush now. It's what your mother would have wanted. She loved a good party."

At the thought of my mom, new tears formed. Thanks to Mimi I'd see my mom's face tonight. I'd finally remember it. I could hardly wait.

"Now stop these tears," Ve said. "There's a handsome man waiting for you."

Godfrey preened and said, "I'll wait. Take as much time as you need, Darcy."

Ve frowned at him but said to me, "It's *Nick* who is waiting for you, dear."

Swiping my eyes, I started piecing things together. "The gloves and crystals."

Ve beamed. "I almost had myself a heart attack when you opened that box."

I gasped again. "The Elder set me up, sending me over here!"

"That she did," Ve said, smiling. "She's a very good accomplice. Everyone's been in on the secret."

"There is no nudie dance competition, is there?"

She laughed. "Heavens no! Nobody wants to see Godfrey naked."

"Now see here, Velma," he blustered.

Patting his cheek, she said to him, "Work your magic, Godfrey. I will go and mingle." She smiled warmly at me. "Enjoy the night, dear."

As the door closed behind her, I pressed my hands to my hot face. "I can't believe this is happening."

"Believe it, my dear." He pulled a drape off a dress form, and I couldn't help from crying out in glee.

"The dress!" Now that I could place it in its proper context it was easy to see it was fashioned after the dress Audrey Hepburn had worn to the ball at the end of *My Fair Lady.* "It's beyond gorgeous."

The white silk dress with sheer overlay had been

painstakingly crusted with crystals, sequins, and threads of silver that made it sparkle like diamonds. It was the most beautiful thing I'd ever seen. I gently touched the jeweled cap sleeve and kept shaking my head as though I was about to wake from a dream I didn't want to leave.

"It's yours. A gift from Pepe and myself." He bowed.

I kissed his cheek. "Thank you so much." I glanced around. "Is Pepe here?"

He fussed with his tie. "He'll be along in a little while."

"Is he okay?"

He wouldn't look me in the eye. "Don't you worry about him. He's just fine. Just fine."

I didn't believe it for a second, but accepted that Godfrey didn't want to put a damper on my party.

"Let's get you all dolled up and get you out there," he said. "Or there's bound to be a mutiny."

Fifteen minutes later, I stared at the image in the mirror, hardly believing my own eyes. Godfrey had not only helped me dress but also fixed my hair (who knew he had such talent), using jeweled combs to keep it off my face. But I drew the line when he suggested bright pink eye shadow for my makeup. He fastened an elaborate diamond choker around my neck, an amazing replica of the one from the movie, and handed me a pair of long white gloves.

He took my hand and gave it a kiss. "You're a vision."

"Thank you, Godfrey," I said, my voice catching. "For everything."

He smiled. "If you ever change your mind about that stodgy policeman . . ."

I kissed his cheek. "I know where to find you."

"No more tears," he ordered. "It is a happy night."

"I promise." I'd probably cried more tears in the past week than my whole life up until this point. I'd be glad to shed no more.

He gave my hand another kiss and was gone. I quickly swiped on some makeup and couldn't keep from touching the dress. I wasn't sure that I'd ever take it off.

Chapter Thirty-seven

A few minutes later, a knock sounded on the door and Nick and Mimi peered inside and Mimi squealed. Nick just stared, and I could have sworn I saw a little moisture in his eyes.

I couldn't keep my heart from racing.

Nick said, "You're stunning."

"Totally," Mimi said.

"And you two are devious. You could have warned me about this party."

"And ruin the surprise?" Mimi smiled. "Never!"

"I forgive you. Now spin around and let me see your dress."

She twirled, her smile lighting her from inside out. "You look beautiful, Mimi."

She hugged me.

"And you," I said to Nick.

"Not bad, eh?" He rocked on his heels.

Not bad? More like amazing. "Not bad at all."

Mimi held up two boxes. "We brought presents."

Nick said, "We know everyone's waiting for you, but Mimi insisted we give these to you now."

I eyed the boxes. "The night's long. No one will mind waiting just a little bit longer."

We sat, Mimi on my right, Nick on my left.

"The little one's from me. The bigger one's from Dad. He won't tell me what's in it." She arched a disapproving eyebrow.

"Patience," he said.

"Which should I open first?"

"Mine!" Mimi said.

Nick laughed. "Definitely hers."

I carefully unwrapped the small square box and my heart melted as I pulled out a charm bracelet.

"For now there are three charms, but we'll keep adding to it. Cool, right?"

"Right," I said, my voice catching. "It's perfect."

"The paintbrush is because of how artsy you are," Mimi said. She leaned against my shoulder. "The book is because that's where Dad and I first met you. At the bookstore. I made both those charms at Wickedly Creative."

I kissed her forehead. "You did an amazing job. They're perfect."

"Dad bought the other one."

I fumbled with the charm, which had flipped backward. My hopes were high that it was a heart, symbolizing love, but as I turned it around, I saw it was the sun.

He said, "It's for the light you bring into our lives. We're not sure what we'd do without you, Darcy."

It wasn't the profession of love I'd been hoping for, but the sentiment still tugged at my emotions. "I love the bracelet. Help me put it on."

Mimi's nose wrinkled. "It doesn't go with your dress."

"I think it does, and it's my birthday so no one gets to argue with me."

She giggled and fastened the clasp. "There. Now open Dad's present."

The charms jangled prettily as I shook the box and heard a *thunking* from within. I glanced at Nick, but he kept his face neutral.

"Open it!" Mimi urged.

I laughed. "Okay, okay." I slowly peeled back the paper to reveal a nondescript shoe box. I stole another look at Nick, but he still wore his poker face.

I lifted the box top in one quick motion and blinked at the contents nestled inside delicate tissue paper.

"Slippers!" Mimi cried, frowning. "What kind of present are slippers? Is there something in them? Like a diamond ring?"

"Subtle, she isn't," Nick said, smiling.

Mimi picked up a slipper and shook it. Nothing fell out. "I don't get it."

"That's okay," I said softly. "I do."

I recalled a conversation Nick and I had recently.

I'd said, *"Not everyone needs grand gestures. Sometimes it's the little things that show someone how much they're loved."*

"I agree, but don't you think he should have—I don't know—said 'I love you' or at least brought her a pair of slippers?"

"Slippers?"

"Like you said, it's the little things."

"I'll remember that."

I remembered. Glancing at Nick, what I saw in his eyes took my breath away. Love. Trust. Promises.

"Could you explain it to me?" Mimi said. "Because I don't get it."

"Sometimes it's the little things," I said, then threw my arms around his neck.

"Hey now," Mimi said. "If you two are going to get all lovey-dovey, I'm just going to go. I'm too young to see stuff like this. I have tender sensibilities."

Nick kissed me.

Mimi giggled and groaned at the same time. "I'm leaving!"

A second later, I heard the door slam closed.

A long second later, I broke the kiss and said, "I think we traumatized her."

"She'll recover."

He stared at me.

I stared at him.

Finally, I said, "We should probably go to the party."

"Probably."

Neither of us stood up.

Suddenly I heard a loud "*Psst!*"

Nick froze. "What was that?"

"I think it's a who more than a what. Pepe?" I asked, peering downward. "Is that you?"

"Over here, *ma chère*. Come, come. I have a present for you."

I gave Nick a quizzical look as we stood up and walked over to a niche in the wall. A piece of the molding had been pushed aside, a hidden mouse passageway. Pepe stood there, a mischievous look in his eyes. "You've already given me a present. This dress . . . I can't tell you how much I love it."

"The dress is nothing," Pepe said, waving away my comment with a swipe of his hand. "The present I have for you now . . ."

There was something different about him. I couldn't quite put my finger on it. . . .

"Just tell her!" a female voice said from within the wall.

He laughed. "I believe you just did, my love."

My love? "What's going on?" I said, thoroughly confused.

"I did, didn't I?" A loud cackling laugh filtered through the wall.

"No . . ." I said, immediately recognizing the sound.

"Oh yes!" A beautiful white mouse popped out of the wall and yelled, "Ta-da!" She wore a pink velour dress, and had long lashes and spiky hair sticking up between her ears. "I told you I'd see you later, doll."

"Mrs. P?" Nick said in wonder.

"In the flesh. Mouse flesh," she said, cackling again, "but still. Like I told Darcy: Sometimes endings are just new beginnings. I'm baaaack." She took hold of Pepe's hand. "And I'm here to stay."

And despite my promise to Godfrey, for the second time that day, I burst into tears.

*   *   *

Outside the Will-o'-the-Wisp, a small dog sat by a window looking in on the dance. She watched the party closely, feeling a swell of emotion as Nick and Darcy sailed across the room, smiles stretching from ear to ear.

"I think my work here as Missy is done," Melina Sawyer said to her companion. "It might be time for me to go." All along she'd planned to help Nick find love again, find someone who could be a proper mother figure for Mimi, and move on.

She'd more than succeeded, and it was time to go.

"Do you really want to leave?" the Elder asked her.

"Not especially, but as they grow closer, the more awkward it will become for me. What happens if they move in together? I'm happy Nick has found love again, but I don't know if I can bear witness to it every day. I still have feelings, you know."

The Elder smiled. "It is a complex situation. There are options available. You can change forms, for instance."

"Perhaps," Melina said.

"Give it some time," the Elder said, echoing the words she'd heard Darcy tell Starla earlier. "You don't need to make a decision tonight. By the way, I've been meaning to tell you job well done assisting Darcy in finding the Good-bye Spell."

Melina smiled. "It helped that I knew right where it was, having used it myself."

No one but the Elder knew Melina had created the journal with the intent to leave it behind to help her daughter learn her Craft.

"They look happy, don't they?" Melina said after watching Darcy and Nick for a while.

"The happiest."

"Nick deserves it."

"Darcy, too. They're a good match."

They were, and Darcy continued to prove how much she'd grown to love Mimi. Melina focused in on her daughter, who was being waltzed around the room by Evan. Her little girl had her head tilted back laughing, and it was easy for her to imagine the sound. Her soul ached to have more time with her.

No, she didn't have to decide her fate tonight.

But she knew what she eventually had to do.

Until then, she'd enjoy the time she had before saying good-bye.

Many hours later, after dancing till my feet hurt and laughing until my cheeks ached, I lay in bed, trying hard to fall asleep—but sleep was being elusive.

Starlight filtered in from the skylight above my head as I snuggled closer to Nick's bare chest and breathed in his scent. Instinctively he tightened his arm around me, and I basked in the feeling of being loved.

"Darcy?" he whispered sleepily. "You okay?"

"Perfect," I said, smiling. "Go back to sleep." We were at his house—Aunt Ve had insisted Mimi and Higgins spend the night with her—and I had hours and hours before I had to face the real world again.

Right now I felt a little bit like I was living in a fairy tale. I knew that wasn't true, but I was quite content with feeling that way for a while.

Unbidden, a snippet of Glinda's voice popped into my head.

You get everything you want.

After tonight it was hard to argue her point. I'd had the best birthday ever. Nick loved me. Mrs. P was back. Starla was on her way to being happy again.

I was happy. I had everything my heart had ever desired.

Plus, I still had the memory spell to use.

You get everything you want.

No, I wanted to argue. I have everything I *deserve*.

With a sigh, I resolutely pushed Glinda out of my head. Tonight was a night to celebrate. I wouldn't let her spoil any of it for me.

"Mind blank; Conscious spark; Lost memories; Return to me." I whispered the words and a chill swept down my spine. All I had to do was say it two more times and I'd see my mom.

But as I lay there, I decided not to cast the spell. Not tonight. I was already full to bursting with happiness—I would save the spell for another day. It was enough to know I'd see her soon.

I finally fell asleep with a smile on my face and the memories of my mom in my heart.

I dreamed. Of Nick. Of weddings and babies. Of a happily-ever-after to my fairy tale.

And of a mourning dove with a perfect blue ring around its eye.

Read on for a sneak peek
at the next novel in Heather Blake's
Magic Potion Mystery series,

One Potion in the Grave

Coming from Obsidian in Fall 2014.

My nerves rocketed to high alert the moment the woman glided into my shop, her eyes masked by a large pair of black designer sunglasses, a gauzy scarf draped theatrically over sleek blond hair and then loosely wound around her neck.

She looked very Jackie O, and in Hitching Post, Alabama, the official wedding capital of the South, people like Jackie O stood out like peacocks among sparrows.

Despite our wedding flair, we were casual folks.

Her peacockiness didn't explain the jumpy nerves. That only happened when danger was near. My *witchy senses*—labeled so by my best friend, Ainsley, when we were teenagers—were at work.

The customer didn't look all that dangerous, but I'd been fooled by people before. Lesson learned. However, I also had to keep in mind that the danger I felt might not come directly from her—it could just be associated with her. My witchy senses weren't finely honed, so I couldn't tell which it was. All I knew was that this woman meant trouble to me.

Poly, one of my two cats, lumbered over to greet the customer and assess whether the elegant newcomer had any hidden treats lurking beneath the flowing designer caftan that swished dramatically around her thin body. Poly was forever starving to death, as his twenty-five-pound frame could attest. Roly, my other (much lighter) cat, stayed curled up on the counter, basking in a puddle of sunshine, preferring naps to treats. The siblings' breed was of unknown origin, but I suspected a mix of calico, white-and-gray ragdoll, and lethargy. Both were long-haired fluff balls of orange, gray, and white, their diluted coloring more pastel than bold. Besides their weight, another way to tell them apart was that Poly had more orange while Roly was mostly gray. They often came to work with me here at the Little Shop of Potions, and I adored each and every one of their lazy bones.

I wondered what this customer knew of my shop, a place that on first look appeared to be a blend of an herbalist and a bath-and-body boutique. On a daily basis, tourists wandered inside, drawn in by the colors, their curiosity, the allure of the window vignette, and the store's tagline written on the window: MIND, BODY, HEART, AND SOUL.

Early-morning light streamed through the display window, glinting off the treasures I'd collected over the years: the weights and measures, the apothecary scale, the mortar and pestle my grandma Adelaide had used in this very store. The sunbeams also bounced off the wall of colorful potion bottles, splashing prismatic arcs across the shop.

I inhaled the various earthy smells from the fresh and dried herbs I used in my potion making and absorbed the vibrant colors, the simple charm, and the magic in the air.

That was the most important part: the magic.

Most tourists didn't know that I hailed from an unusual combination of hoodoo and voodoo practitioners and was a healer who used my inherited magic to treat what ailed. From sore throats to broken hearts, I could cure most anything—thanks to a dose of magical lily dewdrops (Leilara tears) and the recipe book of potions left by my great-great-grandmother Leila Bell.

The customer bent to scratch Poly's head, and he flopped onto his back to playfully paw her hand. The big flirt. He lacked basic moral principles and would do just about anything for the possibility of a treat.

Another surge of warning tingles crept up my spine and spread to my limbs. Instinctively, I latched onto the engraved silver locket that dangled from a long chain around my neck. The orb was a protective charm given to me when I was just a baby, not to defend me from others but from *myself*. Being an empath, someone who can experience another's physical and emotional feelings, was something else I'd inherited from Leila. The locket engraved with two entwined lilies wasn't foolproof, but in most cases, it blocked other people's emotions, so I wasn't bombarded with everyone else's feelings. It was also something of a security blanket—offering me solace and comfort when I was troubled.

Like now.

"Feel free to browse around, and let me know if you need any help," I offered, though really I just wished she'd walk out the door. I didn't know what had kindled my witchy senses, but those warnings were rarely wrong. If she stuck around, I had to prepare for the proverbial anvil to drop on my head.

The woman lowered her sunglasses a fraction and peered at me over the dark rims. "Will do."

A flash of recognition sparked within me but didn't flame. I had the feeling I knew her somehow, yet I couldn't place her for the life of me. She certainly wasn't local.

"Nice shop you have here," she said, her slow cadence that of a cultured Southern belle, one who'd been raised up prim and proper.

Still alert, I said proudly, "It'll do." I just hoped she hadn't heard about the murder that had taken place in the back room not that long ago. There were some things tourists needn't know. Fortunately, that case had been solved, the culprit brought to justice, and my reputation restored, and life went on.

Slowly the woman stood, leaving Poly splayed out on the floor (treatless), his chubby belly the only proof needed that he was well fed. He wasn't that good an actor to be able to cover the pudge.

Her strappy designer gold high heels clacked on the wooden floor as she wandered over to a display of bath oils and surreptitiously glanced over her shoulder.

Although I usually only read people's energy to create a perfect potion, I didn't like waiting for that anvil—I'd had my fill of trouble with that murder and all, thank you kindly—and thought it best to be proactive. I let go of my locket and let down my guard to feel what she was feeling.

I sensed no danger toward me at all, so the danger swirling around was most likely due to the same reason her anxiety level was through the roof. Her stress coursed through my veins, increasing my blood pressure as surely as it did hers.

Taking hold of my locket again, I let out a breath. If she was interested, I had some calming cures and sleeping potions that might soothe her a bit. Temporary fixes to an obviously bigger issue but helpful nonetheless.

As she continued to wander around the store, browsing, touching, perusing, and generally acting suspiciously, I eyed the big fancy bag on her arm and wondered if she was a shoplifter. Over the years, I'd learned that they came in all shapes, sizes, and pedigrees.

When she picked up a handmade soap, I walked over to keep a closer eye on her and said, "The lilac is nice."

Sniffing a bar of honeysuckle soap wrapped in a muslin bag and tagged with a custom label, she said, "I prefer the honeysuckle myself. It brings back sweet memories."

Clear polish coated her short, professionally manicured fingernails. She wore only one ring—an enormous pink star sapphire on her right hand—so apparently she wasn't in town to get hitched this weekend. Most likely she was a wedding guest. Probably the big Calhoun affair. The town was buzzing from the excitement of those nuptials. Especially my mama. She was in a full-blown tizzy because the wedding was being held at her chapel, Without a Hitch.

Mama in a tizzy was quite the dizzying experience—one I'd get to witness firsthand, as she'd roped me into helping her get the chapel ready this afternoon for the big to-do. My arm hadn't needed much twisting. It was, after all, the Calhouns, and I'd have to be dead not to want an up-close peek at the family.

Headed by patriarch Warren (a U.S. senator who had an eye on the White House), and his wife, Louisa, the rich and powerful (and somewhat corrupt) Calhoun family was Southern royalty. They were firmly rooted in politics and had recently branched out into the entertainment industry via their son, Landry, who was a rising country music star. News of Landry's speedy engagement to college beauty and former pageant queen Gabriella "Gabi" Greenleigh had sent shock waves through the whole country, hitting the front pages of every tabloid in the checkout stands. "Little Orphan Gabi," as she had been called in the press, was the only child of one of the wealthiest couples in the state, a couple who had died in a tragic plane crash several years ago. Gabi's father, an oil executive, had been one of Warren's biggest supporters, and her mother had been best friends with Louisa. After their deaths, Louisa vowed to care for the girl, to take her under her wing. During this past year, Landry and Gabi had fallen in love. The picture-perfect couple was due to be married right here in Hitching Post in two days' time—this Saturday.

"Can't go wrong with either." I handed the woman a small wooden basket so she could shop. Might as well make some money off this strange encounter.

Turning to face me straight on, she said, "Carly Bell Hartwell, do you remember that one time you dared me to sneak into your aunt Marjie's yard, knock on her door, and run? Only I got all tangled up in her honeysuckle vines, and she caught me? My rear still aches sometimes from the switching she gave me. But I still love the scent of honeysuckle, so don't be pushing your lilac wares on me."

In a split second, the woman's voice shifted from high class to a local twang. I stared in shock at her and finally said, "Hush your mouth! Katie Sue Perrywinkle? Is that truly you under all that fanciness?"

Katie Sue whipped off her sunglasses, and her familiar blue eyes danced with mischief. Throwing her arms wide, she rushed at me, wrapping me in a tight hug.

We spun in a circle, our squeals scaring Poly out of his stupor. His belly hung low to the ground as he dashed behind the counter.

"Just look at you!" I said. "How long's it been?"

Without missing a beat, she said, "Ten years."

"Tell me everything." I pulled two stools over to a worktable. "Did you get to college like you wanted? Are you a full-fledged doctor now?"

Laughing, she glanced at her diamond-faced watch and said, "I only have but a minute."

"Talk fast, then." So, Katie Sue was back. I'll be damned.

I drank in the sight of her, trying to note the many changes. Her hair had gone from brown to blond, her skin from deeply tanned to pale cream, and her whole countenance from hillbilly to high society. "I'm so shocked you're here." I stumbled for words. "You're . . . unrecognizable. The hair, the clothes, the accent."

"Everything," she said firmly. "It took years, too, with thousands paid to a finishing school, voice coaches, a stylist. . . . The list goes on. Oh, and my name's Kathryn Perry now. I had it legally changed right after I left town." Her voice dropped to a melancholy whisper. "I didn't want them to find me."

Them.

Her family.

My stomach twisted at the old memories. Katie Sue had had what my mama would call an "unfortunate" childhood. Her daddy had died in prison after being sent there for killin' a man in a bar fight. Her mama liked the hooch a little too much and hadn't been above raising her hand—or any other object in the vicinity—to keep her three daughters, Lyla, Katie Sue, and Jamie Lynn, in line.

And when she remarried? *Whoo-ee.* Her new husband had an even bigger problem with the bottle and a hair-trigger temper. And after one particularly bad fight with each other, the state stepped in and awarded custody of the girls to Katie Sue's granddaddy, a hardworking man who lived simply and loved those girls fiercely. It was a move that had probably saved the lives of all three sisters but had eventually torn the siblings apart.

Last I'd heard, Katie Sue's mama, Dinah Perrywinkle Cobb, and her husband, Cletus Cobb, had been released from the local pen, having served two years each for cooking up drugs in their trailer near the river. They'd been free going on five months now and had managed to stay out of trouble.

With wide eyes, Katie Sue glanced around the shop. "I can't tell you how much I've missed this place. It was more my home than that old ramshackle trailer."

As a young girl, Katie Sue had spent hours and hours here, learning about herbal medicine at the knee of Grandma Adelaide, same as I had. Katie Sue would talk on and on about how one day she was going to become a doctor and use the knowledge Grammy had taught her to help others.

Grammy had always encouraged her lofty goals, though truthfully, I'd never thought Katie Sue would leave. Hitching Post had a way of holding on to its own. "Did you get your MD?" I asked, hoping her dreams had come true.

She smiled. "It surely wasn't easy, and I'm still in my residency down in Birmingham, but I did it."

Though she spoke softly, the pride in her voice came across loud and clear. I squeezed her hand. "Good on you."

Taking another peek at her watch, she said, "I have to get going. I have an appointment. Can we meet up later to continue catching up? I want to hear what you've been up to. Anyone special in your life?"

"It's complicated," I said.

She lifted both eyebrows. "*That* sounds like a story. Let's get coffee later, okay?"

I wasn't the least bit surprised she didn't want to meet for drinks. She'd sworn off alcohol as a teenager after seeing what it had done to her mama and daddy.

"Are you back in town to see Jamie Lynn?" I asked, referring to Katie's Sue's baby sister. She'd been just ten years old when Katie Sue left. "I heard she's bad sick."

Pain flitted across her eyes, and she paled.

"You didn't know?" I said, cursing the foot I'd just stuck in my big mouth.

She shook her head.

I should have realized as much. It never ceased to amaze me how money could tear a family apart. Lyla, the eldest Perrywinkle sister, had married straight out of high school and never looked back, leaving Katie Sue and Jamie Lynn to mind their granddaddy when his heart began to fail. Mostly the task fell on a teenage Katie Sue, since Jamie Lynn was so young, and she never once complained about it, though it sopped up what was left of her already pathetic childhood. No other family offered to help and in fact seemed to abandon the three to their own devices. The community picked up some of the slack, but Katie Sue was always on the go. Between schooling and caring for Jamie Lynn and her granddaddy . . . life was hard.

After the man died, the whole town was shocked to learn that the old coot had been buying stocks and stashing away money all his years. In his will, he left all his worldly goods solely to his full-time caretaker—his granddaughter Katie Sue, who at that time had just turned twenty. She inherited almost two million dollars.

No one was more stunned than Katie Sue's own kin, who crawled from the woodwork without a lick of shame, their palms out. When met with a firm refusal— Katie Sue proclaimed the only other person who deserved a share of the inheritance was Jamie Lynn—her mama and stepdaddy made horrible threats, but it was Lyla who dealt the most painful blow. She filed for custody of Jamie Lynn, hoping to get her hands on the money that way. The court agreed that the older, married, and more settled sister deserved custody. When Katie Sue refused to let Lyla be the guardian of Jamie Lynn's share of the inheritance, Lyla retaliated by not letting Katie Sue see her sister. Katie Sue tried to fight the matter in court again and again but lost every time. The injustice of it all near to killed her.

Eventually, she gave up trying. A heartbroken Katie Sue set up a trust fund for Jamie Lynn to access when she turned twenty-one, then did the only other thing she could think of. She took the rest of the money and ran, leaving town and never looking back.

No one in town blamed her. Not even a little.

Katie Sue's voice cracked as she said, "What's wrong with her?"

"No one knows. It's a bit of a mystery illness from what I hear."

"Why hasn't she come to see you? At least for a diagnosis?"

By tapping into Jamie Lynn's energy, I'd easily be able to pinpoint what was wrong. But that didn't necessarily mean I could fix it. There were some limitations to my magic. "My guess is Lyla. She keeps a tight rein on Jamie Lynn," I answered. Katie Sue's older sister didn't care for me much, knowing how close Katie Sue and I had once been, but she tolerated me just fine when I bought herbs from her massive gardens. Business was business, after all. Plus, she didn't care much for anyone, so I didn't take her bad attitude too personal.

"But Jamie Lynn's almost twenty-one and able to make her own choices."

I bit my nail. "It's not so easy to break some ties. Especially when it comes to family."

"Don't I know it." Anger tightened the corners of Katie Sue's mouth. "I'll try to sneak in a visit with Jamie Lynn while I'm here. Do you think you can get her a message without Lyla catching wind of it?"

"What kind of question is that, Katie Sue? Of course I can."

"Kathryn," she corrected with a smile.

"That'll take some getting used to."

"Try, Carly. I worked too hard to make Katie Sue disappear for her to be popping up now." She sighed. "It doesn't help that this town brings back a whole host of bad memories I'd rather forget. Fortunately, my stay is only until Saturday. Then I can return to Shady Hollow and go back to forgetting this place even exists."

I raised an eyebrow at the mention of Shady Hollow. A suburb of Birmingham, it was the wealthiest city in the state. Things sure had changed for her.

Reaching into her bag, she moved aside a small manila envelope that had a coffee stain on the edge and pulled out a notepad and scribbled a quick letter. She folded the note in half, then in half again. Absently, she stared at it for a second before saying, "When I first left, I set up a PO box and wrote letters to Jamie Lynn every week for years. They all came back unopened." Giving her head a shake, she handed the note to me. "I asked her to meet me tonight at my hotel room, so the sooner you can get that to her, the better."

"Where are you staying?"

She smiled, and I realized she'd had her teeth corrected, too. They were now perfectly straight, perfectly white, and perfectly perfect. Which described all of her, not just her teeth. It was a little unsettling.

"At the Crazy Loon. I'm fairly sure your aunt Hazel recognized me but couldn't put a name to my face."

All three of my aunts, Marjie, Eulalie, and Hazel Fowl (my mama's sisters), collectively known as the Odd Ducks, owned aptly named inns in town. All four Fowl sisters were matrimonial cynics and weren't too keen on ever gettin' married, which was kind of ironic, considering where they lived. My daddy, a hopeless romantic, was still counting on my mama to come around, but so far she hadn't changed her mind. She was happy as the day was long to stay engaged forever.

"I'm surprised you got a room," I said. "Everything's booked up."

"Friends in high places," Katie Sue said in a strange tone.

I took the note. "Well, don't you worry none. I'll see Jamie Lynn gets this." I only hoped that she hadn't been so brainwashed by Lyla that she would refuse to see Katie Sue.

"Thank you, Carly. You and your family are the only things that make this town the least bit bearable for me."

"Quit it now. You know we're always here for you."

She gave me another hug, we set a time to meet for coffee at my house, and she headed for the door.

"Wait! Katie—Kathryn?"

She turned. "Hmm?"

"If not for Jamie Lynn, why *did* you come back to town?" Now that I knew who she was, I couldn't help but wonder—and worry—about the dangerous energy she carried.

Something dark flashed in her eyes, and a wry smile creased her lips. "I'll tell you all about it later, Carly, but for now I'll say this." She put on her sunglasses and pulled open the door. "As a doctor, I may have taken an oath to do no harm, but as a country girl who's done had it up to here with that family and their lies, I'm fixin' to give the Calhouns a taste of their own bitter medicine."

Also available from

Heather Blake

A POTION TO DIE FOR
A Wishcraft Mystery

Carly Bell Hartwell, owner of a magic potion shop
specializing in love potions, is in high demand. The
residents of Hitching Post, Alabama, are frantic to stock
up on Carly's love potions after a local soothsayer predicts
that a local couple will soon be divorced. Carly is happy
for new business but her popularity is put on pause when
she finds a dead body on the floor of her shop, clutching
one of her potion bottles in his cold, dead hand.

The murder investigation becomes a witch hunt and all
fingers are pointing to Carly as the prime suspect. With
her business in trouble, Carly has to brew up some serious
sleuthing skills to reveal the true killer's identity before the
whole town believes that her potions are truly to die for...

**"Blake has taken the paranormal mystery
to a whole new fun, yet intriguing, level."**
—Once Upon a Romance

Available wherever books are sold or at
penguin.com

facebook.com/TheCrimeSceneBooks